THE YEAR'S BEST AFRICAN SPECULATIVE FICTION 2023

THE YEAR'S BEST AFRICAN SPECULATIVE FICTION 2023

Edited by

Oghenechovwe Donald Ekpeki
& Chinaza Eziaghighala

Caezik SF & Fantasy
in partnership with
O.D. Ekpeki Presents

ISBN: 978-1-64710-145-9
First Caezik/O. D. Ekpeki Edition. First Printing November 2024
1 2 3 4 5 6 7 8 9 10

An imprint of Arc Manor LLC
www.CaezikSF.com

An imprint of Jembefola Press
www.odekpeki.com

CONTENTS

WHAT DOES IT MEAN TO BE AN AFRICAN STORYTELLER?

by Chinaza Eziaghighala

Last year, I had the privilege of being invited by Oghenechovwe Donald Ekpeki to guest edit *The Year's Best Speculative Fiction Anthology Vol. 3* at Ake Festival in Lagos, Nigeria. The day was electric—surrounded by fellow storytellers, book lovers, and literary enthusiasts, I felt a deep sense of belonging. Immersed in the world of African literary voices, accepting this opportunity felt natural. It allowed me to contribute to the ongoing mission of spotlighting African speculative fiction talent.

Fast-forward to today, and this anthology is now out in the world, brimming with the names of some of the brightest stars in African speculative fiction. The process of reading, selecting, and curating these stories was a labor of love—one that made me reflect on what it truly means to be an African storyteller.

What does it mean to be an African storyteller?

First, it means striving for excellence despite impossible odds. Writing from Africa often means battling harsh realities—unreliable power, unstable socio-economic conditions, political unrest—yet, the writers in this anthology overcame these barriers. They not only wrote; they wrote brilliantly. For those in the diaspora, the challenges may be different, yet no less daunting—racism, inequality, and the isolation of being a minority. Still, they rise, they write, and their stories resonate. That's the essence of the African spirit: thriving against the odds.

Second, the African storyteller carries the soul of the original storyteller—the poet. Many of these stories feel like epic poems waiting to be fully realized. From the Gothic horror of Tendai Huchu's "Hollowed People" to the adventurous fantasy of Uchechukwu Nwaka's "Rainbow Bank," each narrative is unique, infused with the writer's distinct voice and vision. Yet they all share a common goal: to educate, entertain, and inspire.

Third, an African storyteller is free to be whoever they want and to tell their story in whatever form speaks to them. The medium might be visual art, music, dance, film, or television. A diasporan recalling their history through music, a new immigrant documenting their current reality through prose, or a continental African exploring the nuances of their culture through film. Every perspective is valid, because while our experiences may differ, we are bound by the shared roots of our ancestry.

Ultimately, I hope you find as much joy in reading this anthology as I did in curating it. The stories here, along with those in the recommended reading list, offer a glimpse into the incredible work that African storytellers—both on the continent and in the diaspora—are doing. These voices are among the finest, and their stories have the power to transcend time.

THE HOLLOWED PEOPLE

by T.L. Huchu

The strangemare was etched in the pulsating soundcode of djumba drums, whole notes punctuated by foreboding silence, echoing in Ruu'vim's mind, but the sound grew ever more scrambled whenever they tried deciphering the traces of the shadow song leached into the disturbing chrono-dismorphation megascape of dead Mahwè, the corpse world.

There were those of the forbidden faith, a small but significant cult, who claimed that on Mahwè the beat of the Mothersound, the fundamental essence of being itself, had been mangled and deformed until it was unrecognizable to the inhabitants of Pinaa, the nearby moon, who'd long since turned their backs on the magical heartbeat that thrummed through the depths of space. Despite their sophisticated scientific instrumentation and sound theorizations, they saw nothing of worth taking place there. They were blinded from the ultimate truth that something beyond their rigid logic was taking place in the world next door, hiding instead behind the safety of their equations and formulae.

Below was the shredded body of the warrior Ngano, deep cuts and grooves in his fading body as if a thousand spears had flown into him. His short but broad musculature was now just ribbons of flesh and a stream of blood seeping into the bare brown dirt.

Eyes wide open, Ruu'vim stared into the blindness of temporo-spatial oblivion, an event horizon hiding the wretchedness of Mahwè. This was why all good scientists, maadiregi, and thinkers avoided probing too deeply into the mysteries of the planet. Dead things deserved to be buried, hidden from view, but Mahwè refused. Instead, it acted for some as a beacon even seeping into the dreamworld of cybernetic beings as readily as fleshlings, corrupting data until Ruu'vim had been forced to go there, against safety protocols, algorithms, dictates, and even the remnants of their non-existent gut. Base instincts remained encoded even within a grade-three, extensively modified being like them.

Ruu'vim hadn't expected the sickness, but now they were here, they realized the aagoo suits barely kept the dismorphation under control. Sickness was something fleshlings experienced, despite millennia of medical advancement. A cybernetic being like them should have been upgraded beyond such base evolutionary concerns, and this had been true before they had landed on Mahwè.

Regret.

Fear.

Despair.

This is something new. Raw feeling instead of data inputs. They couldn't trust anything about their judgment anymore. Multiple streams of thought collapsed into a single coherent, overriding imperative: **SURVIVAL**

<<Reboot initiated>>

No, not yet, please, Ruu'vim bargained with gods and ancestors of the dead world that had summoned them. Their limbs, made of organometallic composites, glistened copper and ebony as they quivered. They were glitching. Near the horizon, a dust storm was rolling toward them. A great mass of brown dust towering higher than any constructions on Pinaa, moving with incredible speed, was the last thing logged into Ruu'vim's memory banks before the abominable cycle began anew …

"The answers we all seek, the cure for our intolerable suffering, is down there on that planet," Ngano said, pointing out the faux window of the unregistered station Feja orbiting in Mahwè's shadow. The craft was a non-reflective sphere, darker than the blackest shadow, hidden among the masses of space junk, military-grade stealth technology masking its energy signal, so that even the vigilant authorities on Pinaa were unaware of its existence.

"We don't even know whose vessel this is," Xuda replied anxiously. She was ashen, red-eyed, and weary, a far cry from her usual elegant demeanor. "I don't know how you do things in the depths of Ekwukwe, but Zezépfeni has knowledge of things that would make you void your bowels despite you being the warrior you claim to be."

"Of course, because you Sangenis believe you're the descendants of the original people, and so you should lord it over the 'cave crawlers' of my home world. Let's see how well you do that with my shoe deep inside your rectum," Ngano replied, looking to the lovers Baba Do and Adelolade for support. The two were from Órino-Rin and Wiimb-ó, which orbited different stars, and so they might have been more receptive to his indignation at Zezépfenian arrogance, which only the less emotive people of Pinaa seemed immune to.

Xuda scowled, but before she could make a response a holoprojection began aggregating in blue and green light, interrupting her riposte. The time it took to compose itself was an indicator it was being transmitted from a ship at some distance, too far to be Pinaa, but too close to be from the next planet in the system. But Xuda's wary words had been flagged as a potential problem with Ruu'vim, who, drawing on their downloaded files on ship construction and maintenance, had noted that the parts used in the design of the Feja Station seemed to be cannibalized from the best tech from the five planets in their binary system. Great resources had obviously been expended in its construction, but who would have the connections to access classified tech from each of the authorities system-wide? Though the planets cooperated, centuries-old rivalries meant it was impossible for any legitimate actor to coordinate something on this scale.

"Nge, you all gin know one 'em all, nice-well," the hologram said when it had settled.

"No amount of pay would have had me here if I'd known these Zezépfeni scum were also invited. What do you want in return?" Ngano asked, brusque as was the warrior's way.

"Petty plus haste is gon' crush me and you, fight brother. This mission be special for vex dreams drag all sides cross space an' tribe." The hologram had no discernible features apart from being a humanoid analog, carefully proportioned not to give away its identity, but its accent was distinctly a Drifter one.

The Drifters, sometimes called the untethered, were clans that traversed the vastness of the binary system in their assorted spacecraft, trading and occasionally raiding. They had their own codes, and while they were frowned upon by authorities on all five worlds who had their own fleets, their facilitation of commerce and travel made them indispensable assets. As such, the savviest of them accumulated obscene quantities of wealth.

"This no me reality voice. Sound power me no surrender to none," the hologram said and chuckled, turning its eyeless gaze to Ruu'vim.

Ruu'vim, chastened, shrunk back and disconnected themself from the system. They had been trying to cross-reference the oral signature through the station's database to identify the speaker. This discovery forced them to run a purge program in case their duo-thought system, which integrated organic brain to synthetic intelligence, had been compromised.

"I don't care about any of this shit, people," Adelolade said, throwing off her lover's arm, which caused them to disentangle in zero-g. "I can't live like this. I'll do anything to make these terrible dreams go away. Please."

"Corrective no easy with no sacrificial, me tell," the hologram replied.

"But you promised us a cure!" Baba Do said. His wide nostrils flared and then he calmed, reaching his hand across to reconnect with his partner.

"The great Obanje Kami, may him soul sing forever, preach-say: 'Promise be like the oba-worm fruit; beauty outer skin, rot discovered in the bite.' Me no charlatan, ngi. Fair chance is all me offer plus good reward for go carry out."

"We can do whatever it is you need to make these strangemare end, so we can wake whole again," Xuda said. "My song voice is hoarse and magic refuses to answer me."

Ruu'vim shuddered but kept to themself, folding their composite material arms to stop glitching—this started when the dreams seeped into their artificial bio-architecture, corrupting the sophisticated programming that was melded into them, and formed their unified consciousness. They were already an outcast on their home moon; a scientist who dabbled in the esoteric would never find a foothold in that society. But now they were moved from abstract studies and thrown in a room with these traditionalists. It used to be much simpler. Their vocation had been the study of chronospherics, the temporal, ever-shifting shroud of Mahwè's remnant atmosphere and surface, which defied theorization and any attempt at explanation or categorization. There was a running joke that there were more ways to describe what Mahwè was not, compared to methods of describing what it was.

"I no force nobody. Choose free, quick, quick," the hologram said.

"Even relic raiders fear Mahwè," Xuda said, reorienting herself into a cross-legged sitting position as she floated in the room, her garments flowing and rippling. "No one who's ever attempted landing there comes back."

"Coward," Ngano replied with a snort.

"Luck for you and every, Ruu'vim's research offer perfect solution built into this craft plus five aagoo suits expensive made."

The screen on the wall lit up with a red display of three powerful M2D class patrol vessels from Pinaa, with a calculated trajectory toward the Feja Station. That meant they had been detected. The moon's authority forbade unauthorized vessels to approach Mahwè. A metallic sound of disentangling grapplers from their hull shocked them as it traveled the length of the hull.

"Dwa'ndenki sisterfucker! The shuttle is taking off without us. I knew I shouldn't have trusted these Drifter scum," Ngano said, kicking the wall to launch himself out of the room, but the door slid shut, sealing perfectly flush as though the entrance had never been there in the first place. All that remained were the smooth silver walls and the screens, which still flashed images of the approaching vessels.

"Patience. Patrol detect your transport here. I gon' draw 'em away from you."

The screen showed the shuttle which had brought them here was accelerating away. But only one of the M2D vessels peeled away in pursuit; the other two remained on course for Feja Station.

"Is it true you have no jails on Pinaa?" Baba Do asked Ruu'vim.

"We heard you lobotomize your criminals and give their bodies as hosts for your AI. That's why there are no pure organics left on your world. Is that what they're going to do to us if they catch us here?" Adelolade added, raising a single eyebrow.

Ruu'vim did not reply because the premise was manifestly absurd, and they consumed vast quantities of processing power simulating alternative scenarios, none yielding a desirable outcome. But a subroutine detected a line the hologram had said about them offering a solution, and this was associated into their visual data on the makeup of Feja Station, until it dawned on them that their classified scientific recorded oration on aagoometic materials must have been hacked and the results used to construct this spherical vessel. Ruu'vim's great insight, in a world where sound was central to science and magic, was to theorize that time (aagoo) could be described as the frequency of longitudinal energy waves. Therefore, they had postulated in their oration of an exotic material arranged in a similar manner to the convoluted acoustic foam used for physical soundproofing as a way of dampening chrono-dysmorphatic effects. They knew the material structure would have to be uneven, perhaps in the pattern of an egg box at the microscopic scale, but they couldn't find a suitable candidate from the resources available to them at the time. It seemed someone else had cracked the practical solution to this problem. Ruu'vim was flattered that their work had been taken forward, though somewhat disappointed they'd not been the one to do it themselves.

The thought came too late, and they gasped—an anomaly. Sound expelled involuntarily was an indignity only organic children should do, not a grade-three like Ruu'vim.

"The Mother has decided for you," the hologram said.

"Kyi á yikho," Xuda cursed, but it was too late.

They all felt the acceleration of their craft as it threw them against the wall, holding them fast as the screen showed it was headed toward the dreaded Mahwè. The vessel was out of their control. Ruu'vim tried to connect to Feja Station's AI but found themself locked out. They couldn't stop it from plunging into the atmosphere, just as they couldn't shut out the cacophony of panicked voices shouting at the now vanished hologram.

Xuda's mother, Afeni, had been a maadiregi who was also an instructor of the high language on Zezépfeni. The language created resonances in the atmosphere which could be harnessed for powerful magic.

Afeni was often away on pilgrimages to Órino-Rin, where she used this knowledge to secretly craft and weave spells for the ruling elites in three of the five worlds. Órino-Rin's resonant and variable atmosphere could be harnessed to create the most devastating sonics. Though she was a busy woman with little affection for her spawn, Afeni still found snatches of time, over many juzu, to orally instruct Xuda in the rudiments of the high language. By the time Afeni ascended to join the ancestors in Eh'wauizo, the spirit realm, she had bequeathed her daughter the memorized dictionary and grammar of high language which was their most precious heritage.

A younger Xuda had rebelled and rejected the worship of the womb of The Mother Goddess.

She'd been tempted by those who believed that existence spoke itself into being, nothing becoming something out of nothing. It was good for the young to rebel, for only in the act of rejecting tradition could they come to see the value of the very customs they had cast aside. Through this way, in the practical accumulation of many juzu, the straitjacket they sought to rid themselves of would, with wisdom, transmute into the custom-made warm winter coat.

Xuda could have become a maadiregi specializing in using the high language to mix magic and tech for pay, but instead she got lost within the language itself. There was something devastatingly beautiful in the syntax and flow of high language that she would spend hours spinning verse and formulations inside of her head, abstract notations which were stunning creations in and of themselves but lacked any real, practical application for anyone to bother paying for them. Her relatives feared she was going mad for it was not unknown for the high language to turn the brains of lesser maadiregi into mush, gradually devouring their higher cortical functions until nothing was left. Knowledge was power and power had a price. This is why most preferred to limit their learnings to the specialty of their varied industries.

Xuda couldn't tell anyone of her headache-inducing strangemares. Grotesque scenes played out every night which etched themselves as scars in her gray matter, and she woke up with welts on her skin each morning. It was driving her mad, and she thought the language was doing this to her, until she learned of another, a non-maadigeri who was exhibiting the same symptoms.

Few carried a significant catalog of high language words in their heads.

And so it was, as Feja Station plummeted like a meteor through the remnant atmosphere of Mahwè, toward their certain doom, Xuda sensed the subsonic probing of the cybernetic being from Pinaa, Ruu'vim, who was desperately trying to interface with the station's AI.

Caught up in the planet's gravity with the station spinning dangerously, Xuda tried not to pass out. The centrifugal forces acting on them pinned them against the walls of the station. Their holographic employer had erred. Whatever signals they were using to control the station couldn't penetrate the damaged chronosphere of Mahwè, and so they wouldn't be able to control the descent. A strange noise, something akin to a shriek from an unnatural abattoir, rang out in the craft. It rattled through every molecule in Xuda's body, stunning her. She was shaken by its wrongness. It seemed to lodge itself into her entire being.

The station was heating up.

Ngano was praying to the god of war to grant him passage into the Huts of the Valiant.

Baba Do and Adelolade whispered soothing words of eternal devotion, promising to reunite in the next world, as they hoped they were soul-tied to one another. But what did that mean in this dead world? The screens which had shown their descent now only showed a restless grayness, as though the cameras were unable to process the images coming into them.

"They used a standard spacefaring AI from a transit tanker. Those carry bulk and are not designed with re-entry protocols. It doesn't know what to do in gravity and is unable to patch new piloting code. The ship will hold, but we will crash and burn," Ruu'vim said, jerking everyone back to the problem at hand.

"I can get you in if you can fly us," Xuda said.

"You have nil augmentation, and even if you could make it to a manual control panel, it would take months for you to crack the security encryptions using an organic brain alone," Ruu'vim replied.

Xuda couldn't help but smile, even as it felt like her chest was compressed by a dreamstealer sitting atop it. She'd never been to Pinaa but knew they were averse to the use of magic, preferring technological innovation alone.

She opened her mouth and uttered the recitation of R'asasa Akooka, *The Lost Key,* in the high language.

Baba Do and Adelolade cried out in anguish, whilst Ngano gritted his teeth. Blood trickled out of their ears. The sound came out mangled, in the wrong key. Even Ruu'vim, whose chassis was built of composites and could withstand the harshness of space without a suit, shut their sonic receptors. They could still feel the overwhelming power of the language pummeling their body, for vibrations can touch. It seemed like it was going on forever until Xuda's head slumped as she passed out, but Ruu'vim found at last they were patched into the station's AI and could take control of the craft.

Ruu'vim took charge and they crashed.

That moment was the last they saw one another alive.

The ruins of Mahwè were a temporal maze, better still, a labyrinth, and there were multiple stories, counted in powers of five, that happened on the bès the Feja Station landed there. Some Raevaagi, those griots, claimed there were thousands of versions of this tale that played out in an instant. Others argued there were infinite versions instead. The most extreme contended that the story truly never ended, rather it was locked within echoes of itself that were a hall of mirrors which reflected back to one another until the last note of the song of the Saußtiverse was sung.

The peculiar nature of time on the ruins of Mahwè meant the narrative had to be collapsed into a single wave function, a solitary coherent narrative, rather than the played out range of possibilities, else no griot could contain it in their mind, and no audience could live long enough to listen to it all. But what was time, that untouchable essence commonly divided into seconds, minutes, hours, bès, juzu, and so forth, unto the Yu'uxu which is twenty-five juzu, and from there growing ever higher?

Baba Do emerged from the wrecked Feja Station as the sole survivor; he surveyed the carnage, the pureed bodies of his companions, their blood painting the silver walls of the craft. What wasn't glop were bits of bone, teeth, and the composite materials making Ruu'vim scattered through the room.

How Baba Do survived could be hailed a miracle, by believers of such events.

Or it could simply be the same probabilistic property of the universe that meant if you walked into a wall an infinite number of times, on at least one occasion, your atoms and the wall's atoms would be so perfectly aligned that you walk right through it as though it were not there at all.

Such vapid explanations mattered little to Baba Do as he attempted to gather the splattered remains of his love, Adelolade. He wept and wished he too had died, and he had elsewhere, in a different time, but all he knew was this single reality, the same one in which he alone had survived.

It was all so unfair.

The hologram reappeared and said, "This is not a live link but a recording. If you are seeing this then congratulations, you may well be the first to survive entry into the ruins of Mahwè. A historic moment—"

"Fuck you," Baba Do said.

"This recording cannot interact with you directly. Please wait to hear the full message," the station instructed. "—and if you wish to return, you must first find a precious artifact, the Codex of Qu'laaba believed to be lost in the ancient capital of ..."

Baba Do didn't care. Though the message went on and on and then returned in a loop, all he could do was stay in the carnage and grieve the loss of his beloved Adelolade.

Time passed, or didn't, as it does on Mahwè, until he felt hungry, and the baser functions of his body compelled him to seek food and water, which the station had in abundance. He remained within its aagoo reinforced shell, until that too nearly drove him to despair. Eventually he resolved to live so he could seek vengeance on their mysterious benefactor who'd lured them here on the promise of a cure to their strangemares.

On the bés Baba Do decided to venture outside, he noticed there were five black suits on the ship and five white ones. He was not familiar with the fabric of the black suits, which felt strange beneath his fingertips. There were bumps on them, something like a skin with bad acne. Disgusted by it, Baba Do chose one of the white space suits instead. It was logical to conclude that if it was strong enough to protect the human body in the void of space, it would protect him from this hostile planet.

He donned a space suit, clicked on the helmet with a wide visor, and walked into the airlock. Through the faux port window of the hatch, Baba Do glimpsed the brown, barren landscape of the planet. It was awe inspiring, even as a wave of repulsion forced his breakfast back up to his throat. He swallowed. Then he opened the door and stepped outside.

Baba Do blinked, seeing shapes that looked like people spontaneously emerging in the desolation before him. It was as though the waves of the ages were swirling around, rising and falling, churning in incomprehensible shapes. The planet changed and was unmade faster than anything his mind could keep up with. This was impossible. He closed his eyes and opened them again and saw nothing.

In this distraction, he had not realized what was broken was the fundamental quality of time as a dimension which was the stuff that kept everything from happening at once. It was orderly like a river of glue, holding events fast in their place yet simultaneously moving unidirectionally. Everyone understood the limits of what one could do with time: measure it, slow it down with a massive gravitational force, almost suspend it by moving toward the speed of light, and so forth. But on Mahwè, their ancient forbidden experiment had tempered with this order carefully sung by The Mother Goddess.

Here, with their civilization at its zenith, the people of Mahwè had played goddess with time and reaped the whirlwind.

Baba Do's choice of the white space suit was unfortunate. For on this one world the glue of time was rendered unsticky and flowed chaotically so that, agonizingly, his very subatomic constituents were ripped into different eras, shredding him from the beginning of the universe to its very end. It happened slowly and it happened quickly, everything at once.

Baba Do died a scream suspended across the length of all time, becoming a wrong note in the Mothersound. Some griots have claimed this corruption is how pain and suffering first entered the universe.

In another splintered branch of the river of time, Xuda found herself as the sole survivor of the descent to the surface of the corpse world. Since everything issues from the Mothersound, this was her solo; even though the hero should have been the cybernetic child of Pinaa, Ruu'vim who, with mere minutes to impact, successfully stabilized the craft by forcing the ship's AI to reroute the non-positive fuel, thus creating an antigravity thrust in the nozzles and then bringing the ship to a soft landing.

Once on the ground, they surveyed the mess of pulverized bodies staining the craft. It looked like a child had smeared jelly on the walls. But the smell was horrible. "What have you done?" Ruu'vim said before they slumped to the ground and shut down for the last time.

Xuda was aghast.

"We were going to crash."

She wanted to cry out but feared the very sound of her own voice, of what it could do. Instead of saving them, she'd killed everyone in the most horrible way imaginable. Her magic had not worked right since the strangemares intensified. Not on Zezépfeni, or even when she went on pilgrimage to the incredible atmosphere of Órino-Rin. It was there she'd met Adelolade, whom she'd heard singing in the Divine Temple of the Talking Drum, which was the largest cave set within a mountain. The others were much smaller in scale, though they all had their own special harmonics. The acoustic setup amplified magic, making the caves sacred spaces.

Adelolade, a songstress, was wealthy and independent, for the people of Órino-Rin valued nothing more than a golden voice. When she was silent, she had a dreamy air about her, but when she spoke, she could be highly animated.

"You are an incredible singer," Xuda said.

"I sing better when I get a good night's sleep, but something strange and sorrowful has troubled my dreams of late," she replied, right hand touching her collarbone.

And there in the Divine Temple of the Talking Drum, the two women had exchanged dreams, the most intimate thing two people can share. On Órino-Rin and Ekwukwe, both planets which orbited the fiery sun Juah-āju, it was commonly known that sharing one's dreams opened up the possibility they would be stolen if the other party was a dreadful dreamstealer. To share them was to show trust, even if the dreams were strangemares which no one wanted. There was the old Ekwukwe proverb which went: "To cast aside one's strangemare is to lose the nugget of gold within."

Good things can come from bad experiences. Discomfort was a part of life. But nothing positive was to be found in the soul shuddering despair their strangemares held in common. The rocky walls of the cave echoed their terrors back to them. And as the two women spoke, they realized they had been tied into a common dream.

"There are others," Adelolade said. "My partner has been contacted by someone who claims to have a cure. We are going to them on the tenth bès hence."

"Are they an uroh-ogi?"

"We have tried all those doctors and healers, spending a fortune in the process. No one can help us but this man who claims he has answers. Will you come?"

How could Xuda refuse this offer when her mother's inheritance had been stolen from her?

But she was in shock; she could do nothing but stare at the bodies. She eventually made her way to a comms panel and tried to send a signal for aid, knowing full well the planet's field wouldn't allow that. No signals came in or left. She was on her own with nothing but the high language. It was this incredible magic that had worked in ways she'd never seen it work before when she uttered *The Lost Key*, pulverizing her companions.

Now she understood why the inhabitants of the moon Pinaa were so wary of magic. They were, of course, the descendants of the inhabitants of Mahwè. The events that destroyed the planet shattered their trust in magic.

The hologram started up, urging her to find "the Codex of Qu'laaba, believed to be lost in the lost capital of Jenne."

This was her only way to get off the planet.

Multiple voices streaming different thoughts played in her head. It was as if she was hearing people other than herself conversing inside of her skull.

I have gone mad, she thought.

A cybernetic being with integrated quantum AI could think multiple thoughts simultaneously. These thoughts, however disparate, would be harmonized eventually like the different sections of an orchestra. One of the things Ruu'vim ran in their mind was a background check of the four others on Feja Station. They could assign different compartments of their intelligence to do this, including a systemwide scan of government databases to identify their companions.

That was easy.

Then they'd performed an ancestral trace which kept running as the station hurtled toward Mahwè, the planet looming larger on their screens. Two parents make four grandparents who make eight great-grandparents, and so forth, until they'd been cut off from the system as they entered into the planet's atmosphere.

Now they were the lone survivor after the loss of the four descendants of thousands of foremothers and ancestors stretching back generations. They felt sorrow and glitched, collapsing their thought streams into muddled error soundcodes.

They cleared the cache and composed themself in time for the hologram to play its message.

A mission equals purpose which increases chances of survival.

It was not unknown on Pinaa for cybernetic beings without clear life-goal to self-terminate. Usually this was linked to a degradation of the organic gray matter, especially with grades one and two types.

As Ruu'vim started up their various thought streams, they were surprised to find a voice unlike theirs embedded within.

<<Isolate and run diagnostics>>

. . .

..

.

<<ALIEN STREAM DETECTED>>

Another life form here on Mahwè? Impossible. There was nothing out there but desolation beyond imagining. Ruu'vim was about to attempt a flush of the alien stream when they experienced déjà vu for the first time, which was impossible for a being that remembered everything. Someone else was on this world and as secondary diagnostics reported, it seemed they were temporally adrift.

— *Who's there?*

— *I'm going crazy. I'm going to die.* Though the internal voice was richer since it reflected the inner tone of the speaker mediated through bone, rather than air, Ruu'vim recognized it was Xuda's, which was strange, as she had been pulverized.

— *Listen carefully. This is Ruu'vim. I am in your mind, and you are in mine.*

— *Okay, I'm definitely nuts now. Everyone's dead. So many voices. Make it stop.*

Ruu'vim reluctantly collapsed their thoughts into a singular stream.

— *Is that better for you, Xuda? We are temporally dissociated but when you used your high language magic to help me break into the station's AI our consciousness must have become entangled. That's why I can hear you and you can hear me.*

— *I can only hear one of you now.*

— *Listen to me very carefully. We have to work together if we plan to survive this.*

— *Everyone's dead!*

— *Focus.*

— *You're dead. I am insane.*

— *Focus, Xuda.*

Ruu'vim, who specialized in chronospherics, explained various theorizations on the workings of time on Mahwè. This was the reason the planet was so dangerous. Then they asked Xuda to don her aagoo suit as soon as she could.

— *It's the black suit, not the white one. They are designed to keep your atoms in a single, stable chronology.*

Ruu'vim did the same; though their body could endure outer space, the composite material was not designed for withstanding the ravages of chrono-dismorphation. They jettisoned their oxygen pack as they recycled an internal supply to sustain their meager organics. It would be thirty bès before that needed topping up. And they did not hesitate to open both doors, negating the airlock.

Gases from Mahwè's toxic atmosphere streamed in, but without fleshlings on board, Ruu'vim no longer required the life support, powering it down to save energy. Their sensors registered an odd coldness as though death had kissed their suit. But what they saw as they left the vessel and walked were the ruins of the old industrial district of

Jenne, conjured back by a temporal leap. This couldn't be right at all. Nothing should be here. It was impossible to tell if this was real or a simulation as they cross-referenced the sights of old warehouses with internally saved historical records. Ruu'vim grew unsettled, worried a sonic error was affecting their system. Dissonance.

— *You're making my head hurt.*

— *Almost done. I know you're not used to running multiple thought streams, but this is important.*

— *Wait, I can see what you see. Where are you?*

— *Sometime in this planet's past. I can't locate the exact juzu yet.*

Xuda nervously stepped out of her hatch into the eerie dead world.

She blinked and they appeared in front of her, seemingly spontaneously emerging from the desolation into wisps. They were ghosts, but deformed, unlike the ancestors from Eh'wauizo, who were full of vitality, these were hollow projections. They were grotesque, as souls who had neither gone to the spirit realm nor received poured libations tended to be.

— *I've never seen ghosts before.*

— *That's because you view everything from behind your sensors and gizmos. On Zezépfeni they are a fairly common nuisance.*

— *This was a research hub.*

— *Are you still in the past?*

— *They did some sort of psychic experiments in the labs here.*

But Xuda did not hear because the ghosts had approached, a mass of spectral men, women, and children pressed around her. Their faces were contorted in anger and pain as they came at her clawing. She tried to turn back and run to the ship, but she was disoriented. It should have been behind her; now she could no longer find it.

— *Don't panic.*

— *I've never seen so many at once.*

— *What do they want?*

Ruu'vim was jerked from the warehouses into a blur of temporal zones at speeds which taxed their processing capabilities. But their organic mind was buffered from this incomprehensible mesh of data.

Mahwè was simultaneously dead and undead.

It all depended on which timestream in the planet's mangled history or future you wound up in. Without the aagoo suits stabilizing the observer, everything would be a blur. But even with the suit's protection, cognitively, it was very difficult to process what exactly was happening on the planet at any given moment.

Their processors were aggregating collated information. The Codex of Qu'laaba was more than an artifact. Zankara Qu'laaba was a trailblazing scientist, regarded as the father of AI on Pinaa. And while the different planets had eventually developed their own independent artificial minds, Pinaa's central AI got there first because it had been built using the insights from Qu'laaba's experiments.

Hundreds of men, women, and children, including babies and infants were subjected to cruel and inhumane experiments by Qu'laaba and his assistants. Minds were flayed, connectomes extracted, nervous systems shredded to the last neuron, in his quest for mastery over the mysteries of the brain. These people were hollowed out, so they could fill his research orations with novel ideas. Ruu'vim realized this sin was buried deep in Mahwè's and Pinaa's history. Their revered ancestor had ruined lives. He had been a monster.

— *The ghosts say because of these experiments which hollowed them out and made them unwhole, stripped them of their fragment of the Mothersound, they were denied entry into Eh'wauizo. They are stuck here. Uncleansed and shunned.*

— *While we reap the benefits of their suffering.*

Ruu'vim's interrupted background check flashed in their screenview. The five people aboard Feja Station were but leaves on a tall tree, whose fibers dug deep in history, winding down to common roots on this dead world. They might have come from different planets, separated from one another, but everyone having the strangemares was a descendent of Qu'laaba. Ruu'vim was yanked into the alternate present in which Ngano lay dead at their feet.

The sight of him made their circuits freeze, for now he was no longer a stranger but kin.

— *We are here because—*

— *I heard your thoughts loud and clear, Ruu'vim. We are here for our reckoning.*

And so the ghosts spoke to Xuda with Ruu'vim listening across time. They demanded to be heard. So many of them. Their anguish rolled through like a storm across the desert.

"Since Zankara Qu'laaba robbed us of our lives and souls, we demand the same from his descendants," the hollowed people insisted.

"If our deaths will give you peace then we accept. Let this end now," Xuda replied, resigned. She, more than anyone else, was tired of the torment.

"There are thousands more of Qu'laaba's descendants out there. This will not stop here, my sister," Ruu'vim cautioned.

"You will both die, as will they all," the hollowed people said. "Every single one, until Qu'laaba's bloodline is extinguished."

"No, please, there is another way," Xuda replied. "Let us pay off this blood debt another way."

"There is no other way except blood for blood!"

"Truth!" Xuda shouted. "Let us trade blood for truth. We can be your mediums, menagari, through which you can speak, and we will take your story back to the five worlds, so they will know what was done to you. So that the truth will persist. If you kill us then your song dies with us too. But with a medium out there in the five worlds, a host for what remains of you, then you will in effect become living ancestors yourselves. No longer trapped here, lost in time."

Silence. And then, "Two sisters. We only need one. One must live and the other must die so this soil tastes the blood of our enemy. Which shall it be? Choose."

Ruu'vim projected thoughts into Xuda's mind:

— Don't offer them anything. We did nothing wrong.

— They did nothing wrong either. Now it is our responsibility to make it right. And if we do this, at least one of us will survive to tell this tale to the Raevaagi so that they may repeat it and we will not be forgotten. Let us at least have that.

The hollowed people got angrier the longer the two took to think. Their collective rage, fueled by their pain, burned the broken world red, threatening to explode like a dying star.

"Choose, choose, choose, choose, choose," they chanted.

The traveling cybernetic menagari on Wiimb-ó drew a crowd that jostled to see this new wonder. From mountain peak to mountain peak, through the cloud-stained crests, along the slippery slopes, between the passes and spurs that made up the habitable parts of this world, this wandering menagari's reputation had spread. Their fame extended throughout the system and some people came with problems, while others simply wanted to witness the spectacle of the cybernetic being sitting on a reed mat, dressed in their animal skin regalia, casting bones to divine futures.

They wore a crown of feathers on their head.

It was whispered they had abandoned a conventional research post on Pinaa to travel the system from planet to moon to planet bringing stories, healing, and lost wisdom.

Whenever the choice was made on that fateful bès on Mahwè, it was always Ruu'vim who emerged out of the fractured timelines. It could only have been them, for their mind could carry far many more ancestors and cope with those voices singing disparate songs all at once. They were made for this.

And when they were done divining for the public, they withdrew into the recesses of the Divine Temple of the Talking Drum. The great cave's uneven walls loomed over them. It resembled an open mouth crying out. An acute sense of déjà vu washed over them.

We remember this place, a voice in their head said.

Ruu'vim couldn't now ever see the temple with new eyes. This was the same of many places they'd never been to that now felt familiar as were the new memories stored in their drives. Before the hollowed people took possession of them, they made a bargain to also host the souls of Ngano, Baba Do, Adelolade, and dearest to them, Xuda. One bés Ruu'vim too would die and then all would be free to ascend to Eh'wauizo to join the others who came before them whose voices whispered in the wind.

For now, they would carry the souls of these old and new ancestors, healing and teaching, the only living being that had ever crossed the mangled time-threshold of Mahwè and returned.

LOST IN THE ECHOES

by Xan van Rooyen

Magurgurma: a lost Word from The Mother, a sonic tatter carried by the cosmic wind, shaped by storm and whittled by planetary forces, snagged by needle of earth and stone. A demigod born of a broken whisper.

—from "Threnody for a Mother-Fragment," a story of the Ts'jenene

Like blood in water, the music ribboned through the dense atmosphere of the sub-meridian club. Ruk'ugrukun *felt* it: a subtle change in the texture of the air—a thicker current winnowing past his outstretched fingers, triggering the afferent sensors where he'd once had nails. The nanotech heightened his natural sensitivity as if his body were a drum and the world a fist pounding on his skin.

Patrons danced, gyrations loosening flakes of sound from the sonic auras encasing their bodies in invisible scales. No two auras felt alike: this one a sting and judder beneath Ruk's skin, another an itch on his shoulder or an ache between his toes. His own, little more than a subdued murmur—a small mercy for those born Taq'qerara.

The frequencies pummeled his ribs, captured and channeled by the biotech enhancing his nervous system. With his nanoware active and his usual pain ameliorated, he could endure the tumult, sculpting songs from the sonic dandruff patrons shook free. Like this, he could weave subtle healing frequencies into the music already spilling through the speakers.

Ruk glanced down at the writhing crowd from his vantage point on the DJ dais. Nausea roiled through his gut, bitter gorge rising in his throat. Hadn't he run away to escape this? And yet here he stood, bathed in the implicit adoration of the club goers high on the polyrhythmic panacea of his devising.

Braced for the beat drop, he still winced when it happened—his masochism born of guilt and the need to atone. He'd failed his family, but here he did what he could to alleviate fear and angst and tribulation, to replace exhaustion with euphoria in those desperate to escape reality. A few hours gentle reprieve was better than none.

Ruk shuddered and curled his fingers, magic sizzling through his sinews. He was trying to do the right thing even if it might be too late to earn his people's forgiveness, to repair the trust he'd shattered when he'd broken the rules governing his power.

The club would be closing soon as one sun set and the other rose somewhere far above the mire of the city's lower levels. The patrons would have to emerge groggy and disorientated, disgorged from reverie but hopefully rejuvenated. Ruk surrendered to sensation as he embroidered the air with a final rising melody over the pounding bass.

The dancers contorted, limbs plucked by melismatic tendrils of power, faces seized in ecstasy. When it was over, the club goers staggered, released by magic but still drunk on music: their auras more consonant, their souls soothed.

Perhaps if the club owners understood what made Ruk's sets so popular, they'd pay him more, but he was glad he earned enough owo to keep his head above the meridian murk, the threat of eviction as constant as the sonic storms battering the planet.

He deserved nothing more. And he certainly didn't want to draw attention from the Korps that ran the city. He already abused his power for his own gain; he didn't want to become a weapon in Korp hands.

Having reduced the efficacy of his implants, Ruk fled before the house lights incinerated the gloom. He headed down the narrow street leading to one of the numerous elevators. Mist tinged teal and vermilion by the sun-swap billowed in ropy coils, snaking around him like a hungry constrictor. Clouds tumescent with yet to be harvested sound-energy kept the cold trapped in the valleys cut between the planet's peaks. Ruk shivered in the frigid air as heavy footsteps thumped behind him—the sensation ratcheting through his bones.

The elevator doors opened, and figures draped in white boubou emerged, their faces obscured by breathing apparatus and their auras resonating in the stagnant air, already shedding frequencies. On Órino-Rin, the very air chafed auras raw, leaving weeping gaps in the personal orchestration enveloping every human.

Korp members, Ruk surmised. Or maybe members of an upper echelon lowering themselves for the thrill of partying in the slums. But the clubs were closing now, the inhabitants of the underworld slinking back to their dens to recover from yet another night of sensory ravaging.

Ruk cast a suspicious glance over his shoulder. The figure behind him stood with feet planted, legs like boa'oba trees, and arms folded across a barrel chest, the hilt of their dagger on display at their hip. Their aura thrummed and unease curdled Ruk's insides. His hands balled into instinctual fists, muscles tensed and ready for flight or fight. He had nowhere to run, hemmed in by walls and flesh.

The white-clad person at the elevator gestured with a flick of gloved fingers, the movements stiff and awkward but at least discernible. With the breathing apparatus, there was no way for Ruk to interpret their expression, but the hand gestures were at least a passable attempt at Sign. Not the visual language used in the city, but the dialect exclusive to his people: the Ts'jenene.

Ruk shook his head, using his hands to tell them they had the wrong guy.

They spelled out Ruk's name, phoneme for phoneme: Ruk'ugrukun kel Az'zagru. And then, the sign he most despised, a swirl of wrist and flutter of fingers naming him Taq'qerara. They knew what he could do.

Come with us, they signed before their hand drifted to the weapon on their hip.

Ruk's shoulders slumped in defeat. Meekly, he allowed himself to be ushered into the elevator. He worked for whomever offered the better pay, trawling the clubs scattered across all eight extensions of the sprawling city, deliberately never loyal to any one Korp. For the sake of self-preservation, he kept everyone at a distance.

In the elevator, the one who'd signed pressed their wrist to the biometric panel, paying a sum that made Ruk giddy with disbelief. The doors closed and the elevator began to rise. They were packed in tight, shoulders brushing and vibrations clamoring—a sharp stone caught in his shoe rubbing away restless echoes that swirled and lingered in the confines. He resisted the urge to reach for the aural effluvia, to hook them with a careful finger, shaping them with Mother-given signs into magical melodies. Instead, he buried his hands in his pockets, jaw clenched at the waste.

As they rose up the extension, so the clouds thinned and the sky brightened, but Ruk's heart grew heavy with dread. When they switched elevators at the meridian station where the atmospheric density decreased, Ruk sucked in a dizzying breath, savoring the lighter air few could afford to live in. They were still a long way from the towers where the truly wealthy made their homes.

Once inside the next elevator, the white-clad group finally revealed their pristine faces. Each had the chrome of the Kor'ebibi Korp embedded in their left temples.

Ruk tasted blood as he choked on his fear.

Magurgurma, upon the mountain: impaled and impregnated by a bombastic storm. From the dissonant clash of forces—air and earth—tumbled two daughters. Each carried within them a fragment of the Mother's word, a healing utterance, and yet they could not staunch the wound of the one who birthed them.

—from "Threnody for a Mother-Fragment," a story of the Ts'jenene

Ruk had seen Órino-Rin from above.

He'd grown up a nomad, in a home floating through the proximal zone between spires and storm clouds.

The planet was a sea of verticals, wave upon wave of needles all pointed at the sky where the suns courted each other in a fiery dance.

It was the larger star that Órino-Rin orbited and that now illuminated the morning with its superior glow.

Squinting against the glare, he remembered his childhood view of the planet where still uninhabited mountain peaks punctuated those capped with cities, all connected by rhizomatic highways. These the Ts'jenene traced for ease of their own aerial navigation, drifting in their tent-ships from one city to another in search of trade.

But Ruk had never set foot on one of the spires.

Now he stood at a floor-to-ceiling window east of central Mokigu. The city spilled like an impaled pwezapwe—its eight tentacle extensions trailing down the mountainside, latched to the bedrock in defiance of the atmosphere.

Again, a tide of nausea rolled from his toes to his temples as he gazed down.

A disturbance in the atoms, a vacillating vibration of approaching feet—small, light, determined.

Ruk turned to face the newcomer, their aura already gnawing like broken teeth at his nerves.

Short, petite, spine straight, hair an ebony torrent, eyes twin black holes of jet and glimmer.

The vertigo will pass, the person signed with deft fingers. *I'm Iya Kor'ebibi.* She used a sign audaciously similar to the one reserved for The Mother, before shaping the phonemes of her kin name.

Ruk tried not to react to the almost-blasphemy. He was in the presence of the Kor'ebibi matriarch, one of the most powerful Korps on the planet. He, who was less than one of the scuttling memedede bugs infesting the squalid crannies of every extension. And, unlike the memedede bugs, Ruk was not all that hard to kill. He would not survive this woman's ire should he provoke it. He inclined his head in a polite gesture of greeting.

Iya Kor'ebibi glided toward the wall opposite the window where the light from the sun turned her sharp-cut suit a blinding white, lapels gleaming silver to match the kin patterns embroidered in shiny thread on cuffs and hems. Ruk squinted against the rays reflecting from elaborate display cases housing a variety of artifacts, a timeline of the five planets rendered in slivers and shards.

One statuette caught his attention, the figurine fully intact and meticulously carved from wood most likely sourced from Wiimb-o. He recognized it as one of the legendary Kali-twins, Kali-Yeh perhaps, given the typically female anatomy. While Ruk knew the Órino-Rin-born twins had been living, breathing people capable of incredible feats of sound magic, he'd always questioned the part about their ability to tear through the veil of unreality. Hearing the legends as a child, he'd always wondered if the twins also carried splinter-sounds from Magurgurma, and if so, had their shards festered as his did?

Iya Kor'ebibi caught him studying the figurine, her gaze searing as she began to sign. *I'm a big fan of your work. Your abilities are almost as impressive as theirs.* She gestured to the Kali figure.

Ruk shook his head, palms sweaty as her aura continued to trill across his skin. *I'm honored. I didn't think you'd enjoy the extension clubbing scene.*

Cute. She brushed her chin with index and middle fingers, her mouth a thin slit of a smile. *I meant your* other *work. I keep my eyes on the maadiregi, in all extensions, especially my own.*

He'd never meant to reveal the power that had earned him venerated status with his tribe, but the tech required to soften the blow of sound even as it amplified internal sensation was expensive and could only be installed by a maadiregi, an engineer trained in the ways of both magic and technology.

Desperate, Ruk had sought out a maadiregi with questionable scruples and an even more malleable aura. And so he'd once again broken the first tenet governing the use of the Taq'qerara's power. It had been easier to pretend he felt nothing when he didn't have to look his worshipers in the eyes. Even so, abusing his power had only amplified his guilt. He'd promised himself then it would be the last time he did it for selfish gain.

But he was weak, and the magic came too easy.

Iya Kor'ebibi regarded him with a raised eyebrow. She had delicate chrome laced across her forehead in a fractal topography reminiscent of the scars marking Ruk's own face, a cauterized geometry worn by the women of the Az'zagru tribe. At fifteen, when the tribal healer had cut and sung his breasts to thin lines of keloid, the patterns had been altered and *she* became *he*. If only the uroh-ogi could've also excised the Mother-sliver embedded in his soul; if only the healer could've sung away the power he didn't deserve.

Surprised by an unusual wave of homesickness, Ruk flexed his fingers. *I don't know*—but Iya Kor'ebibi grabbed his hand, tapping her thumb on the sensors in his fingertips before continuing to sign.

Don't lie to me. I know what you did. I know what you are. That sign again naming him Taq'qerara.

Ruk crossed his arms as if he could hide his hands and his guilt.

Do what I ask, and you'll never know poverty again. Iya Kor'ebibi's face turned granite and steel. *You'll never have to worry about rent or food. You'll be able to keep your head above the clouds and upgrade your sensors.* So she'd noticed his fingers capped in rusting tech. *All I ask is that you do for me what you did to the maadiregi.*

What you're asking me to do is illegal, he signed.

Her lips peeled back to reveal blunt but perfect teeth, incisors capped in silver to match her forehead. The laughter trickled over Ruk's skin like drizzle.

Didn't stop you before. Her fingers moved deftly.

What you're asking me to do is … wrong. He knew it, felt it twist deep down in his organ meat as a familiar self-loathing simmered to the surface.

Now you care? she signed, as if she knew the rules he'd broken, the bonds he'd severed the moment he'd touched another's aura without their consent. And wasn't he still doing that near nightly in the club, even if he was doing it for their benefit? If he truly wanted to make things right, he would forfeit his power altogether and never shape another soul-sound again.

But Ruk couldn't seem to help himself. Why give him this power only to stifle it? And yet, the wrongness of what he'd done—and continued to do—flogged his insides.

For several moments, Ruk floundered. When had deceit become routine? When had lies replaced his Mother-tongue? He'd only wanted to escape his tribe and their constant demands, the pain he'd had to endure answering others' pleas, the disappointment he would've been when they discovered how he'd ground their trust and hope to ashes. But what if this was the answer to his own prayers—one final sound-shaping granting him so much owo he'd never be tempted to touch another person's aura?

Did he even have a choice?

If I refuse? he asked.

She tilted her head, long hair swaying, fingers dancing across her throat.

Instinctively, Ruk swallowed then sucked in a mouthful of rarefied air, hypocrisy fermenting in his gut as he nodded, his conscience already bleeding.

Magurgurma, bleeding out: a trail of echoes slip-sliding down cliff and soaking into valley; fractured echoes whipped away by fingers of blue lightning, flung across the sky to burrow through ears and settle in the bones of the Ts'jenene—wanderers of the firmament, captives of the echoes. An honor to be so soul-burdened; an honor to be born Taq'qerara.

—from "Threnody for a Mother-Fragment," a story of the Ts'jenene

The body lay inert, imprisoned by sound.

Ruk felt it before he saw it, a pattering against his ribs as if someone were playing his bones like the wooden slats of a mari'imba. The person lay supine, pillows cradling their shoulders and propping up their knees. They seemed at peace, face slack beneath the intricate tattoo spilling from their right temple to disappear beneath the arrow-cut neckline of their colorful dashiki. Blue, black, and red—like the web of ink decorating their skin.

Ruk could almost believe they were merely asleep instead of being held captive, except for the headphones clinging to their ears like the city itself clung to the mountain. Sound magic to render a body inert and disrupt the signal from the comm chip embedded in their wrist.

Taji'iba Kor'ochoyo, Iya Kor'ebibi signed out the phonemes. *Heir apparent to the Kor'ochoyo korp. She's the one you need to—* The matriarch made a swirling motion with her hand as if stirring a pot.

Kor'ochoyo. One of the few families who stood between Kor'ebibi and dominion over all the other Órino-Rin Korps.

Why? Ruk asked, gaze flicking to Taji'iba.

War, so old-fashioned, Iya Kor'ebibi began, *but unavoidable, and I'd rather spare the city unnecessary bloodshed.*

The Korps were known for territorial disputes, but as long as the casualties remained below the cloud meridian, city officials rarely did much to contain the violence.

I've always preferred more subtle strategies, she continued. *The scalpel, not the hammer.* She smoothed down the baby hairs at her temples as she regarded Ruk with a measured gaze. *You will be my scalpel. Change Taji'iba, like you did the maadiregi.*

Ruk wiped the sweat from his hands before moving his fingers. *That was a small, temporary change.* He'd never made significant or lasting adjustments. Only minor tweaks to get him what he wanted without raising too much suspicion in his victim.

This must be permanent, Iya Kor'ebibi gave an emphatic twist of her wrist. *I need this to be slow. I need Kor'ochoyo to crumble from the inside and* she *will make that happen, thanks to you.*

I can only tweak what's already there. I can't alter the nature of a person. Ruk suppressed a shudder as he approached the bed. To permanently alter an aura—a soul—would sever their connection from Mother, perhaps even deny the person access to the afterlife.

Iya Kor'ebibi wore an affable expression, but her gaze was calculating. *You do it every night in the clubs.*

What he did with the music, picking up dropped fragments and recombining them into entirely new soundscapes—that was different. He did it to help the patrons, to minimize anguish, to heal sore hearts, and return those who'd lost the beat to a steady rhythm. A paltry attempt at making up for all the times he'd abused his power.

Ruk shook his head as he touched the fingers of his right hand to his forehead and pulled them away again. The pattering of Taji'iba's aura became knuckles knocking at his bones, while Iya Kor'ebibi's continued to grate at his flesh like a lover's teeth eager to devour, a disorientating mix of pain and pleasure.

Iya Kor'ebibi stamped her foot to get his attention, the vibration tickling the soles of his feet.

Unlike Taji here, she pointed at the body on the bed, *I wasn't born into power. I've fought for every scrap and clawed my way to the top.* Her gaze drifted to the windows. *You might not believe that I was once like you, some city*—she hesitated before using the sign for rat, for vermin—*drowning below the meridian, but I believed in my ability to bend the world to my will.* There was a threat in her gestures. Ruk would bend to her will or be broken. *Now it's your turn to seize this opportunity.*

An acid effervescence scorched his insides as Iya Kor'ebibi sashayed closer. She smelled faintly of thiouraye, a traditional mix of wood shavings and spices common among the Ts'jenene yet so highly prized among the city dwellers.

On this world, you don't get what you deserve, she signed, every gesture slow and deliberate. *You get what you take, so … take it.* She snapped her fingers into a fist before jerking her chin at the unconscious body.

Her words looped through Ruk's mind, a ligation of dark intent and even darker understanding. He squeezed his eyes shut, breathing deep against the battering of the women's auras.

He opened his eyes, decided.

One more time and then never again. He stamped the last shreds of his conscience into the guilt-ridden mire of his past knowing he could never be forgiven for what he was about to do.

You can't be here for this.

She raised a questioning brow.

Your aura is … distracting. He wouldn't let it be the blunt-force trauma he'd inflicted on the maadiregi. *And it might be dangerous for you to be so close when—* He hesitated before swirling his fingers, trying hard not to grimace at the gesture.

Fine. I'll leave you two, but we'll be watching. Iya Kor'ebibi pointed to an orb recessed in the ceiling, a single eye ensuring he did as commanded.

Ruk perched gingerly on the edge of the bed and raised his hands. Braced for the onslaught of sensation, he increased the sensitivity of the sensors and let himself explore the sonorous landscape of Taji'iba Kor'ochoyo.

Magurgurma, decayed and tacet: waiting for the Taq'qerara, for the one Mother-touched and born of silence, who might hold the echoes, reshape the sound, and one day wake Magurgurma who will sing the Word and make Mother whole again.

—from "Threnody for a Mother-Fragment," a story of the Ts'jenene

Ruk sank into an ocean of vibration.

A thrill in his marrow and winnows of electricity swimming through his blood—he exhaled, smoothing the staggered thudding in his chest into an aching hemiola as he and Taji'iba became entrained to the primal beat all children of The Mother carried within. Even as the Taq'qerara, as hollow as a gutted kalabash, Ruk felt the throb that was the heart of the universe, of The Mother.

Taji'iba was a stew of oscillation and Ruk rode those waveforms, sliding up every peak and delving into every trough, her aura so like the jagged landscape of Órino-Rin.

Echoes upon echoes, filling up his hollows.

Ruk relinquished the last of his control and his senses flared, fingertip sensors channeling his natural ability.

He luxuriated in her sound, marinating in the ebb and flow of her soul as he traced the stitches of her symphonic tapestry, analyzing themes and composing the variations that would leave her changed. Her aura was layered in melodies looping lazy serpentines through harmony both consonant and dissonant. Moments of darkness balanced with light, a harshness gentled with gliding harmonics—for every punch, a caress—a morass of profound complexity. How dare he think to muddy such an exquisite rendition of Mother-sound.

He couldn't do it. He wouldn't, even if it meant being tossed from a city balustrade and shattered against the cliff, feeding the scavengers before being eroded to dust by the planet's heavy air, to be swallowed by the spreading silence drenching the valleys, subsumed into absence. He didn't expect he'd be granted entry to Eh'wauizo and allowed to walk among the spirits of his ancestors.

He deserved to rot and decay, to vanish, forgotten and unmourned.

Ruk withdrew, delicately untangling himself from Taji'iba's aura. He signed so those watching would see, *Not yet, I still need time,* before angling his back to the eye above and slipping the headphones from Taji's ears.

Taji'iba blinked open dark eyes. Her gaze flicked across the room before settling on Ruk, mouth pressed into a tight line as her body tensed.

"You're not Kor'ebibi," she said, and Ruk read the shapes of her lips.

He shook his head, wondering how to explain if she didn't know Sign.

"I've seen you in the clubs. Extension Six. I've ..." She added something Ruk didn't catch.

Kor'ebibi hired me. He signed the phonemes refusing to use the gesture so close for Mother to name the matriarch. *She wanted me to change you, so you'd sabotage your Korp.* He added the stirring motion of his hand, hoping Taji would understand.

Her expression darkened, lines knitting across her forehead in a scowl as she tapped her wrist where the comm chip shimmered beneath her skin.

I didn't. I couldn't, Ruk signed, careful to keep his gestures hidden from those who were watching.

Taji raised a subtle finger to the ceiling and whispered, "They'll kill you."

I deserve it. I am not a good person.

"Are any of us?" Taji asked. "But even the worst people can still do good things. So how about ..."

A change in air pressure, the retort of heavy steps, hands on his shoulders, and the pleasurable resonance of Iya Kor'ebibi's aura. Ruk groaned, his sensors still heightening all aural sensation. He turned them down, tension draining from his shoulders as the ache of aura-exposure was attenuated.

Is it done? she asked, glaring at Taji'iba.

Ruk hesitated, casting a surreptitious glance at Taji who had managed to smooth her expression into one of docile compliance.

I tried. We'll only know with time.

The accompanying Korp members hauled Taji from the bed as Iya Kor'ebibi perched beside Ruk. Her hands had only just begun to shape her words when blood splattered her face and peppered her white suit crimson.

Ruk watched the stains spread, breath caught in his throat, heart seized in a fist of fear. Sticky heat dribbled down his own face where he too had been spattered.

Bodies slumped, flesh hitting hard floor with a thud Ruk felt in his jaw. Finally, he turned, following Iya Kor'ebibi's gaze to Taji. She stood over the corpses, a dripping Òbe in her hand, no doubt slipped from one of her captors who'd assumed she'd be compliant. She pointed the blade at Iya Kor'ebibi, speaking words Ruk couldn't parse, though each felt like gashes in his skin.

"You won't get out of this building alive," Iya Kor'ebibi said, signing simultaneously for Ruk's benefit. "Neither of you. My people are watching." She raised a finger. "You're both already dead."

"So are you." Taji advanced, her intention clear.

The blade glinted in the rays from Juah-āju slicing across the floorboards. Ruk braced for a scream, for pleading and tears, but Iya Kor'ebibi canted her head, revealing the vulnerable flesh of her throat.

"Before I go, tell me why." She spoke out loud and with her hands, her question directed at Ruk. "You could've had everything."

Ruk studied his fingers, trying to understand why he'd failed to do what had been so easy so many times before.

It would've been wrong. It wasn't what my power was intended for. I want to do good. I want to do better.

How he wished he'd taken a different route home, that he could fold back time and return to the life he'd known before. Perhaps he never should've left the Ts'jenene and instead admitted his failings, endured their wrath and disappointment.

"You have so much power," Iya Kor'ebibi said. "What a waste."

Taji slit the woman's throat with the Kor'ebibi blade and eased her onto the bed as her last breath bubbled red across her lips.

Ruk felt himself screaming, the scrape and shear of ragged breath in his throat, the formless syllable catching at his teeth as it spewed from his tongue. The scent of fresh iron filled his nose along with the sharp tang of excrement as the matriarch's body surrendered to death.

Battling involuntary tears with eyes burning as if they'd been scrubbed with black pepper, Ruk reached for Iya Kor'ebibi's hand. Her aura was quieting now, the sensation dulled to the patter of an echo.

He wasn't familiar with their customs; he didn't know what rites the Kor'ebibi family might grant their recently deceased or how they might call to the spirits of Eh'wauizo to come and claim one of their own.

"You weep for her?" Taji wiped blood from the knife before stowing it in a stolen sheath on her hip. "Her Korp has hurt people all over this city," Taji continued. "Without her, the Kor'ebibi Korp will fall. Things will be better."

With Kor'ochoyo in power? His fingers trembled.

Taji'iba regarded him, gaze intense. "You could've done as she asked and ensured my family failed."

I didn't want to use my power, not for this. Ruk staggered away from the bed.

"We all make choices." Taji's tone was indiscernible with his sensors dialed down, her expression inscrutable.

I've been trying to help people.

"Me too. I killed a tyrant. The people of Moki-gu will thank me. Well, some might not." She grinned at that and folded her arms.

I never wanted any of this.

Taq'qerara. Sound-shaper.

To be Taq'qerara was to be a walking wound assaulted by sound, with scabs scraped raw by every murmur.

He studied Iya Kor'ebibi, her throat a second mouth peeled open in wet ribbons, watched as Taji'iba picked drying blood from her fingers as if they were no more than specks of dirt. His own skin itched with magic and shame, guilt and a gnawing sense of duty.

He was meant to search, to give and give and never want more than gratitude in return, until the day he fulfilled the prophecy and returned the syllables dropped and scattered from Mother's tongue. It had never been enough. He'd always wanted more, thought he *deserved* more, and resented being denied the opportunity to use his power as he saw fit. He wasn't worthy to bear the mantle The Mother had bestowed upon him.

Ruk flinched when Taji's hand touched his shoulder.

"As long as you have power," she said, "there will always be those who want it for themselves, or to exploit it."

You included? He flicked his fingers, hoping she could sense his animosity.

She shrugged. "I can see many ways we could use you. For good, as you claim to want."

He bristled at that but had no time to respond. Her lips were still moving.

"Power will always be a double-edged sword." She traced the tattoo on her face with her thumb. "We're all fallible, despite our good intentions." Her gaze dropped to the corpse of her rival. "No matter how hard we try, we all fail. And having good intentions doesn't exonerate us from that failure, and you—"

Ruk looked away, not wanting to read the words on her lips.

Instead, he slid to the floor between puddles of gore. A rush of footsteps, shouts reaching him like blows to the shins. Kor'ochoyo forces summoned by Taji'iba come to the rescue, and now Korps members were no doubt slaughtering each other just beyond the closed doors.

You don't get what you deserve, Iya Kor'ebibi's words echoed in his skull. *You get what you take.*

Take, take, take. All he'd ever done because he'd been asked to give.

When he'd first been named Taq'qerara and placed upon a skewering pedestal, his people had come to him in supplication, their adoration like sonic caresses soothing his aching flesh. *You must search, must find, release, heal, you must fulfill the prophecy.* Their adulation became like nails, leaving him bloodied and suffocating beneath the weight of their expectation.

Perhaps he could indeed use his power one last time.

He would remake himself. He would unbecome what he'd never wanted to be—a scar to finally seal the hurt, numbing his senses to the world.

The Mother had made a mistake before and Ruk had had to correct his anatomy.

It had been another mistake to make him Taq'qerara. But no more.

As the sound of fighting escalated, assaulting every nerve, Ruk used the pain to sink deep within himself. There, the sliver that had invaded him. A splinter sloughed from Magurgurma and blown like a feathered seed to lodge within him: Mother's orphaned utterance.

The lost syllables became a sonic storm within the confines of his flesh as violent and tumultuous as those lambasting the planet. His body convulsed—a symphony of cataclysmic sensation, and yet, the agony helped him to focus.

Take it, take it, take it.

His mind met with the slicing heat of the echo. He took hold, wrenching the fragment from where it vibrated in agitation in the thicket of his soul. Perhaps it would be enough, he thought as he plucked and unraveled, tearing the parasitic sound loose from its improper host.

Take it—and let it go.

He relaxed, every strained sinew releasing tension as he loosened his grip on the sound fragment. It slid and slithered through his insides, a trail of raw iron in its wake as it clawed up his throat and across his tongue, cracking teeth in its desperate need for liberation.

Ruk opened his mouth in a scream he couldn't hear and felt the echo of terror from others in close proximity.

Glass shattered and the tower lurched. Ruk opened his eyes when strong hands wrenched him to his feet.

"Go now if you want to live." Taji'iba yelled into his face even as the floor tipped beneath their feet. He saw her lips move but felt nothing. Not even the faintest ghost tickle though she continued to scream orders at the various Korp members scrambling for purchase while the tower swayed.

Ruk wanted to live.

He gathered his limbs and ran.

The music pulsed through the dense atmosphere of the club. Ruk felt it in the coils of his guts, an extraneous thumping behind his ribs and buzz in his back teeth. He raised his arms in mimetic movement of those around him, scarred fingers capped in gel tips painted black.

He danced, every gyration no doubt loosening flakes of sound from the sonic auras of the dancers, but he heard nothing, his body buoyed by pleasant tides of throbbing bass.

He glanced up at the DJ weaving music and magic through the sweat-soaked air, watching as they raised their arm in anticipation of the beat drop.

He still braced for pain, still flinched whenever someone opened their mouth, but he was no longer assaulted by the sounds he couldn't hear, his soul a gentle ripple in the sea of silence in which he floated. When the DJ's fist dropped, a flood of cooling relief soused Ruk's veins.

He'd managed to escape, and here he stood—ignored and unknown—one more murk-dweller spending precious owo on a sensory soothing in a club now owned by the Kor'ochoyo Korp, the walls daubed blue, black, and red.

Kor'ebibi was no more. Iya Kor'ebibi had been crushed in the rubble of her own tower, destroyed by a sophisticated magic attack some sources speculated. Others suspected the Kor'ochoyo Korp had deployed a high-tech energy weapon to bring down their enemies in a terrifying display of ruthless power.

Only Ruk and Taji'iba knew the truth.

He checked the time. The transport would be leaving soon, his seat secured courtesy of the Kor'ochoyo Korp.

Wreathed in blissfully numb silence, Ruk rode the elevators up and out of the extension, disembarking at a mid-tier station where an assortment of ships awaited myriad cargo. And there, the one marked in Korp colors that would take him to the flotilla of Ts'jenene crafts drifting above the city.

Home, he thought. Home to face his people, their ire and whatever reparations they deemed necessary, though he wouldn't be returning an utter failure. Ruk strode toward the waiting transport, hesitating when the now familiar quake juddered up through his feet, a constant quiver across the skin of the planet as Órino-Rin cracked its spine, mountains shivering.

Ruk smiled before finding his seat. Magurgurma had been stirred to waking.

NCHETA

by Chisom Umeh

Ncheta does his best to help the man remember. He tries to connect the dots, pull strings of memories together, mend the broken web of long-held moments and cherished experiences. But even he, the spirit of the past and the present, cannot save his host's mind. So he watches. He watches the memories of the man's children and grandchildren become motes of dust in a whirlwind. He sees the family gather around his host's bed, the daughter and her child, his mother and her sister. But the man does not know them anymore and would breathe his last not even knowing himself.

Ncheta drifts out before the man draws his final breath lest he be trapped in a decaying corpse. Because no matter how much a spirit loves their host, in the end, they must love themselves. It is the one thing the Benevolent shares with the Malevolent. But while the latter accepts this fact and easily moves on, the former often mourns as their host is interred into the ground.

Five moons later, Ncheta is in a tavern on the edge of Ana Mmuo. Beside this inn flows the interminable waters of River Mmirioma, stretching across the length of the realm, giving life to those who are beyond life themselves. This river is supposed to mark the boundaries between this world and that of humans, but rumors have it that these lines, in recent days, have begun to smother each other. Apparently, a virtual realm grows from the bowels of the sacred waters, reaching out, forcing its way into Ana Mmuo.

"I've seen it," says Asiri, sitting across from Ncheta. "It exists, and it's the humans who built it."

Ncheta is barely listening, his mind wandering off to places far beyond the bicker and chatter of the numerous beings in the tavern. Ncheta can see his former host again, smiling at a woman, telling her she looks beautiful and that he'd like to marry her again. This woman, with her smile so soft and her scent so strong, plays along. To him, she stretches her finger and asks that he slides the wedding band on it. He searches his pockets for the ring, even though he never bought one. When he finds nothing, she laughs and says, "Daddy, just pretend you have one."

"No such thing exists," Ncheta finally says to Asiri, shrugging off the caressing touch of his memories. "Humans aren't capable of building such a thing."

"Oh, it's been millennia since the First One created you," Asiri says, "and yet you're still naïve."

"And you've been what, seven-hundred years?" he retorts. "Yet you think yourself more knowledgeable than I am."

Asiri lets out a wry laugh, and Ncheta can only wonder if it was just the gossip spirit laughing or everyone in the tavern. Sometimes it's hard to tell. She does this thing where she speaks in many voices at the same time, and but for close attention, a listener would likely mistake it for the speech of a multitude.

"With you, age is really numbers," she says and shakes her head, her droopy cheeks wiggling. "They call it virtual reality. They attach themselves to it and their minds wander off. They don't know it yet, they often think they remain in their rooms even, but they've been intruding into the heart of our world."

"I only just left my host several moons back," Ncheta says, the initial confidence slowly escaping his voice. "So when did they advance enough to build such an impossible thing?"

Asiri leans in, her body mass tilting the table. Ncheta beholds her eyes—in every one of them, he finds a deathly seriousness. "You've been living in your head for so long," she says, "that you've failed to see how things are changing. You've forgotten that a lifetime to them is but a moon to us. And in that time, they've become more efficient at engineering their doom. It took centuries for them to build boats to cross seas, now they need only decades to build machines to cross worlds."

Ncheta leans back and considers this for a second. Could it be possible that humans have built a machine that interferes with Ana Mmuo? Speculations of such a device did reach him before he left, but it was only a pipe dream even his host didn't take seriously. But if Ncheta is being honest, he'd remember that through the innumerable hosts he has lived in, he has beheld them walk out of caves and lay waste to creatures three times their size. Then watched them do the same to lands and water bodies a million times their size. He's seen them spread even beyond the planet itself to touch the moon. If he is to attempt honesty, he'd admit that it was only a matter of time before this ravenous species found his world and sank their teeth into it.

This is why Ncheta used to hate them. Or, perhaps, how he justified his hatred for them. Because something about these bipeds always reaches for destruction, even their own. And, by Ana, Ncheta never understood this. And for a long time, it kept him angry—not at *them*, just their propensity to forge chaos from order.

"It started as a small spot on the far side of the river," Asiri says, "like a tear in the fabric of our world. Then it began to grow. And soon it was twice the size of a human village."

Ncheta stares at Asiri then takes a swig of his drink brewed from the essence of the river herself, feeling her energy course through him. Tainted by a foreignness, it is now extra bitter. Ncheta used to think it was a new flavor, or that the barkeep had lost his touch, or that something in the alchemic workings of Ana Mmuo's breweries just wasn't right. Only now is he learning that it is the river herself who is getting sick, infected by the meeting of parallel worlds.

"I can take you to see it," Asiri says. "If you're willing to leave your ego by the door."

Ncheta empties his cup and is about to rise when an energy fills the tavern. Every other being feels it too, and the chatter seizes in response. An Old Deity manifests at the doorway, their aura vibrant and thick. They proceed slowly, their feet digging into the ground even though they can glide right over it.

Agwu likes to draw attention to themself and grows more arrogant with each passing moon. They do not walk around tables like sane beings do, rather, they move in a straight line from the door and tables are adjusted for them.

They are not here to have a drink though, just come to allow others to drink in their presence. Ncheta keeps his eyes focused on his empty cup as Agwu passes, sure enough that Asiri is doing the same, neither of them wanting any trouble, because with this deity as little as eye contact can bring fire and brimstone.

Agwu crosses the room and stands, and Ncheta feels their aura halt.

"I am the one humans thank when they have clarity of mind," they say, "and the one they beg in supplication when their son is feeding from a dumpster. But humans are no longer praying, so you must forgive me for seeking attention elsewhere."

The tension Ncheta feels breaks and a sliver of anger slips through the cracks. A memory takes him prisoner and in its dark cages, he sees a man. No, many men. They look sickly, their skins leathery and dotted with black spots. Ncheta sees them all, hands stretching from between iron bars, begging him to free them. Each of them he has once lived in, each he has taken something from. Watching them, he is tempted by their pleas, almost gives in.

"Leave them be," a voice says from behind, and Ncheta turns to meet Agwu. "They have transgressed, so this is their fate. Come, Malevolent, there's much work to be done."

"These people rely more on their phantom world and tech, now," Agwu continues in the tavern, their words calm yet powerful, quiet yet omnipresent. "And have left our worship places untended. I used to visit their children because they failed to pour libations on my altar, and sometimes after I was done, chains weren't enough to shackle them."

The words rattle in Ncheta's ears, and he sees the rusty chains dragging on sand. To keep himself from hearing, he presses his hands to his ears, but Agwu has a way of making themself heard even if you don't want to listen. The words pry Ncheta's fingers apart and register themselves in his consciousness. They feed him grief and force regret down his throat till he quivers in his seat.

Agwu raises a wine-filled cup and says, "But now, not a single prayer has been offered in moons to replenish my power, and so I must drink this sour concoction with the rest of you lowly things." The last words in Agwu's sentence come off firmer and louder than the rest. The deity looks like they're angry, their jaw tight and their face wrinkling, but you'd be ignorant of Agwu's nature to assume their disposition from the arrangement of their face. Their clothes are not really clothes, just projections of Agwu's aura wrapped around them like a halo. So the clothes change with each new decibel Agwu's voice reaches and, some even say, are a better reflection of the deity's countenance.

Ncheta looks around the tavern, and every being is pretending not to listen. Benevolents are bad at this game though, shifting and turning and fidgeting. Malevolents are better, their eyes following Agwu's every movement. Ncheta wonders if any of the Malevolents would be valiant or stupid enough to take on Agwu. The deity did say that prayers to them have dwindled and supposedly their energy too, so it might not be entirely stupid for a Malevolent to push their luck. A mere spirit taking on an Old Deity would be a spectacle in these small corners of Ana Mmuo. Or it'd be an execution; a quick absorbing of an unfortunate spirit's energy, boring and uneventful.

Agwu's eyes catch Ncheta's, and the spirit looks away, at his table, tracing the jagged markings on the old wood. He shouldn't have raised his head. He shouldn't have taken his eyes from his cup.

"Some of you want to live like them now," he hears Agwu say. "Even though you had all the potential to walk beside us as gods. Right, Ncheta?"

Ncheta answers in a memory. An old memory. "Yes, Agwu." He bows to the Old Deity and disconnects his host from his past, his memories, leaving the man an ember of his former self. The man, an illustrious merchant who had traveled across seas bringing back ornaments and stories, bales of clothes and the histories of the people who once wore them, now wanders the streets unclad, speaking tongues even the gods do not understand. He feeds from dumpsters and fishes with his bare hands. He is caught stealing from someone's farm and judged to be a nuisance fit to be hanged among the village's outlaws.

On the day of the execution, Ncheta prepares himself to drift out, Agwu standing beside him.

"He saw too much," the Old Deity mutters. "Began to convince people they no longer needed us. You did well, Malevolent."

Ncheta wants to question this deity, wants to plead mercy for his host. But they call Ncheta a Malevolent, so how can things like these bother him? How can a spirit war against his own spiritedness, the very same thing for which he exists? It'd be like a man engaging his chi in combat, a river drinking itself, fire burning its own flames.

The noose is inches from his host's neck when confusion spreads among the crowd. They are watching a man about to wear his death like a neckpiece. Like the gold chains he once sold them. But now they seem to have found something more interesting. A slender woman with a wrapper on her breasts. She raises her voice above the din, yelling something.

"I saw them with my eyes," she says, pointing two fingers to her bulged eyeballs. "Ananka, they are at the gates. Their soldiers can kill us with their stare alone. We need every man we can spare, even that one about to hang himself."

Ncheta catches Agwu's eyes, and although they hold no emotions, their flowing robe has taken the shade of a blood moon, fiery and thick. Ncheta sees the spirit in the slender woman, a Benevolent. The spirit sees him too, and Ncheta knows this young creature just made herself an eternal enemy of Agwu's.

"Antibalance Season is here," Agwu says now in the tavern. "The First One has seen it, and we can feel its energy spreading fast through the ether."

Ncheta checks again, and now everyone is shuddering. Asiri's eyes are starting to retreat into their sockets, hiding themselves in her face. She sees Ncheta looking and turns away as if her fear isn't mutual.

"In a short while, you cretins will begin to feel it too," Agwu continues. "So if you think we gods and goddesses are the only ones who should be worried about humans' indifference about us, then think again, because when Antibalance comes, there'll be no place for you to hide."

When Asiri leads Ncheta through the banks of River Mmirioma, passing over the waterfall and tributary where the water is both boiling hot and freezing cold, and the caves where the giants live, she is no longer chatty. They move quietly, each contemplating Agwu's words.

If Antibalance is here then it means only one thing—a mad scramble for bodies, frantic searches for human spaces to be tenanted in because unembodied spirits at this time will be removed from existence and their energies recycled.

Every twenty-fifth moon it used to show up and was due five moons back when Ncheta was still embodied, but recent happenings have made it unpredictable, and now it is here, like a man heading for his farm on the heels of dusk.

Ncheta and Asiri reach the burgeoning dome that is the new world. This high on a hill, they can see how the phantom realm sits on the southern shoulder of River Mmirioma. If they didn't know this place very well, having existed for centuries and millennia, they wouldn't have believed the river once passed through this road. The dome is fifty or sixty feet tall and stretches hundreds of kilometers across. It is from this river that the First One formed the first spirit beings before leaving it to Antibalance to carry on creation. From her depths came Ncheta's essence. But now she is birthing something else, something strange and perplexing.

The skin of the dome is translucent, glowing aquamarine and lapis lazuli. Inside, small blob-like figures are flying around: the self-images of the humans. They fluctuate and dissipate. They move and halt and swirl.

"It was smaller when I last saw it," Asiri says, "with only a couple hundred minds. Now … now … it looks almost like a city."

"Can we get in?" Ncheta asks.

"No, we can't. We can't even inhabit any human when they are in this world, meaning surviving Antibalance would be twice as hard this season."

"Can we at least get closer?"

They descend the hill and come within twenty feet of the dome. They see a being standing closer to it, watching from the outside. They move closer and stand beside her. Ncheta can see from his peripheral vision that Mmirioma is no longer shimmering as much as she used to. She's still intimidatingly tall though, standing eight feet above Ncheta and Asiri. But her aura isn't as domineering; it shifts and fluctuates like the human minds within the dome. The fact that they had to come this close to notice her is a testament to her waning powers.

"Is Antibalance season really here?" Ncheta breaks the silence.

"It is," says Mmirioma without turning to look at him. Her voice is like the calling of a whale, loud and poignant, reaching the skies and back, compensating for her dying aura. Her apparel is luminescent liquid, flowing from her neck to her feet. Staying close to her feels like riding waves and drowning at the same time. "I can smell it now," she says.

Ncheta and Asiri exchange glances. "Everything's unstable now," Ncheta says. "I can't even believe this is happening to you."

Mmirioma turns, not a full turn, just enough to look at Ncheta, then she faces the dome again. "You spirits practically live inside the humans. You should be the least surprised about what they can do. How they can alter their world and ours."

"But this has never happened before," says Asiri.

"It has always been happening. Their actions have always been leading up to this. They corrupt everything they touch. Why do you think Ana never let them back on the moon?"

Ncheta remembers. Trash and junk and dirt on the First Mother's hallowed grounds. The goddess later revolted and forced Agwu to sow discord and disinterest in their minds so that they never returned to the celestial body.

"Sadly," says Asiri, "we still depend on them. The gods still need their supplication, and we still dress up in their skin."

"Yes, yes. Very true." Mmirioma turns fully now and looks at them, her aura expanding beyond her, her hair billowing on nonexistent winds. "I must go now. Good luck with Antibalance. Don't worry about me, I'll be fine. Or not." She manages a laugh, weak and forced. But, coming from her, the incarnate of the endless river herself, it is reassuring nevertheless. With that, her aura grows and grows, then shrinks almost immediately. And she's gone.

"Do me a favor, Ncheta," Asiri says.

"What?"

"The big A is going to keep getting harder as these people keep entering our world like this. If I don't make it past this one and you do, try to convince them to stop."

"I want to say yes," Ncheta says, "but it is you who always says: 'We're Benevolents. We can't even turn their minds away even if we tried.'"

Disturbed only by the gentle hum of the expanding dome, a silence passes between the spirits.

"You know," Asiri finally speaks up, "you never told me what happened."

"What happened with what?"

"You used to be a Malevolent."

Even though there's bubbling pain in his heart from memories threatening to claim him whole, Ncheta lets a small smile stretch his lips. "Maybe when you live as long as I do, my friend," he says, "you'll understand that life isn't as neat as we try to make it. Or as the gods try to arrange it so that we can be simple enough for them to control."

Asiri's multiple eyes dim, and Ncheta can see that she's trying to parse his words.

"Those moons ago," Ncheta says, "you knew I was a Malevolent, yet you chose to help me."

"I wasn't trying to help you," Asiri says, looking away. "I just thought your host deserved better. He was a good man."

"Either way, you knew helping him would mean helping me too, and also pitting you against a capricious Old Deity like Agwu."

Asiri shrugs.

Ncheta casts his gaze high as if trying to take in the scale of the dome at once. "The line blurs most times, Asiri. Sometimes we become them, sometimes they become us. Sometimes we both become something else. If you carry on like that long enough, then someday you'll forget where you start and where they begin."

When Antibalance comes, a wave of dark energy begins to spread across Ana Mmuo. It is a sweeping wall of black light, reaching from the skies to the ground, from one edge to another, menacing and all encompassing. The spirits travel ahead of the wall, hoping to find a human body to inhabit before it catches up with them.

Ncheta has survived this event for millennia, each inhabitation strengthening him for the next. The more cycles a spirit completes, the stronger they become and the more their chances of getting embodied when next Antibalance comes. Ncheta holds the memories of many and has preserved the histories of generations. So he is easily summoned by someone, and even if he isn't, can always find a mind yearning for him to fill. But it has been an unpredictable time these past moons, so finding a matching human has become tough even for him. The new world is now inhabited by billions of minds, and the dome can almost be seen from anywhere on Ana Mmuo.

They are fleeing in groups of tens and fives, all thousands of unembodied beings, spread across the vastness of Ana Mmuo. It helps to move this way because the added numbers improve collective energy and make their connection stronger. Each being's energy bleeding into the next. But Ncheta and Asiri's group has shrunk to eight spirits, two having found hosts within the last twelve hours.

There are Malevolents among them, but it hardly matters now. In a short while, if they don't get embodied, the moving wall will restore equilibrium. But they do carry gourds filled with River Mmirioma's essence from which they drink from time to time—this they must protect from the Malevolents, because more energy equals more time to flee, and more time to flee means more chance to search for a host.

Ncheta feels through millions of human minds, searching, querying, looking for a suitable host. He can hear them talk, see them walk, and feel the aura of those already inhabited. The spirits within them sneer at him, warning him off. The humans, at such moments, would feel a surge of unexplainable rage and anger, suddenly talking back at their boss or punching a bus conductor in the face. Some of those humans need him, but Ncheta doesn't intend to fight for space with spirits. But some other beings, desperate enough, would. Such duels often leave the human mind permanently harmed. But a Malevolent would hardly care; whether their host is in an asylum or a palace is of little importance.

Ncheta remembers his last host, a man who as a child could tell the names of the constellations in the night sky. The boy who was curious about everything, and whose quest for knowledge was insatiable. Ncheta sees him now, standing in front of a class. His uniform is torn in several places, and his hair is bushy. He is flipping through his biology textbook, trying to show his teacher why fresh and saltwater fish wouldn't survive in a biblical worldwide flood. But the class and the teacher are having none of it, laughing uncontrollably till Ncheta's host goes back to his seat hanging his head, defeated.

Ncheta rushes through memories till when his host has his first sex. The young man insists on not putting his mouth to his girlfriend's pubic area, naming every type of germ that can be transmitted from her to him until the girl gets disgusted and storms out of the room. Ncheta watches his host beg her to stay and isn't surprised when the young man rushes into the bathroom to take his bath the minute she slams the door shut.

Then there's this moment when Ncheta's host is receiving an award for being part of the three-man team that finally mapped the nature of dark matter. He's on the cover of magazines, hailed in science journals, and revered in the scientific community.

But he's sixty-eight now and he's starting to forget things. He remembers with perfect clarity those moments when he first had sex, trying to wash the girl's smell off him in the shower, but he can't remember what he had for breakfast and can't recall his own daughter's name. He gets worse by the year and soon starts to lose himself. Ncheta tries but can't help him, shakes but can't stir him. His body has succumbed to an illness from which even Ncheta can't save him. So, against all odds, the spirit of the past and present reaches out to Agwu, the deity of mental acuity and madness for help, at least for old times' sake. Agwu agrees but does so on a condition; that Ncheta surrenders to Agwu's whims and allows himself to be the tool of the gods once more.

"I can't help him otherwise," the Old Deity says, "because your host never believed in deities, much less prayed to us."

Rather than go back to the way things were before, Ncheta resorts to letting his host go the natural way. "My host," Ncheta tells Asiri, "if he can hear me, will prefer to not keep his mind if doing so would mean he's the reason many others will lose theirs."

"I'm sorry," Asiri says.

"It's the price I must pay for all the harm I've done."

So Ncheta watches and watches, till there's nothing left of his beloved host to anchor himself to.

"They're ancient spirits," says Asiri now in Ana Mmuo.

"Who?"

"Those who just left. I hear some of them have been with humans since they walked on all fours."

Ncheta looks at his friend. Her voice is becoming weak. Her tentacles are shrinking and most of her eyes have retreated into her face. She might not be able to make it. One Malevolent has left, disappearing without drama or consequence, as if they were never here in the first place. So that leaves seven of them, and the wall is gaining fast.

It is as if Ana Mmuo itself is conspiring against them, shrinking and pressing from all sides. Roads they used to travel no longer exist, and pathways they usually take are now dead ends.

Asiri is lagging behind now, struggling to keep pace with the group. Ncheta slows down and hefts her onto his back. She's murmuring now and Ncheta tells her to stop, to use the energy to find a host.

They can see the wall now, five times as fast as it was when they took off from the other end of Ana Mmuo. Ncheta tries again, reaching across worlds. Using the remains of his energy. He finally sees someone who is neither plugged into the phantom world nor taken by a spirit. This boy feels a disconnect from his past and ancestral roots. He wants to return to the Motherland to trace his lineage and organize his family history. Ncheta reaches out and the boy's mind is clean, ready for the taking.

But, Asiri.

How hard could it be to find someone who likes to know things they're not supposed to know and isn't inhabited already? Ncheta leaves the boy he just found and widens his search. This is risky—the boy could soon be inhabited by another spirit who cares less about suitability and just wants to survive. But Ncheta can't leave his friend behind. It'd be the last time he'd ever see her again if he does so.

He keeps searching, an eye on his potential host. Billions of humans are plugged in at this moment, reality no longer real enough for them. Antibalance is closing in. The wind it brings slows Ncheta and his group down. Their movement is now a slog. Like wading through quicksand. Ncheta feels the boy receding from him and Asiri slipping from his grasp, pulled back by the force that is Antibalance. He feels caught between this world and the next, between saving his friend and himself.

But Ncheta knows he has to save himself in the end. Like he does before his hosts die. Like all spirits do before their hosts die.

The wall is here now, rampaging through the spirit world and taking every unembodied being with it. One spirit is sucked in and absorbed by the wall. Another follows. And another. And Ncheta lets go. He tries to connect with the boy, but the human is now beyond his reach. He pushes with all his energy, but it is like swimming against a tide. Like the world is a giant treadmill. Centrifugal force kicks in and he loses balance and is carried through the air.

Ncheta looks back just in time to see the wall swallow Asiri. His longtime friend now is no more. He shuts his eyes and drifts on the currents, no longer fighting, no longer struggling. The end will come soon enough. Six-thousand years of human history about to be wiped clean.

He lets it come. And the world goes dark.

First, Ncheta sees light. Bright, golden light expanding in all directions. Then, he feels solid ground beneath him, ethereal materials that have been melted into other ethereal materials until they became sturdy and dense. It shouldn't be so. He shouldn't be able to feel himself, much less anything else. But here he is.

There's fog wrapped around him, but it's lifting by the second and the world is becoming clearer and clearer. He's in something like a throne room. The golden light from torches on the walls is the source of illumination. He looks up and the ceiling is made of clouds and stars and night. He tries to move but something is holding him back. He checks and sees his arms are spread apart, held firm by chains tethered to the walls on either side.

Strong energies suddenly permeate the atmosphere. They're so powerful Ncheta feels like his insides are about to melt. In a second, there are gods and goddesses in the room. Amadioha, Ana, Ikenga, Ekwensu, Agwu, all stand before him. First, he can't look at them without squinting. Then his eyes adjust, and he can no longer avert his gaze. The shortest one among them is seven feet tall. The goddess is the least beautiful. And they all have fire in their eyes.

"Why didn't you go?" Agwu speaks first. "We could have let Antibalance claim you and it'd be over."

Ncheta stares at them, not understanding.

"He wanted to save the gossip thing, of course," Ana says, and her voice is like metals clanging against each other.

"Still doesn't make any sense," Agwu replies.

"What is going on here?" Ncheta asks.

"We saved you if you haven't realized," says Amadioha.

"Why? And how? How can you save someone from Antibalance?"

"Oh, we can do a lot of things," Agwu says again, and Ncheta's eyes flit across deities. "We can keep some of you pitiful things to ourselves as a source of energy since, you know, the humans are no longer responding." Agwu holds their fingernails to the light and examines them as if they were recently manicured. The deity has a new shine about them too. Ncheta hadn't met the other gods in a long while, but he can tell they feel as renewed as Agwu.

Unconsciously, Ncheta tugs at the chains fastened to his arms. There's a fire cackling in his belly, reaching and clawing up to his mouth. He feels it stir his insides, and he knows the deities feel it too. "So why am I still here, then? Why am I still here when my friend and the rest of the beings who couldn't make it have been used as food for you hopeless swine?"

"Watch your mouth, Benevolent," Ikenga bellows.

"Is this what you've been doing all along," Ncheta continues, "hiding behind the wall to siphon the energies of lowly beings like us? Did the First One approve of this?"

The gods and goddesses exchange glances and laugh. "Your friend is still with us," Ana says, and Ncheta's eyes widen. "We're still keeping you alive because you're of immense value to the humans. You matter so much to them, especially in times like these when they're beginning to forget themselves."

"I thought they don't mean anything to you any longer?" Ncheta asks.

"We'll let you go now," Agwu says. "But the next time you don't embody during Antibalance, you might not be so lucky."

"Where's Asiri?"

"We'll keep her," Agwu says, "so that when next you stand before Old Deities like ourselves, you'd learn to not speak out of place."

Ncheta's energies roil. They rise and fall like the tides of a sea, his entire being wrestling to keep them in check, fighting to rein him in. If he were still Malevolent, they would have broken free by now. But he's supposed to be the personification of goodness and goodwill now, so his nature is his own enemy.

Part of his struggle is Agwu's aura rubbing off on him, pulling him at the seams, finding weak spots and tugging at them, so that he becomes a paradox, a self-deprecating joke. They want to see him break so that they'd remake him in the image they choose. And they're laughing. Watching him struggle is a source of amusement.

"I challenge you to a duel," Ncheta says, and the laughter ceases.

"Challenge who?" they ask in unison.

"You, Agwu. Let's settle this the old way once and for all. I win, you give her back. You win, you take her, and I become your servant forever."

Agwu guffaws, but the deity is laughing alone. The other beings are quiet, trying to gauge Ncheta's level of seriousness. The deities know that if Ncheta takes on Agwu, though the deity of madness and mental acuity is newly recharged, the fight wouldn't be about energy. The Ancient Law states: If, for any reason, an Old Deity must engage a Benevolent spirit in combat, the duel mustn't be based on strength of arm, but rather, strength of mind. And when it comes to mind, against the deity of madness and mental acuity, the spirit of the past and present has fair ground.

Everyone knows this, and that is why they aren't laughing.

"Come on," Agwu says, "you don't all think this vermin can beat me, do you?"

Silence.

"Do you accept the challenge, Agwu?" Ana asks. Of course, Agwu can't decline a fight with a lowly Benevolent. Their ego wouldn't be this high above Ana Mmuo if they went about declining challenges from lowly spirits.

Agwu glances at Ncheta and their jaw tightens. Then, their lips spread into a smile. "When do we duel?"

The deity and the spirit are in Chukwu's temple. Chukwu isn't present, but if the spirit and deity are here, then it means the First One gave consent. The stone structure is set on the top of the highest point of Ana Mmuo, from which the entire realm is at a glance. All around them is rock, and a few pillars on the edges hold up nothing. They're both standing facing each other. They can see themselves, but they're not themselves. The other Old Deities stand around, bearing witness.

"I am the first thing that shines," Agwu starts, "and the last thing that goes out. Who am I?"

"You are Anyanwu Ututu," Ncheta says, "the Morning Star. Now riddle me this. I am the slice of yam that can feed a multitude. What am I?"

"You are the crescent moon," says Agwu. "Now tell me, I am they that gather regardless of the position of the moon. Who am I?"

"You are the red-cap chiefs. Now tell me, I am he that can make you gather regardless of when you want. Who am I?"

"You are the King," Agwu says with a smile, and Ncheta wonders if he spoke in haste. Whether Agwu has backed him into a corner.

"Riddle me this," Agwu continues, "I am the thing that makes the King lick ash. What am I?"

Ncheta almost hesitates. He wants to give himself room to weigh his options before speaking. But in this game hesitation means defeat. A few seconds of lag is all it takes, and you're done. "You are roasted pear," he says. "Riddle me this. I am the thing from which all pear trees grow. What am I?"

"You are the Earth," Agwu says. "Ana herself, mother of all life."

Ncheta's eyes cut to Ana standing on the edge of the temple, and he sees her shift uneasily. A smile crosses his lips. He has thrown Agwu into defense.

"I am the life who formed the mother of all life," Agwu says, launching another attack. "Who am I?"

Ncheta digs his heels into the rock, stands firm, and sharpens his mind. "You are the First One, Chukwu himself."

Agwu enters into Ncheta's mindspace. "Your host would have done better," they say. "Give up now, and I might not make you suffer."

"You let him die alone and unaware of himself when you could have helped," Ncheta says.

"Of course, the fool thought he knew more than the gods. How do you think his madness began?"

"You had no hand in it," says Ncheta.

"You can't be sure of that."

Ncheta feels his energies concentrating. The dregs of River Mmirioma in him are churning and undulating. He's losing touch with reality. Time is unspooling, one second spilling into the next. There's an abyss in his consciousness that he almost falls into. No. No. He pulls from the brink just in time to rebut Agwu. "I am the wind that restores balance to the universe. The force without which order cannot exist. What am I?"

"You are Antibalance," Agwu says, their face a combination of surprise and disappointment. "You are the opposite of life and destroyer of non-life. But I am that in which Antibalance exists, within which everything exists."

"You are the universe itself," Ncheta says. "The beginning and the end of all things. But then, I am that without which there is no beginning and no end, no past and no present, no now and no never. What am I?"

"You are ... time ..."

"And you are ... out of time."

Ncheta and Asiri are in the tavern. Some spirits have returned from their short-lived trips, their hosts either dead while being birthed or as infants. Antibalance has created new spirits and beings, and some show up at the door looking clueless and brimming with energy. For some reason, the dome has stopped expanding, either because humans have grown tired of it, or someone has influenced lawmakers to put restrictions on the trillion-dollar companies. Some spirits speculate that it has shrunk a little too, but it can still be seen from the tavern without standing, its colors lighting up the room like an aurora.

"I hear Agwu became a spirit and entered into America's president," Asiri says.

"That doesn't make any sense," Ncheta says. "Isn't it rather ... lowly of him to possess a human?"

Asiri's many eyes light up, expanding to almost merge into one big globe on her face. "Well, what can be more lowly than being humiliated by a spirit in Chukwu's temple?"

Ncheta smiles and takes a sip from his drink, which seems to be improving in taste too.

Asiri takes her cup and stands, and Ncheta wonders what she's about to do.

"Hey newcomers and returning spirits, listen up," she says, speaking in multiple voices. "Raise your cups and let's make a toast to the latest New Deity in town. The First One has deemed him worthy of deification, and henceforth he no longer will be running around with spirits when the big A comes."

Ncheta looks around and the entire tavern has raised a cup, and at Asiri's word, they pour their drinks on the ground in honor of Ncheta's new status as the god of the past and the present.

SUPPERTIME

by Tananarive Due

Summer, 1909
Gracetown, Florida

A mother's scream pierced through the barn planks, near human enough to bring hot tears to Mat's eyes. And Mat hated to cry, especially in front of her father. The lamb wriggling on the straw-dusted floor bleated with pathetic agitation, but his mother wailed outside as if she knew how sharp her father's blade was. And what Mama wanted for Sunday supper.

"Firm hand, Mat. Don't let 'im suffer."

Mat tightened her gloved grip on the struggling lamb's legs, still powerful despite being tied, wishing she could let him run free. He must weigh seventy-five pounds—the biggest autumn lamb they had left, one she'd secretly named Buster. "It's all right," Mat told Buster in her sweetest voice, close to his ear. "Don't be scared."

Buster believed her lie and quieted. His thrashing stopped. Then came a barely audible, expert slicing sound and gurgling. Mat swallowed back a sob as she felt the creature's life seep from her fingertips. Against her will, she imagined herself feeding him hay from her hand when he was small. His mother's scream outside grew more terrible.

Papa looked down at her with pride. "Good girl," he said. "You did better with it than your brother. Go wash. I'll hang him up."

Mat looked down at her clothes: Blood had sprayed her shirt beyond the borders of the leather apron she'd worn. And her trouser cuffs. She would need to wash the blood out quickly or Mama would put her in a dress all day tomorrow, not just for supper. Confound it!

But Pa's approval gave her walk to the house a bounce. *You did better with it than your brother.* Now she would have something else to tease Calvin about when he came home from Howard for the summer on Sunday. Mat's tears had not yet dried, but a smile found her lips as she ran down the dirt path through the stand of thin Florida pines to the two-story wood plank farmhouse Papa and a crew had built two years ago when Mat was eleven. The oak planks remained richly dark, not sun faded, and some corners of the house still smelled like sap. Mama said some ladies from church were so envious of her roomy, two-story house with a water closet instead of an outhouse that they hadn't spoken to her since they moved in. And Pa said some white men were so jealous of his prize hogs that he sat by the window with his rifle most nights to make sure no one would try to steal them or burn his new house down from spite.

The kitchen was hot from Mama's stew pot, and the baby carriage hinges squeaked as her young siblings whined with complaints that reminded her of the lamb. Booker had just turned a year old, and Harriet was two; both were identically insufferable. Mat knew she should relieve Mama of the babies, but Booker and Harriet were squalling in the carriage, and a glimpse of Mama's huge belly pulling her house dress taut made Mat back away instead, toward the stairs. And freedom.

Another baby on the way! Mama had been only fifteen when she had Calvin, twenty-three when she had her. Thirty-five when she had Booker, and thirty-six with Harriet—when Mat heard her swear to Papa that her days of carrying babies were over. But she was with child *again*, now a woman near forty, and every time Mat thought about the new baby she felt a combination of pity and rage for Mama. How could Mama stretch and twist her body time after time with such terrible agony, tying herself more firmly to her stove and sewing machine?

Sunday she'd teased Mat with remarks about one of the Stephens boys asking how old her daughter was because she was so tall, and how

Mat would be sixteen in three years, a fit age for marriage. *Marriage!* What made Mama think marriage was anywhere in her heart? Did she only want to punish her because she dressed as she pleased and Papa relied on her just as much as he'd ever relied on Calvin? (Or more, since Calvin could not stand the sight of blood.)

Mat would go to college like her brother. Calvin had promised to help pay her way, since he got a good stipend from the aging writer whose memoir he was typing. Mama was old fashioned and didn't believe girls needed schooling, but Papa had said to wait and see if she could keep up her grades. That wouldn't be hard: She could read and figure better than her teacher, for what that was worth.

The biggest godsend in the new house was her own bedroom, so Mat fled there and closed her door as if a bear had chased her. The oak wasn't sturdy enough to completely mute the whining of her brother and sister, but it helped. A surge of guilt replaced her anxiousness. Mama was standing over a hot stove almost ready to give birth, and Mat should have rolled the carriage out to the "parlor," as Mama now called their front room. (Booker and Harriet stopped fussing when she played happy music on the Victrola.) *You care more about sheep and goats than your brother and sister*, Mama always said. *But after this baby comes, they'll be your responsibility. Who knows how long it'll be 'fore I'm back on my feet? Better start learning now.* Mama's weary desperation had chilled Mat to her toes.

Mat's precious stereoscope goggles were waiting on her desk where she'd left them. After lighting her lamp, Mat pressed the velvet-lined mask to the bridge of her nose. Just like that, the narrow room around her melted and she was *inside* the slide glowing to life in her lamp's flame. The Palace of Electricity—a night view of a regal mansion draped in strings of stars, lit up from corner to corner as if it might burn off her eyelids if she got too close. The Palace of Electricity seemed as far from Gracetown as the sun itself, but the magical pictures from the '05 World's Fair reminded Mat how big the world and its wonders were. Calvin had written as much on his Christmas note when he gifted her with the wonderful contraption and a handful of slides: *The world is a big place, Matty. Here's a good peek at it!*

During his last visit, Calvin had described how he was boarding in a house full of electricity where his writer patron lived; no need for kerosene lamps, with switches that turned on lights above like a wish, a machine that washed his clothes, and hot coils that toasted his bread. And a telephone, of course. If not for the stereoscope where Mat could see so many wonders for herself, she might not have believed his stories of casual magic.

Mat didn't know how long she'd been dreaming of the Palace of Electricity when she heard the *thump* against her window. A flurry of determined scratching shook her windowpane. She pulled the mask away, startled—and was staring into green-gold eyes that were not human. A bobcat was at her window! The large cat was light reddish brown, with only black spots on his ears and coat to distinguish him from the bricks that camouflaged him. He had climbed up the uneven bricks of the chimney to find her window on the second floor. The bobcat yowled, massive paws scratching against the frame.

Mat gasped. The stereoscope nearly tumbled from her startled hands.

"Bobby?" Mat whispered. She froze, not sure. Four months had passed since she'd seen the bobcat kitten she'd raised until it got too big and Mama told Papa to chase him away, and his coat had been more gray than red then. He was far bigger than when she'd found him under a rock ledge and carried him away in her palm. She'd kept him alive with one of Mama's baby bottles. She'd lied to herself and decided his mother was dead—but the truth was, she didn't know if she'd rescued or stolen him.

Heart pounding with anticipation—and a drop of fear, since she wasn't *sure*—Mat cracked her window open. The big cat did the rest, slinking snakelike through a gap that should have been too small. The cat leaped to her shoulders, wrapping around her neck. His fur smelled filthy, like carrion, not like when she'd bathed him in warm water and rose oil. Much bigger claws now raked through her plaited hair to her scalp with such strength that Mat felt her neck crack, and then the cat nibbled at her earlobe with teeth and tongue, nicking her until she bled.

"Stop it, that's too hard!" Mat said, but she was giggling as they tumbled to her bed, rolling in a ball that sometimes put her on top, sometimes the wild cat, their play wrestling so fierce that her bed frame thumped the floor. His gravelly purr roared in her ear. As if no time at all had passed!

Mat assessed her injuries, breathless, while Bobby romped through her room in search of mischief, tugging at her desk drawers and swatting savagely at the scarf hanging on her wall. She noted her bleeding earlobe, a bold white scratch across the dark skin of her arm (not bleeding), another on her back (maybe spotting a little). Bobby had forgotten his lessons on gentle play, if he ever truly had learned. Their reunion had over-excited him. The constant scratches were the reason her parents had made her send him away—*You think you're playing games, but that's a wild beast, and his nature will always come out,* Papa said. The times Mama had caught him peeing in her kitchen sink, his favorite place to relieve himself, had not helped his case for being a house cat either. Mostly, Mama had been afraid he might hurt one of the babies, which Mat could not say was unreasonable. But she had missed him. Soon after her parents stopped allowing him in the house, he had vanished into the woods.

And now he was back—a fully grown bobcat! She couldn't wait to tell Calvin.

But Papa would tear off a switch if he found Bobby in her room now. Joy quickly turned to panic: How would she get him out of the house? She couldn't hope to hide him. It was a wonder Mama hadn't already called after her to see what the ruckus was. Bobby would have to go back out the way he came, and fast.

Mat went to her window and opened it wide. "Come on, Bobby."

Bobby stared, his stumpy tail lashing with irritation at the interruption of their play. Mat almost, *almost* felt a twinge of fright, reminding herself that she did not truly know Bobby anymore, so it might be dangerous to try to poke and prod him. His staring eyes brimmed with his history of killing. But she was more afraid of Papa's hickory switch, so she stuck her head out of the window as an example. "See? You gotta go back outside."

Mat's mattress creaked as Bobby stood on all fours, intrigued now.

"You want me to go out there with you? Is that it?"

Mat didn't believe Bobby couldn't understand spoken words, not *quite*, but Bobby sprang so quickly that Mat had to move aside so he could reach the windowsill. But then he only stared at the chimney's descent. Why did cats love climbing up and hate climbing down?

"You go on," Mat said. "I'll meet you outside, all right?"

Bobby made a sound that could have been agreement or cussing.

And so their night's adventure began.

Mat would be expected at the supper table in thirty minutes and had no business going outside to chase after a bobcat, but that didn't stop her from grabbing her Brownie camera—Calvin's Christmas gift from his first year in college—and shoving against Bobby's weight to close her door so he could not follow her into the hall. His massive claws poked under the door. He swiped back and forth, shaking the door, rattling her doorknob.

"*Shhhhh.*"

Mat snuck back downstairs, past the loud kitchen, and out of the house.

Outside, she saw Bobby was staring down from her window. Mat tried to coax him without being loud enough for Mama to hear her from the open kitchen window, or Papa from the barn. His loud complaints from her window floated through the woods, halfway between whining and growling. He'd be lucky if Papa didn't come running out with his shotgun.

"Come on down," Mat said. "Stop being a baby."

She remembered a trick from when he was younger: If she pretended to walk away, he might chase her. So, she followed the deer path past Papa's wagon deeper into the woods, walking until her house was out of sight. Sure enough, a twig cracked, and Bobby soon was upon her, tangling her legs until she lost her balance, sending her rolling in prickly fir needles. The fall hurt her elbow. Mat held Bobby's mouth away from her face, noticing his sharp, yellow teeth, pushing back against the fur of his muscular shoulders. She wondered for the barest instant if Bobby had turned wild after all. But with a playful burr, Bobby jumped away and let Mat rise to her feet again. Now Mat had a scraped elbow to add to her scratches.

"*No*," Mat said sharply. "You play too rough. Stop it."

Bobby talked back to her in his bobcat language and ran ahead. He didn't stick to the trail, but he never ventured far from it, leaping from bush to bush, sometimes scrambling halfway up a pine tree because he could. Just when she thought he might disappear over the hill, he turned his head to make sure she wasn't falling behind.

"I gotta get dressed for supper. I don't got time to be playin' with you," Mat said.

Bobby ignored her and ran on. Mat stood for a moment and thought it over, noticing how coppery the daylight had become, the sun hanging low in the sky. Then she heard Bobby's familiar call from shivering milkweed a few yards ahead, still close to the path, and nothing could rival the giddiness of seeing Bobby so eager to play. She'd cried for a week straight after Papa chased him away, and she'd stared at the trees hoping he would come back for nearly a month before she gave up. Calvin had confided to her at Christmas that he might not have survived the wild because he'd been raised by a human hand. And here he was!

She would go home in five minutes. The sun wouldn't fall below the tree line for at least fifteen minutes, so if she started back in five minutes, she might make it to the table on time.

Another lie. She knew it even then.

But she needed to capture Bobby in a photograph with her camera! How else would anyone ever believe she'd tamed an honest-to-goodness fully grown bobcat?

Bobby was too quick for her camera. He would need to sit still—*real* still—for her to be able to set up a good shot with her Brownie. Every time she'd pointed the lens and could make out Bobby's fur in the viewfinder, he was gone long before she could click the shutter. Time after time, her viewfinder showed her a tree stump or empty boulder instead.

"Hold still, would you?"

Bobby would not. He raced on with such purpose that she had no choice; she followed.

By the time they reached the first dampness of swamp water turning the soil to mud, Mat realized that Bobby was leading her to a spot where she had found him, a rocky ledge that had given her shade on hot afternoons while he lunged at the tadpoles and water lilies floating just beyond them. It wasn't a cave, exactly, because it was open on both sides, but their secret spot had felt like a castle to her. Papa could walk within five feet of her and never know she was there until he heard her giggles.

Mat was breathless by the time she reached Bobby. True to his camouflage, she had trouble making him out at first in the shadow, but the sight of him made her grin. Bobby was still at last, his haunches lowered as he chewed on something in the dark. His flanks were in shadow, but the twilight made his coat shine and his eyes glow like marbles when he gazed up at her. With trembling fingers, Mat pointed her Brownie again, expecting to find he had already leaped away, but Bobby was framed like a painting in a museum. Heart pounding, she pressed the shutter and heard the satisfying *CLICK.* She had her photograph!

She took a step closer to see if she could take an even better photo when she noticed the poor creature struggling in Brownie's jaw: At first she'd thought it might be a snake, but it was too broad, and she'd never seen a snake this odd color of slick gray-brown mud. Sometimes it looked like a tube, sometimes flat, and it kept wriggling although Bobby never stopped eating its other half. By the look of it, whatever it was might be two or three feet long. Or it *had* been.

CLICK. Mat pushed the shutter button again accidentally, startling herself in the same instant she realized she had never seen a creature like it. If it had legs, it might be a weasel. But it didn't look warm-blooded. If not for its giant size, it might have looked like …

Mat's mouth fell open, and she took a step back when her memory formed the word: *a leech.* She'd heard her mother and grandmother talk about giant leeches that crawled from the swamp and nested inside babies during the summer. Swamp leeches, people called them. But Mama had never been able to point out anyone who'd ever *seen* one. Was this …?

Mat remembered her camera and raised it again, trying to see the last of the creature before it disappeared in Bobby's mouth, but Bobby's eyes had perked up and he'd dropped what was left of it, staring toward the edge of the swamp where he had once played. Bobby growled—not in the playful way he did with her. Like he meant it. His teeth were fully bared as he scrambled to his feet, charging toward the water. Then came horrific splashing: a sound so loud that it could only be a gator.

"Bobby—no!" she said.

That furious sliver of last daylight gave Mat a good enough view for her to realize that Mat was *not* tussling with a gator. This creature was also a gray-brown color, with the same slimy skin, but it had long, wiry tendrils that whipped at Bobby's hide, making him yowl.

The mama, Mat thought.

That was the last thing she thought before she turned and ran.

It was dark by the time Mat reached her doorstep.

She'd wasted many minutes lost in the graying woods, unable to see past her tears as she tried to stumble toward the sanctuary of their sturdy oak house. She ran inside and leaned against the door while she pulled the deadbolt Papa had built, breathless and sweating. She was so glad to be home, her knees were watery with gratitude. The door propped her while she gasped, shaking with worry for Bobby. And the memory of the thing she had seen.

From the doorway, she could see the table where Mama and Papa were already in their seats, holding hands to say grace. Papa's face was stern. Mama's was more like enraged.

Papa stood up when he saw her. "Matty! Where were you?"

"Matilda Lydia Powell, you are in a heap of hot water!" Mama said.

Papa walked close to her with the lantern from the table to get a closer look at her face.

"I swear, this child is so spoiled she thinks she can just run off and—" Mama was saying, but Papa's face softened as he looked at Mat. He held up his arm to silence Mama.

"What's happened?" he said in a tight voice she had only heard once or twice, and only now did she realize it was the way he sounded when he was afraid.

Mat hadn't thought up a story yet, so she didn't know how to answer. What was the point of telling them what she'd seen? Mama would accuse her of making up stories. And what if Papa went hunting for Bobby at the mention of him?

Papa moved his face closer to her, his jaw trembling. "*Who hurt you?*"

"No one," Mat finally said. "I saw a gator and I ran off. I tripped and fell."

"So you were off playing by the swamp?" Mama said, clarifying her transgression.

"Yes, ma'am," Mat said.

Papa held the lamp even closer to her face, trying to see any lies in her eyes. He stared at her a long time. When he noticed the camera she was clutching close, he seemed to believe her at last. His jaw's trembling stopped, replaced by ironclad anger.

"Shame on you," he said, the words Mat most hated to hear. "Hurry up and go upstairs and get dressed. I've got half a mind to send you to bed without supper."

"That's all right, sir, if that's what I deserve." Mat hadn't had any appetite since the barn.

"Oh, I bet you'd like that," Papa said. "Come right back down to the table proper."

"And you better look like a *young lady*," Mama said.

More hot tears escaped as Mat climbed up the stairs, but she hoped Papa hadn't seen.

"Look what you've done!" Mama said to Papa as Mat walked upstairs. "Calling her by that boyish name. Letting her dress any kind of way. She's half wild. No man will know what to do with her!"

Mat waited at the top landing to hear if Papa would say *Stop worrying so much* or *She'll grow out of it* like he usually did, but Papa was stone silent.

Five minutes of scrubbing in the upstairs sink and the pleated dress from her closet worked a small miracle, wiping away all signs of blood and the creatures outside. Mat took extra care to brush her hair down flat where she'd already sweated out Mama's pressing from last Sunday. Her image in the mirror looked like the biggest lie ever told.

Mama did not look her way when Mat sat at the table, said her silent grace, and spooned chicken stew into her bowl. The only one who seemed happy to see her was Harriet, who squealed "Matty! Matty! Matty!" and gave her a hug from her high chair. Mat made a show of buttering corn bread and breaking it into bite-sized pieces for her, and Harriet squealed from her big sister's attention. Booker was equally delighted to be bouncing on Papa's knee while he ate handfuls of a soft mash from a bowl beside Papa's plate. Gazing upon her family—including Calvin's empty seat—made Mat feel the shame Papa had uttered at her like a curse. Mama looked weary enough to fall asleep upright, rubbing her swollen belly's discomfort. Was it so wrong for Mama to expect her to be more of a helper? Was it fair that Mat spent so much time outside with Papa, leaving Mama to fend for herself with Booker and Harriet?

Mat was opening her mouth to announce an apology when a *THUMP* shook the door.

"What the blazes—" Papa said.

Papa handed Booker over to Mama and was on his feet, producing his hunting rifle so fast that Mat realized he'd moved it from the closet to be near him, expecting trouble from the time she was late. He took a step toward the door, but she jumped in front of him.

"Papa, no!" she said. "It's only Bobby! I saw him outside. He's come back!"

"Is *that* what you were doing out there?" Mama said. "Fooling with that bobcat?"

Another *THUMP*, and this time it sounded like buckling wood.

"He's back to break down our door?" Papa said. "And steal our livestock?"

Papa had delighted in Bobby as a kitten, but no love showed in his eyes now.

"Bobby wouldn't do that!" Mat said, then she reminded herself that she didn't know Bobby anymore. But it felt true in her heart, anyway. And she was just glad he was all right.

Another *THUMP* shook the door while a loud feline screech and growling came from the other side of the house, closer to the kitchen. Papa snapped a look to Mat; they both knew that bobcats did not travel in packs. *That* was Bobby. On the other side of the house.

Then Bobby wasn't at the door. The room felt frigid as Mat's world went askew.

Papa took long strides toward the door while Mat tried to keep pace with him. Her mind fumbled for words to explain the monstrous creature that might have followed her and Bobby from the swamp. "Papa, wait—"

Papa flung the draperies aside to try to see outside, but Mat could tell it was too dark. A hog squealed from the barn, setting off a cascade of panicked cries.

"He's in the barn now!" Papa said.

"That's not Bobby," Mat said. "I swear it isn't, Papa. Be careful! I saw something—"

"Stay here with your Mama," he said.

Mat grabbed Papa's arm with all her strength before he could go outside in ignorance. "Listen to me!" she said, and her tone was so grown that he turned to her. "I saw something by the swamp. Not a bobcat. Bobby was eating some kind of big, ugly leech, and its mama came out of the water, big as a gator. Mean as one too. It was whipping Bobby with these … big whiskers? No—tentacles. Thick as ropes. I don't know what it was. But I think it followed me!"

"What's she talking about?" Mama said in a tiny voice, her anger revealed for the fright it truly was. The hogs and sheep in the barn were in a frenzy.

Papa stared down at Mat, truly wanting to make sense of her babbling. "I have no damn idea," he said, speaking to Mama. "All of you go hide upstairs—*now*. She's right about one thing; it ain't a bobcat. Someone's after the hogs." He probably thought it was white men from town, and white men from town might not be satisfied with stealing or killing hogs. Papa was wrong, but whatever that thing was might be just as bad. It might even be worse than jealous white men.

"Be careful, Papa. Please."

"Don't you let no crackers kill you over a hog!" Mama said.

"Go on, I said!" Papa waved to Mama at the table. "Hurry up, Belle!"

He waited until he saw Mama pull herself to her feet, Booker in her arms. Mat ran back to the table to scoop up Harriet so Papa would know he could count on her. Harriet cried in the commotion, clinging so hard to Mat's collar that the lacy fabric chafed her neck.

Satisfied, Papa finally opened the door and peeked outside. She prayed he wouldn't shoot Bobby. But if Papa saw anything, he didn't let on.

"Pull the bolt," he called back to them and slammed the door behind him.

Tears fell from Mama's eyes, and Mat realized it was all her fault. If she hadn't followed Bobby when she was supposed to be getting ready for supper, the Leech Monster never would have come after her. Had it tracked her by scent? Or had Bobby led it here?

With a trembling hand, Mat bolted the door while she held Harriet close with her other arm, bouncing her gently to assure her. A peek through the curtains only showed Papa running toward the barn before he was out of sight. Mat's heart shook with worry for him.

"Come up to my room, Mama," she said.

Mama blinked as if she hadn't heard her. Then Mama followed her up the stairs.

Mat pushed her desk against the door to barricade it while Mama opened her closet, still holding tight to Booker while Harriet clung to her skirt. Mama was replaying a bad memory, her face slack with terror while they braced for gunfire and angry voices outside. So far, they only heard Bobby's snarling, sometimes more distant, sometimes very near.

"Tell me again," Mama said, hushed. "What did you see?"

Mat remembered her camera, lifting it from her desk as if Mama could see her evidence captured inside. "I think I took a picture of it! It was big, Mama. And these long ... whatchacallit ... *tentacles* on it. Like an octopus, almost, but it wasn't no octopus. It was the swamp leech's mama! It came after Bobby when he was eating its baby."

Mama's face flickered with relief. Her shoulders sank as she exhaled the breath she'd been holding.

"You know what that thing is, Mama?"

"Shhhh," Mama said, nodding toward Harriet, not wanting to scare her. "Heard stories about swamp leeches. Never seen one, though. Never heard of one big as this."

"But you believe me?"

"I want to, child. Your daddy can hold his own against a beast." Like Papa, Mama was more scared of lynching.

But they hadn't seen the thing. And it dawned on Mat that there might be more than one.

"Who's there?" Papa's voice boomed from outside. If there *were* white men in the barn, that thunder in Papa's voice would get him killed.

Scratching came from Mat's windowpane, which she'd closed as soon as they ran into the room. Mama gasped, which set Harriet off crying. Mat turned up her lamp's light, but she already knew before she saw the eyes gleaming on the other side of the glass.

"It's only Bobby! Mama, please let me let him in—he's hurt."

Mama backed further into the closet, bringing both Booker and Harriet with her. She kept the closet door open only a crack. "Yes, but hurry up," she said. "If you're *sure* it's Bobby."

If Mat had been closer, she would have given Mama a tight hug. Mama casting her complaints aside reminded Mat of when Mama had laughed and daydreamed with her—before the whispers embarrassed her.

Mat pulled the window an inch, and Bobby did the rest, forcing his body inside. He left a thin streak of blood against the white paint. Two raw stripes in his coat looking like a whip's lashes.

"Come on, it's all right," Mat said, and shoved the window closed behind him.

Bobby jumped on the bed, then off again, pacing the floor. Mat was relieved that he seemed like himself despite the blood. When he padded toward the closet, Mama pulled it shut.

"Keep him away from the babies!" Mama said, her voice slightly muffled, so Mat patted the mattress and Bobby came back toward her. He jumped on the bed and licked his wounds.

"This is all your fault," Mat said softly to Bobby.

Then the rifle shot came. Mat's heart stuffed her throat.

"Get in here, Matilda!" Mama called in a wire-thin voice.

But Mat barely heard her, creeping back to the window to see outside. Lamplight flickered inside the barn, roaming between the cracks in the wood panels. A second shot flared in the dark like a fireball, making her wince. A high-pitched sound she had never heard before seemed to echo against every tree trunk for miles.

"Goddamn!" she heard Papa say faintly. His blasphemy was shocking. "What in the goddamn hell …?"

"Mat!" Mama called from the closet, frantic.

"I'm all right, Mama. I think Papa got it. I'm just trying to see—"

Bobby leaped off the bed, growling low in his throat.

A movement in the dark through the window made Mat instinctively pull back right before the grass cracked to pieces and flew into her room, one shard scraping her nose. The odd black tendrils lashed into the room, squirming like snakes. The rest of the creature's body was pressed against the top half of the window, which had not broken—the only barrier keeping it out. This thing was bigger than a gator; bigger than the one she'd seen at the swamp. Its skin slithered across the remaining glass pane as it tried to bulge into the room. The upper pane shivered and cracked.

Bobby pounced, but he whined when a lash caught his ear.

Mat wanted to turn and run for the closet like Mama had said—to be her child instead of her protector—but she doubted that Bobby would have fled into the house if he could beat the thing back by himself.

"*Papa—help*!" Mat screamed with all the strength in her lungs.

But she didn't have time to wait for Papa. The beast was already tensing thick tendrils across Bobby's middle while Bobby struggled and whined, slashing with his paws. Mat whirled to look for anything that could be a weapon, and she remembered the oyster knife in her desk drawer. It wasn't big, but she kept it sharp. She would have to get in close to try to hurt the thing, but Mat had to protect her family. Bobby was her family too.

With a yell, Mat charged with her knife and plunged it toward a tendril, but the slimy flesh snapped away so fast that her blade sank deeply into wood. *Dammit*! Sharp pain lanced her forehead as she realized the tendril had touched her, slicing through her skin. If Mama could see from the closet, she would faint. Mat felt ready to faint herself.

But Bobby's snarling and the cries of her brother and sister from the closet forced Mat to push aside her horror at her own warm blood. Half-blinded from blood stinging her eyes, Mat fumbled until she felt the knife's handle, tugging to free it. She'd stabbed the wood so hard that she needed two hands for a strong enough grip, and she nearly lost her balance when it came free. This time, instead of trying to hit one of the fast-moving tentacles, Mat stabbed through the crack in the glass, like Papa had taught her when she was hunting: Aim for the body's center.

She couldn't see the body well, much less know where its center was, but the creature let out a piercing screech like the one from the barn, so loud that Mat backed away and covered her ears. The tentacles flapped and then retreated, releasing Bobby—but Bobby snuck in a ferocious slice with his claws that left one of the odd tentacles severed on her floor.

"Get away from the window!" Papa shouted from outside.

Mat ducked, hooking her arm around Bobby to try to pull him down too—enough to surprise him off-balance. He wriggled free, though thankfully he didn't rake her with his claws.

Another rifle shot. More glass rained in Mat's room. The otherworldly shriek came, and something big fell to the ground outside before it went silent.

"We did it, Bobby," she whispered to the big cat beside her. "And I saved you!"

Bobby bumped his head against hers, knocking her teeth together so hard that she saw sparks, the closest he came to saying *thank you*.

When Papa finally agreed that it was safe for her to come outside, Mat understood why no one had ever spotted a Leech Monster with their own eyes. Papa had covered both corpses with tarp after he shot them, but by dawn the tarp beneath her window had sunk to the soil, with only an oily black spot remaining where the creature had been. It was *gone*, tentacles and all.

The same slick spot was all that remained in the barn.

"But you saw it, Papa? Didn't you?" Mat said. In the morning light, their story felt fragile. Since Mama had stayed hidden in the closet, Calvin would never believe her without Papa's corroboration. And who knew how long it would take for her photographs to come back?

"I wouldn't know how to describe it to folks, Matty," Papa confided. "It was so dark in the barn, and it moved so fast. I was hoping to get a better look after daylight."

That was how Mat knew they would not talk about it, not outside of family. Not ever. Many things happened in Gracetown that no one talked about, or so she had heard. Mama probably had heard stories about swamp leeches from her grandmother and cousins that she'd never bothered to tell Mat until one came to the door.

The new baby came early, two days before Calvin's homecoming. The baby might have died if Miz Effie, the midwife, hadn't unwrapped the umbilical cord from the baby's neck to help her gasp her first air from the world. Mama went from screaming to crying with joy, swearing it was her last—again. Just as Mama had warned, the birth and bleeding had weakened her, so she couldn't stand to cook and clean and care for Harriet and Booker the way she usually did. Those tasks fell to Mat, of course. So instead of slopping hogs and raking hay and helping Papa fix broken rails in the fence, Mat stirred oatmeal on the stove and washed clothes and played the Victrola for Harriet and Booker, doing silly dances for them until they squealed with laughter.

Calvin had gained at least ten pounds and looked five years older since he left for school, much more a man than a boy. Papa cooked the lamb for his supper so well that Mat had two servings although she had promised herself she wouldn't eat any. Calvin asked Mat how she'd gotten the scar across her forehead, and Mat shared a look with

Papa and said he wouldn't believe her, so she would wait for her photographs to come back.

It was six weeks before a package from the Kodak Company arrived, almost time for Calvin to return to school, and she ripped it open as soon as Papa handed it to her, eager to see what images she had captured.

But all she could clearly see was Bobby, his eyes shining in the dusk light. The shadows beneath the ledge obscured the tiny swamp leech clamped between his jaws. Worse, she must have been too frightened to click the shutter when she'd seen the Leech Monster, because the last two photos were a horrific blur. And then came a photo of weary Mama smiling with the new baby in her arms.

"Well, will you look at that?" Calvin said, peering over her shoulder. "What a family record! You said you had a special one to show me, and you weren't lying. You could take photographs as a trade one day, you know. Just keep practicing. I'm proud of you, Matty."

A future taking photographs! Mat had never imagined such a notion, but it filled her with a sense of possibility. She might be the first Negro photographer for the *Saturday Evening Post*! Mat swallowed back her bitter disappointment that she had no record of the creatures that had attacked her family, that she and Papa would have to rely on memories that surely would fade one day. She wondered how anyone remembered their own family's faces—every crease, the hairstyle, the *exact* smiles—in the days before photographs.

But photographs, no matter how marvelous they were, did not substitute for life.

When Mama was sleeping, Mat cradled the new baby and stared into her peculiar little face and bright, hungry eyes and remembered the odd creature Bobby had been eating under the ledge. And she imagined how horrible it would be if someone came and stole the new baby away, and how she, too, would track down any creature who hurt her.

In later years, Mat would reflect upon that as her favorite summer of childhood.

Bobby never visited once while Calvin was back at home, but he was back at Mat's window two days after Calvin left, early in the morning. Even the babies were sleeping, the house silent except for Bobby's fuss. Mat rushed to pull on her overalls and the sturdy boots she had inherited from her brother. She grabbed her Brownie camera and raced outside to join Bobby in the woods washed in the gray dawn.

If she could capture the right image, her career in photography could begin now!

But Bobby, as usual, did not cooperate. He found every shadow and obstruction.

"Would you hold still for once in your life?"

Bobby playfully leaped against her side, pushing himself away with his powerful legs. His claws did not prick her this time, but she could feel the strong tips. Mat swayed and stumbled, relieved that she did not drop her camera and that her bottom landed in soft moss. Bobby licked the top of her head. He was far too close for a good photo now. Unless ...

Inspiration struck Mat: she turned her Brownie's lens toward her face, the viewfinder on the other side. She could not see what image was framed from this side, but the angle *should* be right, shouldn't it? And if the camera could see her face, could it also see Bobby nuzzling her? She didn't know. But she fumbled to reach the button. *CLICK.*

It might just be a photo of the sky or a tree trunk, for all she knew. But maybe she had a keepsake of her and Bobby together. When Bobby finally stepped away from her, head upturned because of a dull crack from a small twig overhead, Mat knew this was the perfect image without seeing the film. His head was slightly above hers from where she sat, regal, his coat glorious in the rising sun.

"I've finally got you now, Bobby," she said as her camera clicked.

It might be the best photograph she had ever made. Or ever would.

But when Mat blinked, Bobby was gone.

A NAME IS A PLEA AND A PROPHECY

by Gabrielle Emem Harry

Kuyom stood at Death's door, shuffling from one foot to the other. She patted her head impatiently. She had gotten rid of the lice a week ago, but she still felt the phantom itch. They'd crawled into her hair while she was sleeping under a mango tree in the evil forest on the outskirts of Dianku, just outside Death's domain. She'd had to cut her hair. It had gone uncombed and uncut since the first time she bled, as was the custom for servants of Adeh. It had locked into thick cords that grazed her shoulders like a reassuring hand. Now she was as bald as a child again. It unsettled her but did not matter in the end. Everyone goes to death like a child, unknowing and afraid.

Death came out of the house with a chewing stick in its mouth and a calabash in its hand.

"Have you risen?" Kuyom greeted it, hand on her hip. There was no need for respect now.

Death sighed, gripping its white wrapper at the armpit.

"Why are you here?"

"My name is Kuyomnkpa."

"I said why are you at my door, Don't Seek Death?" it asked, turning her name into a sentence on its tongue.

"I am disobedient." She shrugged.

...❖...

Death sat on a low stool, cleaning its teeth. Kuyom sat on the ground sharpening her dagger on a stone, getting harmattan dust on her wrapper. It would join the layers of dirt and sweat and blood already covering her. She had climbed seven hills, crossed seven rivers, and braved seven forests, uncovered secrets and offered sacrifices, to find Death's home.

Kuyom sat in the shadow of a dozen lifeless palm trees, the dust-brown, drooping fronds reaching down mournfully toward her. The air was as dry as a final cough, and the stones were brittle, ready to crumble at the slightest touch.

"If you want me to return a lost lover to you, I cannot," Death said in a flat voice.

"That's not why I am here."

"A parent?"

"No."

"A debtor?"

"No."

"A talented palm wine tapper?"

Kuyom stared at Death in irritation.

"People have asked." Death shrugged.

"I don't want to bring anyone back. I want to leave."

"Leave where?"

"Life."

"You want to die? You could have waited for the sun to rise. I would have come to you."

"I don't just want to die. I know that when you die you have to wait in Mfre until you forget your last life. You can't come back to this world again until you've forgotten. I can't afford to forget."

"Hm," Death said, scrubbing its teeth with the stick. "What must you remember?"

"A deal."

"What was this deal?"

Kuyom sat in stubborn silence.

"Ah, so it's a secret. Tell it to me, and I might let you keep it when you die."

Kuyom looked to her left and right and sensed no living thing, but land and wind and water, they are curious too, so she gripped Death by the arm, drew it in close, and whispered, "Help me, and I will show you something you've never seen."

When she pulled away, Death licked its lips and laughed. And across rivers and hills and forests, some heard that laugh in dreams or in dark corners, and they were struck with dread as sharp as lightning and as sure as thunder.

"Something I have never seen? Well," Death said, "I will grant you this favor, because I am curious. I will tell you how to remember. You see, you must die a raw death. Come, I will show you how."

Kuyom was an orphan, like many of Adeh's servants were in those days. Her mother had died in childbirth and her father had followed shortly after. She did not know much about them, except that they had been cast out. Cut off from family and community, her parents had no one to leave her to. Kuyom did not know who had left her at the shrine of Adeh. It was taboo to help or touch or talk to an outcast or their offspring, but someone had risked it and saved her.

Adeh accepted anyone with a strong enough spirit, and a strong enough need, whether outcast or accused or abomination. One of Adeh's praise names was "The One Who Wipes Spit From My Face." Adeh took shame and shaped it into a shield for his servants, blessing them with luck and strength and speed, lengthening their lives … if they were willing to pay the price. Adeh had two conditions for initiates. The first: need. They had to smell of a desperation so strong that it tasted like death. The second was sacrifice. It always came down to sacrifice with these gods.

Adeh's outcasts, having been thrown out of families and clans and age grades and villages, formed a community of their own on Adeh's sacred land. On the outskirts, it was mostly overgrown bush which they left untended to maintain a sense of awe for visiting worshippers who came to leave offerings. People did not have to dedicate themselves completely to Adeh to worship him. Not everyone was so desperate. Adeh's chosen were a rare few. Those who committed the most heinous offenses, who did grievous harm, were almost always killed instead of exiled. Those who managed to escape that kind of death and came looking for respite in Adeh were met with unfathomable agony. Adeh contorted those he found wanting into grotesque shapes of anguish, fingers bent backward over cracked spines to clutch at toes, limbs folded over and under each other to compress a person into a broken, bleeding pulse of pain. Adeh could weave bones with flesh and make a body nothing but a braid begging for a swift death.

You know a god by its doings, by what it punishes, and how. By whom it accepts, and why. Adeh was vengeful and unforgiving and eloquent in torment, and in spite of this, because of this, he was a god of the helpless, a hider, a home. Adeh took in those cast out, those possessed by unknown spirits, called evil because it was the closest word accusing hands could grasp. He remembered those who were forgotten, who lived between realms, who had lived too many lives, whose eyes saw too much, who the world had called broken and then proceeded to break. He wiped the spit from their faces.

Kuyom was raised by abominations. Others came to Adeh as a result of mistakes or misfortune; they came crawling and limping or running, but always as a last resort. Kuyom's case was different. She was an outcast who had never been cast out. She was born unbelonging. All she'd ever had was all she would ever have.

Kuyom was a killer from the day she learned to love. The first thing she loved was an udara tree. It was only her third harmattan, and someone had handed her the smooth orange fruit, unthinking. No one had ever put much thought into raising her. She was a child, true, but she was practically invulnerable due to Adeh's blessing. Every bit of sweetness in Kuyom's life was handed to her carelessly and could be taken away with just as little consideration.

Kuyom had bitten into the udara from the side, because no one had taught her to bite out the stem and spit it out, then lick the pale pink juice before tearing the skin to get at the sweet-sour flesh and finally sucking on the seeds. She had bitten into the rubbery skin and chewed the flesh with it, sticky and sandy and sweet, and she'd been content. So, from a young age, Kuyom learned that sweetness meant sand in your teeth.

Kuyom learned to climb the next morning, because she did not know when next someone would place udara in her hand. She decided she would pluck it for herself. She climbed the tree as the sun climbed the sky, falling five times and standing up by herself. She reached the branch with the fruit the sixth time, and she plucked an armful. She hid them in a calabash, planning to eat them at night.

By the next afternoon, the tree had withered. Have you ever seen something die in full bloom? It's a different kind of rot.

Kuyom did not understand what had happened, but she sought consolation instead of answers, as children often do. That night when she went to eat her udara, she found that the fruits were so sour that they turned her mouth inside out. No one had told her that you need to wait for them to fall from the tree.

After the tree came the bad-tempered old black goat that had been given as an offering to Adeh. It was a living offering, not meant to be eaten. Kuyom had seen the sun reflect on its smooth black coat, and it was the first time her child's eyes had seen darkness catch light and hold it.

She would dig up immature cocoyam from the farms some of Adeh's people kept, to feed to the goat and lay her head on its round stomach on hot afternoons, until her low-cut hair took on its musk. Whenever the goat licked her hand between bites of cocoyam, Kuyom's stomach felt warm, and her chest felt light. She learned then that sometimes if you give away something solid, you can get lightness in return.

And then one day, she came to the goat pen to find her goat stiff on the ground, harmattan dust covering its coat, eyes wide open and staring at her in accusation. Some people had complained about the waste of meat. It would have to be buried instead of eaten, since it belonged to Adeh.

It was not the last to die by her unknowing hand. This was Kuyom's curse, the sacrifice Adeh demanded: Where she went, death followed.

Kuyom visited the river when she could, and she often could, since Ndia ran like a vein through the seven towns. It was a killer like her, and a safe thing to love. River people were suspicious and quick to hire servants of Adeh to break curses and seek out evil medicine causing illness and misfortune. It was an easy living, and most of the time she didn't have to do much work. Kuyom hated ease. She persistently sought out harder tasks, joining parties venturing into evil forests, seeking strange creatures, finding lost royal stools and staffs and heirs. She entertained no suitors. Not the wealthy farmer from Ikoro, which was far enough inland for people there to scoff at riverine taboos, who sought to marry her and keep her as a conquest in his home, an adventure in a basket, for his kin to gawk at over palm wine, pork, and edita-iwa. Not the imperious trader from the city of Kuwo, who had first wanted Kuyom for her son, and then herself, promising her the most exquisite cloth and coral and a life of endless pampering. Not the servant-vessel of Itamke, the goddess of birds, who had abandoned life on land and all its rigidity, white robes and chalk, god-bound, yet untethered, and promised to teach Kuyom how to fly. Especially not that one. Kuyom told them all that she was a hard built, sharp thing. A soft life would dull her to despair.

Kuyom was not supposed to accept offerings. Nkoyo was not supposed to go to Adeh's shrine alone. Their disobedience had collided on a rainy day, while Nkoyo's father was asleep, and no one could be bothered to be beaten by rain to receive offerings. Kuyom was bored and restless, and lonely, so she offered to go.

Children were not supposed to give offerings, but they weren't supposed to receive them either, so the girls had assumed it would balance out. Nkoyo had brought a dirty yellow chick. It was stolen. Her father did not keep chickens, and her mother had gone to sell yellow pepper in Kuwo. She'd been selling that same pepper in that same Kuwo for twelve seasons now, half as long as Nkoyo had been alive. Nkoyo confided this to Kuyom over fresh palm wine offered to Adeh by Ekere, the best tapper in Isino, who had been born a twin, and had a brother in Adeh's sanctuary. He brought two fresh calabashes every market week, and Kuyom had been stealing sips of it with Nkoyo from one of Adeh's sacred gourds since the beginning of the rainy season. It was almost harmattan now, and they knew everything worth knowing about each other. Nkoyo helped Kuyom find out more about herself than she ever could have in Adeh's sanctuary.

Kuyom knew that Nkoyo would not eat smoked catfish unless it was in afang soup and that she was more loyal to Adeh than any of her family gods and that Nkoyo dreamed of going to Kuwo when she was old enough, to ask her mother whether she still hadn't finished selling that pepper. Nkoyo knew that Kuyom loved udara, and her favorite part of serving Adeh was how strong she was, and that Kuyom dreamed of death. In some of the dreams, she was reunited with people she had never met. Kuyom told Nkoyo that the dreams were not sad or bad omens, that they comforted her, and Nkoyo accepted that, and said she would listen to Kuyom talk about her dreams until the day they both died, and even after that.

Not every untrue thing is a lie.

On a cold harmattan morning, Nkoyo's father came to Adeh's shrine with no offering. The first thing Kuyom saw through the fog was his eyes, red and searching; the second was his hands on his head. She listened to him offer his curses to Adeh. He screamed until he was hoarse that Adeh was an ingrate who had killed his daughter after she had served him so diligently.

For the first time, it occurred to Kuyom to pity a god. What did Adeh know of Nkoyo? Of how she always hummed after yawning, of how resentment and understanding could both fit in snugly in her chest, one never overpowering the other, of how she could look at you and know you entirely and choose to come back day after day, to help you know yourself, of how she had taught Kuyom that udara was sweetest when you waited for it to fall on its own.

Kuyom stood with Death at a crossroads, watching the woman in the indigo wrapper.

"What is she doing?" Kuyom asked Death, scratching her head.

"Sealing her fate," Death said softly, almost affectionately.

The woman was only beginning to gray. Her wrapper was worn and faded, and her jaw and arms were carved in the sinewy shape of suffering. She dropped a covered calabash where the road split, and she turned her back to it, walking purposefully away. She did not look back even once.

"She just traded her life for her child's."

"Her child was meant to die?"

"The child was never meant to live." Death laughed.

"So now it will?"

"Yes. She will die the day the child stops nursing, and it will have no choice but to live."

"Who did she make this trade with?"

"You don't know them. And it's a good thing you don't. You're too troublesome for that kind of knowledge."

Kuyom hissed. "Stop talking like you know me."

"Ah, of course I know you." Death laughed, turning to her. "And you know me. We have met several times. Don't you remember? When you were almost beheaded in Amana for cutting off the tip of a cobra's tail, the sunlight reflecting on the cutlass caught my eye. When you fell from an iroko tree in the evil forest in Nka, I heard the sound your bones made when they broke. When you angered that stubborn goat of a god in Ubok Akan, and he cursed you, I watched and laughed. When you were summoned by Ndia, I—"

"That's enough," Kuyom said.

"Is it?" Death asked, deceptively soft.

It lifted her chin with one finger.

"I don't think you understand yet. I own all deaths, but you? Even your life belonged to me. When you were born, your father saw your face and your future, and he screamed. Your name was a plea, and a prophecy. And yet you chased me until you found me. Maybe you are lying to yourself that you're here because of a friend or a promise or a deal, but you are not. You are here because of destiny."

Death held Kuyom's neck and whispered in her ear, "I told you that you would need to die a raw death to remember a past life. Do you know what that is? It is what that woman just did. She looked her end in the eye and chose it. Can you do that, Kuyom? What will you choose, now that you've finally found me?"

Kuyom drew back, her teeth carving her face into a smile. She gripped Death tightly by the neck, looking into its eyes.

"Is that all?"

Kuyom took her newly sharpened dagger, and led it to her heart, the question still on her lips. She fell where the road split in two, her left hand still wrapped around the crocodile-leather handle. When the blood came, the dry crackled ground tasted it first, and it traveled in thin red streams down the two roads.

Death only laughed.

…❖…

The day Kuyom first saw the face of Adeh, she'd been plucking palm-oil-stained feathers off a guinea fowl she'd found in a chalk-marked calabash under a tree. It was obviously an offering to some god or the other, but in Kuyom's experience, gods only had as much power as you believed. At the moment when she'd stolen the fowl, she'd felt the fact of her hunger, and it weighed more than the fear of lightning or affliction striking her. Besides, she'd been struck by lightning once already that rainy season after a member of a search party for a wealthy yam farmer's first son had killed a sacred newborn goat and shared a single roasted ear with her. What were the chances that it would happen again?

Kuyom had woken up two market weeks later, thanks to Adeh's blessing, and found the rotting body of the goat-roaster beside her. The rest of the group had already found the yam farmer's son living with a plantain trader's son in the city of Kuwo. They'd shared the young men's bribe and sent news to the father to show his second son the boundaries of his family land since he would never see the first again.

Since Kuyom had gotten no bribe and no bounty, and fishing during Ndia's feeding season was death, she'd been surviving on goodwill and forest fruits. Since Kuyom was not one to keep friends, and she did not particularly like pawpaw, it didn't take long for her to grow hungry enough to justify stealing from the gods.

She looked at the bony thigh of the roasted fowl, weighing the risks and then, as always, ceded them to Adeh.

She chewed slowly and swallowed cautiously. When nothing happened, she hissed dismissively and took a second bite. She did not get a chance to swallow it.

She woke up to something scratching at the bottom of her foot.

Kuyom sprang up, clutching her dagger, and pointed it at the back of the man in front of her. He looked only a bit older than her, with wide, pretty features, a dark, even complexion and hair neatly braided back. His lean body was stretched out as he sat, palms in the sand and toes fluttering gently in the river. He'd tossed the stick he'd used to scratch her feet to the side when he turned to face the river.

"You're awake. I wasn't sure if I had debased myself enough for her to let you live."

"Who are you?" Kuyom asked.

"Who are you?" the man mimicked, pitching his voice lower and making it coarse like Kuyom's.

"I asked you a question," Kuyom said, touching the top of her dagger to his back.

"So," the man said lazily, turning around to look at her with half-lidded eyes, elbows resting lightly on his knees. "You do not know the god you serve?"

Kuyom hissed, dragging the dagger across his throat. "I serve no god."

He stared at her in annoyance, wiping the thin stream of blood seeping from her killing cut.

"I'm even bleeding!" he said petulantly. "Is your disbelief this deep?"

"You're really him," Kuyom said with a sigh. "You sounded different in my dreams," she muttered, walking away.

Adeh started speaking to Kuyom through dreams after she realized what exactly her curse was. After what happened to Nkoyo.

Most children are taught the praise names of their ancestors, the prayers of their gods or incantations for the spirits they pledge to as soon as they can speak. Kuyom was taught the most searing insults that existed in the river tongue and all the pidgins of Kuwo.

She did not know her lineage, or how to speak to gods or summon spirits. A child who knows what comfort is, not finding it during the day, might seek it at night in other realms. Kuyom did not know what comfort was and did not know to seek it.

But maybe there is something divine about these gods. Because what is it but a miracle, that a god would smell a small girl's sorrow and seek to soften it?

Adeh came to Kuyom as a voice in the night, as warmth and as reassurance, as a lightness in her chest and a heaviness in her eyes. He was the reason she'd always felt safer in the dark. But he was always gone in the morning. And in the sunlight, she would remember that he was the cause of the tears he dried. He was the reason for her curse;

the lives lost to her love were a sacrifice to him. It is a dizzying thing, to be slapped with the right hand, and embraced with the left.

As Kuyom sized Adeh up, she saw that he was smaller than she'd first thought, shorter than her, with a sharp smile and a gap in his teeth like the ones the youths in Kuwo prized so highly. She wondered if the gap was natural or if he had filed it in like they sometimes did in Kuwo.

As he followed her quietly, she decided that he had been born with the gap, if gods are ever born. He walked like someone who was born into beauty, treading lightly as if he was blessing the earth with every step, and staring straight ahead, trusting the ground not to trip him. She wondered if it was his beauty or his power that made his steps so sure. Beauty is a kind of power too, she decided, and power makes you beautiful.

He followed her quietly for a while, humming a song.

"You know, you sound different too."

"What do you mean?"

"I never heard your voice, all those nights. Your spirit is so different from your body."

"What is my spirit like?"

"Timid, and strong. But here you are bold, and so weak."

"What do you want from me?"

"I want you to do something for me."

"No," Kuyom said, happy to deny him.

"You would refuse me? Your savior and provider?" Adeh asked, placing a palm on his chest and giving her a beseeching look.

"Yes," Kuyom said with a smile.

"Do you know whose guinea fowl you ate today? Who I had to beg to save your life?"

"I don't care," Kuyom said, turning around to walk away from him.

"I will give you something in exchange."

Kuyom turned back slowly, rage simmering. "You. You will give me something. In exchange."

"Kuyom—"

"After all you've taken from me. You've stolen any life I could have had, everything I've ever had, and you won't even let me die! You've made me too strong and brought me back every time I've come close. And you want something else ... in exchange." Kuyom's laugh was bitter.

"I'm sorry. You cannot understand how sorry I am."

"I don't want to."

Adeh did not touch her, he was standing at a distance, but somehow she felt his presence embrace her like it used to when she was a child, a warmth in the darkness.

She threw her dagger at his chest, and it stuck there.

"Never do that again," she hissed through her teeth.

Kuyom saw the bloodstains on Adeh's teeth as he spoke. "Let's make a deal. If you do this for me, I will let you die."

Kuyom was silent for a moment.

"What do I have to do?" Kuyom asked, walking up to him and pulling out her dagger. Adeh winced and smiled, almost as if he enjoyed the pain.

"You have to kill Death."

Kuyom sighed. "Is that all?"

Kuyom woke in Mfre, the before and after, the place of forgetting. There was no dagger in her chest, no gaping wound where there should have been. She could still sense and feel, and she was stronger in spirit, like Adeh had said. She was in front of what looked like a river, sitting in what felt like sand. Except for the fog, thick as a morning in the middle of harmattan, it reminded her of the days she spent sitting on the banks of Ndia.

"Where you go, Death follows," Adeh had said. And he was right. He had made it so.

Surely as the sunrise, Death came after Kuyom.

It appeared beside her, sitting in the sand.

"You did well. In your next life, you will remember your deal, but you must move fast now. The raw death crystalized your memory, but this place will strip it if you stay here too long. Hurry on to your next life. I will find you there as well."

Fast as lightning, Kuyom grabbed Death by the wrist, slamming her knee into its back and holding it over the river of Mfre. In the still water, Death saw its own reflection for the first time.

How do you make a god? By believing, by remembering. How do you kill a god? By forgetting. Death is a god, in its way.

Death choked out a laugh, amusement mixed with shock.

"This … this is the deal you made? You cannot kill me, Kuyomnkpa."

"I can keep you here until you forget what you are. You are nothing if you don't know your name."

Time passes differently in Mfre, but Adeh walked out of the fog just as Kuyom was forgetting her name, and Death its purpose. Adeh found them both sitting in the sand, staring at the water.

The one that was once Death looked at Adeh, face contorted in an effort to remember. "You … I know you. You were—"

"I am Adeh."

"Who am I?" it asked.

"No one important, now. But you might be in your next life."

"Who am I?" the one who was once Kuyom asked.

"You?" Adeh turned to her with a sharp smile. "You are Death."

THE HAUNTING OF KAMBILI

by Amanda Ilozumba

It was the smell of fried plantain, slightly burnt, that roused her. But when Kambili opened her eyes, she wasn't in Nne's kitchen. There was only a filmy darkness—one that left an oily coat on her tongue—and the rusted tap, leaking drops of water.

One, two, three. She counted, closed her eyes, and submerged back into the vision.

The next time she woke, she was in the hotel room, with the duvet's heat smothering her. She lay without moving. Sometime during the night, the power had gone out. Kambili heard the sound of generators—old and tired—and felt a flash of irritation. Why had the hotel not put on its own generator?

Reaching into the duvet, Kambili fumbled around for her phone. She found it, turned on its torchlight, and aimed it at the roof. She blinked. Above, on the cemented ceiling, were wet footprints as if someone had run all over it upside down. And below, on the floor, there was a murky pool of water.

Kambili drew in a ragged breath that was brittle and harsh against her teeth. She swung her legs over the bed and settled them on the floor. The cold enveloped her feet. *Is the water real?* Something stung her, and she winced, bringing her feet back up. They were covered in cuts, with mud and leaves stuck in the crevices and her toenails. Slowly, she breathed in and out, wondering if she had made the right decision in coming to this place. No matter what she had seen, she should have stayed with Nne. Her lips trembled as she began to pray, "Our Father, Who art in Heaven, Hallowed be Thy Name …"

1: NO ONE LEAVES OBATETE

In the morning as soon as the first rays of sunlight kissed the sky gold, Kambili did makeshift first aid on her cuts; some were deep enough to get infected. She cleaned the wounds with the bottle of water she hadn't finished during the bus ride, then disinfected and slathered them with Vaseline.

There was still no light and no running water either. Kambili had not expected much from a hotel in a middle-of-nowhere shit town, but *ahah*, this one was too much. She cleaned her face, neck, armpits, and "down there" with wipes and changed her underwear, begrudgingly wearing a bra because she knew how villagers could be. Then she shrugged on a long blue cotton skirt—a lone ranger in her sea of jeans—and her hoodie (formerly white). She checked her phone for messages, but the signal was poor, almost nonexistent. She hissed, tucked the phone and some cash into her bag, then shoved her feet into her worn-out sneakers. Before leaving the room, she glanced at the ceiling. The footprints were gone and so was the water—disappeared or dried up? She didn't know. But she steeled her shoulders and locked the door.

Kambili was going into the village.

The village was a relatively small place, quiet and picturesque, with muddy hills and muddier grounds. And it was sentient. Kambili could feel it in the thick air, in the bending of the trees, and on the ground in the grass that wrapped around her ankles, pulling. There was darkness lurking. Evil had spoken to this village for a long time, and now it had called her here.

On those rare days when Nne slipped into sudden catalepsy, she had murmured about the village well enough for Kambili to know her way around. It was strange. This was where her mother had grown up, laid her roots, and uprooted herself. Yet, Kambili felt no form of kinship; all she felt was dread. Cold, hard, heart-churning dread.

Kambili passed the market, already bustling with people. She noticed that compared to the men, the women were fewer—one or two in a sea of men. Unlike her, who averted her gaze and kept it to the ground, the villagers stared at her openly, and she could have sworn that one fish seller hissed at her. Their animosity tightened her bones. Did they recognize her? As the daughter of the one who ran away?

A little further, she came upon the settlement. There were rows of mud houses and thatch huts built and spaced intimately, to keep the ajo mmuo from squeezing themselves in, Nne had said. But it made no sense to Kambili; bad spirits could not be stopped by small spaces. The houses were marked with ancient Nsibidi symbols, drawn with white chalk and numbered with red or black chalk.

With a sigh, Kambili wiped the sweat off her forehead; the sun was beginning to lose its morning warmth, and humid heat wrapped around her like a thick blanket. Under her hoodie, rivulets of sweat formed between and underneath her breasts. Kambili tugged at the hoodie, wishing she had worn a camisole underneath. She had expected harsh, village Harmattan weather; this heat was something else.

"That useless hotel had better have water when I get back," she grumbled and picked up the pace. She needed to go to the sixty-sixth hut. Conscious of the villagers who watched her, she adjusted her bag's strap over her shoulders and began to count the houses in Igbo, "ofu, abou, ato, ano, ise ..."

Compared to the others, the hut was downtrodden, with its mud exterior chipping away and a goat tied to a post in front of it. Kambili hesitated, questioning her sanity again before she knocked on the wooden door and pushed it open. The hut was dusty, but there were signs that it was occupied. In the parlor where Kambili stood, she found a used plate—orange with palm oil—sitting precariously on a monochrome TV, a brown, aging wrapper resting carefully on a plastic chair, and a comb on the wooden table with white hairs in its teeth.

"Mama," Kambili called out softly. She checked the rooms—there were only two—and they were empty. The last door led to a backyard. Kambili twisted the door handle open and went outside. That was where she found the woman whose hair matched the strands on the comb, thick and strong despite her age, and a little loose, framing a wickedly wrinkled brown face. The woman shifted, and Kambili noticed she was barefooted, her feet reddened by mud and leaves stuck in her toenails.

Kambili called out, "Mama?"

The woman straightened, moving away from the firewood she was stoking and limped toward Kambili. She held Kambili's face between her hands, smiled (warmly), and said, "Anyi echewo gi ogologo oge." *We have waited for you a long time.*

Kambili supposed she should have brought her grandmother a gift. The Our Lady's Bread the East was known for, or Okpa, but she didn't know what her grandmother liked. She had not even expected the woman to be alive and so strong; Kambili watched in awe as her grandmother pounded ede, showing no exertion as the gummy white cocoyam paste drew in the pestle. She was showing Kambili how to cook ofe onugbu—a soup made from bitter leaves and thickened with ede.

Kambili heard singing—slight at first, then becoming louder—from the other end of the house.

"Okpa. Okpa di okwu!" a hawker called out as she passed. Kambili had eaten Okpa only once when Nne had traveled to see a "friend." Her mouth watered as she thought of the bean meal: yellow, soft, and surely steaming hot. Kambili's stomach rumbled, reminding her she had not eaten the night before, or this morning.

Her grandmother caught the swallowing in her throat. "Agu o na agu gi?" *Are you hungry?* she asked.

Kambili nodded and glanced at the stove where the pot was bubbling, its cover open. They had already washed the bitterness out of the onugbu leaves. It was boiling now, but it would take at least an hour before the meat cooked and the soup was ready.

"Call the woman," her grandmother said, referring to the Okpa seller.

"Okpa o!" Kambili quickly shouted as she searched the thin pockets of her skirt for money.

The seller came from behind the house, through a gate Kambili had not noticed because it was half swallowed by the bushes leading to her grandmother's farm. "Ehei good morning, o," she greeted as she set her tray down. "How many?"

"Two," Kambili answered. Perhaps it was Kambili's voice, but something made the Okpa seller stop short. She eyed Kambili, really looking, for a few seconds before reaching into her tray and selecting two Okpa wrapped in plantain leaves and separated from the rest. The seller made to put them inside a nylon, but Kambili's grandmother shoved a plate at her. "Put it here," she grunted.

A silent exchange went on between the seller and Kambili's grandmother, and Kambili thought she was going mad, but she swore she could hear their voices in her head. Both argued about a Ritual of Purity. Kambili suddenly felt uncomfortable—unsafe. She moved between both women and collected the plate from her grandmother, then pushed a five hundred naira note in the Okpa seller's waiting hand.

"Don't worry about the change." Kambili offered her a reluctant smile.

The seller smiled back, and whatever tension was in the air dissipated. "Are you Nne's daughter?" she asked then, adjusting her wrapper and tightening the knot on her waist.

"Eh, yes," Kambili answered, confused, because this woman clearly knew who she was.

With a speculative gleam in her eyes, the Okpa seller smiled even wider. "Nnoo nwa furu efu." *Welcome back, lost child.*

After the woman left, Kambili's grandmother snatched the plate from her hand and threw the Okpa into the fire.

And Kambili, hungry, tired, and restless, watched it burn, her lips pressed into a thin line.

Evening rolled in, bringing with it storm clouds that Kambili knew she could not allow to catch her on the way back to town. It was time to leave.

Strangely, she felt bereft. Sad that Nne had never brought her to the village. Sure, the village was weird, with it being transmundane and having fast-changing, extreme weather, unfriendly occupants, and that crazy Okpa seller. But finding her grandmother made all of that seem unimportant. They had spent only an afternoon together—she and the grandmother she had just met, but there was an immediate bond. It felt like she had met her grandmother before; there was a familiarity in her touch and in the way her eyes crinkled at the seams when she smiled.

Kambili went over her day again and again in an attempt to sear the memory permanently into her brain. She had learned how to cook onugbu. With the way her grandmother cooked it, Kambili had licked the soup bowl clean. Then they went into the farm to pick corn ripened and goldened by the rich soil. And Kambili fed the goat out front, offering it stalks of dry grass by hand until her grandmother laughed and warned her not to get attached because the goat would soon be boiling inside a pot.

Running her hands over the fresh, flat braids her grandmother had plaited for her, Kambili picked up her phone again. The service bar had two lines, with one going on and off. Kambili sighed and hoped that would be enough to deliver her message. She tapped Nne's number and tried calling, but when the call didn't go through, she opened the messaging app and began to type, hoping that her mother would read it soon.

Kambili's hand hovered over the send button. She bit her lower lip and typed one last thing.

I know you said I shouldn't go, but I had that vision again, and I had to see. Sent: 6:15 p.m.

Her grandmother was still on the farm, so Kambili laced her sneakers and returned there. She found her holding a plastic bottle filled with palm oil and pouring it on a mound of soil, muttering to herself. It looked almost ritualistic. *The oil must be bad*, Kambili nodded to herself. She paused before saying, "Mama, I have to get back now. I'll come again tomorrow, and you can show me around the village."

Stilling, her grandmother dropped the bottle and shifted in front of the mound, blocking it from Kambili's view. Kambili frowned. Her gaze averted to her grandmother's feet, muddied and covered in green. The image flashed, and Kambili was looking at her feet, stinging from the cuts, covered with those leaves and the red mud coating her soles.

Air rushed in and out of Kambili as the world slowed. The images became interweaved and a realization hit her. She'd been here. On her grandmother's farm, she had been here!

"No one leaves Obatete."

"What?" Kambili whispered, finding it hard to breathe.

"Not by this time," her grandmother said, "the bus park closes by 4 p.m. You won't see transport going back."

"Oh," Kambili said, then laughed, feeling very stupid.

Taking her arm, Kambili's grandmother led her out of the farm, back into the parlor, where she pointed at the second room in the hut. "You look tired nwa m. Go and sleep. There is a meeting I have to attend. I'll be back soon. Should I buy corn and pear?"

"Yes, Ma. Thank you."

Wearing a Dunlop slipper that was flat and lifeless, her grandmother tied the brown wrapper over her shift, then hung a bag over her shoulders. Kambili eyed the bag, convinced it was more of a travel bag than a handbag. The thing was bigger than the suitcase she had come with. She held back a snort of laughter.

"Bye-bye, Ma." She waved.

Her grandmother paused at the door. "Kambili," she said, all the light in her eyes gone out, "lock your room door."

God abeg. Kambili sighed. It was probably a safety measure, but why did her grandmother have to say it like that? Still, she turned the key in its hole twice to be sure.

With no service, she couldn't check her Instagram and Snapchat; some statuses had loaded on her WhatsApp though, so she watched those before switching to the offline color puzzle game she was addicted to while listening to her Eric Nam playlist. If there was a way to kidnap the K-pop singer and keep him all to herself, Kambili would have done it without hesitation.

Eric Nam's voice serenaded her to sleep. And when his voice mottled down into a guttural whisper—harsh, grating, and not his—it woke her up.

There was scratching at the window. Panic-stricken by the change in the song she had been listening to, and now this, Kambili called out for her grandmother. "Mama! Are you back?"

As soon as the words left her mouth, Kambili wished she hadn't spoken. She felt a shift in the air. The song (although she had stopped it) started playing again, with the melody shifting between the singer's voice and the forceful whispering.

Scratching, again, at the window. Kambili swallowed, her tongue stuck to the roof of her mouth like a dry husk. She got up and padded to the window.

Scratch.

Scratch.

Scrawl!

Two knobby, bony fingers appeared on the window, followed by three others, then another hand—skeletal and ghostly. Kambili bit back a scream and backed away from the window slowly.

A face took shape behind the fingers, stretching and filling until it had eyes that watched Kambili with unbridled malevolence. It had rotten flesh, with pieces falling away to reveal white bone underneath. The Thing's mouth opened, and it blew on the window. Then it continued scrawling.

Kambili read the letters. It said n-w-u-o. *Die.*

She screamed then because the Thing was starting to open the window.

"Oh God. Oh shit!" she prayed and cursed at once. Then she hoped God would smite her down for using a curse word with his name. That was better than facing whatever hell forsaken thing was at the window.

A white light flashed, blinding her. This was it, Kambili thought. Nne had warned her about the village; she had told Kambili it was demonic and dangerous, but she hadn't listened, had she? Kambili had gone with her coconut head to the one place her mother had told her never to step foot in.

The window stopped opening.

Kambili paused. Swallowing the knot in her throat, she went to the window and looked through it. In the small space between her grandmother's hut and the next, two Nsibidi symbols were glowing. The Thing had disappeared. Nne's words came back to her: Small spaces keep the ajo mmuo away.

So the symbol between her grandmother's and the next hut was some sort of protection? Kambili slammed the window shut and locked it. Whatever it was, the Thing, the symbols, the village, she would leave first thing in the morning and never come back. Fuck what she had seen in the dream.

She was going to check whether her grandmother had come back when the door handle began to move up and down like someone was trying to open it and was failing. The key twisted in the hole—in, out, then a click. It was open. Kambili felt hot liquid on her face and realized she was crying. She ran into the bed and huddled at its corner, folding into herself. She bit on her left arm, and with her right, she held her phone tight, cracking its screen protector.

The door didn't open, but wet footsteps came in. They were tiny at first, like those of a child (five or six), coming toward the bed. Then, as the footsteps stopped and changed course, climbing the walls, they grew in size into those of an adult—an adult with two toes missing on the right foot.

"Our Father, Who art in Heaven, Hallowed be Thy name." As Kambili shook, she switched to Psalm 91. "Whoever goes to the Lord for safety, whoever remains under the protection of the almighty can say to him—" She looked up at the roof. The footsteps had stopped right above her head.

Water dripped onto her forehead and rolled down to the tip of her nose. She sniffed. It smelled metallic. Kambili continued praying, her voice steady. "You are my defender and protector. You are my God; in You I trust."

The water was dripping down faster, soaking her and the bed.

"You will keep me safe from all hidden dangers. I need not fear any dangers at night."

Her phone vibrated, startling her. She flung it away by reflex, and the phone landed on the floor. The phone screen lit up; she had a message. Kambili crawled to the edge of the bed. The message was from her mother. She leaned over and snatched the phone, unlocking it with shaking fingers.

Only two words:

Kambili. Run.

All at once, the ceiling cracked and water poured in—no longer in baby drops but in torrents that swirled around her—choking, drowning, and swallowing her screams.

Slimy and cadaverous hands clasped her legs, gripping like a hook into a fish's gills. Kambili saw herself standing in a sea of dead women. Their bodies were blue and bloated and rotting. All with open eyes; eyes that were dead but gleamed with jealousy because she was alive, and they weren't. They wanted her.

Someone was calling Kambili's name. Her grandmother.

"Mama!" she cried out, "Mama please."

"Kambili nwa m." *I'm coming!* The door opened, with her grandmother behind, eyes blazing with a circlet of fire around her right arm, and a kerosene lantern in the other hand.

At that moment, the hands holding Kambili's legs tightened, twisted, and dragged her under.

2: A PSALM, A CURSE, A DREAM, THE THING

It was in 1930-something that the first cairn that formed Obatete's foundations was laid. It was a pile of rocks, tainted with the blood of its women, wet with their tears, and held together by a psalm of their cries.

The curse (although Obatete's people would not admit it was a curse) started with the mutilation of the witch girl, Imelda. Obatete's women, at the moment of their first bleeding, were circumcised, and the blood from their privates was collected and offered to Obara, their god. In return for their purity, Obara granted the sacrificed women Theurgy; through him they were able to wield oku—*fire*—to nurture life in the village and keep warm when the biting cold of Harmattan came. Because of this, they believed it was the virtue of their women that kept Obatete's rivers flowing and its soil pregnant with harvest. To refuse this rite of passage was to become an outcast, an unclean person, a curse on the village.

There were those who died: girls who did not survive the cutting, and women who bled to death during childbirth. And there was Imelda, the witch girl. Perhaps it was because of the darkness that rested in her bosom, or the evil that often clouded her thoughts, but when Imelda died during the cutting, she came back.

It was Imelda that Kambili saw in her dream in the night, bleeding into a small dirt hole, crying. And she was afraid, not of the dark as a child should have been, but of the woman kneeling beside her, holding a knife and whispering of purity. Her nine-year-old body had trembled violently with resentment toward her people. Imelda had vowed to return and not stop until she put an end to Obatete's atrocities against its women. She would destroy the village and everyone who lived there. She had to, so they would not spread their dreadful traditions to the rest of the world.

With each person she took, Imelda became the Thing—a spirit of retribution and bloodlust.

3: THE GIRL WHO RAN, THE WOMAN WHO RETURNED

Nne was going to kill her daughter. But first, she would kill every single person in that village if even a single strand of hair was missing from Kambili's head.

After everything she had done to keep Kambili away: running off at nineteen with a four-year-old daughter, starting a new life in Lagos with nothing but a primary school degree, fighting off her people's spiritual attacks because God forbid anyone left Obatete and talked about what they did to those girls. Nne had struggled, and Kambili had gone and thrown everything she had worked for away, and for what? A vision!

Nne twisted her finger rosary, her lips downturned as she gripped her car's wheel harder and leaned her head on it. She started to nod her head back and forth in an attempt to calm down. Anger would do her no good. Nne shook her head. She wasn't really angry; she was scared. She hoped the woman who had cut her then was dead. She felt a pang in her chest, and she brushed it away. It didn't matter if her mother was the one who did the cutting; she still wanted her to be dead.

With a sigh, she got down from the car, went over to the other side to get her stuff, then locked the car and stuffed the key into her jeans. She shouldered the small backpack she had brought. She didn't plan to stay long. "In and out, Nne," she breathed and started trekking.

Surrounding Obatete's boundary was a shield of fire that had not been there when Kambili arrived, built more to keep its people in than to ward off outsiders. Nne paused at the shield before tentatively stretching her hand forward and into the flames. It parted for her, recognizing her as Obatete's own; it was an identity engraved into her very being, one she could never shed. The minute she stepped past the boundary, Nne felt the shift in the air. Everything felt wrong, darker, suffocating. It was hard for her to breathe, and she twisted at the heat that roiled beneath her veins. Her fire was returning. She had despised her oku; it was another thing that tied her to Obatete, but now that it was licking at her veins, just waiting to be released from her fingertips, Nne welcomed it like an old friend.

She decided to cut through the main road and take a shortcut, one that led through the forest and straight to her mother's farm. Nne was jogging now. Her body protested the exertion. It had been ages since she had done anything more than stretch. She ducked under a tree branch, hissing when its leaves slapped her face. She blinked away the stinging in her eyes and moved faster.

Another set of footsteps joined hers—they were swift but light. She heard them somehow, over the roaring in her head, and deduced that whoever it was, was chasing her. She stopped and shifted deeper into the bushes, where the grass was tall enough to hide her. Nne's chest heaved as she glanced around, squinting because she had forgotten to bring her glasses.

Her pursuer came into view. It was a man; he was tall, barrel chested, and thick bearded. He did a 360° turn, scratched his head, and hissed, "Was it not my two eyes I used to see that woman?" he muttered to himself.

Nne watched him. Flames licked at her fingertips, and she had half the mind to throw them at the man. She laughed to herself, cursing her luck. Of course, the first person who spotted her was Afam, the husband she had left behind. The stupid, stupid man who chose Obatete over her. He was still handsome. She noticed the cleft on his chin had become less visible with age. Nne crouched to start crawling away, only for something cold to slither up her legs. It was sudden, and her mouth opened to let out a shrill scream before she could bite it back.

"Nne!" Afam shouted and rushed into the bushes, following her scream. Before she could fix her backpack and run, Afam was there, reaching into her jeans and bringing out the caterpillar that was crawling up her pants.

"Get away from me," she said, and backed away.

Afam laughed and raised his hands in surrender. "I thought my eyes were seeing double. You're still as strongheaded as ever. I can't believe it's you."

Nne's throat constricted. She hated that she had missed this man. It felt like she was betraying herself. She turned her head so he would not see the tears burning her eyes, but Afam held her chin and turned her face to his. Leaning in, he cleaned her face with the sleeve of his shirt, then pressed his lip to her forehead. Nne clicked her tongue and pushed him away. "Where is my daughter?"

"Our daughter."

She eyed him up and down, then rolled her eyes. "Biko, where is she?" she asked again as she got up and adjusted her shirt where it had ridden up her stomach. She did not miss the way Afam's gaze lingered on her skin.

He hesitated before he spoke, his eyes not meeting hers. "I—see eh, I only just found out she was here yesterday …"

"Afam."

His lips pressed into a thin line, and he stepped away from Nne, carefully watching the flames shadowing her fingers as he said, "She was taken."

Afam nursed the bruise on his temple where Nne had hit him. The skin there was tender and slightly burned. He sighed. Twenty-two years later, she had returned to give him another wound that matched the one on his left chin. He rubbed the scar, a habit he had developed while it was healing and itching like hell.

He glanced at Nne again for the umpteenth time. She had changed a lot. There was a hardness in her gait that had not been there when they were younger. Whatever she faced after leaving Obatete had strengthened her in more ways than one. Something slithered in his chest, and he realized it was jealousy. A part of him wished he had gone with her. Maybe this time he would be brave enough to.

They trudged through the forest in silence, with Nne doing her best to pretend he was not there. Her brows were furrowed, the only indication of her annoyance.

Nne forced herself to concentrate on saving her daughter. She had come back for Kambili, nothing more.

They reached the thinner part of the forest. Obatete's main square came into view. Nne's breath caught in her throat. Not much had changed; it was like the village was caught in a state of limbo. The huge iroko tree at the center of the square was only a little thicker and weathered. The Theurgy school building just behind it, where the village girls learned to control their fire. The small kiosk (the only one that sold provisions). And the people milling around the square—still as wretched looking as ever. She recognized all of them, surprised their names came to her so easily.

"Let's go further down," Nne said to Afam, pointing to the path that would take them past the main square and right into the village settlement instead. The fewer people that saw her, the better. That was why she had not ditched Afam. Who knew what he would tell people if she let him go?

"Okay." Afam nodded and took the lead. The path had changed a little over the years, curving in a snakelike pattern where it had once been straight. He couldn't bear the silence anymore, so he faced her. Walking backward, he said, "Nne . . ." But as soon as he called her name, his courage dissipated, and he realized he did not know what to say.

How have you been?

Where did you go?

What is it like outside of Obatete?

Nne waited and then sighed when he did not speak. "Nwoke m, what do you want to ask?"

"Nothing," he said to her questioning stare. "Wait!" he blurted. "Why did you leave?"

Hissing, Nne came to a stop. She stood with her arms on her waist. "Lee onwe gi anya—look at yourself Afam, then look around you. Why do you think I left?"

Fair enough. He nodded. "I should have gone with you. I regret it every day. Drowned myself in palm wine too"—he laughed—"they even said you used juju on me because I refused to look at any other woman."

Nne paused at that. "You did not remarry?"

"*Mhm mhm.*" He shook his head with a smile, the same boyish grin she had once loved him for.

With a noncommittal grunt, she said, "Me too."

Afam clamped down on the surge of happiness he felt at her answer. "What are you going to do when we get there?" By "there" he meant her mother's house. Despite Nne's reluctance to go, Afam had explained to her that since it was the place Kambili disappeared, it would only make sense to start their search from there, see if she left anything behind that would give them a clue.

"I'm going to find my daughter any way I can. Then get out of this place. And God help anyone who tries to stop me." Nne answered and continued walking, leaving a trail of fire-tinged grass beneath her feet.

4: TO FIGHT AGAINST WHAT YOU BELIEVE IN

Obatete's people reckoned that fire was life, a living thing, human like them but formless and powerful. Perhaps it was because the fire that Obara granted their women appeared to live and breathe and consume anything in its path, or maybe it was that it felt warm enough to heat up the blood beneath their veins. Either way, they were wrong. Their fire was not alive; neither was it life itself. It was a tool, one that lay dormant until it was awakened.

Something burned within Kambili. She stirred, groaning from the headache pulsing at the side of her head. The night chill had seeped into her bones, stiffening her body so moving was painful. She shifted up from the ground where her face was pressed into the marshy earth. She sniffed and grimaced. She was lying in manure.

Kambili shivered violently. Someone had taken off her hoodie and skirt, leaving her in only her underwear, bound her hands and feet with ropes, and blindfolded her. She folded her lips to keep her tears at bay. *Think first, panic later.* That's what she should have done at her grandmother's house.

Crickets chirped somewhere nearby, and it was dark all around her, thickly so. She could feel that even with the blindfold on. But where was she? Her memory was hazy after the bodies dragged her in. It was as if they had transported her through a spirit portal of some sort. Kambili was sure she was still in Obatete, just not where.

Raising her knees, she tried to sit up, but the rope that had been used to tie her up dug into her skin, tearing the flesh open the more she moved. Kambili sucked in a deep breath, then screamed. She hated that tears were burning the corners of her eyes; she hated that she was scared; she hated that she had ignored her mother's warning. She should never have come to Obatete.

A prayer started to rise from her lips, but Kambili stopped herself. This wasn't God's fight, it was hers.

She screamed again and continued until her voice was cracked and hoarse. It was only then that she calmed down enough to process everything that had happened. *Kambili, think first, panic later*—it was what Nne had always told her because she tended to get overwhelmed by the littlest things.

Where the hell am I? Kambili thought. Ignoring the pain in her ankles and wrists, she started rolling sideways, worming her way around until she hit a wall. She stretched out her hands to feel around. "Wood," she murmured. The wall was made of wood. She pushed herself into a half-sitting position that burned her core, but years of sit-ups kept her steady. She pressed her hands onto the wood. It was soft, slimy, and cracked at the edges. Pushing her left hand into one of the holes, she pulled, hoping to break off a piece and use it to cut her bonds. The wood held despite being rotten. She grunted in annoyance and gave up on that idea.

She went back to worming around, figuring that if she was on the ground and there was a wooden wall, then she was probably in a shed. And the shed had to have an exit. After scraping her head on sharp stones and getting multiple splinters in her palms, Kambili was ready to give up, right until she hit a body. The body was frigid, too cold to be alive, but it stirred when she brushed against it. Kambili's stomach dropped, with her heart beating so hard she was sure it would stop any minute. She brushed against the body again, and whoever it was let out a small feminine whimper.

Kambili wet her lips and spoke hesitantly. "I—who are you?"

The girl whimpered again.

"Were you taken too? By the bodies?" Kambili asked, only to realize how ridiculous she sounded seconds later.

The girl coughed, heavy and dry. "Others," she said, "anyi di otutu." *We are many taken.*

Oh God. Kambili gasped. The girl sounded so small that she had to be younger than ten. There was a great deal of pain in her voice, and from how cold she felt, it was obvious she had been in here for days.

"Okay," Kambili said, "listen to me carefully. I'm going to roll closer to you and bring my hands to yours. You have to untie me, okay. Then I'll do the same for you."

"Okay, Aunty."

Little by little, Kambili scooted over to the girl, not wanting to move too much at once so she would not accidentally roll on her. "Am I close enough?"

The girl did not answer. Instead, nimble fingers began to work on Kambili's bonds. Kambili gritted her teeth. The girl's fingers were so cold that they left imprints of ice where they touched Kambili's flesh. A brief flash of anger ran through Kambili. How could anyone treat a child this way?

She felt the knots loosening, so she flexed her wrists to make the rope come off faster. Kambili hissed in relief when the rope came off. She rubbed the welts on her wrists, then ripped off her blindfold, untied her feet, and immediately went to work on the girl's ropes.

Thin lines of moonlight filtered into the shed, making it easier for Kambili's eyes to adjust to the darkness and allowing her to see bits of the girl's features. The girl was a tiny little thing with a clean-shaven head, sunken dark eyes, and bones jutting out of places where flesh should have been. Her skin had a bluish tint to it, with an almost translucent glow. Kambili's eyes watered, not just because of the state the girl was in but because, somehow, she was feeling her pain too. Kambili had the nagging feeling that she knew this girl. There was something familiar about the way the girl shrunk into herself, something about the mud that stained her slender, hardened feet.

"Do you know where the others are?" Kambili asked, remembering that the girl had said they were many, yet the shed was empty, with the exception of both of them.

"Gone," the girl whispered.

A shiver passed through Kambili. She chewed on her bottom lip, thinking of what to do next. Whatever it was that took them was probably still out there. They couldn't escape the shed without a weapon to protect themselves, but then, what could she use to fight ajo mmuo?

Kambili froze. She had heard footsteps, soft and calculative, approaching the shed. She put a finger to her lips, warning the girl to stay quiet. Together, they watched as a figure came to the shed. Kambili was not sure, but it looked like the person was pouring something outside the door. Then they started making clicking noises, and others joined. Kambili listened to the distinctive clicks. There were at least four people out there.

The clicking faded away, and so did the figure, until it was deathly silent. Kambili's chest rose and fell; fear was starting to cloud her mind, but she shook her head. She had a little girl to protect, and she could not afford to be afraid at this moment. She took the girl's hand in hers and whispered, "I don't know who's out there, but I promise, I won't let them harm you. Everything is going to be okay. I'll keep you safe."

The girl shook her head. "No, Aunty. I'll protect you."

With a pause, Kambili turned to her. What did the girl mean she would protect her? She could barely stand. Yet she seemed so sure of what she said. The girl shifted, moving directly under a strip of moonlight. Kambili peered closer, squinting and using her imagination to fill in the features she could not see. She mentally noted the translucence of the girl's skin; her not shivering despite how cold she was to the touch; the malevolence (and warmth?) that rested beneath the girl's eyes, at odds with the fear that lined her dirty face.

Kambili blinked multiple times, sure that her eyes were playing tricks on her, but the more she looked, the more she saw the resemblance between this girl and the one in her dream—the one that had told her to come to Obatete.

"W-what is your name? I'm Kambili," she stammered.

The girl hesitated before she spoke. Kambili thought it was because she was scared to say who she was until the girl said, "Amam gi—I know you, Aunty, and you know me. I am Imelda."

A scream rose in Kambili's throat, but only a haggard gasp escaped past her lips. She dropped the girl's hand and backed away from her. Dread settled in her chest, as well as the unavoidable cognizance that she was talking to a ghost.

Outside, drumming and singing started mingling with the unmistakable sound of girls crying in pain. Kambili whimpered and shot to her feet, searching in the darkness for anything she could use as a weapon.

"It's okay, Aunty. I brought you to Obatete. I'll protect you." With that, the girl's features stretched out, becoming distorted—bonier and rotten—until she transformed into the Thing.

N-w-u-o. Kambili could only hiss out the word that the Thing had scratched into her window.

"No, not you," the Thing said in a low guttural voice, "them. I need your help to kill the Cutters."

"Stay the fuck away from me!" Kambili screamed.

Sighing, as if saddened that Kambili did not trust her, the Thing turned and pointed to the shed's door. "The Cutters, ha na-abia." *They're coming.*

The door swung open, and standing at the entrance was an old, almost ancient woman with saggy, wrinkled skin that was collapsing in on itself. Kambili's eyes rested on the knife the woman was holding. It was so sharp that it glinted in the moonlight, with drops of blood streaming down the edges. Then Kambili's gaze traveled to the woman's feet, first to her left, which was skeletal and crooked, then settling on her right (also crooked), where two toes were missing.

What happened next was a blur. Imelda—the Thing—jumped at Kambili and embraced her. Kambili shuddered as their bodies joined. She felt splintered down to her soul like she had been taken apart and put back together, but not quite. There were pieces of her that didn't fit, parts that weren't hers but Imelda's.

Kambili hung onto a line, a single tether that held her to her own body. She wrestled for control with Imelda. "Let me go!"

"Biko Kambili, it is only you that can help us." There was sincerity in Imelda's voice. Kambili knew this because they shared one body now. She sighed. She may have bitten off more than she could chew by coming to Obatete, but she was already here and already in danger. She would not go down without a fight. If Imelda was the only chance she had, then she would take it. Her grip on the tether faltered.

"What do you mean, only I can help?"

"I've seen Obara, the god we worship. I've seen him, that wretched creature!" Imelda spat. "He's not what they think he is. My people were deceived into thinking Obatete was sustained by virtue, but our village would have prospered with or without him."

"He's feeding off the girls."

Nodding, Imelda said, "Ee—yes. Virgin blood is what fuels his existence, and so does our unwavering belief in the customs he formed. We are bound by our tradition, unable to break free. All of us, except you, Kambili. The Cutter's knife has not touched you. You have not been poisoned by this … falseness."

If this was true …

Kambili thought of her mother, now completely understanding why she had run away. Kambili could not imagine living with the terror of being held down by a tradition such as Obatete's. Her heart broke at the thought of those women holding Nne down and cutting her. She wondered who had done it. Her lips pursed. She would kill whoever it was. *Wait*, she thought. "But what of the fire? In the dream, you showed me the fire from Obara."

Imelda shook her head. "I showed you my fire. It has always been ours; we were just made to believe otherwise."

Shoulders strengthened with resolve, Kambili released her grip. "I'll do it. For Nne and you and the other girls."

"Daalu." *Thank you.*

Then Kambili was falling.

She landed in the same place they had been, outside the shed, but everything was different. Her eyes now easily picked out the incorporeality of the past, and there was something else she recognized—that filmy darkness that left an oily coat on her tongue. Slowly, the darkness cleared, and Kambili was able to see. Bile rose in her throat.

Ghostly naked girls were bleeding into little dirt holes. Cutters floated around like wraiths, their mouths firm, eyes blank, and fists clenched with the piety of one who was a proud custodian of their tradition. They placed dried leaves on the girls' private parts, but only those that weren't crying, Kambili noticed. They treated only the girls who did not have defiance in their eyes.

Lightheaded, Kambili watched as they brought in a new girl. She was screaming and thrashing, spewing words that should not have come out of the mouth of a girl her age. Imelda, Kambili mouthed. Imelda was fighting to get to another girl who was being held in the dirt. Imelda broke free and ran toward the woman holding the other girl and pushed her. "Run!" she shouted at the girl. The older woman grabbed the girl by her legs and held her down. She spread the girl's legs and pressed the knife down there. The cutting happened fast. If Kambili had blinked, she would have missed it. The girl let out a piercing shriek.

Someone pushed Imelda out of the way, and that was when Kambili saw their faces clearly. The girl and the older woman—Nne and her grandmother. Then the vision was cut off. "Wait." Kambili gasped. "What—"

"Ndo Kambili, I tried to bring you back before you saw."

"You knew my mother?"

"Nne bu enyi m—my only friend. O ya bu onye liri m—it was she who buried me."

Then, Kambili fell again. Juxtaposed somewhere between the past and the present.

5: FIRE

Rain drizzled, cloying the air with the scent of petrichor.

Kambili was back to the present, no phantom girls and no phantom cutters, just a shallow darkness that told Kambili she was outside and that it was almost dawn. There was a persistent pressure on her chest. Three women were restraining her. One sat on her stomach, lodging her hands in Kambili's braids and gripping tight enough to push her head into the wet earth.

Leathery hands clamped over Kambili's mouth so that she could not scream. The second woman pinned both of Kambili's hands, and the last woman spread Kambili's legs open and bent poised over her. "Jide si ya ike," *Hold her well,* she hissed.

"Be fast, Mama Chi! Before the other girls hear."

Gasping for air, Kambili tried to twist away from under the woman. The pressure in her chest increased, her lungs strained for air, and her eyes watered as she felt the Cutter's clammy touch between the valleys in her thighs. Kambili remembered how swift the cutting was; all it would take was one slash of the Cutter's knife.

Something unfurled like a fire seed in Kambili. Rage blossomed in her stomach, spreading through her veins like a wildfire. Kambili focused on her anger, poking around in her soul for Imelda. The ghost girl was still there, waiting for Kambili to realize what she had to do.

Kambili latched on to Imelda's essence, drawing strength from her, accepting her heritage in all its good and bad.

Pieces of Kambili locked into place, the parts that had always wondered where she was from, why she could see ghosts, why she dreamed of a girl she had never met. And her fire, the one that had lain dormant in Kambili, she cradled it in her palms, sang to it, and awakened the flames.

Snapping her eyes open, Kambili twisted her hip, brought up her left leg and slammed it into the Cutter that stood between her legs. Bones connected with bone, feet with the neck, and a crack followed. The Cutter fell to the ground with a thud, moaning in pain.

"Mama Chi!"

Kambili ignored the pain in her ankle and reached for the other Cutter closest to her. The women were still shocked by the vicious flames that lit up Kambili's body, and that was the opening Kambili needed. She latched onto the Cutter's leg—the one that had sat on her stomach—and dragged her down. Kambili flipped over so that she was the one on top of the woman this time.

The woman gurgled. "You're spitting in the face of tradition. Kambili I ma ihe I na eme—do you know what you're doing? Are you ready for the consequences!"

Somewhere within Kambili, Imelda tugged, asking Kambili for control.

No. Kambili shook her head. This was her fight. Hers and hers alone.

Kneeling over the cutter, Kambili pried the woman's mouth open. Consequences be damned. "Thunder fire you people and your barbaric tradition!" she spat, swallowed a lungful of air, then screamed. A flood of flames poured out of Kambili's mouth and into the Cutter's, burning the woman from the inside out.

Kambili pushed away from the woman, staring at her. Her face was burned and disfigured, but somehow Kambili recognized her—the Okpa seller. She felt nausea rise in her throat. What if her grandmother was here? Her insides contracted and she retched, but instead of vomit, smoke came out. Kambili covered her mouth and breathed in the petrichor, letting it calm her. She had always loved the scent of air marrying mud.

Where was the last Cutter? She turned. Kambili found the woman sniveling in a corner beside the shed where they had kept the other girls. A sharp snort escaped Kambili's lips as she bent to pick up the Cutter's knife.

She went to the woman and thrust the knife in her face. "Open the door," Kambili said, pointing to the shed. Her hands itched to burn the woman too, but she needed her alive to lead her and the girls back to the village.

"B-b-biko nwa m," the woman begged.

Kambili hissed and waved the knife. "Aunty Biko, don't waste my time. Open the door." Kambili's patience was running thin; she had the spirit of an angry dead girl in her, and her stomach was starting to growl, reminding her that she was hungry.

Rays of light were starting to cut across the sky as morning came. Kambili wanted the morning to bring hope; she wanted it to taste like freedom. She needed to feel like she had survived and come out on top, but she couldn't. The thing she had come to Obatete for, the person who had brought her here, told her it was just the beginning. Imelda wanted more from Kambili; she wanted her to end Obatete. With a tired sigh, Kambili nudged the Cutter to open the door faster.

Her ears pricked at the crackle of twigs. "Kambili!" someone shouted. Kambili swiveled and squinted into the bushes. Was that?

"Nne!"

It was a mistake—a grave one—to shift her attention away from the Cutter. Kambili did not see the Cutter reaching into her wrapper and bringing out a small dagger. Her gaze was focused on the man helping Nne out of the bushes. Her mother held a cutlass in one hand and a gun in the other.

"Nne," Kambili breathed, watching as her mother raised her hand and trained the gun on her.

In a split second, the gun went off, and coppery warmth splattered on Kambili. She felt blood trail down her neck, down her back, and between her butt cheeks. Kambili was suddenly aware that she was still naked. She turned back, just as the Cutter fell lifeless, her hand still tightly gripping the dagger that would have found solace in Kambili's neck. Then Nne was there, covering Kambili with a wrapper.

"We need to leave now!" Nne shook her.

Kambili pointed to the shed. "The girls. There are girls in the shed."

Nne hissed. "Afam, open the door," she said, her voice tinged with impatience.

Remembering the man, Kambili shifted for him to get to the door. She watched him, noticing the cleft on his chin and how much he looked like her. "Who is that man?"

"He's from the village."

"Nne, I'm not stupid," Kambili said.

Nne knocked Kambili on the head and smacked her arm. "You think you're too big for me to beat you. You're not stupid, but you came to this place after I warned you. What do you think is going to happen now? Do you think they will let us leave in peace! Ah, what am I going to do with this girl?"

"Start by not shouting at her. Look at her, Nne. She has been through a lot." Afam reprimanded Nne as he kicked the door open.

Kambili shot him a look of gratitude. She slid away from her mother's grip and walked into the shed. The girls in there had terror in their eyes. Some of them had already been cut. They were bare and bleeding in a corner, their mouths gagged. The ones that had not been cut were bound and gagged just as Kambili had been.

"Jesus," Nne cried. It was different, seeing this as an observer. Her vagina ached as if remembering when it had been she in that shed, crying, and watching as her only friend bled to death. "Go and wait outside," Nne said, pushing Afam away. His hulking frame would terrify the girls even more.

Nne went to the girls and started hacking away the ropes that had been used to tie them up. Her body was rigid with anger, and something else—shame. She had tried to stop Kambili from helping these girls. She looked at her daughter, who was silently comforting a sickly looking girl, and her heart swelled with pride. "I mere nke oma Kambili." *You did well.*

Smiling, Kambili held the girl in her arms tighter—perhaps it was because of Imelda, but she could feel the girl's life slipping away.

Kambili wasn't sure where she would start. There was a lot to do in Obatete. She could start by convincing her mother to help or maybe bonding with the man she knew was her father (killing her grandmother also seemed like a good place to begin). Then there was the matter of being possessed. The longer Imelda stayed in her, the more Kambili wasn't sure where she began and where the ghost girl ended. But Kambili didn't mind, the fire in her veins spurred her. This felt right.

No one leaves Obatete, and Kambili did not plan to.

PARODY OF THE SOWER

by Michelle Enehiwealu Iruobe

Nene decides to transplant her embryo seedlings into the cocoyam farm at the back of our house, where the fertile soil is a luxuriant black, and large gray-pink earthworms slither and burrow like limbless moles.

It is a cool, late afternoon when she brings the seedlings home in a pot of fired clay. Only three weeks old, yet they've already started sprouting leafy ears. Nene informs us that they are improved varieties, her face alight with joy and pride. Can we believe it? The embryos would grow and become mature in just six months!

"Congratulations!" Mummy says to Nene happily. She is certain that with Nene's expertise, the seedlings would be healthy babies at harvest.

Daddy is furious. His ears and nose emit vapor, and his hand quivers as he points at the three sprouting embryo seeds in the pot. "How on earth is my grandmother going to take care of babies at her old age?" he yells. Young couples do not even apply for embryo seeds anymore. All the necessary paperwork involved is exhausting, nursing the seedlings till harvest requires per-minute attention, and the fetuses do not always turn out well in the end. Many of them perish when the rains become too heavy, and the few that survive either get scorched to death by the merciless sun or become shriveled, disabled babies at harvest. Does she want them to end up like the one-and-a-half-legged child of the Onaiwu couple living in the opposite flat? Does she?

But Nene is resolute. She holds her drooping breasts with her hands and looks Daddy in the eye. What does Daddy know, *ehn*? What does he who was uprooted yesterday from her cassava farm back in the village know? She is still healthy enough to raise a child. Her nipples leaked a few days ago! She thought she was going crazy, but it was true. Her nipples, which seven children, including Daddy, suckled as infants and which have been dry for three decades, miraculously released milk. She knew then, after she'd absorbed the sight of the drops of creamy liquid on her blouse, that she still had "work" to do. And didn't she cultivate Daddy and his siblings many years before? Did she ever complain about how hard it was to nurture them before they were harvested? And what about Daddy's own children: me and Sam? Isn't he enjoying the fruits of his and Mummy's toils now? Can he remember just how tremulous those early days were? So, because climatic conditions were becoming more unfavorable by the day, people shouldn't have babies anymore? Humankind should go extinct?

No, she declares emphatically. She is going to nurse her embryos. There is nothing Daddy or anybody for that matter can do about it.

Daddy swallows any words he might have to say after Nene speaks. His shoulders droop and he trudges to his room like a man soaked in cold water.

Much too early the next morning, I awaken to our dog, Checkers, howling wildly in between spurts of loud barks. I sit bolt upright and listen closely in the stark darkness of my bedroom. There are more sounds: owls hooting, leaves rustling, and feet sinking in mushy soil in the garden just behind my window.

My door bursts open and I jerk up, but I catch the faint outline of my brother, Sam standing in the doorway in his striped pajamas.

"Jesus, you scared me!"

A bright white light beams on—Sam's phone torch.

"Won't you come outside? Nene wants to transplant the embryos," he announces, and even in the darkness, I can see the excitement illuminating his features. I fumble with the thick bedding and jump out of bed, my heart beating excitedly in my chest at the same moment betrayal creeps in. I can't believe Nene would've gone on to transplant them without me.

Outside, the sky is a darker sheet of blue than I thought—almost midnight black. Sam's bright torch leads the way, casting long shadows behind us as we walk to the garden, the cool breeze seeping through our pajamas.

Checkers's howling switches to relieved whimpering on seeing us, and he starts turning in circles, vigorously wagging his curled tail. I pat his large head reassuringly.

Nene is crouched inside one of the "boxes" demarcating one part of the garden from the other, in a wrapper tied around her waist, leaving her upper body bare, her breasts as flat as slippers dangling from her chest. It looks like she's performing a ritual—holding the clay pot containing the seedlings with one arm and mechanically pulling out weeds from the soil, her forehead wrinkled in concentration. She doesn't even glance at us.

"Nene, *Aisan*," Sam greets.

"*Oya, vhare,* come and help me pull these things," she says. Sam lowers the torch to the ground, and we squat under the umbrella-like leaves of the cocoyams and uproot the leaves wet with dew. Checkers inspects the growing heap of dead, limp foliage as we work, scratching and clawing at the earthworms still clinging to them. My hands are covered in wet loam by the time we are done.

Nene carefully sets the pot of seedlings down and digs three holes in the weeded ground with her fingers. Sam takes pictures randomly with his phone camera, the shutter sounding like mini thunderclaps in the still darkness. Nene takes out two of the three seedlings one by one from the clay pot and lays them in their bed holes. Their sprouted leaves stick out of the soil even when the seeds are completely buried. Then, she hands me the last one. I cradle the embryo—bean sized and a faded pink—with both palms, and I feel something throb rhythmically against my palm like a faint heartbeat. I tune out all the sounds around me until I can hear only the seedling's heart beating underneath its sensitive, pulsating skin, and then mine, both beating together in a harmony that spreads pleasant warmth through my body.

Sam's shutter clicks madly, bursts of light settling on me and the little one in my hands for a second before vanishing.

When Nene takes the seedling away to be buried in the ground, my hand feels very empty, hollow even.

It is a full, bubbly house by the time I finish wiping dirt off my body and changing my soiled clothes. It is Sam's tenth harvest-day anniversary. The delicious aroma of jollof rice, grilled fish, and dodo fills the house's air. My little cousins run around the house bursting balloons and giggling in excitement, eliciting occasional cautionary shrieks of "Esosa!" and "Oghogho!" from my Aunt and Uncle Parents. Even Checkers won't stop twirling happily around in circles.

Daddy's guests talk and laugh loudly in the living room over the blaring music, but Daddy sits with hunched, dejected shoulders and doesn't join in whatever conversation they are having. He seems to grow smaller every hour, watching Nene cheerfully exchange pleasantries with his friends. He goes particularly small when Nene starts to talk about her seedlings in the cocoyam garden, trying to get some of the guests to examine her exposed breasts to find where milk had come out from. It is here, yes, this spot. Do you see it? Feel it, full and ripe with milk.

Daddy's other siblings who are present do not seem to mind Nene cultivating children at her age. Aunty Ofure squeals in delight and inspects Nene's nipples. I see it, Nene. May the gods let me lactate even in old age! Aunty Bridget laughs and jokes about Nene acting like an *Ovbiaha* about to harvest her first child, and Uncle Ehigiator stares at Nene with a slackened jaw on hearing the news but doesn't utter a word of objection.

Mr. and Mrs. Ohaito, our next-door neighbors, congratulate Nene most enthusiastically. Mrs. Ohaito weeps when Nene talks about being "dry" for thirty years (she too had never lactated until recently) and Mr. Ohaito says that he and her his wife would harvest their baby tomorrow, and that we were all invited for the ceremony.

Nene congratulates them and prays that they should harvest more children. Then, she makes use of the opportunity to narrate the story of how Daddy and his seven siblings were cultivated. They were quite a lucky set; all seven were alive and healthy at the time of transplant, and alive and healthy at harvest. Baba, my grandfather, had thrown a feast of the century to celebrate them.

"I never used a drop of inorganic fertilizers like some people did," Nene says proudly. "How do you expect fetuses to grow well in the soil when the only thing you do is to let them chuck down chemicals?"

Toward the end of the party, after almost all of Mummy's jollof rice is licked off the pots, all the balloons are either removed or burst, and half of the birthday cake disappears, Sam brings out his photo album (which he allows to be in the public gaze only once a year), and the visitors *ooh* and *ahh* at his photographs. Mummy and Daddy worked very hard at documenting my brother's early memories. There are photos of him at his transplanting; Daddy holding a black cellophane filled with sand and Sam's ready-to-be-relocated seedling and grinning lavishly at the camera, Mummy in rubber gloves dirty with grime, all stages of Sam's growth in the soil, photos from his bud-nipping ceremony ...

My mind wanders again for the one-thousandth time since the party started, to the feel of the embryo in my palm, and the heartbeat—the little hint that it was real, that life, whole and powerful, was within that thin strip of fragile skin.

The next day, my family goes to see the Ohaitos. Mrs. Ohaito welcomes us gleefully at the door, smelling pleasantly of flour and sugar. We are ushered into the living room where a handful of other guests are milling around. Daddy snorts disapprovingly at the crowd and mutters something like a child harvest day/bud-nipping was usually a private family affair, so there weren't supposed to be so many people present. Mummy coolly chides him by saying that it is only natural for the Ohaitos, who weren't granted the right to cultivate their own babies for a very long time, to want to celebrate their success in a grand style. Besides, richer couples throw more extravagant parties nowadays, or doesn't he know?

"It's just God that said I should start lactating and then be granted rights around the same time," Mrs. Ohaito says to the women over and over again, after she changes from her kitchen work clothes into a pretty, flowery dress.

"It's really the work of God," Mummy says.

"You deserve it, my sister," one woman says, noisily munching some chin-chin.

"Yes o!" says another. "You think nine years is a joke?"

"We all know that getting those idiots at the ministry to accept your application and grant you rights on the first try is almost as impossible as trying to get a return ticket to the afterlife," says a woman; the female version of Mr. Ohiato. "But for a woman's breasts to respond to her pleas as well is even tougher."

The women murmur their agreement. Aunty Omogui, a talkative woman with messy brown hair who lives in the apartment directly opposite the Ohaitos, says, after downing a glass of wine: "It is like the day someone would die. Does anyone know when their time would come? Look at Edede. How old is she? I've known her since I walked with my knees on the ground. She was around Mama Samuel's age then." She glances at Mummy. "Over forty years have passed now. And to my knowledge, not a single drop of milk . . ."

And so, the discussion drags on until the late afternoon, when we all troop outside for the main event—the harvest. Luckily, the weather is as cool as evening time. No one will complain about staying out in the sun for too long.

The full-grown baby plant is as tall as me, with a heavily muscled trunk, luscious green leaves, and red and pink flowers that remind me of the hibiscus. There is a sweet smell wafting off the flowers. The crowd inhales, sighing collectively in appreciation.

The harvesters, two burly men stripped to the waist, take their positions on both sides of the plant while the expectant couple stands nearby, beads of sweat clinging to their foreheads in trepidation. The men pull hard, and the crowd comes alive, chanting words and singing songs of encouragement. Sweat flows down the harvesters' tense backs, and the ground below the plant tremors. Mrs. Ohaito grips her husband's hands so tightly that his veins pop out. Even when babies were healthy from their early days, many things could go wrong during harvest.

"Isn't it taking too long?" Sam asks me.

I shrug. How should I know? I haven't witnessed a harvest before.

The crowd's singing intensifies as the plant slowly begins to move, its tangle of roots rupturing the earth. Slowly, slowly, slowly, it comes up until with one final yank by a harvester, the plant is off the ground, and a small, dirt-brown baby is wailing open-mouthed underneath.

"It's a boy!" one of the harvesters screams. The happy cheering of the crowd is deafening. Aunty Omogui and a few other women begin to sing and dance. Mrs. Ohaito half slumps on her husband in relief before recovering herself and taking her baby from a harvester. Sam takes a series of photographs in rapid succession.

I stare at the newborn being jostled around happily by the guests even with mud caking his skin, his plant bud still clinging to his navel, and with a surge of warmth I think of how someday Nene's seedlings—now as small as peas—would grow and become like this.

Mrs. Ohaito hands her baby over to Nene, the oldest person around, to nip the bud with a broad smile. Nene rubs her hands with red oil and salt and deftly yanks the bud off the uncleaned baby's navel. The baby's cries increase in pitch. Nene hands him over to his mother who immediately thrusts her nipple into his open mouth.

Three mornings after the Ohaitos harvest their baby, our family awakens to Nene's loud, strangulated screaming. We all rush to the backyard to find Nene sitting on the bare earth, legs astride, still wailing. The sun is high up in the sky, casting everywhere in a golden light too bright for so early in the morning. Some yards away, under the newspaper-wide cocoyam leaves, Checkers is still digging up the holes where Nene's embryos were buried. Everything that happens next happens in a blur. Mummy joins Nene in the wailing. Sam dashes forward, dog chain in hand and a vicious look on his face. I search the black soil for the seedlings, heart racing. The chain in Sam's hands locks around the dog's neck. The first seedling suddenly pops out of the dug-up soil like an orange seed spat out of a child's mouth. Sam smacks Checkers so hard that he lets out a yelp. I find the second seedling. Checkers continues to whimper as Sam drags him to the porch. Nene's voice echoes off the porch. Her cries are mixed with choking sounds. I can hear Daddy telling her sternly to keep quiet. I find the third one.

I kneel in the dirt, turning the seedlings over in my palm, their newly sprouted leaves already wilting and sprinkled with soil. I wonder which embryo I held that day Nene planted them. My hands shake. Was it this one? Or this one? I pause to feel their heartbeats, to grasp faint evidences of life within their now shriveled skin. There is none.

HOW TO RAISE A KRAKEN IN YOUR BATHTUB

by P. Djèlí Clark

"Ambition!" Trevor emphasized, rapping knuckles hard on the wood table. "That is what makes the great men!" He took a satisfied swallow from his mug.

Across from him, Barnaby put down the daily he'd been reading and sipped from his own beer. Pulling out a handkerchief to dab froth from his lips, he scratched thoughtfully at a set of ginger muttonchops.

"If it is ambition alone that lifts up men, then why friend Trevor are you here?" He motioned to the noisy pub—not one of the dives frequented by the soot-stained shabby types of London, yet certainly not a place for gentlemen.

Trevor traced the edges of a waxed brown mustache as he always did before saying something he thought profound. "Because ambition takes proper planning. Take me: a young clerk at a prestigious firm, and recently married."

"To a beautiful wife from a family of some means," Barnaby added cheeringly.

"Yet not *great* means. I can bide my time certainly, work my way to even chief clerk. But that could take up the entirety of my life in this drab attire." He motioned to his black suit, favored by the business class. "And I am a man of ambition."

Barnaby laughed, patting the belly beneath his tweed jacket. "If only my aspirations were greater than finishing this mug of ale! And how, dear Trevor, do you intend to set about fulfilling your lofty goals? Have you fabricated some confounding new contraption of spinning gears and cogs? A wondrous mechanical contrivance that will catch our attention, like this fellow?" He tapped the daily on the table. In a bold headline and fantastic detail, it recounted news of a submersible craft sighted by Her Majesty's Navies in the far seas.

But Trevor waved it off. There were always new machines, one churned out after another in these times. They had become expected, commonplace. People yearned for more than that. And he would give it to them.

Barnaby thought he glimpsed a twinkle in his friend's blue eyes as the corners of his mouth lifted into a smile.

"Ambition abhors convention, dear Barnaby—and repetition. I intend to be quite unconventional." Taking another gulp of beer, Trevor let the cold liquid slide down his throat and dreamed—ambitiously.

The package came on a Tuesday. Trevor rushed home at message of its arrival. Margaret greeted him at the entry, her eyebrows raised in surprise.

"Goodness! Did you run all the way here?"

"Only the last bit," he puffed as she took his coat and hat. His eyes searched about.

"Well, it seems you haven't come to see me." She pouted.

Trevor looked down, smiling as he stopped to stroke her red-gold curls. "Forgive my rudeness, dear Margaret. It's just I've been expecting this for weeks. I hardly want to waste another minute."

"I know. Your great and secret project. It's in the back parlor."

Giving her a thankful squeeze, Trevor made his way hurriedly to the double parlor.

Clutching the sides of her blue bustle skirt, Margaret followed fast behind.

When Trevor reached the back room, he stopped, staring down at a long wooden crate. Burned onto its planks was pyrographic lettering scorched in black:

FANTASTIC AND BIZARRE SEA PEARLS, BAUBLES, AND COLLECTIBLES

"It was delivered by two Mermen," Margaret commented, coming to stand beside him. "They gave me this." She handed him a thick brown envelope.

Trevor turned quizzically. "Mermen?"

She nodded with a grimace. "With those green scales and horrid tattoos. I almost fainted when I saw them! But they spoke your name plain enough—Trevor Hemley. What could you possibly have bought from Mermen?" When he didn't answer, she went on as she often did to fill his silences. "Arthur says their kind should be run out and put back to sea. We didn't conquer them just to have them infest our cities."

Trevor walked around to inspect the crate. "Your brother's fought in Her Majesty's Navies against the Mermen, so perhaps he knows the right of it. Can you fetch me my crowbar?"

Margaret gestured to the tool already waiting on a nearby table. He smiled at her forethought. "I suppose you're still not going to tell me what this is all about?"

"It wouldn't be much of a secret if I did. I have a plan here, Margaret, one that I must see to myself."

Her amber eyes took on a piteous look, and he clenched his jaw against it. He detested that look. "I've told you before, Trevor, there's no need to prove yourself to me. We do well as it is. We have a home, money—"

"A home gifted to us by your family," he cut in. "Money provided by your father. Don't mistake me, I'm thankful. But I want to do more than well, Margaret. I want to be great. Now if you wouldn't mind?"

Margaret sighed but said no more. Gathering up her skirts, she turned and strode from the parlor, closing the doors behind her.

Throwing down the envelope, Trevor rolled up his sleeves and grabbed the crowbar. With little effort, he wrenched open the crate lid one nail at a time. It slid off, revealing a bed of slick, green seaweed. He hesitated a moment before plunging his hands inside, pushing apart wet kelp to get at what lay beneath and lifting it out.

The thing resembled an overly large egg, big enough so that he had to hold it in both hands. But where eggshell was smooth and fragile, this was segmented and hard, not exactly like stone but more so the shell of a crab. Here and there bony barbs and tangerine streaks dotted its dark ochre surface. It was weighty as well, with a solid feel.

Flush with excitement, Trevor nestled his prize gently back into the bed of seaweed and kelp. Wiping hands on his pants he picked up the envelope and tore it open, extracting a page of tan parchment. At each corner was the imprint of a creature, like an octopus or squid, but with a head of sharp ridges and tentacles displaying curved hooks. The words were addressed to him:

> Dear Mr. Trevor Hemley,
>
> Welcome industrious and intrepid adventurer! Those of us who dream, place ourselves above the more ordinary of men. And you have chosen to do that which most men only dream and do not dare—to give life to one of the most magnificent creatures ever to roam this glorious earth! Enclosed you will find a manual to aid in your task, providing you with all you need to know.
>
> Yours Respectfully,
> Doctor P.D. Bundelkund
> Fantastic and Bizarre Sea Pearls, Baubles, and Collectibles

Trevor repeated the name. Bundelkund. German perhaps? But he was too thrilled to give it much mind. Already he was reaching into the envelope and withdrawing what remained: a book, bound in heavy aquamarine cloth patterned as fish scales. Emblazoned on its front in gold leaf like a billhead were the words:

HOW TO RAISE A KRAKEN IN YOUR BATHTUB
A GUIDE FOR USERS

Sitting on the edge of the crate, he opened the manual and glanced through the table of contents, turning pages before stopping at an image. It was a monster. Its fleshy skin was a pale pink, only showing beneath bone-ridged armor like a thick gray barnacle. Lengthy tentacles festooned with suckers and hooks stretched out from a bulbous head with two eyes round as dinner plates. The appendages wrapped about an antiquated wooden galleon, reaching around broad sails and tall masts to drag the ship into the sea. He read the words beneath:

> The kraken is an ancient creature that inhabited the deep waters of the world. Once thought to be the stuff of sailors' stories and legends, the first reputable kraken sighting was reported almost three hundred years ago.
>
> During that time, the creatures harassed and attacked seabound vessels. Little solution was found for this continuing problem until their numbers began to dwindle dramatically in the past century. The last sighted kraken was found dead, washed up on a beach thirty years ago. None have been reported or seen since.
>
> Doctor. P.D. Bundelkund, however, has discovered the only cache of kraken eggs known to be in existence, found in a dark part of the sea and unspoiled by time. He is willing to make these available to a select few. Through careful study and research Doctor Bundelkund has perfected the means by which to hatch these eggs, and thus resurrect the species. He has made it possible so that even you can raise a kraken in your very home, in your very bathtub, with the simplest of tools and instructions …

Trevor read on in fascination. He'd stumbled upon the advert in the back of a penny dreadful, which he snuck between his dailies. He was intrigued at once. The notion of such fantastic creatures, and the means to bring them back to life had taken up his every waking moment. But he had even greater plans.

He'd been to fairs and circuses in London since he was a boy. He'd seen their many curios: barbaric peoples of the colonies in their native dress, strange beasts from far-off lands, small primitive men who lived in forests among the apes. Millions flocked to these exhibits. They wanted to see more than the cold machines that had grown so ubiquitous in their lives. They wanted a glimpse at the unfamiliar, the alien, the grotesque.

And he would give it to them!

He could see it now: Trevor Hemley Presents the Great and Monstrous Kraken! They would come from far away and pay much for such a sight. His name would grace all the papers and every tongue. And they would all say: By God, that Trevor Hemley! There goes a man of ambition!

He smiled a satisfied smile and read on.

"Where the devil have you been?" Barnaby lowered his newspaper as his friend took a seat across from him. "It's been two weeks man!"

Trevor called out an order and smiled. "That I can't tell you yet. But I'll be able to show you soon enough."

Barnaby put on a wounded look. "Keeping secrets from old friends?"

"Men of ambition can't always share their dreams."

Barnaby scoffed, handing over the daily. "Men of ambition seem to be in abundance these days."

Trevor read the headline: Mysterious Submergible Dreadnought Chased Across the Seas by Her Majesty's Navies and Airships.

"He calls himself Captain Nobody," Barnaby related. "How fantastic is that? He's sunken several of our ships. Built this infernal metal machine himself. It moves leagues *beneath* the waters, surfacing like a whale only to attack! Would you believe they say he's a Hindoo? His crew are Mermen! Travels the seas, he says, to free the oppressed."

"Free them? Free them from who?"

"Why, from us it would seem—we imperialists and would-be civilizers of the world. The enemies of freedom, he names us."

Trevor scowled, throwing the paper down. "And what do the darker races of this world know of freedom? Where would they be without our guiding hand?"

Barnaby accepted the mugs of beer placed on the table and shrugged his round shoulders. "Some question our deeds. They say it's not progress we bring the world, but the chains of industry—by way of the Maxim gun."

"And is there any language better understood by the unattained Huns than that bap-bap-bap of the Maxim?" Trevor took a strong swallow and traced his mustache with a finger. "Much as a woman is endowed the weaker sex, so are the darker races weaker forms of men. We overestimate their capacities and burden ourselves unduly with these civilizing efforts. Make them a servile class I say. Teach them to be hewers of coal, drawers of gas, and harvesters of rubber. But they will never know thrift and industry."

Barnaby didn't reply, knowing better than to engage his friend when his dander was up. He returned to their original subject. "Well at least have me over. For a peek at this plan of yours. Perhaps I can be of help?"

Trevor grinned toothily. "Not to worry, dear Barnaby. I'll have you over soon enough. When my plans … hatch and … grow to fruition, I'll likely need your prodigious assistance." Trevor leaned forward. "Tell me, does your uncle still collect and import specimens of men and beasts for display at the zoologiques?"

Barnaby's eyebrows arched. "Indeed. The old codger remains exceedingly well-honed in his peculiar trade."

As his friend sat back and drank with a rakish smile, Barnaby sipped from his own mug and wracked his brain to ponder on this most curious question.

Trevor knelt beside the long copper tub that sat in the room behind the kitchen. It was an odd place for a bathroom. But the design had been Margaret's father's wishes, and who knew his reasoning—perhaps to assure servants saw to their cleanliness. The stoic man had been reluctantly eased into the young clerk's courtship of his daughter and offered the house to them as a wedding gift. Now this odd space was perfect for him to conduct his business.

Margaret rarely came back here, except to give brief instruction to the domestic she insisted on hiring. It was an expense to which Trevor readily acquiesced. It was unseemly that his wife would cook, any more than he would expect her to be out working. Let those insufferable suffrage societies that were popping up tell it, and women were ready to proclaim themselves the equal of men. Thankfully, Margaret had shown no inclination toward such strange desires.

None of that of course dampened her curiosity, and he'd taken to locking the door to the bathroom and keeping a key. The cook only needed firm instruction, which she followed to the letter. So, as it was, only he entered this room to look upon his wondrous plans.

His fingers disturbed the waters of the tub where the kraken egg sat submerged like a hoary seed, yet unmoving. Glancing over to the manual sprawled open on the floor, he read the same page for perhaps the hundredth time:

> Contrary to popular notion, kraken did not birth their young in the seas. Doctor Bundelkund came by this revelation in his research. The infant kraken must be weaned on freshwater before it can imbibe and breathe seawater. He believes that after mating, kraken delivered their egg sac along estuaries. The eggs would then float into freshwater streams where they could hatch and develop before the infant kraken returned to the sea.
>
> This, Doctor Bundelkund believes, accounts chiefly for the destruction of the species. As the industries of our age grew, estuaries became filled with pollutants hazardous to the infant krakens. Robbed of these viable offspring, the species was decimated. To revive them Doctor Bundelkund has devised a method by which kraken eggs can be nurtured in safe, protective environs.

Trevor had followed that method. The water was clean of pollutants and kept at 55° Fahrenheit. Fresh soil had been spread along the tub's bottom and a complex mix of organic compounds kept the water a tinge of green. Yet after three weeks the kraken egg lay as dormant as it had upon arrival. And he found his impatience growing.

He'd invested a hefty sum in this undertaking, taken from money set aside for them by Margaret's parents. As he exercised control of their finances, she was none the wiser. That was best, for her contented mind would never understand his plans. He intended to recoup it all anyway when his venture proved profitable.

But what if he'd been had? A seed of doubt had taken root in these past days, and it now grew up deep inside him like a troublesome weed. There was no shortage of flimflam men out there. What if he'd been taken in by a swindle—like strength tonics and healing elixirs? The thought made his stomach knot.

It was during these misgivings that Trevor heard the gurgling. He looked down to see bubbles breaking the water's surface. Along a tangerine streak on that ochre shell there was a crack, through which a thin, almost translucent arm peeked out, tentatively searching.

Trevor gripped the edge of the tub, watching, willing, and coaxing his prize to enter the world. As if hearing him it did—slow at first and then in a frenzy. More arms appeared tearing the crack wider. Bits of shell broke away in jagged chunks. With a sudden heave, a fleshy mass pushed itself free in a burst of milky albumen.

The infant kraken stared up with round black eyes ringed in silver. For a long while it simply floated unmoving in the water. Then in a blur, ten tentacles twirled like a ballet dancer doing a pirouette. They reached for a piece of shell that was brought to the base of its soft bulbous head. What looked like a beaked mouth with teeth opened and quickly devoured it.

Trevor stared, mesmerized, as the infant kraken consumed the rest of its former home. It was beautiful, in its own monstrous way. And it was his very own. As he stared, it occurred to him that he should name it. He'd had a parakeet once named Rupert. No. He needed something greater to speak to the magnificent beast this would one day become.

Khan, he thought suddenly. An exotic and grand name. He could envision it, emblazoned on a banner: Come! Witness! See the Wondrous and Terrible Khan!

He smiled as he dreamed of greatness to come. That would do perfectly.

The kraken is ravenous by nature. Medium specimens were known to devour sharks, and their larger kin were sighted engaged in battle with whales. The most monstrous, that attacked sailing vessels, would not only tear apart the ships but tumble the unfortunate sailors into the waters. There it plucked and devoured them at leisure. Over the years, kraken showed an amazing aptitude to luring and baiting ships, sometimes disguising themselves as islands by covering their heads with bits of sand. Doctor Bundelkund has surmised that krakens are not mindless beasts but thinking beings with an alarming awareness that approaches that of men. This intelligence is focused singularly on hunting. It is not unlikely then to conclude that a kraken's size is directly related to its cleverness in increasing its diet.

"Trevor?" The knock came again. "Trevor dear?"

Trevor jumped up, draping a sheet over the tub. Hastily arranging himself he unlocked the door and peeked his head out. Margaret stood in a long violet dress with a trail of gold buttons down the center. She looked up at him from beneath a hat covered in lavender lilacs.

"There's another order from the butcher." She pointed to a dresser strewn with brown paper bundles wrapped in twine.

Trevor eased himself out the door, closing it behind. Checking over the bundles he inspected their stamps. Last time they'd neglected to bring the hog jowl, which Khan enjoyed especially.

"I had to show the butcher in as the cook's left for the day," Margaret said. He nodded absently. The cook had already gone? Was it so late?

"Will you be much longer?" Margaret asked. "We don't want to keep the Harrisons waiting." Trevor turned to her, puzzled. Harrisons? She put on a distressed face. "Oh Trevor! Don't tell me you've forgotten our afternoon stroll with the Harrisons?"

Only now did he notice her yellow gloves and matching parasol. He didn't remember being told—though it was entirely possible that she had. Of late he'd been preoccupied.

He barely made it to work now, lessening his hours at the firm daily—something that wouldn't long be tolerated he knew. But Khan demanded so much of his attention. The hatchling had grown exponentially in the past four weeks. More than he thought possible! Its fleshy body covered with a bony barbed armor took up almost the whole length of the tub now. And it was always hungry! The creature devoured everything—meat and bone alike, then thrashed about for more. At this rate, he'd have to talk to Barnaby about his uncle soon, to find some new space. Thinking on that work left little time for afternoon strolls.

Margaret made an exasperated face when he informed her he couldn't go. "What will that look like?" she lamented. "Me alone with a married couple, like some old maid! That Patsy Harrison is a church-bell as it is, and her husband's not so much better. Why they'll talk my ear—"

Trevor silenced her with a finger to the lips. "It will look as if you are married to a very busied man." He planted a kiss on her forehead before grabbing up the butcher's bundles and sliding back into the door.

Outside Margaret watched it close, hearing the lock tumble. And her eyes narrowed.

Trevor burst through the front door, running to the parlor. Margaret lay on a brocaded rose-hued couch face down in tears. She looked up with eyes red with misery, and he knelt to place his arms around her.

"I came as soon as I got your message!" he exclaimed, still laboring from his run. "It said something about an attack?"

She shook her head. "Oh, Trevor, I'm so sorry."

He frowned. "Sorry? What about?"

"I'm a vain and meddlesome woman. You've been so absorbed in your secret project these past weeks. All your spare time is spent there. You don't even come to bed until late. I had to know." She paused. "I made a key—"

Trevor jumped up abruptly. Turning, he ran to the back parlor, through the kitchen and stopped. The door to the bathroom lay open and hanging on one hinge. Green tinged water was splashed all along the floor, creating a trail. He followed it to a broken sash window through which a steady rain now fell. Khan was gone.

He turned to find Margaret behind him, wringing her hands. "I made the key days ago but hadn't used it. Only today there was this terrible squealing and thumping against the bathroom door. It frightened the cook off. I should have called you, but I picked up a broom handle and opened the door instead—"

"Did you hurt it?" Trevor asked tightly. "With the broom handle?" Margaret blinked, taken aback by the question. "No. I opened the door and .... It happened so fast. I just remember falling and something running past me, through the kitchen and out the windows." She paused. "Why were you keeping a dog in there?"

Trevor blinked. A dog? Whatever she'd seen, it seemed her mind now grasped onto the most convenient answer.

He sighed. "It was part of my project. Are you alright? Were you hurt?" She shook her head, and he drew her close. His eyes however remained locked on the broken window, through which his ambition and chance at greatness had fled.

Once he'd fixed Margaret a hot brandy and put her to bed, Trevor went immediately to the manual. He searched the Table of Contents, finding a chapter titled "Possible Troubles." Trevor passed by the headings: Asphyxiation, Biting, Dehydration, until he found what he was looking for—Escape. Flipping to the appropriate page he read in earnest:

> It is more than likely that your kraken will eventually escape. Krakens are after all crafty creatures. Even the most careful enclosures cannot always prevent flight. It is not advised you report your loss to the authorities, however, as krakens are not state-sanctioned animals to which discretion will be granted. Your kraken will probably sustain fatal injuries upon apprehension, and you will lose your valuable investment. The best means of retrieving a lost kraken is through the use of Mermen. Mermen have long experience with the creatures in their underwater environs and are especially suited for this task. You should be able to secure their services for a moderate sum.

Trevor read over the brief passage several times with incredulity.

Escape was more than likely? Damn fine place to mention that! And Mermen? Then again, it made a perverse type of sense. Who better understood the ways of sea creatures? He set out to look for them that very evening.

It wasn't hard to find Mermen. They inhabited London's docks and harbors, performing menial tasks such as hauling goods of ships and diving for wreckage. Mostly they sat around idle, imbibing opium and causing a public nuisance. He found several at Canary Wharf as expected. Four in total. Their moss-green bodies were almost bare, save for the outlandish wide-bottomed pants favored by jack tars.

He called out to them firmly—as he'd heard this was the only way to deal with such near-men, lest they think him weak. They turned as one from where they knelt playing some barbaric game that included the tossing of fish heads. One of them walked forward on bare feet, a muscular brute with black tattoos inked across his chest. No Merman stood shorter than seven feet, and this one was a few inches more. Their chieftain likely. His large oval eyes stared down, with black pupils set in dull yellow.

Trevor cleared his throat. "I wish to hire you and your men."

"Yes!" The Merman grinned, showing block white teeth.

Well, that was easy enough. "You should know the nature of this—"

"Yes!"

"I should explain—"

"Yes!"

Trevor frowned, looking into those yellow unblinking eyes. Was this Merman a simpleton? There was laughter, and another of their number sauntered up—smaller than the first, but still broad shouldered with a spidery tattoo veiling half his face. There was a smile on his dark lips.

"Mwal is no great speaker," he slurred, setting the gill flaps on his neck to flutter. "We make joke on you."

Trevor's face heated. But he stifled his anger away, keeping to his task. "I wish to hire you and your men."

"For what?"

Trevor held up the manual. The Merman took it in a webbed hand, running bony talons across the cover before looking up blankly. Of course. He'd forgotten these wretches couldn't read. He took the book back and turned to a page of an old naturalist sketch inked in red.

"I've lost one of these. This very day. In the city. I wish to get it back." The Merman narrowed his yellow eyes. "You want us find a Lok-Lok? In city that belches smoke?"

Trevor frowned. *Lok-Lok?* "Yes. I need you to find a kra—a Lok-Lok—that's escaped. Can you?"

The Merman turned and began talking to his companions in their slurring tongue, making ornate hand gestures that flowed like water.

Trevor watched, all too aware of Mwal, who had not moved but glared his way. When it was done the Merman turned back and smiled.

"We find Lok-Lok for you. Come. I am called Shan. We talk price now." Trevor sniffed. He supposed that was one bit of industry the savages had picked up. Joining Shan and his men in their circle, he began his barter.

"I don't understand why I have to go," Margaret said, tying the bonnet under her chin.

"You've said you wanted to visit your parents," Trevor reminded, handing off a set of bags to a Merman by their entry.

"Yes, but this is sudden. It seems everything is so sudden of late. You barely go to work. You seem to be here most of the day. You get no sleep." She gazed about, her voice lowering. "And there are four Mermen almost constantly in our home!"

"I hired them to fix the broken window and bathroom. I told you, they come cheap."

Margaret frowned, biting her lip. "I suppose. They've been remarkably kind, not at all as I expected. Especially Shan. He's noble in his barbarous way." She smiled to the Merman chieftain who was hoisting a lacquered traveling chest onto his broad shoulders. He grinned back, and Trevor couldn't help but notice how Margaret's eyes tracked his bare, muscular torso.

"Did you know that among the Mermen women hold high places?" she went on. "Shan says they are ruled by a queen, and Merwomen hold all the titles of generals. The women there even take multiple husbands! Can you imagine?"

"Probably why they lost the war," Trevor murmured. Such fool nonsense these Mermen were putting into his woman's head. All the more reason for her to go. "It will only be a month. Then everything will return to normal."

Margaret never took the worry from her eyes, but she nodded. She reached a gloved hand to his cheek, stroking the unkempt beard that was growing in odd patches on his face. "Take care of yourself, Trevor." He saw her off and then returned to the waiting Mermen.

"Well? Any news? It's been weeks!"

"We still look," Shan slurred. "Find signs of Lok-Lok. Follow those." Trevor ground his teeth. Signs they had in plenty. Butcheries broken into at night. Missing pets. Sightings of some odd bear or wild pig. Thank heavens for the limited imaginations of the masses. But time was slipping away. Sooner or later, someone was going to catch a good glimpse, then the secret would be out. If Khan wasn't killed someone else would capture it—and claim the credit! He'd lose his prize! He'd lose everything. Just paying these Mermen was exhausting what funds he still had.

He sighed, lowering himself into a chair. Not for the first time he wondered if he was in over his head. He could stop now, stem the bleeding, and accept his losses. But what then? Admit his failure? Tell Margaret he'd gambled away their finances? The very thought of her piteous look disgusted him. No, it was too late to turn back. Men of ambition pushed on.

A Merman walked up, hovering over where Trevor sat. Tilting his head down, the Merman said, "Yes!"

"What? Oh, it's you."

Trevor called Shan over. The Merman chieftain made a few hand gestures to which his companion answered back in kind. Then he turned to Trevor and grinned.

"Mwal find your Lok-Lok."

The Mermen took Trevor to a building in the middle of the city. He recognized it—one that held an indoor pool created by the Swimming Association, for public use. Mwal had tracked Khan to the sewers. The wily kraken was using the drainage tunnels to travel, careful to come out only at night to feed. Clever. Now it had ended up here.

The pool was closed this time of year, and the Mermen had to cut the chains that secured the doors. Following them inside Trevor was greeted by stifling darkness and the strong scent of mold, from a pool that hadn't been drained during disuse. He followed the Mermen along a walkway before stopping. There, one of them held up an old kerosene lamp, illuminating the space below.

Trevor gaped.

It was Khan. Only Khan had become a true monster.

The kraken had grown tenfold or more. Trevor estimated the pool to be well over twenty yards long, and that was still not enough to contain the creature's immense bulk. Tentacles, some wide around as small trees, spilled out in a fleshy mass of curved hooks and round suckers. The bulbous head was like the hull of an armored airship ending in a sharp honed point and covered in jutting barbs like tusks. Submerged in the murky water, under a ridge of protected bone, a black eye ringed in silver stared up at the glowing lantern. There was an ear-piercing shriek that echoed through the dark, and Trevor staggered back into a wall.

How had this creature grown so massive? Could dogs, cats, and whatever was found in the sewers do this? A sinking feeling crept into the pit of his stomach. Had there been any missing persons of late?

"Your Lok-Lok," Shan commented, yellow eyes flickering devilishly in the lantern light. "It is hungry."

Trevor blanched. What was he going to do? He willed himself calm. Men of ambition didn't panic when faced with such things. There was still a way to make this work. He just needed to find a place to house this monster. Barnaby! Of course! There was already a plan for this! He needed to find Barnaby!

"Trevor!" Barnaby greeted, putting down his evening paper. "Good to see you ..." He trailed off, taking in his friend's appearance. His suit was soiled and torn, his hair and mustache grown wild. When he sat down, he leaned forward, peering with haggard eyes that begged for sleep.

"Where have you been, Barnaby? I've been searching for you for almost two weeks!"

"I'm sorry, Trevor," he stammered. "Was off visiting a great aunt in Huntingdonshire. Dreadful place. Thought she was dying, but the old biddy will be around for a while. But why all this rush? I haven't seen you in over a month! You haven't answered any of my messages." He tilted closer, lowering his voice. "I've heard Margaret left you, and you've lost your employment. Is it true?"

Trevor frowned. "What? No. I sent Margaret away. But yes, I was let go. None of that matters now, I have other business."

"Ah! Your grand ambitious project?"

"You remember, Barnaby, I told you I might need your uncle's help? Well, it's much sooner than expected. Can you place me in touch with him?"

"My uncle? Well yes. But not now. He's just left the country."

Trevor's face fell. He put his head in his hands, muttering beneath his breath as his eyes took on a hunted look. "What now? God knows, it can't stay there! Gotten so big! Always hungry! And that Shan just keeps feeding it!"

Barnaby frowned. What was the man going on about? Had losing his work so injured his mind? "He'll be back in several months, I'm sure. Gone off to collect more natives is all—as far as Bundelkund it seems." Trevor snapped his head up, breaking from his trance. "What did you say?"

"My uncle. He's gone off to find natives, for the zoologique—"

"Where?" Trevor broke in. His eyes had grown feverish. "*Where* did you say?"

Barnaby reared back. "Bundelkund. With that name in the news, the old codger set out immediately."

Trevor looked poleaxed. "Bundelkund ... it's a place?"

"Why yes. Where that Captain Nobody is from. Haven't you been reading the papers?" He held up the daily. "It's all they can talk about, even in droll Huntingdonshire. They've found out his true name—Prince Dakkar, the son of a Hindoo ruler of the kingdom of Bundelkund. One of our provinces in the Indies. Why that's what his war is all about—to bring down Her Majesty's Empire. The madman's even released a Manifesto:

> I pledge to throw off your iniquitous laws by all means available. To free those beneath the colonial yoke. To undo the damage the earthly horrors of industry have released into the air and seas. I will make you the tools of your destruction, so that the many-headed hydra that consumes you arises by your own hands, and from your very depths.

Barnaby shook his head in amazement as he finished reading. "Quite a dramatic flair! He certainly knows how to—Trevor? But where are you going Trevor? You've only just arrived! Trevor!"

Trevor barely heard his name called as he ran from the pub. His mind reeled. Doctor P.D. Bundelkund. Prince Dakkar of Bundelkund.

A man who lived in the sea, who declared it his dominion, who conspired with Mermen—a man of great ambition, who now waged a war upon the Crown. What elaborate scheme could such a devious mind concoct?

Screams and shouts broke his thoughts, and Trevor fast found himself in a sea of humanity. People streamed by in a flood, heedless, terror marring their faces. He pushed past them, dread gnawing his insides to shreds. When he rounded a corner, he stopped and stared at a nightmare.

The kraken was pushing up from the building that housed it, sending mortar and brick crashing in a plume of blinding dust. From within that billowing cloud came a bestial roar—a mighty bellowing that shook the very air and struck Trevor to his core. Fleshy tentacles writhed about within the haze, lashing out like fierce whips. A policeman raised a truncheon in some pointless gesture and was crushed beneath an armored limb. A screaming socialite was plucked from a carriage as her terrified horse bolted. The brown dun didn't get far before a fleshy appendage wrapped about it, bony hooks gouging flesh as it kicked futilely. Another tentacle ripped a man right off his high-wheeled velocipede, sending the vehicle flying and lifting him twenty feet into the air. All three were dragged to where a ravenous beaked maw waited—soon rendering hair, bone, and flesh, to gory pulp in moments.

Trevor watched in stunned horror as the Great and Terrible Khan cut a swath of destruction through London's streets. A round black eye ringed in silver stared out, surveying the people fleeing before it like so many ants—or a movable feast. It turned his way, locking on him, and within that monstrous glare Trevor saw a mind beyond a beast. An intelligence resided there, one that hinted at knowing and recognition. The mere thought near sent him mad—and he fled.

Trevor ran now with the escaping crowds, tripping and stumbling in his haste, turning down an alleyway. In his head, that infernal Manifesto whispered: *I will make you the tools of your destruction.* Dear God! What had he done? He needed to tell the authorities! He couldn't have been the only one to read that advert. There were other eggs. This could be happening all over London. People had to be warned!

But what would he say? That he had been a dupe of this Prince Dakkar? That he'd been made an unwitting tool? And now he'd helped release untold terror upon them all? *They'll lock you up for a traitor*, a voice warned in his head. *Or a fool.* What would Margaret's family say? No, he could tell no one. He had to get home, destroy everything so that there would be no trace. His name wouldn't be known as the pawn in some madman's scheme.

So frantic and fast was his running, that when he struck the figure in front of him, he fell back, sprawling onto the alley floor. Scrambling to sit, he looked up as a face hovered over him. A familiar face, with dull and yellow eyes.

Trevor gasped. "You!"

"Yes!" the Merman said.

"I know your schemes! You and that Shan! You fed that monster! Then let it go!"

"Yes!"

"It will destroy half the city!"

"Yes!"

The Merman stepped closer, and suddenly to Trevor those unblinking eyes no longer seemed simple at all. He paled. "You don't have to do this," he whispered. "I won't tell. I won't tell anyone! I promise I won't tell."

The Merman cocked his head and then smiled, his mouth folding back to reveal an inner jaw with jagged triangular teeth like a shark. "No," he said in a guttural growl.

Trevor trembled. Then he began to cry. This was not supposed to happen. Not to him. Not to Trevor Hemley. He was a man of ambition! He was still crying as the Merman's terrible mouth came closer.

Barnaby sat in the parlor, where Margaret poured black tea into a porcelain cup. She wore a blue striped dress—though for all the sadness in her face, it might have well been a black mourning gown.

"Thank you for coming," she told him wearily.

"Of course." He sipped the tea and grimaced. Trevor had said his wife was not a cook. It seemed she was not good with tea either.

"I'm just at my wits' end over Trevor. The police won't investigate his disappearance. My family believes he's abandoned me. I just can't believe .... I fear something dire has befallen him. Have you heard anything?"

Barnaby shook his head. "I would tell you if I did, believe me. I've tried to find out what I can, but Trevor was often . . ." He chose delicate words. "A man of secrets."

She sighed heavily. "I didn't even know he was let go from the firm. He'd become so obsessed with this secret project. Father says he emptied the bank of all our money! And believes he's now absconded like a common thief. I don't want to even think on such a thing. Yet . . ." Her teeth worried at her bottom lip. "I wonder how much I knew Trevor at all."

Barnaby sat awkwardly, holding the small porcelain cup. What was one supposed to say? In the silence, his eyes roamed to the morning paper that sat open on a table, and he found himself reading its contents.

"It's awful, isn't it?" Margaret said, catching his gaze. "All these kraken attacks. The fifth ship this week! It's created havoc with trade. Why the stores are practically empty. People are hoarding and boarding themselves indoors! That kraken that rampaged through the streets and tore through Parliament—it ate almost half the House of Lords before disappearing into the Thames!"

"And a good number of MPs," Barnaby added. "Though, only Unionists."

Margaret didn't appear to share his joke, and he buried his face back into the awful tea. She shook her head in exasperation. "Where are these monsters coming from like some plague? Now the Mermen are in open rebellion, fighting alongside this Captain Nobody. My brother Arthur has been called back up for service. I fear it will be war!"

Barnaby nodded gravely. "We are entering dire times," he agreed. She sighed again, then hesitated, playing with a bit of paper in her hands. "In those last weeks, before Trevor sent me off, he'd hired several Mermen. He claimed it was for odd jobs about the house, but I know it had to do with his project."

Barnaby frowned. Mermen? This was new.

"I can't find any trace of it now. Someone seems to have burned most of his things. But this was in the fireplace." She gingerly handed him the bit of paper, a scrap of singed tan parchment. On it was the imprint of a creature with long tentacles. He inhaled at the sight.

"I know!" Margaret said, reading his look. She leaned in, her face anxious and her voice a whisper. "Trevor's secret project, I saw it once … I told myself it was a dog. I knew it couldn't be, but I convinced myself it was all the same. Now I've been fretting these days and nights, on what it might have been. Oh Barnaby, do you think our Trevor is …" She swallowed. "A traitor?"

Barnaby fumbled for words, but none came. Instead, he stared at the monstrous imprint and pondered the desperate acts of a man of ambition.

IN THE FOREST OF TALKING ANIMALS

by Makena Onjerika

The girl watches as the forest takes over the street, transforming it in awkward, uneven progression. Buildings, people, and clumps of rubbish change into hills, trees, and animals. The world elongates, darkens, and gains new shades of green, brown, and burnt orange.

The girl, crouching on a heap of quarry stones, tries not to panic as her older brother and his best friend Sammy trade insults nearby in a scathing game of mchogoano. Unaware that they are changing into trees, the boys rub their hands together, each giving the other maniacal grins, each proud of his cleverness: "You are so black, when a stone is thrown at you, it goes back to the thrower to ask for a torch."

"Only that? You are so ugly when devils see you, they shout 'Jesus!'"

Their foreheads are luminous with the sweat of vigorous gesticulation as the sun drifts down to the land of the dead. The girl watches, trembling, as Sammy's head grows into a majestic crown of branches and leaves on a thick-barked neck, his eyes still dancing and alive with excitement, set in rough bark. Her brother's skin starts to turn into bark too, his arms branching out and sprouting thick green leaves as he dances around Sammy, hurling another insult. In motion, his eyes catch the girl's eyes for a moment, but he does not see the old woman sitting on her back, sucking out her spirit.

"Kim," she calls out.

He is too immersed in his game to hear her.

Across the street, Eric from upstairs is counting against the wall of Building Four and growing viny branches through his ears. The other children who live on the street have become startled antelopes, running in zigzags and trying to find good hiding places.

"Kim," the girl tries again, more urgently now.

The old woman whispers a stale breath against her cheek, "You have only me now, little one."

The girl closes her eyes and shakes her head. The motion clears parts of her vision and she regains pieces of the real world: Kim and Sammy, half a building, a fishmonger sitting on a stool nearby, dropping tilapia into a pan full of sizzling oil. But the forest still stalks the edges of the world, blurring its way back in slowly, steadily, trying to take over again.

The old woman on the girl's back cackles at her attempt to restore the world. Then she spits toward the boys; a thick brown glob of ugly phlegm hits the ground between them. And suddenly, they are no longer playing; their faces harden, their bodies bend to war. Kim throws the first punch. They fight like lumps of clay pounding each other into shape, and the old woman laughs and digs her nails into the girl's shoulders.

"What are you doing?" shouts the tailor from where she sits inside her shop in Ebenezer Shopping Center, her feet spreading fractal roots into the cracked concrete floor. In her hair, yellow weaver birds go in and out of their nests, chirping. The little girl shakes her head again.

"Nyinyi," shouts the tailor as she throws an empty tin at the boys. They stop and consider each other, surprised at their actions. Then Sammy flashes his pink tongue at the siblings and runs off to play hide-and-seek with the other antelope-children.

"Only me, little girl," says the old woman, pushing the girl's head aside to attack her neck like a calf coming to its mother's tit for the first time.

"Only me."

She is gelatinous in the girl's head, poisoning her with visions of the forest and encroaching on all her secret territories. The girl reaches a hand toward her brother but cannot seem to reach him.

"Kim," she cries.

"Stop disturbing me. Just go home if you want." The girl's brother kicks a rock and sticks his hands in his pockets as he stares longingly at Sammy who is now at the center of the hide-and-seek group.

When the sky opens, phosphorescence bounces off the muddy water of a disturbed pothole nearby, and an eager bush grows out of it. The girl's eyes blur; she is evaporating. She has been evaporating since Saturday morning when she saw her Daddy for the first time in almost two years, on the front page of the Nation Newspaper, standing under the bold, black headline: "Doctors Strike Again!"

That afternoon, her brother stole the newspaper from their mother's bedroom and brought it out into the street to show off. While the girl crouched at the swamp just past the row of shops, dropping pebbles into the black water to scatter tadpoles, the other children who live on the street besieged her brother and gushed, "*Waah.*"

"I am going to be a doctor too," he said.

Frog eggs lay like strings of mucus on the swamp's turfs of grass, sparkling, and the place smelled of rotten eggs. The girl put her hand into the murky waters, caught a tadpole, and squeezed it to death.

When a still, small voice called her name, she shot to her feet thinking that a neighbor had caught her red-handed, playing with dirty water, and would tell her mother.

But it was only a strange-looking old woman, who challenged her to a riddle: "Kitendawili?" she asked.

The girl should have wondered at this stranger knowing her name, but the world was a nauseating color that afternoon, and the girl's Daddy had missed two of her birthdays and had not bought her any new Christmas dresses, even though he was on the front page of the newspaper. And so, although she noted the woman's short stature and her shriveled skin and her small head full of thick black hair and her too-white teeth and the sticky-sweet smell wafting off her, and even despite her mother's warning her about talking to strangers, the girl answered, "Tega."

"When it goes out, it cannot be brought back in," said the old woman.

The girl was the best riddle solver in her class at school, and this was the easiest of riddles. "A word," she said.

That was all the consent the old woman required. She leaped onto the girl's back, and before the girl could gasp, she planted her lips on the soft, young neck. The girl felt the hurt of seeing her uncaring Daddy in the newspaper leave her, suctioned away. Such relief. At that moment, she thought she would not mind being emptied.

"I have given you everything. Please," the girl says to the old woman now. "Everything. Please."

"Yes, but you must give me something even better."

"No."

The old woman is pointing a bony finger at the girl's brother who has just kicked another rock and is now seemingly weighing whether or not to go beg his friend to come back to their game of insults. He looks so much like their Daddy with the widow's peak and the broad nose and the deep-set eyes.

There were other men standing near Daddy in the newspaper, holding placards, and wearing lab coats, but their faces and bodies were turned away. Only Daddy looked straight into the camera as if knowing the girl and the boy would shove each other to look at him for the first time since their mother moved them from the bungalow in Kahawa West to Building Ten here in Zimmerman. The boy passed his hand over Daddy's printed face. The girl cried; their mother thought it was because she missed Daddy.

The old woman fills the girl's mouth and speaks. "Kim, let's go see Daddy. I know where he is right now,"

"No, don't," the girl tries to say, but she has been relegated to a small person inside herself. The forest has again colored her vision.

"We can go see him and come back quickly," the old woman says in the girl's voice. "No one will ever know."

When her brother leans in, curious, the girl knows there is only one way to save him. She runs away. Over sharp, uneven stones studding the murram road to the market. Past the bare-chested men hammering the stones into the road to fill potholes. The little girl runs as fast as she can with an old woman on her back and even faster when she hears her brother shouting her name. The forest chases her, transforming everything she passes by.

Coming down the road from the market is the milkman who sells milk in plastic bags to the families on the street. He slows his bicycle and grabs the girl's arm.

"Where are you going, kaschana?" he asks, standing on one leg to keep his bicycle and the plastic bucket tied to its carrier, upright.

She sees that his fingers are gnarled twigs, his eyes are river-smoothed stones, and from his mouth darts the long, curled tongue of a chameleon. The girl pulls away sharply, almost tripping him and his fur-covered bicycle over.

She runs past the market, past the vegetable stalls, past the plastic items seller and the madman who lives under a tree near the butchery, past the butcher, and the cassette tape hawker playing loud gospel music on a radio, past the mini supermarket that throws out a net of clean new-item smells to trap her, past the shoe repairman, and a porter pulling a mkokoteni piled high with sacks of potatoes. Someone calls her name, but she ignores it; she must take the cackling old woman far, far away, and keep her brother safe.

Only when the forest suddenly overtakes and engulfs her in a rush of trees and undergrowth does she understand that the old woman has tricked her into crossing the divide between worlds. The forest of the underworld grabs the girl into its darkness, and for a long moment, there is nothing but her scream. Then there are birds in twitter, a stream babbling to itself, insects quarreling, and the wind shaking down leaves as though a cascade of seeds over the dry reed casing of a kayamba. A wet spider's web traps and breaks the sunlight. Decay and dampness fill the girl's nose.

But she is no longer herself. She is shriveled, bent over, and barely able to carry her weight. Her mouth tastes of dirt. She feels devoid of some concrete beingness.

"Thank you for bringing me back home, little one," says the old woman who is no longer old. She is taller, smoother, and standing on strong legs in beaded calf skins.

"Give it back," cries the girl, although she does not know what "it" is.

"You don't need it."

"It's mine." Whatever the woman has taken is important, the girl knows.

The woman lifts the girl by her neck. "Ungrateful little animal. I have helped you; I have saved you."

She begins squeezing; the girl fights for air, but the woman's fingers only tighten, and she seems to grow even younger. Then something catches her attention. She stops to listen and scan the curtain of trees. A minute passes as a girl struggles, then suddenly, the woman drops her and takes off in a sprint.

A deafening roar. Something jumps out of the trees and chases after the woman: a long-toothed beast with bright-yellow eyes.

The girl scampers away on hands and knees until she is safe among the giant roots of a giant tree. From there, panting, she peeks out. All is menacing shadow. The trees rise far above her head, their barks ribbed and crisscrossed with termite mud tunnels. A quilt of leaves shutters off the sun.

The forest is speaking; the girl can hear it. Trees lean in to whisper to each other about her and shake their heads. She hears the scratching of insects biting into the sapling and ripe fruit and the beat of butterfly wings too. Birds startle into cacophonic flight in the canopy. Monkeys screech, scurry, and leap. But nothing comes near her. Minutes or hours or perhaps days pass.

"Poor child," someone says finally.

The girl startles. An Antelope with a clear brown and white coat and spiraling horns emerges from the trees to her left, then a Hyena, its fur ragged and its mouth wide. A giant brown Tortoise follows, from the right side, with a smoothed, polished black shell. A Hornbill caws, "Intruder. Trespasser." Drawing the girl's attention to the canopy as it lands on a nearby branch, its black wings spread out around the shock of color on its head, like protest.

"It is much too late," says the Tortoise with sympathetic clicks of its tongue.

The girl's mind is full of screaming; she has gone mad.

"What are we to do with her?" asks the Hyena. "She is but an empty shell now."

This is how adults talk about the girl sometimes, even though she is in the room, as if she were too small or too unimportant. She opens her mouth and lets the scream out of her head. The Hornbill jumps, flapping its wings, and spews curses in loud caws.

"I am full of things," she says, more to herself than to the parliament of impossible animals.

The Hyena looks about to laugh. "Not anymore," he says. "All gone. No more heart."

"No heart, no heart, no heart, empty," the Hornbill sings.

The girl's hand goes to her chest. True, there is no ndu-ndu-ndu, nothing to mark her as alive.

"Where is it? Where is my heart?"

The Hyena barks laughter. "You gave it to the Trickster." The pity in his voice makes the girl want to curl into a ball.

"No," she refuses his words, waving her hands. "No, give it back."

Then out of the trees jumps a Leopard to silence her shouts.

Resplendent in the majesty of a spotted coat, his golden, slit eyes shine even in the forest's dimness. His muscles stretch and tense under his fur, and the bones of his shoulders articulate in their sockets as he steps forward.

"The Trickster escaped," he says.

"You would not have caught her anyway," says the Antelope, stripping a young sapling of its bark with tongue and teeth.

The Leopard growls, setting the girl aquiver.

"We must kill her," he says, pointing a claw at the girl. "If she remains here, she will infect the entire forest with her emptiness."

"Evil. Evil. Evil," caws the Hornbill.

"Please. Please, no."

"It is a mercy, little one. You will still die if we leave you here, but you will die cruelly," says the Tortoise, its small head shaking.

The Hyena laughs again. He has found an old bone on which to gnaw. The girl searches her whole landscape for an escape. She is painful joints. She is a heavy head full of thoughts. She is a hungry stomach eating her from the inside out,

"Help ... help me get back my heart, please. Help me kill the Trickster."

"The Trickster is part of the forest. She does not die," says the Antelope around a mouthful. "We found a way to banish her, but you helped her return."

"Traitor. Traitor. Traitor."

"I did not know. She tricked me."

The Tortoise smacks her lips as if tasting the air then gives the girl a long stare.

"Please. I can make it right. I can. Please." The girl is on her knees.

"Impossible!" yells the Leopard.

"Please," she says, although even she knows she is too tired and too confused to fight the Trickster. If she could only lay down and sleep for a while, just enough rest to help her rearrange the world and make it make sense again. She bends and rests her head on her knees and closes her eyes.

Why is she here, far from home and joy? She did nothing to make Daddy go away. She was always a good girl; she kept her clothes and shoes clean and pretty when they went for outings. Her hair stayed in its ribbon, and Daddy told her brother to eat his ice cream properly like she did, without making messes. If she could only understand why Daddy chose his other children. She feels herself falling asleep, leaning to one side, about to fall over. But the trees, the trees are talking. Louder now. They are trying to say something. Shaking their branches and leaves madly. Throwing accusations. No, not accusations. She raises her head. She listens. She frowns and listens harder. Riddle, riddle, riddle, they say.

A riddle, the realization comes to her as sharp as a sting. She considers the five animals with narrowed eyes.

"I know you," she says. The animals all fall silent. The Hyena drops his bone, the Tortoise's neck shrinks toward its shell, the Leopard's eyes burn, the Hornbill knocks his bill against a tree.

"But how ...?" whispers the Antelope.

The girl is the best riddle solver in her class, after all, and here is a riddle, the most important riddle, the riddle of herself. The answers come to her fast.

To the Antelope, slender and long horned with a wet nose, she says, "I know you. I know all of you."

She cocks her head, feeling very clever as things finally begin to make some kind of sense to her.

She points at the Antelope. "You are the only one of them who is kind. You must be Hope. Because of you I will search for the Trickster everywhere. I will never give up."

"Cheat. Cheat. Cheat," screams the Hornbill.

The girl points at him. "I know you too. You are Confusion and Doubt. I will have to overcome you to win."

"Lies. Lies. Lies," caws the bird.

"Enough, Hornbill," says the Tortoise. "Let her finish."

"You, you must be Wisdom. You always are in the stories. You know how to find the Trickster, don't you?"

"Ke-ke-ke," laughs the Hyena.

"You are Cunning. You know how to kill the Trickster. You will show me how."

"It does not matter what you know. The Trickster does not die," protests the Leopard.

The girl turns to him. "You are Strength. You will help me run faster, and you will help me fight her."

A strong wind blows through, and the trees of the forest shake their branches in clapping. The air thickens with the excitement of insects.

"Help me get back my heart," says the girl, feeling more in control. "Help me, and I will take the Trickster away from the forest forever."

"It is more difficult than that, little girl. More difficult than you imagine," mutters the Hyena.

"But she has solved the riddle. She is clever. She may be able to trick the Trickster," argues the Antelope.

"Weak and small. Weak and very small," spits the Hornbill.

Leopard growls and leaps up onto a branch and stretches out his body. "If I cannot kill the Trickster, how can this child do it?"

"Dead, dead, dead girl."

"Not if we show her the way," says the Tortoise.

The Leopard swings his tail. The Hyena smiles greedily. The Hornbill pulls a worm out of the wood of a tree and swallows it. The Antelope nods her head. The Tortoise explains:

"Long ago, the Trickster poisoned part of the forest so that only she could enter it, a place of memory. There, she traps and feeds on the hearts of those who try to avoid pain, those who seek stories to hide away from the things that trouble them." The tortoise scratches at the fallen leaves and soil below. "But pain is part of the soil of the forest. We need it; it cannot be avoided any more than the Trickster can be killed. Do you understand?"

The girl nods, even though she doesn't, not completely.

"She has taken your heart but was foolish to leave you here alive," says the Tortoise. "Because now she has left a little of herself in you, and you can enter her part of the forest."

The Tortoise plucks out her left eye, which is a lurid marble of swirling colors. "Take it. It will help you see the truth."

The Antelope pulls out one of its horns. "Hold it in your strong hand and stab."

The Hyena hacks out a necklace of wet bones. "They won't protect you from the Trickster's power for long. You must be clever and fast," he says and winks.

The Leopard jumps from the branch and reluctantly slashes his leg with a long claw, opening a stream of bright red blood that shines in the dim light. "Drink," he says.

The girl drinks his blood and feels her young body return; she feels her bones grow strong, her skin become supple and taut.

"This will not last. You have little time to take back what the Trickster has stolen. You will fail and I will kill you," says the Leopard, then he stalks away.

The girl looks at the Tortoise's eye, watching its colors swirl and bleed into each other. She and the other animals turn in unison to look up at the Hornbill.

"You are going to tell her I'm coming," says the girl.

"Catch me. Catch me. If you can," he caws, taking flight.

The girl is fast. She launches the Tortoise's eye and strikes true, hitting the Hornbill in the side of the head. He falls with a muted thud.

"Madness," coughs the Hornbill, before the girl breaks its neck.

How much time passes before she finds the river? Bringing trembling lips to the cold water, she feels she has walked longer than she has lived. A large forest pig and her piglets watch her. Baboons emerge from the trees to gawk at her and whisper, "She is the one." Curious eyes follow her, but only the elephants further down the riverbank trumpet when she begins wading through the water, following the beat of her stolen heart.

"Don't go," they warn.

Seeing the bungalow again, even with a tree growing through one of its walls, brings a lump to the girl's throat. The tiles on the roof of her old home are of black clay and overgrown with moss, and the metal door has ax marks from when thieves tried to break in at night. Her Daddy's old Peugeot 504, which he inherited from his own father, is parked outside the house, its white and blue paint peeling.

The little girl now understands. They left—her mother, her brother, and her—they left, and everything died.

Daddy went for Mass that Sunday morning and returned to find men loading furniture onto the back of a Toyota pickup. The girl sees his face now more clearly than she did then. He spoke calmly to the pickup men and supervised the loading, but his eyes were small behind his spectacles.

"Daddy," the girl says, breaking through the sheer curtain at the door.

But there is no Daddy, only an empty sitting room and the switched-off Greatwall TV reflecting the little girl's face. Daddy's slippers are standing at the foot of his favorite sofa and some of the pages of his newspaper have fallen to the floor. The cushions of the sofa have taken the shape of his body. Has he been here all along, waiting for their return?

But the Tortoise's voice comes to her mind: "Is this the truth?"

Her heart grabs when she sees the footprints through the marble eye. They cross the dusty floor toward the inner rooms of the house. They are too large to be Daddy's.

The girl puts on the Hyena's bones and creeps along the walls and into the kitchen, holding out the Antelope's horn. There is a pot of rice bubbling and jumping on the stove, and the food in the store is rotting. Onions and potatoes in a makuti tray have grown into a small garden. Flies are hopping here and there, stopping to drink juices off the rotting pawpaws, oranges, and tomatoes, then rubbing their feet together with glee.

The girl continues her search in the bathroom, which is also a toilet. Then she checks the room where their house girl slept and where she left behind an old bra hanging in the otherwise empty wardrobe. The girl checks under the bed that is mysteriously still here and made, although also in the new house in Zimmerman. She does the same in the room she once shared with her brother. Their small beds stand side by side, and the room smells faintly of urine from all the times they wet their bedding. When they moved, their mother took nothing that Daddy had bought but said they could take their toys, that he was still their Daddy. The girl forgot the teddy bear Daddy had bought her for her last birthday. It is still here. She leaves it where it sits on the bed.

And now the last room. The room she hates most: her parents' bedroom, into which she often snuck in the afternoons to play with her mother's malachite necklace, a green snake among the bottles and jars on the dresser. This is where the girl stole and spritzed her mother's perfume. This is where she wore her mother's clip-on earrings and looked at herself in the triptych of dressing table mirrors. And this is also where her mother told her and her brother the truth one night, almost two years ago: "Your Daddy has another Maami and another Kim and another Kendi," she said.

They were sitting on either side of her, and she had her arms around their shoulders, crying and hugging them to herself, just the same way Daddy is now holding her brother. She ran away to save her brother, but somehow, he still followed her into the forest of talking animals.

The girl watches him and Daddy through the crack between the door and its frame. Daddy's laughter and the softness of his eyes behind his spectacles make the girl ache to fly to his side. She discovers she has never hated him. Missing him has worn a hole through the middle of her. But the Tortoise eye shows her the truth: Daddy never looked back, never missed them, never wanted them back. Here sits the Trickster, feeding on her brother's spirit, even without biting his neck.

Her brother is crystal eyed in the curve of the Trickster's arm. The girl can smell his happiness: Daddy's mixture of sharp Lifebuoy soap and gentle aftershave. She hears the sound of his happiness: Daddy's even, lulling voice. But it is the feel of her brother's happiness that terrifies the girl most: its neediness and vulnerability. She understands then. Her brother never showed it, but he missed their Daddy terribly. She pushes the door open and points the tip of Antelope's horn at the Trickster.

"Give him back and my heart too."

The Trickster smiles Daddy's smile and says, "Your brother loves you, Kendi. You know that? He followed you here, to save you. Look what love did to him."

The girl's brother does not seem to see her. He continues his languid drawl, "Dad, will you take me to Uhuru Park to ride the boats on the water and to eat ice cream and drink Fanta?"

The Trickster pats him on the head. He is two years older than the girl but is now so shrunken that his clothes hang on his frame.

"Will Kendi and Maami come to live with us and all of us be happy again?" he asks.

The girl pleads with him to wake up.

"Run, little girl, run," the Trickster says. "When I am done with him, I will correct the mistake of letting you live. Those Hyena bones will not save you."

The girl makes herself sore from pleading with her brother. He only looks up for a moment then leans back into the Trickster's embrace. Finally, she rushes forward and stabs the Trickster in the heart. She does not expect the Antelope's horn to sink so deep into the Trickster's flesh and burn a hole, charring the skin. She does not expect her brother to scream and the Trickster to laugh. The girl drops the horn and stares at her hands.

"Poor child. They did not tell you the cost, did they? They did not tell you what you would have to destroy?" Trickster brushes a hand over the girl's wet cheek.

"Kim, please."

"*Shuush*, little one. This is his peace. Let him be. You know he does not want the truth, and he never will," says the Trickster.

But the girl must try. She wraps her body around her brother. She presses the tortoise's eye into his palm and tries to make him hold it up to his eye, but he does not see. She pours remembrance into him. She calls him, "Kim. Kim. Kim."

She whispers into his ear about things they have done together, trying to anchor his memory in place to stop it from escaping. She reminds him of the time they stole meat off Maami's plate of nyama choma, of the cat they threw stones at a few months ago, of the games of mchogoano they have played, of the times they've ganged up against the other children on their street. She whispers and whispers but there is no response.

Days or years pass. The Trickster laughs and mocks and feeds on brother and sister. And the house continues to decay around them all.

SATURDAY'S SONG

by Wole Talabi

The seven siblings sit in a place beyond the boundaries of space and time, where everything is made of stories. Even them. Especially them.

People are made of stories too, but only the versions of their stories that they tell themselves. Curated, limited, incomplete. Many of the stories people tell themselves are lies layered on partially perceived things, to give their lives structure and meaning. The siblings who sit beyond, sit true, for they are made of all the stories that were, that are, that are to come. They tell each other these stories, taking them out and examining them in the light like a never-ending self-dissection. They listen to the stories, and as they do, they are made whole again. They exist in narrative equilibrium. In constant flux. They tell each other stories of what has happened, is happening, will happen, because it is their function. They tell these stories because they must.

Sometimes, they sing the stories too.

Saturday likes to sing. She thinks she has a nice voice, and this is true. It is euphonic, lilting, mellow, but strong and full of emotion, so her siblings let her sing her parts of the stories when she wants to.

Some stories demand melody.

"Let us tell another story," Sunday says, breathing the words out more than speaking them. He is the most knowledgeable of the seven siblings, even though none of them know why. He just is, because that is his story. He rakes the tight curls of his beard with his fingers before continuing. "Saturday, it is your turn to choose a story for us to tell and hear."

Saturday stops playing with the thick, long braids of her gold-spun hair. She is still surprised even though she already knew it was her turn before he told her so. She looks around the table, avoiding her siblings' stares, then she closes her eyes and focuses inward, seeking out the story she knows has a good shape, the story that feels right, like she is reading her own bones. When she finds it, the story she knows they need in this moment of non-time, she beams a smile and radiates the choice out to her siblings, passing the story they all know she has chosen for them to hear and tell. None of them react when they receive it, but they know it is a good story.

Monday, who always starts their stories, begins his duty solemnly with clear words, "Saura met Mobola at a financial management conference in—"

"Stop!" Saturday cries, holding up a small hand.

The shock of the interruption leaves Monday's mouth open, like he is a fish removed from water. Sunday's emerald eyes widen. Tuesday, Thursday, and Friday crane their necks toward her, their gazes curious and hard. Only Wednesday does not visibly react because she is bound up in thick clanking chains, punishment for the crime of trying to change a story. The timestone Wednesday used to perform the abomination sits at the center of the mahogany table between two ornate, pewter candelabras like an offering, or a temptation. Its emerald edges reflect and refract the candlelight in peculiar ways, making the bright orange light dance with shadows across the table and the walls.

Saturday feels sad for her sister, but knows she needs to be careful. She does not want to be punished too. Interruptions once a story has begun are mostly forbidden, although not as forbidden as attempting to change a story. The rules that govern the seven are both rigid and flexible, to varying degrees, like the rules of storytelling itself. Still, Saturday knows it is important it be done this way. For Wednesday's sake.

She says, "Forgive me. But I want to begin the story near the middle. Please, can we? We will go back to the beginning, but if we start at the middle it makes the story so much better."

She pulses her story choice again. This time, she radiates not only its substance, but she also gives them its form and structure, the shape of it with all its contours defined. Not just what it is, but also the way she wants them to tell and to hear it.

They receive it as a stream of visions. As a kaleidoscope of images. A swirl of sounds. A spectrum of sensations. A babble of narrator voices. As points of view. As music. As song.

Sunday gives her a look that is both surprised and curious. Tuesday claps her hands with glee. Monday nods with understanding. He looks to Wednesday, the chains wound around her body like perforated metal anacondas. The chains are older than time itself. Saturday wants her shackled sister to tell the part of the story where Saura obtains the chains to bind the Yoruba nightmare god, Shigidi. Resonance. She thinks it gives the middle of the story the reinforcement it needs. Like a good skeleton. Everyone has been allocated their part of the story to undergird it with what is important for the telling and the hearing. The other siblings also nod their approval. This makes Saturday smile. They understand even if they don't fully know her motives. But they know it is not just important to tell and hear the story, it is important to tell and hear it well.

Monday wipes the thin film of sweat from his narrow mustache, adjusts the collar of his pinstripe suit, and starts again.

This is the part of the story that Monday told:

Saura never dreamed before she encountered Shigidi.

For as long as she could remember, she'd never recalled a single dream upon waking. For Saura, sleep was, and had always been, a brief submergence into dappled darkness, her consciousness consumed whole like swallowed fruit. And because of this she never felt completely rested. She always felt lethargic. Unfocused. Persistently exhausted.

When she was eleven, her mother who was magajiya of the local Bori cult in Ungwar Rimi village near Zaria, summoned Barhaza, the sleep spirit, to possess her. The ritual was performed, and the spirit invited into her body to relieve Saura of her ailment and give her rest. But despite their offering of fresh milk from three white goats, the rolling of her eyes in her head, and the convulsions she experienced when the spirt entered her, the possession was unsuccessful, and she remained dreamless and unrested.

Her mother wept and gritted her teeth.

Saura had the gift of sensitivity and was meant to succeed her mother as magajiya. A refusal of the spirits to grant such a simple request counted against her, even though there were other things that counted against her more which her mother would soon come to know.

"I don't want to," Saura protested when her mother announced that they would attempt another possession.

"You must."

"No!" she'd screamed. It took her father two hours to find and retrieve her from the bush beside the market where she had fled to hide.

When Saura was sixteen, her mother tried again, ambushing her in her sleep and tying her down with thick hemp rope so she could not resist. That time, her mother begged Barhaza to not only give Saura dreams and rest but to adjust her subconscious desires, to make her stop looking at other girls with lust in her eyes, to take away her visible attraction for the curve of other women's hips, the swell of their lips, the fullness of their breasts. Once again, the spirit entered Saura's body, rigidifying her limbs, milkening her eyes, and communing with her thoughts, but when it left, there were still no dreams, and her desires were unchanged. That evening, Saura, wounded by her mother's betrayal, ran away from home with nothing on her back but her jalabiya and the light of a full moon.

She only ever returned home once, to attend her father's funeral. She refused to speak with her mother and sat with her lover, Mobola, and her father's family, tears streaming down her cheeks as they lowered his body into the hard red earth.

When she was twenty-five, after struggling her way through university with the help of a local charity, and finally getting a job at the bank, she went to see a doctor in Kaduna City. He was an oddly shaped man with a big head, a small frame, a protruding belly, and a kind smile. On the brick wall of his office hung a yellowing diploma between two hunting knives, like a trophy. His degree was from a university she'd never heard of, in Kansas. He connected a string of electrodes to her head and took measurements on a machine that beeped a steady whine until she fell asleep.

"No REM sleep," he announced, poring over his notes and charts when she was awake and back in the office chair. She'd never gone into REM sleep. After three more sessions with electrodes and needles and charts and uncomfortable sleep, he concluded that she was incapable of it. He told her she was a highly unusual case, prescribed a series of medications, and asked her to sign a release form so he could study her more. None of his medications worked, and so Saura didn't sign his forms. She simply got used to empty sleep, to never being fully rested, to never dreaming.

That is why, even before waking, she knew something was wrong that night Shigidi entered the master bedroom of the house in the heart of Surulere which she shared with Mobola. She knew something was wrong because she dreamed for the first time.

In her dream, she saw a small dark orb hovering above them as they lay naked in bed entwined in a postcoital embrace. The orb was dense and powerful, like an evil star. It settled on Mobola's chest and tugged at her flesh with an inexorable force like gravity. It tugged at Saura's too. She resisted the pull of it, tossing and turning and sweating profusely on the bed, caught in a night terror she could not escape. But she saw the dreamy, ethereal version of Mobola in her mind, yielding to the pull of the orb, being fragmented, stripped down to fine gray particles that were absorbed by the thing. When there was nothing of dream-Mobola left, the orb disappeared and Saura sank back into darkness. On Monday morning, when the heat of the sun on her face finally woke Saura up, Mobola was cold to the touch, her skin pale and dry. She'd been dead for three hours.

Saura screamed.

Monday stops speaking, and Saturday gathers into her chest what Monday has said, each word is a bird that she swallows, expanding with it. In-breath. It is important for her song.

Tuesday's pale face is unusually blushed bright pink, and her lustrous auburn hair seems to gain volume as she prepares to speak. She knows, has known, will know, that she has the best part of the story. The part that begins with lust and ends with something like love. Saturday winks at her sister. She has given it to her by design. Tuesday likes description and dialogue and the cadence of human speech, which is important in conveying emotion. A smile cuts across Tuesday's freckled face.

This is the part of the story that Tuesday told:

Saura met Mobola at a financial management conference in Abuja just before the cold harmattan of 2005.

It was break time in between an endless stream of panel discussions, and Saura was standing by the tall windows that overlooked a stone fountain, its water flecked gold with sunlight as it flowed up toward the sky. When she turned around to go back, she caught Mobola staring at her from across the hall. The moment their eyes met, there was a surge of something intangible within her, like an emotional arc discharge. Saura smiled and beckoned her over. For two days they'd been stealing glances at each other, occasionally catching each other's eyes. It was the seventh time it had happened, and Saura had learned enough of herself to recognize the surge, the feeling, the signs. She was ready. Mobola flashed her a sweet smileful of white teeth and approached. She had bright, inquisitive eyes with an anxious look in them. Her hair was natural and curly, and her wide hips strained against the gray of her skirt. Saura thought she looked stunning.

"Hi. I'm Mobola. I manage the Trust Bank office in Surulere," she said. Saura told her she was the logistics manager for all the Kaduna offices, and that if she had to listen to another discussion on foreign exchange approval procedures, she would go downstairs and drown herself in the fountain. They both laughed at that, carefree, like wind. There was something about the way Mobola laughed, the way she threw her head back, the way she almost hiccupped between breaths, her chest heaving against the cashmere blouse, the way she closed her eyes at the peak of her mirth, that Saura found deeply attractive.

They talked for a few minutes. There was a deliberate softness to everything about Mobola. The curves of her body, the cadence of her words. Saura was lost in Mobola's eyes, unable to look away. Brown, big, glistening, and full of a look which was a strange mix of sadness, grittiness, and hope. The look of someone who had seen the worst of the world, had stared into the dark heart of humanity, but had survived and resolved to live, love, and laugh freely despite it.

They pulled out their phones and exchanged numbers, laughing when they realized they both used the same model of BlackBerry, a bold, and agreed to meet at the delegate hotel bar at nine.

Saura watched Mobola leave, the sway of her hips hypnotizing her like magic. She could barely breathe, the air suddenly seemed thinner, oxygen harder to take in. She knew she had to be careful. If she had read the situation wrongly, she could end up in prison for years. Nigerian law was not kind to sapphic romance.

Saura arrived early at the bar and had two Irish coffees to wake herself up. She knew she wasn't wrong when Mobola showed up and waved. She wore a blue dress that was so tight in her fuller places it could have been painted on. There was a gap showing between her front teeth, some cleavage, and a bit of a belly. Legs shaved smooth and feet encased in black pumps. Saura thought she was even more stunning than before.

They had three gin and tonics, making fun of the parade of boring panel speakers and the other conference delegates who pretended to be interested in the minutiae of interbank financial processes before Saura pulled Mobola up to her feet.

"Do you want to go somewhere more interesting?" Saura asked, finishing her drink in one gulp.

Mobola smiled at her, lips red and glistening, mouth full of piano key teeth. "Sure."

Saura took Mobola to a club she'd heard about from one of the online forums she'd joined when she'd first started trying to understand herself. It was called The Cave and was a ten-minute taxi ride away. When they entered, it was into a rainbow chaos. Strobe lights. Colorful décor with bizarre shapes that challenged the very concept of geometry. Sweaty people pressed together at tables, on the dance floor, on barstools, running over with feeling. They made their way to the bar, ordered shots of something the bartender told them was tequila but didn't taste like it, and then merged with the mass of flesh on the dance floor. Mobola turned her back to Saura and began to rock from side to side slowly, sensually, following the beat of the music. Saura wrapped her hands around Mobola's waist and swayed with her so that they moved to the music together like a single creature.

Saura's head was a cloud. In that moment, she was sure she knew what it was like to dream.

The next morning, they woke up in each other's arms fully clothed and in the same position they'd danced in.

"Good morning, beautiful." Mobola said.

"Good morning."

"I had so much fun last night."

"Me too."

Mobola turned around to face her. "Did we …?"

Her face was close. Saura could see for the first time that she had a solitary dimple on her left cheek. It was faint, but there. Mobola was staring intently, and Saura could not look away, lost in her eyes. Her hair had bunched up and tangled, pressed against the hotel room pillow, loose strands dancing in front of her face. When she smiled, Saura's heart took flight.

She reached for the question hanging in space between them. "No."

They were both quiet for what seemed like a long time. An unbearably long time. And then she pulled Mobola closer so that they were chest to chest, inhaling each other's alcohol-scented breath and asked, "Did you want to?"

Mobola smiled. "Yes."

There was no hesitation. None.

Saura kissed Mobola and the cloud in her head ascended, rising beyond the ceiling and the roof and the sky, to the place where hearts go when they are buoyed by love.

It stayed there, never coming down. It only ever rose higher. For ten years, that feeling never sank. Not even when they fought and accidentally hurt each other and cried and made up and laughed like all good lovers do. Not when Mobola fell asleep one night and didn't answer Saura's calls for help after her car overheated and broke down on Third Mainland bridge. Not even when they argued about Mobola's not telling her before applying for a residence pass for both of them to leave the country. Not even when Saura's mother had refused to speak to Mobola at Saura's father's funeral or to acknowledge her existence. She tried to convince Saura to come back home, telling her that she was throwing her life away and bringing shame to the family.

No, Saura was always sure of the cloud of them. For ten years, she was sure. Through all the vicissitudes and the accusations and the arguments, she knew with all the certainty of entropy's irreversibility that she loved Mobola and that nothing would ever change that. Not even death.

…❖…

Tuesday is done speaking.

She is standing now. Her thin, pale hands are thrust out in front of her like the bones of a large bird. She'd allowed herself to become swept up in the story, infused with it, become one with it. And because she had, so had all the siblings. There is a solitary tear running down Thursday's face. And Sunday has a glazed look in his eyes that makes him seem much older than his hair, gray at the temples, would indicate, even though time is meaningless to the siblings. Saturday is pleased. They need this for the story. The emotion. She has taken in all of Tuesday's words, the sensations, the feelings, all of it. Her chest is filling up with power of the story, and the first melodies of her song are beginning to take shape within her lungs. Sunday turns to face Wednesday, whose turn has come. Wednesday must go back to the middle of the story, because that is where the chains first appear. Chains not unlike the ones wrapped around Wednesday's torso, snaking through shackles that bind her hands and feet, tethering her to the stone ground so that the only parts of her that can move are her head and chest and most importantly, her mouth. It's hard to tell or hear a story without a mouth.

Saturday waits, watching her sister. Wednesday has already received her section of the story. She just needs to accept it. She is hesitating, but it is not like last time when she rejected a story midway through and entered it, trying to change it—the crime for which she is now bound. The middle of the story is where the chains and the refusal to accept fate are waiting like familiar stalking animals.

Wednesday begins to shake and Saturday knows the story is coming. Erupting from the deepest volcano of suppressed emotion.

This is the part of the story that Wednesday told:

A month after Mobola's funeral, Saura went to see a babalawo in Badagry, at the mouth of a waterway that kisses two countries. She hadn't slept in days. Her friend Junia, who was also a colleague at work, had recommended him, claiming he'd given her a charm that helped her deal with depression after a miscarriage. Saura took his contact details from Junia but hadn't planned to use them. If Barhaza of the Bori, a spirit historically linked to her people and family, couldn't give her rest, then there was nothing a Yoruba babalawo unfamiliar with the shape of her spirit would be able to do. The yellow piece of paper with his number written on it in blue ink remained unused on her table, until one afternoon, watching traffic glide past her window, she realized that while he would not be able to give her peace of mind, he might be able to give her information. To help her understand why ten years of love and companionship and joy had ended at the speed of a bad dream.

The babalawo was a thickset man, with a long graying beard and calm eyes, who spoke perfect English. Three white dots were chalked onto his forehead, at the center of the space just above his eyebrows, and the string of beads around his neck rattled as he shook his head when he heard her explain what had happened to Mobola. When she was done, he removed the beads and threw them onto the raffia mat between them, rapidly whispering an incantation.

"This is the work of Shigidi," he said with his eyes still on the beads as he explained to her that Shigidi was the Yoruba deification of nightmare, able to enter and manipulate the human subconscious, especially during sleep when humans' grip on their thoughts was loosest. He could induce night terrors and sleep paralysis in his prey as he sat on their chests and pressed the breath out from them. The babalawo explained that Shigidi was an ambivalent Orisha, protecting those who gave him offerings but also often sent by evil people to kill those they perceived as enemies or threats. "You have communed with spirits before?" the babalawo asked, looking up at her curiously. "To have sensed Shigidi the way you described it, to receive a bleed-over dream when you were not the person he came for, that is very unusual."

Saura's eyes were wide with shock, but she only shook her head. She didn't tell him about her mother or her intimate knowledge of the Bori or her adolescent possessions by myriad spirits. She simply paid him his fee and hired a car to take her home. But not the home she'd shared with Mobola. No. Back to Ungwar Rimi where she knew she could obtain the power to take on the nightmare god that had killed Mobola and find out who'd sent him. To fight fire with fire. Saura hadn't spoken to her mother in more than a decade, but they were bound by blood, and Saura needed her mother's help, her knowledge, to do what she wanted to do. Human families can be made of chains too.

Saura did not go to the family compound to talk privately with her mother. That would have been too personal, too painful, and would have made it too easy for her mother to refuse. She went instead to the market at night, when the moon and the stars hung low and most of the village had retired to their beds, leaving the wide-open spaces of the market to the members of the Bori cult. This was where the council of Bori magajiya—who knew how to summon spirits and invite them to possess the bodies of people for various purposes—held court and heard requests from the sick, the curious, the desperate.

She arrived at the center of the market in a black headscarf and cotton veil atop a flowing black jalabiya like the one she'd been wearing the night she ran away. They were already in the middle of a possession. An unusually tall man, shirtless, with broad shoulders and long wiry arms like a spider, was crawling on the ground, facing up, with his back arched high to an impossible curve. He was singing in a high-pitched voice even though he was foaming lightly at the mouth. He looked like he was leaking tree sap. Saura recognized the signs. He'd been possessed by Kuturu, the leper spirit, the healer of diseases of the flesh. Two men in white kaftans played soft music on white dotted calabashes. A girl who seemed no more than thirteen played an accompanying lute. Saura used to be that girl, the one playing the lute at possessions, before she was compelled to flee and enter the world.

When they were done and the man was helped to his feet by two others, presumably healed of his ailment, Saura removed her veil and made her request before her mother could completely compose herself.

One of the other magajiya, a plump woman with plaited hair, asked in accented Hausa, "Tell us, why do you want the Sarkin Sarkoki to possess you?" It was her aunt, Turai.

For Mobola, Saura thought but didn't say. "I have been wronged. And I want justice." Saura replied.

The third council member, a man with thick white eyebrows whom she had never seen before, asked her why she wanted Sarkin Sarkoki, the lord of the chains, the binding spirit. Why not Kure, he asked, the hyena spirit who could give power and stealth, or Sarkin Rafi, who would give strength to do violence which vengeance often called for.

"Because the one that wronged me is not mortal," she said. At that, they fell silent.

The three members of the Bori council stared at her appraisingly, sifting and weighing her request. Her mother's gaze was unrelenting.

"My daughter, I'm glad you have finally come home. Where you belong. But Sarkin Sarkoki demands a great price." Her mother stood up from the raffia mat to her full height. Saura became acutely aware of just how much they looked alike. The same thin nose and lips. The same ochre skin, even though her mother's was more weathered, beaten to stubborn leather by the Sahara-adjacent sun. The same determined look in the eyes. "The possession is permanent. The lord of the chains will bind himself to you before giving you the power to bind your enemy. You are giving up your body as a vessel forever. What justice could be worth this?"

Beneath the veil, heat rose behind Saura's neck. She did not want to say what she was thinking. There was too much pain in her heart threatening to spill out. If she let even a drop of the decade's worth of resentment within her begin to slip between her lips, it would become a deluge that drowned them all.

"It doesn't matter. I am one of you. Heir to a title. I have a right to commune with the spirits. With Sarkin Sarkoki. And I have made my request."

There was more quiet weighing. More sifting. More appraisal. Finally, her mother turned to face the other two of the council, and they communed briefly before announcing their decision.

"We will grant your request," her mother said, "but on one condition. Once you have had your revenge against whatever spirit has wronged you, you must return home and become a full Bori devotee. We cannot have a vessel of Sarkin Sarkoki roaming free. You will take your place with us, you will marry a good man, and you will bear children and teach them our ways. Do you agree?"

Saura knew this was what her mother had always wanted. To bring her back and bind her to home, even if she had to exploit a tragedy to achieve it. But Saura could not see past her desire to avenge Mobola, to find out why her lover had died, and to make their story make sense again, even if she couldn't change its ending.

"I agree."

Her words, like her heart, had taken on the texture of stone.

Her mother nodded and smiled, teeth cutting a curve like the half-moon beaming down on them from the cloudless sky.

Saura closed her eyes as a woman in a yellow jalabiya, cut like her own, took her by the arms and brought her to the center of the clearing where the two main roads that crossed the market met. The woman stood behind her; she would be her nurse if anything went wrong.

Saura breathed steadily as the men in the white kaftans and the girl on the lute began to play their music and the three members of the council, led by her mother, began to chant words she had not heard for years. Words that made the air feel heavy on her skin, in her lungs.

Saura felt something in her chest open like the blooming of a flower. She felt a flush of heat, saw a flash of light. A rush of charged air entered her and then the world fell away as she was insufflated by the incoming spirit.

In the dark and nebulous place of her mind, Saura saw Sarkin Sarkoki.

He was an impossibly gaunt man, sitting on a stool at the center of the empty space. He had gray skin, and his limbs were like vines. He was bound up in thick, corroded chains that were tethered to something she could not see in the filmy darkness beneath, a few feet away from where he sat. A black cloth was wrapped around his waist and draped over his lower half; it pooled in cascades merging with the nebulous black ground below. His eyes were dark red, like spilled blood, and his stomach was cut open revealing mechanical viscera of chains and gears and roiling iron entrails. All over his skin, scripts were written onto him in chalked scars. He looked like a man that had been tortured and starved. He opened his mouth to reveal rust-colored teeth.

"You offer yourself as a vessel," he said, already knowing why she'd let him into her mind, and what she wanted him to help her do.

"Yes," Saura managed to reply despite her trembling.

"You surrender your body to the chains."

"Yes."

"Then so be it," Sarkin Sarkoki stated, his chains clanking and rattling as he began to vibrate. "We are one. You will have what you desire."

The chains around him unfurled themselves and reached out to seize her. They were heavy and rough. Saura felt them wrap around every part of her, flesh and bone, blood and nerves, mind and spirit. The chains squeezed tight around the very essence of her until the world was nothing but chains and darkness. A full and lovely pain consumed her as Sarkin Sarkoki bonded with her, and it wasn't until the woman in the yellow jalabiya poured water on her face and shook her back into full consciousness that she tasted the sand in her mouth and realized she had been rolling around on the ground, screaming.

Wednesday goes quiet.

Her siblings wait.

She takes in a deep breath and lets out a scream. It is at once a declaration of defiance and an accusation leveled at her siblings, at the family that put her in chains. Her scream is a knife in their hearts.

Saturday will not look away until her sister stops screaming. Wednesday's face, once full of grace, is contorted into an ugly shape with lines like regret, but Saturday does not turn from it. She takes it all in, the words, and the scream, because that too is part of the story.

When the screaming ends, there is a pause as they allow the scream to settle.

And then, the story continues.

Her siblings' words are air in Saturday's lungs, and her song is half complete. Saturday turns to face Thursday. His mahogany skin is pallid in the candlelight. The sadness hanging from the corners of his mouth, and the salt and pepper of his hair, make him look fragile and small in his black fitted suit. He leans forward and places both elbows on the table, settling his jaw on the tip of his fingers, hands pressed together as in prayer.

When Thursday begins to speak, Saturday manages a smile. She likes Thursday's voice. It is steady and powerful and full of purpose, like waves crashing onto a cliff—like vengeance.

This is the part of the story that Thursday told:

When Shigidi arrived, just before midnight, Saura was pretending to be asleep on an uncomfortable spring mattress in a spacious hotel room she'd taken for three nights. She was shivering beneath the duvet, because she didn't know how to adjust the central air conditioning, but she didn't care. There was a "do not disturb" sign outside.

The nightmare god's arrival was sudden, and she felt his presence immediately. The dream sensation of that small dark orb tugging at her subconscious with its evil gravity was one she could never forget.

She waited until he climbed onto the bed and sat on her chest, the weight of him restricting her breath. When she felt his probing at the edges of her mind, noticed a blurring and loosening of her thoughts and memories, she knew he had made the mistake of establishing a connection with her mind, of attempting to slip into her subconscious, as was his way. But she'd set a trap for him. The babalawo in Badagry had given her the number for another, less reputable babalawo who took requests for the nightmare god's assistance from people with such cruelty in their hearts. She'd told him that she wanted someone killed in their sleep, but she didn't say that the name she'd given was her own. And that the location she'd provided was the hotel room she'd booked. The trap was sprung.

She sat up suddenly and came face to face with the god that had murdered Mobola.

Saura was taken aback by how small and ugly Shigidi was. He was just over two feet tall. His head was too big for his body, and his dark ashy skin was covered in pockmarks, rashes, scarification lines, and sores. He wore filthy Ankara print trousers and a plain black cloak that sat on his shoulders and ran down to the back of his ankles, with cowrie shells and lizard skulls sewn into the fabric. Black ash covered his face and made it look so much darker than the rest of him. He looked confused, surprised, a bit stupid and unsure of what to do.

Saura felt a flush of anger that something so hideous had been the one to take Mobola from her.

"Bastard," she spat.

"What is happening?" Shigidi asked as he tried to withdraw from the borders of her consciousnesses.

Saura did not answer; she simply grabbed him and pulled him into the darkness of her mind where her inability to dream had left a vacuum in which the cadaverous and bound Sarkin Sarkoki now dwelled.

Chains shot out of the darkness and latched onto Shigidi's small limbs, binding him to the place. He struggled and pulled, but he could not free himself. Sarkin Sarkoki sat on his stool, watching and making a sound like laughter.

"What is going on? Who are you people?" The nightmare god shouted.

Angry that Shigidi could not even remember her face, she did not give him the satisfaction of understanding.

"You gods and spirits, you are all the same," she said instead. "You think you can enter our lives and ruin them at your whim, taking whatever you want and leaving us to pick up the pieces. No. Not this time. This time, here is what will happen. You will suffer, like you have never suffered before. There will be pain. A lot of it. I will take my time. And even when you begin to thirst for death, when the chains have dug into your ugly body so deeply that they have fused with your nerves so that there is nothing except pain, you will not die. I will watch as you are stripped of every fragment of hope you hold in that body, until you feel as black and as bleak as this place deep inside you. Maybe then you will remember who I am, and you will remember the person you took from me."

As she spoke, the expression on Shigidi's face had morphed from confusion to terror to something beyond both.

And when he whispered, "Why?" Saura silently asked Sarkin Sarkoki to tighten the squeeze of the chains around his neck until his head bulged, and he began to choke. It did not relent until he blacked out.

Thursday lifts his head and withdraws his hands from the intricately patterned mahogany table. Its straight-grained, reddish-brown timber was cut from a tree that once stood at the center of a garden that is not a garden, in the middle of nowhere, everywhere, all at once. He leans back and turns to meet Saturday's gaze. She smiles at him, grateful for the way he told his part of the story which she has also absorbed. She feels it almost bursting out of her now—the song. She just needs one more part. The revelation.

She turns to face Friday who is raking his hands through his thick Afro. He is the most reserved of the siblings and the one who likes the shape that secrets give stories which is why she has arranged it so that he can tell this part, just before her song. Candlelight dances in his large brown eyes and his pitch-black lips are quivering. He is eager to tell and hear.

Saturday nods and Friday opens his mouth, his bass voice booming and bouncing off the walls of the room in powerful waves.

This is the part of the story that Friday told:

Their bodies lay still and silent on the bed in the hotel, slumped over each other in an awkward embrace, but in the darkness of Saura's mind, possessed by Sarkin Sarkoki, Shigidi was screaming. Saura watched dispassionately, refusing to allow him even a waking moment of respite, a single fleeting second where he was not intimately acquainted with the pain from the contracting chains. And with every scream, she asked him the same question.

"Do you remember what you took from me?"

He insisted that he did not know, and so the torment continued. Sarkin Sarkoki's laughter the only other sound in her mind.

Almost twenty hours passed before the screaming stopped. Saura knew that it was not because the pain had ended; she was still commandeering the chains to pull and squeeze, and he was still writhing and whimpering. It was because something in him was breaking. Even a god can only take so much torment.

And yet after all the suffering, when she looked at him, pathetic as he was, she did not feel the satisfaction that she had craved. Underneath her rage was a sense of emptiness and loss and soul-deep weariness. She too was breaking under the weight of vengeance. And she knew that someone else had sent him to their home that night, because the two babalawos had told her it was the only reason Shigidi would kill someone.

"Mobola," she blurted out, eager for resolution. "Her name was Mobola."

Shigidi looked up at her, a glimmer of hope in his eyes for the first time since she'd lured him into the place of chains. He looked around at the darkness as though he were searching her thoughts for something. And then, "Ahh ... Mobola ..." he croaked. "Yes. Omobola Adenusi ... Lotus estate, Surulere. I remember now."

Saura seethed when her name escaped his mouth.

"I'm sorry." Shigidi breathed. "It was just a job. A standard nightmare-and-kill job."

Saura shuddered, she knew how he worked, but she was too angry to care. "Just a job? You took the most precious person in the world from me because it was just a job?"

The chains around his limbs rattled as Shigidi's tortured body sagged with the effort of keeping his head upright. "I'm sorry. I didn't know. It was just a job. It was only a job."

"Who sent you? Who was the client?"

And as she asked that, Sarkin Sarkoki's laughter stopped abruptly.

"I don't know." Shigidi said. "I just do what they ask me."

"Then you must remember." Saura demanded.

The chains tightened again.

"Please ..."

"Tell me."

"I don't know," the nightmare god maintained, each word excavated from him was hoarse and desperate. "But ... but ... wait ... it was a woman. Older. Not Yoruba. I remember she was not Yoruba. She had an accent. She was slender. Thin nose. She had eyes like yours."

Saura clutched at her chest.

"In her prayer, she only said she needed to get rid of the girl to get her daughter back."

A knot like an iron rope formed in her stomach. Saura fell to her knees as the weight of realization settled upon her. The lack of surprise when her mother saw her at the market. The insistence on returning home as a condition of her possession. The guilt in her aunt Turai's eyes. It all made terrible sense to her in that moment.

She asked Sarkin Sarkoki to unshackle him from her mind, and Shigidi fell onto the dark filmy ground with a thud. In an instant, they were back on the bed, in the hotel.

Saura shot up and rolled off the mattress onto the carpeted floor. She felt the iron rope tighten in her stomach and everything constricted, like it was being squeezed by invisible hands. She felt like her insides were about to be torn and exposed, like the hollow clockwork belly of Sarkin Sarkoki. She threw up and began to cry.

"Ah. You know who it was, don't you?" Shigidi whispered.

Her mother's words tolled in her head like a bell.

My daughter.

I'm glad you have finally come home.

Saura straightened up and settled a long stare at Shigidi, who was looking back at her with large yellow eyes full of pity or regret or perhaps both.

"Yes," she whispered back.

"Family?"

"Yes."

"I ... I am sorry. I am truly sorry."

Saura was surprised by the sincerity in his voice.

"I hate my job sometimes," Shigidi continued. "But I need the offerings and prayer requests to survive. Please understand. I didn't mean to cause you pain, but I ... need to survive. I never mean to cause anyone pain. But I ... I don't want to wither and die. I just wish there was another way."

Saura was even more surprised when Shigidi awkwardly clambered down from the bed and lay on the floor in front of her, prostrating in the traditional way, to show respect or profound apology. "I'm sorry."

She placed her hand on his head, and Saura and Shigidi wept together.

The story is near its end when Friday stops speaking.

And Saturday's song is about to begin.

There are no instruments to be played, but the air hums electric with a sense of music, in anticipation.

Her siblings watch, enraptured as her ribs expand, her diaphragm moves up, and her belly hollows out like a cave. The pressure of the melody builds up in her chest and there are vibrations in her throat, her mouth, her lips. Saturday feels like she is full of all the words and feelings and air that her siblings have given her with their words. Like she will never run out of breath. Like she will never run out of story. Like she will never run out of song.

Saturday begins to sing in a clear and loud voice full of energy.

This is the song Saturday sang:

She entered a life
She struck in like lightning
But was taken too soon
Beauty and joy and kindness
Mobola, lost to nightmare's touch
Breath extinguished by a mercenary god
Oh, a dirge for true love
For an embrace lost
A return home
Where Saura's heart is buried
A sacrifice to the essence of binding
The lord of the chains
Gave her the power
Gave her the strength to catch a murderous god
But gods only serve people.
They are made in the minds of men
In Saura's mind the nightmare god revealed a secret
That the umbilical cord can be a noose
That family can be a chain
That seeks to bind at any cost.
How could a mother do this?
Oh, how could she not just accept?
How many tears must be shed to pay for this sin?
How much blood must be spilled?
It's an evil way she has chosen
To show the depth of love.
Oh, a dirge for motherhood
For the poison in the womb
Saura swears that for as long as she lives
She will not let this happen to anyone like her.
The bargain has been struck,
The word-bond is made of iron,
But there are many kinds of homecoming
And sometimes gifts bare teeth.
Saura makes a pact with her lover's killer
An unwitting instrument in a war that began at birth.
He will give her dreams as restitution,
To make amends for stilling her lover's heart.

And she will forgive him
For he knew not what he was doing.
But grief and sorrow must be repaid.
There are many kinds of binding,
And even invited guests can come baring teeth,
If death is the price of her presence
Then let there be music and tears
As she goes home to share a living nightmare from which there is now no escape.
Oh, a dirge for childhood
Of innocence lost
She enters the village like a whirlwind
And blows her way home.
Her mother is sitting in the clearing
Where Saura once played Kagada with friends
Trust-falling into each other's arms and singing
And eating hot tuwo under weekend stars.
Their eyes meet full of determination and knowledge
Tragic corruption of love and affection
Her mother strikes first, possessed by Kure the hyena
No deeper pain than to be struck by the hand that fed you.
Fate is cruel to set blood against blood
She reaches into her mother's mind and ends it quickly
She gives her mother's mind permanent shelter
In the dark place with Sarkin Sarkoki
Where she will always be with her
Trapped in the once-empty darkness now filled with hate
Bound together in their pain
Their new umbilical cord made of spirit-chains
Her mother's body becomes a hollow vessel
Sessile as a tree and just as alive.
She has been given the thing she wanted.
Saura takes her mother's place,
For a paralyzed woman cannot be magajiya
When her daughter has come home.
They are now always together.
In her every waking moment Saura hears her mother's voice
Pleading, railing, crying to be let go

But every night when she goes to bed
She closes her eyes, and silence falls
And in the quiet of her mind, she dreams.

And so, Saturday's song ends.

The euphonic cavalcade of melodies comes to a halt. Saturday is exhausted and feels empty, like a gourd with all its water poured, but she smiles because she thinks it was a good song, and she sang it well.

Her six siblings remain silent, rapturous looks on their faces. They are still lost to the song. Saturday savors the moment. This is why she sings the stories sometimes. To see that look in their eyes that says she has given them something special. And for what she hopes it will evoke within them. She has told, she has heard, she has performed.

She turns to Sunday, whose task it is to complete all their stories, and she sees tears in his sea-green eyes. She smiles and nods.

Sunday sucks in air and lets out his words in a whisper that was loud enough for all of them to hear.

This is all that Sunday said:

"The end."

At that, the seven siblings who were, who are, and always have been, fall silent again and contemplate the story for a moment that is also an eternity. It is a reading of their own entrails, an examination of the essence of all things from which they are woven, and it is the most important part of the story—what it does to those who receive it. Its interpretation, its impact, its legacy.

"Humans are such tragic things," Sunday says. "Little grains of consciousness floating atop an ocean of existence vaster than any of them possibly imagine, barely aware of all the other ways of being, of all that exists outside their perception. And yet their stories are heavy in our bones, written upon us with the brightness of stars. The myriad ways they love and hurt each other are fascinating. They weave such tenderness and cruelty with every fiber of their lives."

He pauses. And then: "This was a good story. We told it well."

He turns to Saturday, the lines of his face converging, his eyes wide and full of realization, of knowledge. "But why did you choose this story for us to tell and hear, sister? Why did you sing this song?"

"For the same reason we tell and hear all our stories. Because that is what happened and thus must be told."

The siblings all echoed the mantra in unison. "That is what happened and thus must be told."

Sunday smiles faintly, maintaining his placid countenance. "Indeed. But there is also another reason, is there not?"

"For Wednesday," Saturday admits, brushing a loose, blond braid behind her ear. She knew he would be the first to understand. "We are not human; we are not like Saura or her mother. We should not continue to bind our own blood so, regardless of her crime. Wednesday is our sister. Yes, she tried to change a story, but which of us has not been tempted to do so?" Saturday pointed at the timestone sitting at the center of the table like an emerald fruit. "Her actions were wrong, but they came from a good place. And in the end the story was not changed. The stories cannot be changed. She knows that now. She is certain of it. As are we all. That is the lesson of her story, and it is complete. Let us release her from her chains."

Saturday sees the gratitude silently forming in the sides of Wednesday's thin mouth, her soft eyes, her broad nose.

Sunday looks at all his siblings. Their eyes reveal what they want even though they are mostly bound by rules carved in the primordial essence of existence, rules older than time itself. But rules, like gods, are only as powerful as their purpose, and the will of those who made them.

"Do you all agree with this? Shall we free our sister?"

"Yes," Monday says.

From Tuesday, "We should."

There is a hopeful nod from Wednesday herself.

"Yes," Thursday says.

Friday echoes his agreement.

"Yes." Saturday cannot hide her joy.

"Then so be it," Sunday says.

Saturday leaps to her feet and lets out a cry as the shackles loosen and fall from Wednesday's limbs, clattering with a noise like songs of freedom, like a sibling's laughter, like the forgiveness of family.

NAIRUKO

by Dennis Mugaa

1

I walk into Old Town. In a curio shop on the promenade, an old man sells paintings, deras, kikois, and ornaments. Tuk-tuks move swiftly along the cabro paving, passing the teapot sculpture at the roundabout. Pushcarts lumber beside the street restaurants and past the old buildings covered by vines. A radio plays "Malaika," the song rising like a wisp of steam. Shouts of children playing football near the sea reach me. I buy a ticket to Fort Jesus, and the seller tells me I am lucky because it is the day of secession.

The Coast Province is seceding from Kenya to form a new country. The fort's history plaque is being replaced; two men drill the new plaque onto the wall with fervor. They acknowledge me with a nod as I stop to look. Now, the plaque traces, with an ancestry tree diagram, the history of the secession movement since the coastal strip was handed over to Kenya from the Sultanate in 1963 till today—the day of freedom.

"Naweza kuelezea historia vizuri," a tour guide tells me, but I ignore him. I climb up to the crenelation. Pigeons take flight when I reach the top. I watch the water. Fishermen paddle along the creek. Two people swim across, and the English Point Marina gleams in the afternoon light.

My name is Nairuko, and I am about to become a horrible person.

2

When I say it like that, it makes me doubt if I'll be able to do what's required of me. It's something all laibons must go through, like my Papa did. But he's not here to witness my initiation. He took his own life when I was eighteen years old, five years ago.

I'm waiting for my friend Rahma; we're going to attend the secession announcement in Diani. She is a journalist and was involved in drafting the Coast Province's new constitution. She supports the secession movement. The movement gained momentum when offshore oil and gas reserves were found here ten years ago and most of the revenue kept going to the central government in Nairobi.

A text comes in from Rahma: *I'm here.*

I walk toward Burhani Gardens, where we're supposed to meet. The street is lined with posters of the movement's leader, Faisal Mazrui, an Islamic lawyer. His family have been prominent people here since the days of the Sultan. Faisal's wife died in a gas explosion when she was in the market. The Kenyan government said it will not recognize the secession and promised war, while also leveling charges of treason against Faisal Mazrui and his new cabinet.

I find Rahma seated, drinking from a bottle of water. She is facing the sky, and her throat bulges with each gulp. Below the bench, the hem of her blue buibui caresses the ground.

She's the only friend I've made since my father died. I feel closer to her than to my elder brother. She's my neighbor. I met her in my first week here on the rooftop of our apartment building. That day, as I watched the sunset, I looked to my left and saw her, through hanging clothes fluttering in the evening breeze, smoking a cigarette. She looked like a chimney, and at the same time, unburdened. When she noticed me, she asked, "Do you smoke?" I lied, took a puff, and started coughing. She was older than me, more assured of herself; there was no trace of malice in her voice—even in her laughter afterward when she realized I'd lied. It was as if by offering me her cigarette, she was offering me friendship, a place in her life. Since then, we've traveled together to Watamu and taken a boat ride through the mangrove forest in Mida Creek. And last November, when we went to her hometown in Lamu for the cultural festival, her parents made us biryani, mahamri, and samosas.

"Rahma!"

Her eyes light up when she sees me, and her dimples show as she smiles. She rises and hugs me.

"Twende?" she asks. I nod and we flag down a tuk-tuk to take us to Likoni ferry.

The ferry we get into is old, rusty, and creaks with each movement forward. I lean on the rails and look out at sea. I notice the city reflected in the water. I imagine that the other city mirrors the one we are in except that everything happens in the opposite. Cars drive backward, gravity acts up, and people walk on the sky. In it, time moves backward too, and I see my father, still alive and carrying me on his shoulders in our garden at home.

He died with so many secrets, and I'm only now finding them out. I'm a laibon, like he was. There are only nine of us from my tribe. After my father died, the council performed a ritual so that my father's ability could be transferred to my elder brother, but it didn't go as planned. It landed on me instead.

That day, I was walking to my bedroom, reading slides on Sans Papier protests in France for my Sociology class, when suddenly I found myself in an apartment in Paris with the Eiffel Tower outside the window. It was winter, snow was falling. I thought it was a dream until my Aunt Sianto—she's a laibon too—found me an hour later. She wrapped a shuka around me and told me my father's spirit had chosen me.

"I should have known Sironka would choose you," Aunt Sianto said. "But why burden his beloved daughter?"

I was confused. I didn't understand what she was saying. "Close your eyes," she said, and she recited something softly to herself. The next moment, I was at home.

"Auntie, what just happened?" I'd asked her in disbelief. "How did I? How did we—"

"My child, I cannot explain now," she said. "I promised your father you would finish your education." And on the day of my graduation from university, Aunt Sianto came, chauffeured in a sleek black car. She walked toward me, with all her elegance and mystery, as I took photographs in my gown, and whispered, "You are ready now."

3

Ripples caused by our ferry's arrival make the city in the water wobble and I lose the vision of my father. We find another tuk-tuk to where they are announcing the secession results. The results mean more to Rahma than they do to me. The council of laibons posted me here to observe how a place disintegrates. It's the first assignment a new laibon gets, so that they are used to seeing war and suffering. The council has, for years, known when a place will descend into war.

"When countries start buying weapons, training soldiers, and politicians throw around ultimatums, that's how you know," Aunt Sianto told me.

I don't know how I will feel when the war does start.

The center for the announcement is a memorial, built on the site of the former market where the explosion happened. The memorial is made up of one hundred three white marble statues with wings as if ascending into heaven. It's breathtaking. I've passed here a few times with Rahma when we were going to nightclubs in Diani. The statues are made in the likeness of those who died. I don't like looking at the statues of children because they remind me of how vulnerable I felt when I was a child and Papa left for work. Beside the statues are inscriptions in Arabic of their names and year of birth in the Hegira. Even though the bodies are not buried here, it has the mournfulness of a graveyard.

Today it's different, however; everyone is in a celebratory mood. People are wearing the yellow scarves of the secession party over kanzus and buibuis. They've come from Lamu, Pate, Malindi, Kilifi, and many like Rahma and I, from Mombasa.

We shove past a man blowing a whistle as we struggle to get to the front. When Faisal Mazrui appears, everyone cheers. He is wearing an embroidered kofia; his graying hair pokes through a little giving him a dignified aura. He is flanked by two men and two women. The results are announced. Ninety-two percent voted for independence. Faisal starts to speak, his Swahili rich with poetry and wisdom. He says the new country of Nazira will not waste money on a grand independence ceremony. "Kutoka siku ya leo, ni sisi tutakao amua mwelekeo wetu." At the end of his speech, the Kenyan flag is lowered and replaced by a yellow, blue, and white flag.

4

Rahma wants to celebrate and so we go to Forty Thieves because we know the DJ. We get in and I immediately take three shots of tequila. Rahma gets a table near a few tourists. When we sit together, she with her shisha and me with my cocktails, we are lightbulbs—men hover around us like moths. They buy us drinks, more shisha, and food. It's not that we can't afford it, but it makes us feel good. I am a different person now. I didn't used to drink or go to nightclubs. Even in university, I was always left studying. I had to be the best student because that is what I felt I owed my father's memory. Nowadays, I can't lie, I like enjoying myself.

The DJ plays Afrobeats. He's an Italian called Giovanni. He's our friend, and he knows what we like to hear when we come. Rahma and I stand up to dance. The men who bought us drinks stand up with us, but we don't want any of them. We hold onto each other, our arms locked. I drop my body down low and someone cheers. I let go of Rahma a little and she pirouettes. I slide across the dance floor toward her. The disco lights explode, and it feels like stars are falling on us. Louder and louder the music plays. I see a boy I might like and give Rahma a signal: a light touch on her shoulder. He approaches me with a smile, his eyes the color of rain at night. I press my body against him and move my waist. He looks beautiful, but I turn away from him in case the alcohol wears off in the middle of my dancing and I find out he is not.

When Giovanni finishes his set, he hands over to another DJ and walks to our table where Rahma is now seated. I know that's my cue. "I'm coming back," I lie to the boy. Rahma and I like Giovanni. He's a sixty-year-old man. He tells us stories of Naples and he treats us as if we were his daughters. He's childless, so perhaps this makes sense.

The three of us walk out and sit on the beach. The sea is dark, nightfall lending it color. A dhow is moored in the distance. Near the sea, I feel free, my spirit imitates the waves and I forget myself.

"Will you two leave if there is a war?" Rahma asks suddenly. Giovanni and I turn to her in surprise. "Would you leave because you are from somewhere else?"

"I would never leave you, Rahma," I tell her.

"This is my home," Giovanni says. "I have lived here for more than twenty-five years."

Rahma scoops a handful of sand but doesn't hold it into a fist, the sand falls through her fingers as if in an hourglass. "I hope there won't be one like they are saying."

"You know, Rahma, when I was your age, I was a stadium announcer in Stadio San Paolo. Dios, Diego Maradona played for us." His gestures morph into his words as he relives his past. He has told us this story before, but we still like it. " 'Di-e-go!' I would shout when he scored." His arms sweep out. Maybe it's the alcohol, but his arms seem to touch the sea. "And thousands of people would scream 'Ma-ra-do-na!' " His gaze fixes on us, and we know what he wants.

"Di-e-go!"

"Ma-ra-do-na!" Rahma and I reply, like the Naples fans of his memory.

"Di-e-go!"

"Ma-ra-do-na!"

We fall into laughter and our voices roar, echoing against the water.

I will miss feeling this free.

We sit watching the waves move calmly against the shore. Behind us, the nightclub explodes into cheer. It starts to drizzle, but the sky is clear—no gray or white clouds; but we don't move. There is no one else around the beach; it's just us three, the moon, the stars, and the sea.

5

The mothers in the apartment building are preparing lunch and the delicious smell of chapati and pilau wafts into my room. "Kwaheri."

Rahma's voice descends the stairs with her footsteps. She always says this to the children running up and down the steps when she's leaving, although they hardly ever reply.

I look at myself in the mirror. My Afro looks like it belongs in a black and white photograph from the sixties. Papa always told me to look at myself in the mirror when I was not sure of who I was. "Ru." He called me Ru. "Ru, look at yourself in the mirror and remember who you are," he would say. I suppose he thought it was something profound, but he only ended up sounding like Mufasa from *The Lion King*. I understood what he meant, however. He meant: Ru, you're my daughter, you're Papa's little girl.

Today, I'm unsure of myself. It's my initiation day. This means I'll be a laibon for the rest of my life. I have to do it whether I like it or not. Honestly, I don't know what else I would have done either way. I have never really figured out my true passion. I once wanted to be a singer, a jazz musician. But I feel like I was born too late. I know everyone says this, but for me it's true. I feel nostalgia for times when I did not exist. I should have been a young, marcelled singer in the Jazz Age.

I hear a knock and open the door. It's my Aunt Sianto. She is Papa's elder cousin, and she is tall and thin. She has an air of authority about her, and whenever she speaks, her voice leaves no room for questioning. She runs the export and import company, that the first laibons to teleport formed a hundred years ago, after almost all the members of our tribe were massacred by the British, and she is chairperson of the council of nine laibons. After my father died, there were eight laibons left. I'll be the ninth.

I'm a little hungover from the nightclub yesterday, and I hope she doesn't notice. I brushed my teeth, but I can't be sure; nothing gets past Aunt Sianto.

"Child," she calls me, but her voice is dry, without affection. I've heard the other laibons say that before my Papa died, he was the only one she shared laughter and secret stories with.

"Auntie!" I hug her and ask if she wants tea.

"We're late," she replies. She notices my blue jeans and white T-shirt. "Nairuko, you need to change. Didn't you get the clothes I sent?"

I did get the clothes, but I found them boring. I reluctantly walk back and put on the ceremony outfit she sent. It's a navy-blue trouser suit and a crisp shirt sewn in shuka patterns. It's something Aunt Sianto would wear, but not me. I hold my Afro with a band around the middle and it forms an hourglass; this way I look more stylish.

Aunt Sianto and I hold hands. She shows me a photograph of where we are going and asks me to visualize it properly. It's not like I have never teleported on my own before, but Aunt Sianto doesn't trust anyone to do the right thing without her guidance. I close my eyes. Every time I teleport, I feel like I've died and then come back to life somewhere else. It's like my cells disintegrate then rearrange when I emerge where I want to go. The coastal humidity disappears and is replaced by clean, crispy mountain air. We emerge on a hill's meadow overlooking a dry riverbed. I feel a chilly wind on my face, and I see the snowy peaks of Mount Kenya in the distance. Below the hill are antelopes and giraffes.

We are in Laikipia. The hill we stand on was where my tribe, the Ilaikipia, made their last stand against the British. We used to be pastoralists before colonization. The British, while building the Uganda Railway, passed across our lands. They were signing treaties with other tribes to get land for the railway and settlers. Our tribe's laibons, back then, possessed the ability to foretell the future, and they had foreseen that we could only win if we secured guns. My tribe's warriors ambushed a caravan and stole their weapons. The fighting which ensued was merciless. The British commanders vowed that none of us would live. They hired our enemy tribes and promised them our wealth. In the five-year resistance, we lost men, women, and children. When some saw that all hope was lost, they went into exile and assimilated into different tribes. We call them the lost descendants because they were never heard of again. The last village to fall was situated here. The laibons had performed one last ritual and begged the spirits for a way out. When the enemy forces came, they led my people to the top of this hill's cliff and ordered them to jump or be shot. Mothers jumped with their children, and men jumped with their wives. Some opted to be shot. Imagine thousands of lives lost like that! The nine laibons jumped together; instead of falling to their deaths, they emerged in the town at the center of the railway line, Nairobi.

The meadow transformed after the genocide. Nine geysers appeared, and odorless white fog emerged from them. The fog is the voices of our ancestors. Anyone who comes here feels immense suffering and misery, and a pull to jump off the cliff.

When Aunt Sianto and I make it to the circle of laibons, I feel a great horror engulf my heart. I hear the screams, and my head starts to spin. I stumble and Aunt Sianto places her arm around my waist.

"It's okay, I know how you feel," she says.

They bring a chair. One of them swirls a mixture in a calabash. It looks like ochre, but he adds tattoo ink into it. I feel the pull of death as if the voices are eating the essence of my spirit.

"Which design, Nairuko?" a clear voice breaks through the screams of horror.

Through the pain, I fumble through pictures on my phone and show him the tattoo design I want. "This one." The tattoo is to be drawn on my left wrist. My design is like henna. It's a floral tendril that leads up from my fingers to the top of my wrist, like Rihanna's. Rahma's mother drew it on me first; she is a henna tattoo artist for weddings.

Aunt Sianto purses her lips as if she is asking: "Is that really your choice?"

The tattoo is history traced on the body; it means a laibon has come here, heard the screams of their ancestors, and knows what it means to survive when people you love die. Yet, it is also a sign of survivor's guilt, the guilt laibons must carry all their lives, as if it were a curse. To learn to live with guilt, to numb emotion when worlds are falling apart, is instrumental to our work.

The idea of the tattoo was founded by the first laibons to teleport. They realized they could no longer foretell the future when they emerged at the train station in Nairobi; instead, their ability had been replaced. And they felt immense guilt. Why hadn't they died? Why had the spirits chosen to give them the power to save only themselves? They had lost children, husbands and wives, and some fell into deep grief. The leader of the council at the time conducted a ritual of remembrance in which they all tattooed themselves to represent what they had been through, their unique identities, and the history which held them together. One could choose whichever tattoo they liked, and it was used in the diaries and history books they wrote of themselves thereafter. Most laibons chose tattoos of things which held meaning to them: the face of a loved one, beaded cherished ornaments, a staff they used while herding cattle, or the stars, arranged as a downward-facing calabash, like they were on the night our first ancestor descended from them with his cattle.

The tattoo is forming on my left wrist. I watch him through a fuzziness as he applies it with an ancient magical thorn.

"Breathe in, Nairuko, allow the sorrow of our ancestors to pass through you," Aunt Sianto says. I take a deep breath. "Now, breathe out. Release the sorrow."

I feel the noises of grief from the geysers disappear slowly, and the taste of blood in my mouth reduces.

When the tattoo is finally drawn, Aunt Sianto looks at me, and the other laibons start to chant. They shake their shoulders in rhythm to the chant and move closer to me.

"Nairuko, this will hurt," she says. I don't understand what she means.

She takes a knife and slashes across the inside of my wrist, on the space where the tattoo ends. I scream. My blood drips to the ground. The nine geysers erupt, turning the air around us misty.

"This connects you to our ancestors forever. It connects you to our suffering," Aunt Sianto says. She treats the cut with antiseptic and bandages it. "Stand."

I feel fearless when I rise. We all go to the cliff where we are supposed to jump. Aunt Sianto says she will go last, after me. The other laibons jump and then teleport, disappearing in midair until it's only Aunt Sianto and me on the cliff. "You shouldn't drink too much, child," she says.

My cheeks heat up in embarrassment. Of course she noticed.

"One more thing. You should be careful with your friend. The one I saw going down the stairs," she says as she turns to face me, her voice soft and low, with the tone of a worried mother.

"Who? Rahma? What's wrong with her?"

"It's not a good idea as a laibon to make close connections in places you're working."

"So, I can't have friends?" I ask Aunt Sianto, surprised at her suggestion.

Aunt Sianto places her palm on my shoulder. "What I mean is, because you're sworn to secrecy about being a laibon, you're not able to be your true self with her. Would she still be your friend if she knew who you really are? And what if she—"

"If she what, Auntie?"

"It would be wise if you listened to me," Aunt Sianto says, then adds that she will send some books to me about laibon history for me to read. "Now, jump!"

When I jump off, I see the white imprint of the moon below thin strips of cloud. Before I hit the ground, I appear in my apartment.

6

I don't know how to feel today. I have been indoors for days. When I close my eyes, sometimes, I hear the sorrow I felt at my ancestors' site.

I'm reading the books about laibon history that Aunt Sianto sent and about our company's business model for the last one hundred years. They are written in Ilaikipia, and because I don't speak it a lot, I'm reading the books slower than usual. The books say there are three rules to teleportation: *A laibon must visualize the place they are going properly, a laibon cannot teleport with another living thing, and a laibon cannot teleport with something heavier than their body weight.*

Rahma calls on me after work. I put my books away and turn on the television before opening the door. She comes in and lays on my couch, her legs spread out in weariness.

"I haven't seen you in days. How are you? Are you still working? What work is it that you do remotely?"

"Do you want a glass of water? Or juice? I have juice." I'm not prepared to answer her questions, so I walk to the kitchen to get her something to drink.

From the news, the Kenyan government declines to recognize the sovereignty of the Coast Province and considers the secession a call to war. They give Faisal Mazrui's government one week to surrender itself to authorities, if not they will launch an invasion.

"It's because of the oil and gas," Rahma says as she drinks. "They don't care about us."

"Rahma, tusiongee kuhusu habari za vita, tell me how your day was," I say.

"Okay. We had a training on—" She pauses when she notices my tattoo. "You got henna? When?"

"No, it's a tattoo," I tell her, but I don't elaborate, because I don't want to lie to Rahma.

"When? Let me see." She comes closer to touch my arm. I quickly raise it for her to see from where she is. "What happened to your wrist?" she asks when she sees the bandage.

"I cut myself while cooking."

"If you cut yourself like that, maybe you should not be cooking at all," she says, and we both laugh. "Lakini, you've been quiet na your moods look low. Are you sure you're okay?"

"I'm fine," I reply while nodding. It's hard for me to keep things from Rahma. In the past few months, Rahma has been like my sister. I wish I could tell her who I was and why I am here, but what will she think of me when I say: "I am here to watch your city burn and not help." Aunt Sianto's warning rings in my head and I think to myself that maybe I was foolish to have befriended her in the first place, and that I should have stayed alone throughout my time here.

7

When Rahma leaves, I go back to my reading. The laibons, on reaching Nairobi in 1905, didn't have much. To survive, they stole money by teleporting into colonial bank vaults. After some time, they established a small export and import business dealing in rare valuable goods. In the Second World War, they expanded their business internationally, branching out into profiting from conflicts.

I skip through pages and pages of history and stop at the section with my father. The books detail that his first assignments were in the early nineties. He assisted the TPLF in covertly acquiring arms for the overthrow of the Derg. His service was, however, distinguished in the late nineties when he worked in the Congo Desk. Papa directed the sale of diamonds and other valuable minerals like cobalt and coltan from the Eastern region, despite warring rebels and government soldiers. In his final years, he was working with the Syrian government in acquiring chemical weapons during the Arab Spring. He had been on leave from Aleppo when he died.

There is a section on laibons, marriages, and relationships. It says often we have trouble maintaining relationships because of the guilt acquired while working in war-torn areas and the amount of time we spend at work. For me, I'm not sure if I want to be married. I've liked boys before, but I've never loved anyone. I've never truly felt I could inconvenience myself for a boy.

What about the children? Do they love their children? I wonder, but there are no sections about this.

I would like to believe Papa loved my brother and me. My mother had left him a long time ago for reasons I never fully grasped. Therefore, we lived in Karen, the three of us. Papa was often away in different countries, and whenever he came back, he smelled of fantasy worlds. He would relieve our house help from her duties. Then he would make us a recent dish he had learned from the country he was working in and play with us in the garden. I remember his laughter. He didn't laugh a lot, but when he did, he did so with his head leaned back, and his laughter left rings of warmth hanging in the air. He took me on hiking trips, an activity he and I liked to do. We hiked up Ngong' hills, Aberdare ranges, and Mount Kenya. Papa liked silence, and when we were together, although we didn't speak much, he would ask me about my performance in school, about my brother who he didn't get along with very well, and about my sprinting, if my starting off the blocks was getting better. But I loved the silences the hikes gave us because of how comfortable and safe I felt in his presence.

Still, I wonder how I never noticed in my years with him how his silence hid how withdrawn he was, how he was retreating further and further into himself. I know that he loved ruins. I often wandered into his study secretly. There were photographs hung around the walls of places in various states of destruction. Some showed bombed city buildings with bullet holes, some were of cities which had long been abandoned due to a natural calamity, and others were sites of fallen civilizations preserved in a state of ruin. I didn't understand why my father forbade my brother and me from going into his study, and yet all he had were photographs of ruins and books. I would try on his coat from the dresser and walk around with it to feel his presence enveloping me. Now I realize that perhaps being in his study meant being in his heart—a beating heart, full of life, and yet surrounded by ruins.

He is survived by Ru. I close the book when I see my name.

8

On the day before the Kenyan army invades, I walk to the supermarket to get supplies. Long lines stretch outside; everyone seems to be stocking up for the coming war. The new government said it would not be standing down. It has raised an army to fight. It recruits people in mosques, colleges, and public squares. *Nazira bila ukoloni wa Kenya!* This phrase is plastered across the city and repeated on the radios. A newspaper in a stall shows a photograph of young people enlisting in the army in droves—*Jisajili,* the headline reads. On the back page is a story about foreign countries sending planes for the evacuation of their citizens and another about several people from the interior of Kenya moving back to their ancestral homes to escape the incoming conflict. I go to the aisle with rice and then get some meat and spices for Rahma as she has been busy putting out statements for the party.

Outside, on the balconies of various apartments, the flag of Nazira flutters in the wind. On stalls along the road, people speak with exuberance. Despite their excitement, I see fear in their eyes, hear worry in their voices, and sense that they will be so tired and weary for years and years, even after the war. I don't know how to explain it, but maybe it's one of the things I'm here to learn: that death is never far from the thoughts of those faced with imminent war. I realize too that they will fight two wars. The physical one that is coming; and after it, they will fight another war in their memory.

It reminds me of something Aunt Sianto said to me: "Do you know why laibons profit from war? Why we still do so after all these years?" I hadn't answered her. "It's not because of revenge if that's what you're thinking. It's because of trauma, passed down trauma. Our ancestors' memories live with us, and we are afraid of extermination. The only way to protect the tribe is with money, a lot of it; and now with our gift, laibons are good at working in war zones. In many ways laibons are still at the war we lost a hundred years ago, and we are standing on the edge of that cliff, powerless, while the rest of the tribe is being slaughtered. Only now, it's a war within us, with our memory, and we must do what we can to win." It does make sense. Our tribe, from the surviving nine laibons, now has about one hundred and fifty people. Everyone is a millionaire because of the work we do; even the children, because trusts are set up in their name when they are born. There is a clause in the company's articles which states that each descendant of the nine laibons gets a share of the company's profits. Profits, like our ability, are reserved for the survival our tribe.

My conscience is not as clouded as it was before my initiation. My tribe is right to always look out for itself and only itself. Where was everyone when thousands of my ancestors were killed? Even after independence, the Kenyan leaders did not requisition our land. Instead, the colonizers' descendants continue to live there and claim it as their own. We only have ourselves, and our ancestors, to protect us.

When I go back to the apartment, I find Rahma and our dear friend Giovanni. He has two large suitcases.

His shoulders are drooped and instead of looking at Rahma when he speaks to her, he stares at the ground, crestfallen. They are seated on the entrance steps. "I'm leaving," he says to me. "I'm going to Nairobi. I'll come back when peace returns. If it doesn't, I'll go back to Naples."

Rahma and I take him to the railway station. We move with him past the security check and into the waiting area. There are so many people around. The intercom sounds: *Abiria wa gari ya moshi ya kuelekea Nairobi* .... Giovanni rises.

"I'll miss you two," he says through teary eyes. At the turnstile, he turns and smiles at us. "I'll miss how happy we used to be together. I'll miss that so much."

On the way back, Rahma is silent. She shakes her head and then looks at me. "That night on the beach, Giovanni said he would never leave here. Now look," she says. "Why are you staying, Nairuko? You could leave. You should leave."

"I love living here, Rahma. I have found a home here and I would never leave you."

She doesn't say anything, and I doubt I have convinced her. We complete the journey in silence, and I feel my heart growing heavy with the weight of my lie as if I am dragging along an iron ball. "Come stay with me tonight. I'll cook and we'll spend the night talking."

9

At dawn, the invasion begins with airstrikes. It's a shrill sound, like a frightening scream, followed by the crackling of fighter jets.

Rahma leaps from the couch. "It's happening, they are bombing us! It's happening!" She goes to the window and opens the curtains. Black fumes and fire rise in the distance. I rush to her and hug her. She cries into my shoulders.

I don't know what to tell her. I know I am not scared. If an airstrike were to hit our apartment building, I would be safe. But what about her? I am suddenly burdened by deep guilt; it creeps up from my toes into my stomach and I hold Rahma tighter. Now that the war is here my embrace of her feels like I'm holding onto something that is withering. Yet when I ask myself if I would ever abandon her, my heart answers that it wouldn't.

In the afternoon, when the bombs stop dropping, we walk out. The airstrikes were targeted at strategic military points. In the news, they report airport runways and army naval ships along the four coastline towns were destroyed.

As we walk, we notice an apartment building close to ours that was hit. The building has fallen into the road and covered the roadside stalls where Rahma and I sometimes buy vegetables. Men are struggling to get through the rubble. Some people are trapped inside and their shouts pierce through. We hear sirens and see an ambulance and a fire truck parked along the road with a hose and ladders.

"Tusaidie," a man pleads with us. Rahma immediately joins them. The lifeless body of a child, a young boy, is pulled from the rubble, and I suddenly freeze. I feel my stomach constrict. How is the world like this? Are these the places I'm supposed to work in? Who will I be if I am a laibon for the rest of my life?

A man shouts at me after lifting rocks with a crowbar, "What is wrong with you? Help us!"

But I don't move. I can't move.

10

The days fold into each other as the airstrikes continue. Now, however, they give a sixty-second warning. They announce which building will be bombed and we have sixty seconds. Sixty seconds to leave and hide in makeshift bunkers constructed to avoid the airstrikes. Rahma goes out to collect people's stories to send to news networks around the world, highlighting the atrocities of the invading Kenyan army. *The coast has a right to independence in the same way each state has a right to determine its destiny,* she writes.

The government here has refused to surrender. The UN Security Council passed a declaration deploying peacekeeping forces at designated safe zones. These are schools and hospitals. We see them in their blue helmets as they drive, patrolling the safe zones. Every day, I see people fleeing to the south, into a new refugee camp in Tanzania. It's a wondrous sight, a long line of people and cars flowing nonstop, like a river flowing to the ocean.

On the ground, the army invades from two fronts. From the North in Lamu, and from the West in Malindi. They plan to take Mombasa last to end the siege. Rahma's parents now live under occupation.

11

It's raining and the electricity is out. Outside, the football field overlooking my apartment has turned into muddy sand. Rivulets of water cut across it, branching into forks like a river delta. Crows land and peck at surfacing insects. There's no sound of children playing on the staircase anymore, nor the sound of mothers cooking and playing music. The city has acquired the feeling of a ghost town and the quality of ruins, like the photographs in Papa's study.

Suddenly, I hear a knock at the door.

I am startled, but when I open it, I see Aunt Sianto.

"How are you?" she asks me as she comes in.

"I don't know," I reply.

She sits down and looks at me.

"There is so much sadness, Auntie. I don't think I can handle it. And to think I will be working in places like these. Auntie, I can't. I want to help some people. Yesterday—"

"Help? Help who? Is this about Rahma? I warned you about making close connections. We don't help people. Did anyone help our tribe all those years ago? Remember how much we've suffered." Aunt Sianto's face turns into a frown as she speaks, and her voice rises.

"No, it's not about anyone. My heart feels so heavy, it's as if I'm—"

"It's guilt, child. All laibons live with it, you know that. You'll get used to it."

"How did Papa die, Auntie?"

"You already know that, my child."

"No, I mean, why?"

She hesitates and takes a deep breath. "Your assignment is almost over. You will finish when the city has fallen. It is the last step of your initiation." She moves to the door, opens it slightly and then stops.

"Sironka—your Papa, he was depressed. He lived with it for years." She turns to me, her face is now tender, and her wrinkles are clear through the light from the door. I realize how much Aunt Sianto hides about herself and her feelings toward people she cares for. "Sometimes, there's a limit of how much guilt we can take. Your Papa was a good man and he saw too much suffering and grief he felt responsible for. But we are laibons. He knew that, and maybe his heart couldn't bear it. He wouldn't have done what he did unless he felt he didn't have a choice. You'll turn out differently. I promise I'll watch over you more."

12

Our internet access is cut off. Rahma and I are walking to a hospital where civilian casualties are. I have decided to help her with her work, even though Aunt Sianto warned me from being close to her. I don't know what will happen to me if she finds out, if the rest of the council of laibons finds out. But every day I worry about her going out to work as the city is being destroyed. I fear for her life, and I'm going to try and keep her safe.

My top is blotted with sweat; it's a hot, humid day and we are wearing yellow press vests over our clothes. On my wrist down to my fingers, I have covered my tattoo with a white bandage to forget the history traced on my body. Some part of the tattoo is still showing, but I try not to look at it—not to think about it.

"We have to find a way to tell the world," Rahma says. She is carrying a notebook and a camera; I, her microphone and headsets. "Thank you for being here. You are part of us, part of me."

I don't say anything.

We arrive at the hospital and find long queues. A man at the entrance argues with the receptionist. He is holding his daughter. Blood drips from his hand. When I look closer, I realize the blood is his daughter's. She has a cut on her head. "I need to see a doctor."

"Tafadhali, keti chini. Everyone else is waiting."

"My daughter. Please—" He starts to cry. I've never seen a grown man cry before, and I think of my father's sadness.

An elderly woman rises from her seat. "My insulin," she complains, holding up her walking stick. The rest of the patients simply look at her. Every time I look at someone, I feel as if I cannot endure their grief; the grief they transmit to me through their eyes.

In the wards, we find patients lying on beds and the floor. We ask some of them if we can take their pictures. There are so many of them with gunshot wounds and shrapnel lodged in their bodies. A doctor pulls out a stethoscope and checks on a patient. Another in a frayed white coat carries a drip to the farthest end of the room.

Rahma sits on the ground. She breaks down, crying. "This is so painful. The suffering!"

Suddenly, we hear the airstrike siren.

"It can't be this hospital. It's a safe zone. They would never bomb the hospital," Rahma says. But we see people running past us.

A nurse screams at us. "Run! Run outside!"

"It's this hospital, Rahma." I pull her up.

We run. As we run, Rahma is struck by something blunt. I place my arm around her shoulders and assist her to run. But there are too many people.

We run and run but we are not close to the exit.

"I'm scared," Rahma says. "I'm so scared."

Our sixty seconds are almost up.

"Rahma, I'm sorry," I say.

The bomb pierces through the roof of the hospital. I visualize the garden at home where Papa and I played. The air heats up. "Rahma, I'm so sorry." I reveal myself to her before she is engulfed by flames. I emerge lying on the earth and grass of our garden. My hand is stretched out toward an invisible Rahma and hot tears burn my cheeks.

I feel so empty. So hollow.

THE MOST STRONGEST OBEAH WOMAN OF THE WORLD

by Nalo Hopkinson

From the minute Yenderil jumped into that brackish blue hole water, she started out on a journey that could have no good end. She knew from the preacher's sermons every Sunday that Hell was down below her feet, but down is the direction she was determined to go anyway, straight to perdition if she had to. For the beast she was hunting had to be a creation of the Devil's, so downward was where she would find it.

Yenderil had had to watch and wait for days until there was no one near enough to the blue hole to spy what she was up to. That was the thing about a bussa-rassa small village so poor you could scarcely find two rockstones to rub together to make fire; ongle a few hundred people living in Trentwall, and everybody up into everybody's business. But today she finally had her chance.

Truth to tell, though: In that moment of sinking into the saltish water, Yenderil wasn't studying her future any at all. She felt like she was all in pieces, couldn't hold herself together in her head.

The soul case that was her body was feeling the wet splash of blue hole water rising up, rolling from her feet to her head-top. How the water was cool and sky blue, but getting colder as she sank down from sky blue to indigo blue to navy blue till it was blue-black like blood, but still she kept sinking down lower.

It was so dark she wasn't sure her y'eye-them were open. Her lungs were studying how long they could let her keep holding her breath before they would open out like bellows and make her suck in whatever they could, be it life-giving air or death-dealing water. Her two girlchild arms, young and strong as new branches, were studying whether to let go the boulder-stone they were wrapped around, ascording to how the weight of it was pulling her down blue-black down and downer even farther to where girlchildren with lungs instead of gills had no business finding themselves. Her skin was turning to gooseflesh 'cause of how cold the water was this far into the depths of the blue hole. She never knew say cold could burn like fire. Her eyes in her head were looking, looking, twisting her head as far round to either side as they could, seeing nothing but black. Her ears were trying to hear, but the ongle sound in that silence was Yenderil's own heart pounding on her rib cage, trying to find a way out to freedom come.

The leather belt the obeah man had given her to clasp around her middle was thinking the ongle one thing a belt could think: cinchcinchstaytightmydarling. The cutlass the obeah man had told her to slip into the belt was singing itself a song about chopping and cutting. And the knot in the hem of Yenderil's dress was studying one single thing: keeping the dress close and decent around Yenderil's knees. For Yenderil was a good girl. Rather die than expose herself, even to the rahtid devil she had come to kill. And Yenderil herself? She was only studying on finding the blue hole devil that had taken her mother and father and the family's one nanny goat with a sweep of its ten devil snake arms three years before. She wasn't paying no mind to what might come after. She had been living with no "after" for three years already.

Three years before, in the space of four terrified Yenderil breaths, that blue hole devil had flung its long arms out of the water and made Yenderil an orphan, without even a she-goat to give her and its kid warm milk to drink in the cool of morning. Yenderil had given the kid to the obeah man, since it now had no mam to nurse it, and he had agreed to train her in return so she could get her own back at the fish devil.

Three years later, as she dropped down inna that blue hole water this day, Yenderil was ongle studying the words of the obeah man who had taught her how to make that fish devil dead:

You haffe slice that devil, you hear me? You going to be him bait, and that is how you will catch him. Wait till him grab you and hold you good, then take out your cutlass and chop him anywhere you could reach. Chop the arms holding you till him let you go. Then follow him down and jook your cutlass into him eye. Jook it deep, you understand me? Deep into him brain. That will kill him dead.

Some days, Yenderil wondered how he knew how to kill a devil. But he was an obeah man. He knew plenty more than she.

There. Far down below Yenderil. A glowing, flowering green of arms like aloe bush, ten of them, reaching for her, getting long and longing for her, rising fast till she could see they were plenty longer than she. Her heart had found her throat-hole and was trying to jump out that way. Her scared arms let go the boulder-stone right away. The knot in her skirt was so frightened, it expired. Slipped loose and then her skirt was billowing round her head and she couldn't see the green devil good. It came to Yenderil that what she was doing was pure foolishness and her lungs were burning. She tried to kick her way up to the surface, quickquickquick to get away.

But then the devil snatched her and held her fast. Its green arms wrapped around her like rope, and Yenderil realized one thing the obeah man hadn't told her: how to chop the devil if she couldn't get an arm free to reach for her cutlass.

Squashed up close to her like that, the devil's flesh was like wet, clenching rubber. The side of Yenderil's face was pressed into it. Deep inside the soft, bright green she could see black forms moving, linked together. Coils of gut. A pulsing heart, bigger than her head. Two smaller hearts, too. Who could kill a thing with three hearts?

The devil squeezed. Pressure built in Yenderil's chest and pushed upwards till she thought her head was going to burst. She couldn't help it; she opened her mouth to scream. She sucked water in, salt as sweat and cold as death. It burned down the back of her throat, and her whole body began to spasm, caught fast in glowing green.

A bubble of air rising out of her mouth. The gasping, stopping. The pain feeling far away. The arms around her getting loose, holding her away from the body of the devil. Two eyes in its middle, big around as wagon wheels, looking at her. And her floating in that endless black, legs kicking out. Whether head up or head down, she didn't know. And her fading, fading away as she reached weakly for the cutlass.

"Hold 'im good, Gregory."

Her friend struggled to keep the insect still in the cage of his fingers. "I 'fraid I break off a leg."

"That won't hurt it. It will still be able to fly." Yenderil worked the length of some of Ma's waste thread between Gregory's fingers, around the middle of the peenie wally. The steady green light in its batty made it difficult to see what she was doing in the darkening day. It took her three tries, while Gregory wriggled and tittered that the peenie wally was tickling his hand. Finally she had the knot tied. "Good," she said to Gregory. "Let 'im go."

The peenie wally rose into the air, fluttering to get away. But Yenderil held fast to the other end of the string. The best the insect could manage was a few feet above their heads. Yenderil held her hand high, and she and Gregory wandered along the roadside at dusk, following the peenie wally's unblinking glow. The sun wasn't all the way down yet. The top of the peenie wally's body glowed with it, while its underbeneath was dark, except for the light in its tail. Dust had painted red shoes on both her and Gregory's feet. Straggly jasmine bushes bracketing the roadside were releasing the perfume of their white flowers into the air. Trentwall village was laid out on their right. It ended in a low-walled cliff, with the sea below. The waves crashed onto the beach and threw salt smell up into the air. On their left, the garden plots of the people of Trentwall village. Beyond those, bush, bamboo, ebony, live oak, and mahogany trees. And filling all the air, the croaking and scraping of thousands of little frogs and crickets, calling out for wives for the night.

"Gregory?"

"Yeah?"

"What you going to do when you finish school?"

"You mean, four long years from now?"

"Yeah."

"I think I going to make a cart. Pick green coconuts every week from the trees on the beach down the cliff, load them into my cart, and pull it into town. Borrow Daddy's cutlass to cut them open with. Sell coconut water right from my cart to the town people."

She could imagine him doing just that, running to town and back between the traces of his cart. "Is a good idea. Your two brothers and a sister can help your mama and papa grow the cassava and breadfruit for market. So you could do something else." Yenderil grinned into the not-yet-dark. "You going to need a donkey for your cart."

"Maybe I can afford one with the money I make from the coconuts."

"I can help you out there. You know what I'm going to do when school finish?"

Gregory stopped dead on the path. The peenie wally flitted above them in a sad, desperate circle. "Not the Mandeville thing again, Yenderil!"

Yenderil grinned into the darkness. "Of course. I going to Mandeville. More than that, I going to find the Iron Donkey and tame him for you, so you will have a donkey for the rest of your days, and you could pass it on to your children when you too old to be a coconut cart man."

"You mad to rass. This is our life. Right here. This is real."

"It don't have to be!" Old argument between the two of them. "Plenty more out there in the world. We could see the Golden Table in Spanish Town. Or the big ships coming into the docks over by Kingston. And you could come with me!"

Gregory shook his head. "Yenderil, you know I not going to do that. You have nobody here to look after. I not free like you, to just ups and go anywhere I want."

Yenderil felt her blood heating up. She stopped and scowled at him. He said, "I sorry. I shouldn't talk like that."

From above, the peenie wally caught her eye. "Never mind." They started walking again. She looked up at the peenie wally. "What you think it could see from up there?"

He shrugged. "Same as when we climb the alligator pear tree outside your house. Houses. The road. The rum shop. The church. The sea."

"I know," she replied, irritated. "But it must be different, nah true? To see it and fly same time? To go fast-fast to what it could see in the distance? To fly up to the moon and back, even right out of Trentwall?"

"I suppose. You want to go look for that dead hog we saw in the bush this morning?"

"Yes. It was so stink!"

"It had maggots moving under the skin."

"And it was swelled up big. Dare you to poke it with a stick!" They turned off the road and into the bush. The peenie wally right away got snagged in a tree branch, and Yenderil had to leave it behind, fluttering in a circle around the branch. From the trail of its batty light, Yenderil could tell it was winding the piece of thread shorter and shorter.

Chop he. You have to chop he. Yenderil had practiced with the cutlass all these years, preparing for this day, till the obeah man had told her she was strong enough. She knew what to do. So she must have done it, nah true? In her almost-drowned moments she must have pulled out the cutlass from her belt and slashed at the blue hole devil. But after, she couldn't remember.

Moving through the water again, gulping it in but not dying, not dying, not going to heaven to see Ma and Pa. Not yet. Instead, moving through water that shifted from black to navy to indigo to sky blue. Going up.

She broke through into the air, the pit of her belly heavy. Coughed the water out her lungs. Her legs didn't feel like hers, but she managed to kick herself through the water to the bank of the blue hole. She dragged herself out. The cutlass was long gone, sunk into the depths sometime during the battle. Had she killed the fish devil?

Yenderil collapsed on the bank, not just from fatigue, but because she was heavy now. So heavy. More than when she went into the water. But everything was all right now. She had killed it, nah must?

Then she looked down at her body.

Yenderil walked for she didn't know how long. Stumbling. The left foot flopping, catching at rockstones, guinea grass. Brackish water dripping down from her hair, her dress. She dried off quick in the tropical heat, but dry skin felt wrong. The sun too bright. The heat too hot. Sound too loud. And her y'eye-them, trying to look every which way, like she had never seen Trentwall before. She passed one-two villagers. Some called out cheerfully to her, but then they looked at her leg and ran away.

She found herself standing in front of the calabash tree at the edge of Auntie's plot. Then she was rubbing her cheek against the bark, surprised to find it rough. There were round, green calabashes hanging from the trunk of the tree, like a big 'ooman's bubbies. Why was she running her tongue on one? Why was she trying to bite into it? What was this weight upon her, dragging her down? She remembered where she was going. Forced herself into a heavy, slow run. Light too bright! Skin too hot!

She reached her aunt's house, opened the door. A scream came from inside.

Daddy Pa, the village's obeah man, was on his knees behind the hibiscus bush in his backyard, retching. Yenderil made a face at the sound. Same sound she had made when she first saw what the fish devil had done to her. She waited, sitting on the wooden dining table that Daddy Pa kept outside under the awning and kicking her legs over the side; the one good Yenderil leg, barefooted with five little piggy toes, and the one new devil leg, fat and boneless and tall for so; taller more than her by two-three times. It had suckers on the backside of it from the tip all the way up to high on her leg back. It kept curling around things, touching things. The table leg. Yenderil's hair, the plaits tangled now and coming down. Her face.

The table rocked little bit, creaking with each swing of Yenderil's legs; the pavestones under it were cracked and uneven from the patches of grass pushing up between them. Daddy Pa's back was heaving. Yenderil could hear the splatter of his breakfast hitting the ground. She could smell the sourness of it, too. An interesting smell that would have made her feel sick a few days ago. Seemed like she could smell everything since coming up out of that blue hole. More interesting than Daddy Pa's spewed-up breakfast was the fleshy scent of the white hen in a wire cage on the table beside her. Yenderil's belly rumbled. The hen opened and closed its beak in the heat of the morning sun.

Yenderil had rolled her dress up over her tummy, holding it against her chest with one hand so Daddy Pa could see what had happened to her. Her devil leg filled out one leg of her draws, pushing at the seams. With her belly outside like that, she could watch Daddy Pa with her old Yenderil eyes, and at the same time watch the chicken with her new devil eye. Made her dizzy, seeing two different things in different places like that.

The table groaned. Before Yenderil could understand what was about to happen, the table sagged in the middle and snapped in two beneath her, with a crack like a rifle shot. Yenderil landed hard on her bumbo, the squawking chicken on its back in its cage on her lap. Out in the village, dogs had started barking at the sound of the table breaking. That one out by Mickle Road was the hoarse yelp of Mister Pertwee's old red hound, Horseface. From down by Main Street came the quarrelsome yipping of Mister Chong's two black-and-brown sister bitches. Yenderil didn't know their real names or if they had real names. She and the other pickneys just called them Ping and Pong. Ping and Pong and Mister Chong, who sold dry goods the whole day long. Ma used to tell her not to sing that song, that it was wicked to make joke 'pon Mister Chong.

When he heard the table break, Daddy Pa leaped up from behind the hibiscus bush. He ran over, heavy on his feet, wiping his mouth with the back of his hand. He towered over her, smelling like vomit and grown man. Smelling like supper. His big body blocked the sun and threw a cooling shadow over Yenderil. "Get up," he said. "And put your dress back down. Nobody want to see that."

Yenderil smoothed the dress over the wriggling lumps on her belly, covering the devil eye with the fabric. The eye shut, or she shut it her own self, like shutting her own Yenderil eyes. She wasn't sure which, but now she could ongle see with the two Yenderil eyes in her face.

Clucking and scolding, the chicken fought itself back onto its feet. Yenderil handed the chicken cage up to Daddy Pa, when what she really wanted to do was rip the cage open for the sweet meat inside. Daddy Pa took the cage from her, still staring at the place on her belly that she'd covered up with her dress. "What do you?" he asked hoarsely. "How you end up like that?"

Horseface, Ping, and Pong had stopped barking. The hen eyed her suspiciously.

Daddy Pa had asked her a question. Yenderil replied, "Is nuh your obeah do this? I wanted to kill the devil, not stick it to me. Take it off me please, Daddy Pa?"

His mouth dropped open. "My obeah . . . ? Is not me make this happen."

"But is you taught me to go after the devil!"

"Ongle because you were forever bothering out my soul case about it! And ... and that thing in the blue hole kill too much people and livestock in Trentwall already. I thought maybe if you could manage to get rid of it .... Plus, to tell the God's truth, you give me your last kid goat. Your ma and pa gone, and you scarcely ten years old back then, without two quatties to rub together. Eating yourself up with grief. I thought say coming and training with me might take your mind off it ..." He was babbling, different reasons coming out his mouth. He stuttered to a halt and stepped out of reach of her twitching devil leg. "I too sorry, Yenderil. I didn't know you would really go and do it."

He thought she was fool-fool for believing him all this time. But he didn't deserve to die for that. With her hands and her good foot, she pressed down on the devil foot, stilling it. It was like holding back a cow that didn't want to go where she were leading it. "I sorry I break your table," she said. She didn't know how she was going to pay for a new one. Tears started to spring from her eyes, all three of them. A trail of eye water wormed down the front of her dress, her ongle dress, hem torn and coming down from her battle. "But people saying I'm a devil now too, that I had no business in that blue hole. Auntie Mabel won't mek me stay in her house anymore. She tell me I must go back and live in my old house. She say is not for her sake, but I frightening her pickney-them and her man. How I going to live, Daddy Pa? You must take this thing off me."

Daddy Pa took a step back. His fear smelled like dog shit. "But you don't even have a left leg no more. You don't see? You have a devil foot. Is part of you. How I supposed to fix this?"

Fury blinded her. She reached out and pulled. Not with her arms, but with her devil leg. She hooked it around Daddy Pa's ankle and yanked his foot out from under him. With a yell he crashed to the ground, crushing the hen cage under his solid self. Poor hen didn't even have time to squawk. In one quick movement, Yenderil pulled Daddy Pa close to her. He shook, his eyes staring wide and terrified into hers. She hadn't known she could frighten a grown man like that. But she was too vexed to wonder at it right now. "You going to mend me," she growled at him. "Or else—"

"All right, all right," Daddy Pa babbled. "I will do something to fix you. But"—he swallowed bravely—"how you going to pay me?"

The fight went out of Yenderil. He hadn't demanded to be paid before this. "I don't know. I don't have no money." The tears were coming again, and all she wanted to do was bend and lick up the chicken blood trickling over the broken pavement stones from under Daddy Pa's body.

"Hmm," was all Daddy Pa said. Yenderil made the devil foot let go his ankle. There was a space of silence between them, which time Yenderil smelled and heard the village more clear than ever before. Hot cassava scent of fresh bammie bread baking in coal pot from outside Mistress Cadogan's hut near the beach. That meant the fishermen had had a second catch that day, and she was making bammie to sell with fried fish. The shouting and taunting of boys up on the cliff a mile away, jumping or pushing each off the side into the sea below. Earthen smell of fresh-turned soil from the plots up on the hill, where people gossiped and sang as they tended their gungo peas, dasheen, bananas.

Daddy Pa cleared his throat. He sat up, scowled at the flattened cage and compressed hen inside it. He held the bloodied back of his shirt away from his body. He grunted. "Going to owe me for the fowl, too. And for my shirt."

"Owe you?" said Yenderil. "So I can pay you back likkle-mickle?"

He nodded. "Something so." He pushed himself to his feet, then held out a hand to help Yenderil up, watching her devil leg the whole time.

She didn't take the hand. She remembered the length and thickness of the green arms coming for her inside the blue hole. She was wearing those arms on her belly now. Even though they'd smalled up themselves to fit, Yenderil was probably heavier plenty more than even Daddy Pa. She scrambled to her feet.

Daddy Pa said, "I will work an obeah to clean the devil out of you. Come back tomorrow. I will have the obeah ready for you."

Tomorrow? So long?

But she didn't have no choice. "Yes, Daddy Pa. I could have the hen?"

He looked confused. "What?"

"I will pay you back, Daddy Pa. But I could please have the hen? I so hungry."

"Well, waste not, want not, I suppose." He picked the crushed cage up by one clean corner and held it out to her. Inside it, the hen was a mess of blood, bone, and feathers. "She would likely make good soup."

Yenderil agreed. But she had a feeling what she most wanted was to drink the still-hot blood out from the raw hen.

Daddy Pa saw her looking hungrily at the crushed chicken. He swallowed. "Ah, why don't you go and fix yourself some supper with it?" he suggested. "Come by early tomorrow. Fore-day morning."

In the darkness before sunup. So nobody wouldn't see her. "Yes, Daddy Pa."

He watched her all the way to the gate of his compound. When she got around to the front of the house, Daddy Pa's grown son, Stephen, was out there, pretending to sweep the verandah steps with a coconut broom. But really he was staring at her and her devil foot. Yenderil wished horseflies would fly into his foolish open mouth. As she let herself out the gate, she saw one of the front jalousie windows on Daddy Pa's house slam shut. Next thing, the front door opened a mickle, and Daddy Pa's wife called out to her son, "Stephen! You come inside this house this minute!" Like her son was still some young pickney. Fear-smell was blowing out of the woman's mouth, too. Yenderil could taste it from all the way over by the front gate.

She put her head down and made haste along the road that led to the bush, praying the whole while she wouldn't bump into anybody. She didn't intend to go home. Her belly was growling so loud in her ears she almost feared the dogs would hear it and start barking again. Yes, she could pluck the hen and make soup with it, but her belly turned when she thought of eating cooked food. And she used to love chicken too. She couldn't even give the smashed hen to Auntie Mabel. She was forbidden from going back into her aunt's house.

She didn't reach all the way to the bush. Ongle as far as her Aunt Mabel's gungo peas patch. The rankness of the raw hen flesh was making her mouth water. She managed to push her way in among the waist-high plants before hunger pangs dropped her to her knees and she put the cage to her mouth and sucked salty porridge-thick blood from the chicken carcass like she was sucking on a sweetie. She pried open one corner of the cage, stuck both hands inside, and pulled the body out. She gnawed on raw flesh, paying no mind to the feathers in her mouth. She swallowed them down and all. She slurped up slippery entrails full of half-digested matter, and chewy pee-tasting kidneys, and fibrous gizzard. She sucked marrow out of bones. She spit out the cracked-open bones, together with claws and a beak. She belched. Her belly was clenching at what she'd just eaten, but she had never felt so satisfied by food in her life.

No, not her. Wasn't she feeling that. There was another mind growing inside her head. Faint, but it had been getting louder. Yenderil could feel how restless it was. It wanted her to go and do something else, anything else. It didn't know what it wanted. Something.

Yenderil was weary to her bones. She sighed and dropped the cage right there so in the gungo peas patch, on top of what was left of the hen. If somebody found all that nastiness and was frightened, then let them be frightened. She needed rest. She started on the road toward the bush.

On the way, she passed Gregory's daddy, carrying a tied bundle of long sticks of sugarcane on his shoulder. He jumped when he saw her, and cussed, then crossed himself for good measure. He put his head down and scurried on his ways.

Yenderil realized that she hadn't wiped her mouth. There was a bright red ring of blood all around it. That, and her twisty devil leg, and the wriggling lump on her belly under her dress; she must really look like the Devil in truth. She could just imagine what Gregory's daddy would tell Gregory about her. But she didn't want to face her friend just yet.

It was full dark now, cooler than the day, and blessedly restful on Yenderil's eyes. If she held up her dress so the fish devil could see, she had no problems walking in the dark. The fish devil liked darkness. She just prayed nobody would see her holding her dress up so scandalous.

She climbed a live oak and wove some of its branches, still attached to the tree, into a nest. She climbed into it and lay in a crouch. The devil leg wrapped itself around her and wound its tip around the tree's trunk. Dimly, Yenderil sensed the fish devil noticing that the swish and switch of the night breeze were much like floating in its home's deep water. The creaking of frogs and crickets were like the underwater sounds, though much louder. All Yenderil's eyes closed, and she slept.

Yenderil had heard the story one evening when she went to fetch Pa from the rum shop. The men were drinking and talking old-time story. Seem a bounty hunter named Champagnie had made the Iron Donkey long time back, to help him find escaped slaves. More than fifty years ago, before the freedom times. Him make it out of plate iron, held together with nails from the coffins of hanged black men. Carved its jaws from the thigh bones of

those men. Put a terrible engine inside its chest to give it life and wits. The way the story go, once Champagnie sic the Iron Donkey on you, it would never cease chasing you till it sink its jaws into your flesh. "But," said one of the men, "I thought that Champagnie man dead long time ago?"

The one telling the story replied, "Ah-true. But he dead before he could shut down the Iron Donkey. It still out there hunting down black people, never mind we not slaves no more."

Since then, Yenderil had been mad to go look for the Iron Donkey, take it apart to see how the engine inside worked. She wanted to find the Golden Table in the Rio Cobre in Spanish Town. Did it really rise up to the surface at noon every day, float for seven seconds, then sink back down again? And she wanted to go to another country! In a real ship! She wanted to find a duppy and make the ghost talk to her. She wanted Gregory to come with her on her adventures, but he wanted to stay in bussa-rassa Trentwall. Maybe she could get Daddy Pa to make some kind of a "come follow me" powder for her to put in Gregory's food. Gregory would enjoy traveling with her, if ongle she could get him out of Trentwall.

But first she had to repay Daddy Pa for taking the fish devil off her. Then she would see.

When Yenderil got to Daddy Pa's house early the next morning, son Stephen was putting a rickety little table out back, to replace the one that Yenderil had broken. Then he and his mother peered at her and Daddy Pa through the half-closed back door, not even trying to pretend they were minding their own business. There was a short bench, too. Daddy Pa was sitting on it. So Yenderil stood beside the table in silence. The devil leg twitched back and forth. She let it. Let Daddy Pa remember what it could do.

It was fore-day morning, still dark. The sun was just beginning to leak bluing across the black sky. Breeze tickled a blessed coolness over Yenderil's skin. Even so, the devil kept trickling messages through their combined blood about being too hot. Quietly, Yenderil muttered, "Go back home then, nuh? I would be happy to take you."

In reply, the devil sent some rudeness that Yenderil couldn't understand. But it smelled like the kind of facety thing a devil would probably say.

Daddy Pa stood. "Sit on the bench," he said. "We nail some more wood to it last night, so it could hold you."

Crickets kreeked in the darkness all around. On the table, the kerosene lamp flame danced to their music.

Flame. The blue hole devil had never seen it before, flowing like water, but not water. Yenderil refused the devil's urging her to stick her hand down the throat of the lamp to touch the pretty orange water. As she wouldn't, it kept trying to raise up the twisty devil foot to do the task. Yenderil would push the foot back down before it reached more than a few inches. She must have looked impatient, or like she needed to wee-wee.

Daddy Pa cleared his throat, and Yenderil came back from contemplating the strangeness of fire.

"Tell me something," said Daddy Pa. "That thing stick up onto you—if I jook it with a knife, you would feel anything?"

She had already found out the answer to that. "It would hurt. Like if you doing it to me."

Daddy Pa scrunched up his face at that thought. He looked at the ground for a second. Sighed. Looked up again. "Yenderil, I have some things to try. I think I could take the face of that thing off your front, but I don't know what to do about the leg. It might have to stay that way."

Hope sank into the pit of her stomach. But maybe with the face gone, the fish devil thoughts would stop. "All right, Daddy Pa."

He frowned. "I want you to understand what could become of you. If I remove the devil face, the leg might stay healthy, or it might stop working. And then it would be just hanging there."

Dragging after her, weighing her down. A spectacle everywhere she went.

Daddy Pa's two eyes made four with hers. "Hear me good, now. It could be even worse. If the leg die, it could rot and pass the rot to you. It could kill you. We would have to send you to the hospital in town to amputate it before that could happen. So tell me true; you ready for all this?"

She wasn't. But— "I not going to stay this way," she said. "Do it. Work your obeah."

"Very well."

First was the healing bath, with herbs floating in the water. It was Mommy Pa who washed Yenderil, with Daddy Pa standing outside the door and shouting hymns. The fish devil liked the bath. It kept drinking the water through its beak. Mommy Pa shuddered and wouldn't touch that part of Yenderil's belly. "Jesus Lord," she whispered. She filled a small tin with the bathwater and poured it onto the fish devil from high up. She dried Yenderil off with a cloth. Told her to put her draws back on and gave her a loose white flour sack dress to wear. Sent her back outside to Daddy Pa.

Daddy Pa had three plates on the table: What look like herbs mixed together in one; charcoal in another; and a kind of black oil in the third one. Some little twigs lying beside the plates. And a big, sharp knife. When Yenderil see the knife, her breath catch in her throat. Daddy Pa noticed. "Going to smoke it," he told her, "like a beehive. Make it sleepy so it don't feel anything. If it can't feel, you shouldn't feel, either."

Yenderil wasn't so sure, but she lay down on the bench like Daddy Pa showed her and pulled the robe up to expose the fish devil. Daddy Pa pulled back in surprise. "It have skin like yours now?"

"It can change its skin."

"Awoa. I know some fish like that."

He dipped one of the twigs in the oil, lit it from the fire under the coal pot. Black smoke started to pour out the end of the twig. He brought the smoky end close to the fish devil's face. Its eyes blinked. It thought the smoke was funny, that it was trying to look like … something. Yenderil didn't understand what it was saying. Pretty soon, its eyes shut. "It sleeping?" Daddy Pa asked.

"I think so."

"Pinch the devil leg for me. Hard."

She did. She didn't feel anything. Hope blossomed out through her body again.

Daddy Pa picked up the knife and touched the tip of it against one edge of the devil fish face, between it and Yenderil's skin. His hand was shaking. "Anything?"

"Nothing."

Daddy Pa gulped and pushed in a little deeper. Yenderil wanted to shut her y'eye-them, but she wanted to see too.

Daddy Pa said, "Lord help me, I never do anything like this before. Lance a boil, yes. Sometimes even stitch up a deep cut. This is something else."

"Keep going."

"Yes." He began to saw the knife around the edge of the fish devil's face, very gently. One stroke. Two. A trickle of blood came out. He stopped, leaving the knife in. "Anything?" His voice squeaked at the end of the word.

"Nothing. I could feel the knife, but not the pain."

Three strokes. Four. Daddy Pa was saying the Lord's Prayer, tripping over the words. But he continued cutting.

Five strokes. "Easy," he said. "Just like getting an oyster out the shell." He didn't sound sure.

Six strokes, and aiee! A stabbing, catching pain shot through Yenderil's middle. "Stop!" she cried out. He stopped right away, but same time, a trickle of blood ran into the fish devil's free eye. The face shuddered, and Yenderil felt it all through her, right to the devil leg.

It happened so fast. The fish devil's eye opened. It glared at Daddy Pa. A hole opened below and one side of its beak. A purple, sticky juice flew out of the hole, all over Daddy Pa's face and his knife hand. The devil leg pushed Yenderil off the bench and sent her flying through the air. She came crashing down onto her side a few yards away. Daddy Pa had dropped the knife. He was hissing, trying to wipe the purple juice out of his eyes. And his wife and son were rushing out the house to help him.

They turned the bench back over and sat Daddy Pa on it. They got a damp cloth and wiped his face and hand. He kept saying he was all right, but he seemed confused. He asked if a snake bite him. Wife and son took him into the house. Stephen came back out with Yenderil's clothes. "Go," he said, throwing them at her. "Please."

"He going to be all right?"

Stephen pointed at the gate. "We will see to him. Just please to go. Don't hurt us anymore."

Yenderil didn't want to hurt them. She just wanted to be fixed. "All right."

As she stumbled along the path, her skin came out in goose bumps when a voice inside her, not like her own at all, said, ****I haven't had to do that trick in a very long time.**** It sounded pleased with itself.

The fish devil was growing stronger inside her.

She didn't want to go back into the bush again. She couldn't go to her aunt's. Sobbing, sneaking along side paths so nobody wouldn't see her, she went to the only place she knew would let her in.

In her parents' old home there was a bucket of tepid water on the table. It was her aunt's bucket. Auntie must have brought it from the well for her. Some bammie bread and ackee on a plate beside it.

Yenderil sat to eat on the corncob bed with its single thinning flour bag sheet she used to sleep on with Ma and Pa. For a while, that bed had slept four when Ma had added the baby brother who died before he had lived eleven weeks. She hadn't been in this house for years. It smelled of dry rot.

She didn't know what she would do next. She'd cried out all her salt tears for the time being.

At least she had breakfast. The yellow ackee was buttery in her mouth like scrambled eggs, the bammie chewy in the middle and crunchy on the outside. A new set of flavors for the fish devil. She felt its wonderment. She chewed and swallowed for a long time, cogitating. She addressed the fish devil: "You going to punish me to death for trying to kill you?"

No. I'm not punishing you. The voice was hollow and deep, like a church bell ringing underwater.

"Is not a punishment?"

No.

"So why you latch on to me, then? Why you don't stay in the water with your own kind?"

I ate them.

"You ate your family? Your people? Why?"

Do you beings not do the same, then? Is that why there are so many of you?

What had she let into the world? Yenderil put the plate down beside her and wrapped her arms around herself to keep her shaking in. "A-true," she replied softly, "we don't do that."

How then do you gain knowledge? Do you all remain as ignorant as when you quit the egg case?

"I don't understand."

Silence for a moment, as the fish devil shoved and tickled its way through her thoughts and her memories:

Pa finding five-year-old she in the backyard trying to dig up her dead baby brother with a stick. She just wanted to see what he looked like under the ground and to ask him if he could breathe.

Yenderil coming first in a maths test. She beat Gregory by two points. So to make him feel better, she climbed to the top of her auntie's Otaheite apple tree where the bendy branches creaked and swayed with her weight. The sun was warmest there, the Otaheite fat and purple and tender. She picked two and brought them down for Gregory. They were bruised by the time she made it down to the ground. Their maroon skins were pulled back in places, staining the white flesh showing through. Gregory was still sulky, but pretty soon he smiled and took the apple-them from her and sucked them both down to the brown stone in the middle. She beat him in the next test, too. And the one after that. He got used to it, and pretty soon she didn't have to bring him presents afterward anymore.

Yenderil tried to mentally shove the fish devil out of her head where her private rememberings lived. Might as well try to boil the ocean with a match. After a few moments it said: ****I see your way of it now. You don't respect each other enough to give of yourselves!****

The fish devil didn't understand anything at all. She had given her orphaned kid goat to Daddy Pa. She picked fruit for Gregory to make him feel better that she was smarter at maths than he was.

The devil continued, ****My people were once plentiful in our ocean home. The waters slowly sank over millennia and left us stranded in what you call the blue hole. But we could live well there at first. There was food, and there were tunnels where we could spawn our young. We gave ourselves to the most gifted among us, as is our way; no overpopulation and more knowledge consolidated in our wisers. Each of us who is eaten by another passes on its accumulated wisdom to its devourer. Until finally only I, the most canny of our kind, was left. I have lived more than seven hundred orbits of that giant burning in the sky. I have consumed more thousands of my kind than I care to remember. I grew in wisdom and knowledge until I became a great . . . what you might call an obeah . . . woman.****

It was a 'ooman, then.

The voice continued, ****Though the magic of that paltry being who tried to root you out from me does not come close to comparing to mine. My obeah is how I was able to blend my compressed self with your body.****

Words, words. Plenty big words Yenderil didn't care about. But she heard the one important thing in all this speaky-spoking; the fish devil had just told her for certain that it was the last one left in Trentwall's blue hole. She hadn't been sure. And she, Yenderil, had caught it. Down below where it lived, it was queen. Up here in the air, it didn't rule.

Not yet.

She couldn't eat it, though. It was already part of her. "So you eat and eat till none left but you with all this wisdom."

****Yes, that is our way.****

So pleased with itself it sounded!

"What for?"

****Explain, please?****

"Here you are, all smart, with no one to pass it on to no more."

The fish devil had nothing to say to that. It demanded some water from the bucket on the table. Yenderil went to dip some out. The dipper was touching her lips when she stopped dead in her tracks.

The fish devil had a weakness. She knew how to fix its rass.

She didn't drink any water from the bucket. In fact, she emptied the bucket out in the yard, at the root of the Scotch bonnet pepper bush. The fish devil grumbled. Yenderil ignored it. She went back inside. She closed the door. She made sure the jalousie window was shut tight. She put on every bit of clothes in the house, even Ma's good church dress and Pa's heavy canvas dungarees he wore when he went out with the fishermen. The fish devil regarded all this activity curiously. For a little while, it forgot about being too hot. It asked what she was doing—she was beginning to be able to understand it more clearly now. She didn't reply. She dragged the thin bedsheet from off the bed, kept it within reach. Then she knotted their heavy rope around her good ankle, tangled it into a bastard knot she would never be able to untie with just her fingers. She tied the other end around a leg of the table, messy and unloosenable same way. She wrapped herself in the bedsheet, lay on the wooden plank floor, and waited.

And the hotness got hotter in the small one-room house. Yenderil's mouth was parched.

****Just likkle water, **** whispered the devil fish. ****Go beg some from your aunt. You wouldn't even have to drink it, just dip my leg into it. ****

"No," Yenderil whispered. "We staying right here-so."

The devil leg started twitching toward the rope knot around her ankle. Yenderil set her mouth hard. No. I not going anywhere. Sweat was running down her forehead, griming her neck with salt, creeping into the crevices of her skin under all those clothes. She was a crab in a pot of boiling water, steaming inside its own shell. She caught herself throwing off the bedsheet.

No.

She put the sheet back on and tied it around her middle.

Hours went by. Maybe hours. Yenderil was dizzy with how dry she was. She was feeling cold now. But burning up.

More time, the voice in her head sighed, ****I ongle wanted to know the world above and what was in it. I ongle wanted to know.**** It sounded faint.

"That's why you took my family? And all the others?"

****Yes. I thought if I ate them, I would know them. But they couldn't tell me anything about the world of air. That's why I made myself a part of you. Please, let me . . .****

A weak, soundless scream. Not hers. With a squelch, something at Yenderil's middle came unglued. She peeled away the layers of clothing to find the devil fish's face lying in her dress. Its wet jelly inside was facing her. Pink frills of flesh in it trembled. A tendril extended from its brain-part into her navel. Yenderil wailed. Snatched up the stink, rotting thing and pulled, yelping at the answering tug inside her belly. She forced herself to keep a firm, steady force when she rather rip the thing from her. She hissed with the pain but kept at it until she pulled the whole length free, like pulling a carrot up out of the ground. She hoped it was the whole thing. There was something like a root at its end, stained with her blood. Sweating, she threw the face and its root from her and fell back, weeping with the soreness screaming from her belly.

But she had no rest, no triumph yet, for the devil leg began to tear loose from her body. It had gone grey. It smelled like the latrines. It twitched and thrashed, and the agony deep inside her hip joint made her too crazed to think clearly. She tried to grasp it with her hands to pull it out of her, but it was dissolving into nastiness. There was nothing to get a good hold of. All she could do was move backward away from it, using her elbows and good foot.

It didn't come clear cleanly. It thinned, moving with her, till she had dragged herself, keening, around most of the room. She kept thinking of the abandoned peenie wally, flying round and round the branch that had snagged it.

The jelly trail got thinner and thinner. It was attracting flies. When finally there was no more of it melting out of her, she scuttled backward to a corner and lay there, half propped up, keening softly. Pain was like a taste in her mouth, like chewing on rusty iron.

It's done, said the voice in her head. It was fading. **You've consumed me. Thank you for showing me the world above.**

"Trentwall? Here is not the whole world."

It is to me. Blood and a clear, sticky liquid were leaking from the hole where the devil leg had been. **I'll be gone soon. Your brain cannot absorb my knowledge. All that I have learned will be lost with me. But I have one gift I can leave with you.**

The holes left in her were going numb. Her body, even though it was lighter now, felt heavy: heavy as when she'd climbed out of the blue hole. She crumpled to one side. Her mind was full of smoke. Her eyes closed in blessed relief.

When she awoke, her belly button had closed up. The remains of the fish devil were ongle two stink-smelling puddles melting into the floor, all that was left of the face and the leg. In the heat of the room, they were drying up as she watched. The face puddle had a beak in it.

And where the fish devil leg had been growing out of her, there was a floppy human leg. Thin-so like a new ginger stalk when it first poked out from the ground. Yenderil pulled herself up to stand on the good leg. She tried to put her weight on the new one. It collapsed under her. It was not exactly long enough, and it was weak. She could feel bones inside it, but they were too bendy to hold her up. Was this the fish devil's gift, then?

The new leg itched and itched. Yenderil got up again. She hopped over to the bed, gathering her clothes along the way. She got dressed, using the bed for balance. When she was decent, she hopped over to the door and opened it. She knew the midday breeze that flowed in was hot enough to wilt the morning glory blossoms on the vines that were draped on fences and walls all over Trentwall, but it felt cool as seawater as it flowed over her. She hopped and crawled around the yard till she found a stick she could lean on. By then, the new leg was the same length as the other, and she could almost walk with it.

It came to Yenderil's mind that she had won. She had beat out the smartest obeah woman of the world—didn't the fish devil call Trentwall the world, after all? She had freed her village. And the rest of the village would be grateful. The preacher, who had lost his two boys-them to the blue hole devil. Liddy Turkel, widowed when the devil snatched her man down. All the pickney-them whose parents used to beat them for their own good if they played too near the pretty water. No one would have to walk all the way to the standpipe three miles away and back to fetch water. And there would be good fishing in the blue hole again.

She could feel her lips pulling into a smile, like they had forgotten how and were slow to remember. Then she laughed, quietly. What a story to tell Gregory! By the angle of the sun, he would be home from school in a few hours.

But something made her stand still and ponder. Slowly, she understood the fish devil's final lesson. Though she was nearly the old Yenderil again, everybody knew what had happened, and everybody was afraid of her. Yenderil now realized that, like the fish devil, her strongest nature was to get what she wanted, even if that meant pulling others out of their natural stations, causing them distress. A peenie wally. An obeah man. Gregory …

She set her mouth in defiance. "Nothing wrong with wanting to learn," she said. So Pa had always said.

But it wasn't the learning. It was what she was willing to do to get it. Trentwall didn't have no fish devil anymore. But if she didn't watch herself, she would take its place. A girl devil.

Back inside the house, she tore a long strip from the bedsheet. She wrapped her mother's sewing needles and thread and heavy iron scissors inside it. She could hear the school bell ringing from the middle of the village. End of school for the day. She had to leave, now. And she had to do it alone.

She closed the door of her old home behind her. Her leg was already holding her better. She had likkle bit of time before Gregory could run all this way. She set out for the road, in the opposite direction from the school.

Stomp. Thump. Old foot. New foot. Every step leading her to a new life. The blue hole devil behind her. Ahead of her, maybe the Golden Table. The Iron Donkey. The Whooping Boy, riding his three-leg horse. She had beat the most strongest obeah woman of the world. Who knew what she would do next?

THE RAFTING OF JORGE SANTA CRUZ

By Adelehin Ijasan

"¿Dónde está mi hija?" Jorge asked his mother on the little screen in the cramped communications booth. Outside, a long queue of miners washed their faces with tiny, 0.05oz water sachets. Most wanted to speak to their wives or girlfriends, having been mining the pale blue promethium salt in the moon's subsurface for months. Jorge wanted to talk to Maria, his little girl.

"Ven ... con ... padre," his mother said, her image freezing on the dull screen.

"¡Pinche conexión!" Jorge cried, slapping the monitor. At the third smack, his daughter appeared, rubbing her eyes and clutching Sophie, the giraffe doll he'd bought for her three birthdays ago.

"¿Volverás para mi cumpleaños, Papá?" she asked, grinning as she climbed up on her abuela's knees.

"I will, mija," Jorge said. "I will not miss your birthday for the world."

"I am going to be six," she said proudly, rocking Sophie.

"Seis," Abuela told her. "*Voy a cumplir seis años.* Demuéstrale a tu padre lo mucho que has aprendido."

"Seis," Maria said, beaming. "Uno, dos, tres, cuantro, cinco, SEIS!"

"No money for cake, Jorge," Abuela said, covering Maria's ears.

"I've paid up most of the debt, Mama." He glanced at the timer. Only fifteen seconds left. "I will have a little leftover for a cake, I promise."

"You don't have to buy a cake if we can't afford it," Maria said, pulling Abuela's hands down from her ears. "It's okay, Papa. If you can make it, then it's okay. That's all I want."

"I will make it, mija," Jorge said, suddenly breathless, but the connection had dropped again, Maria's smile frozen on the screen, and she didn't hear it. His timer ran to zero, and the message: "*You have exhausted your credits*" popped up in nauseating green.

"¡Puta!" He cursed, slapping the side of the monitor before getting out of the booth. Maria's birthday was in four days. The next shuttle was leaving for Earth the next lunar day. If he got on it, he'd be just in time to make it after a three-day journey to Earth. He had to get on that shuttle. Surely, his manager would understand.

It was his little girl's birthday.

"No," his manager said flatly.

Jorge's heart sank. She printed a ledger of his collection over the past nine months, snatched it from the machine, and showed it to him. "I cannot let you leave until you've paid your debt in full, George."

Jorge adjusted his baseball hat, wiped his sweaty palms on his blue overalls, and took the printout from her. Karen was a stringy, no-nonsense woman who ran a tight crew. She was unmarried, had one estranged young-adult son from some distant period of indiscretion, and was known around these parts as the Iron Lady. Her no's were usually final. She unscrewed the top of the bottle that contained her anti-radiation pills and tossed two into her mouth like peanuts. She chewed, and Jorge frowned. Only psychopaths chewed such bitter medication.

"It … it says my total is 480g, here." Jorge stammered. "That was my agreement with the company, Karen, 480g covers my debt and then some."

"Nine months ago, *George*."

It had stopped irritating him that she called him George.

She typed again on her computer, and the printer came to life. "Your debt has accrued interest in the nine months since you've been here at 2.4 percent representative APR."

Jorge picked up the paper, tears in his eyes.

It said, "*Updated Loan Commitment*" at the top, and after a page of legal jargon, ended with "*Recalculated repayment amount in Promethium: 481g.*"

"1 gram?"

"Yes."

"It's just 1 gram, Karen." He felt the urge to fall to his knees and beg, but he restrained himself. Karen was the sort of psychopath who would like that.

"You want me to overlook 1g, George?" she spat.

"Please, it's my daughter's birthday. I have done my time."

"There are four-hundred miners here on the moon's subsurface. Most, if not all, are gamblers in over their heads with debt. If I overlooked 1g from everyone's quota, that's 400g of promethium!"

Jorge looked at the document again, hoping to find a new total. The number 481 glared back at him.

"You still have time," Karen said, looking at the launch schedule on the whiteboard behind her. "Launch is not for another eight hours."

"Dios mio," Jorge wailed and dashed out of her office.

...❖...

Promethium 147, a lanthanide, was discovered on the moon in the late century by explorer probes mapping the elaborate network of hollow space beneath the moon's surface formed during the eruption of basaltic lava flows in the moon's early formation. Prior, promethium was produced only by the bombardment of uranium and was not found naturally on the Earth's crust. It was the main ingredient for atomic batteries, also known as perpetual batteries. Two thousand grams of promethium could power an entire city for hundreds of years. It was the new *coltan*, the new gold. Every single electronic device ran on promethium-powered batteries. The lava tubes beneath the moon's Mares Serenitatis were deep, connected caverns, and the miners lived and worked in human habitats protected from cosmic radiation, meteors, and extreme temperatures.

Jorge broke into the miners' quarters and began to don the suit that protected him from the gamma decay of the rare mineral. He grabbed his shovel and black light and swallowed two anti-radiation pills—130mg of potassium iodide, which blocked radioactive material from being absorbed by the thyroid gland. The lunar-day miners were back from their shift, lounging in the dormitories, playing whots on double bunks, and returning from the chemical showers.

"Going back out?" Gbenga asked, drying his hair. He was a Nigerian who owed 6000g to a cartel and had been on the moon for twelve years. No one knew how much he'd paid, but it seemed he was never getting out. He was cheerful about it, in any case. Always smiling.

"Thought you were all paid up," Gbenga said, lathering his skin with the recommended anti-radiation cream that left a whitish residue like sunscreen.

"1g more in interest," Jorge muttered, zipping up the yellow suit, his breath fogging the visor.

"Hmm," Gbenga said knowingly.

Jorge brushed past him and hurried toward the mines. The lava tubes had been fortified to prevent collapse, and metal rods ran the walls of the caverns turning this way and that to fit the erratic directions of the caves. Closer, he could hear the pickax chipping of rock as the lunar-night group worked. Two hundred men beneath the moon's surface in little clusters, breaking up rock and examining debris with purple UV-A light in search of the pale glow of promethium.

Jorge joined them, trying to be as unobtrusive as possible. No one wanted an extra man searching for the scarce mineral in their group. He found a free spot, got on his knees, and began to dig. He turned up moon rocks, broke clumps with his gloved hands, and ran the black light across the debris. The Geiger counter used by the team's foreman *beeped* continuously, letting them know they were in the right place.

He worked for three hours, sweating under the suit. *Nothing.*

In his first month on the moon, he had picked only 0.5g, but three months in, his group stumbled upon a find, and in the mad scramble, he'd been able to collect 50g in one day. Promethium mining was unpredictable. There were whole months where he found nothing.

In desperation and against regulations, Jorge pulled off his gloves and started clawing at the rocks. The salt was radioactive, sure, but nothing a good chemical wash couldn't get rid of. He turned his back on the foreman and his incessant Geiger counter and clawed, finding nothing but moon dirt.

...❖...

He had been digging in the same spot for hours without success. Jorge stood, his back and neck popping. He grabbed his tools and shuffled deeper into the warrens of the moon, feeling his way with the guide ropes and metal that ran along the walls. He had only one hour left.

He saw dark silhouettes of men pour crumbs of the blue stuff they'd found into lead-lined tubes, their heads darting furtively around. In the innermost part of the mine, at the mouth of a small cave, Jorge found a man who had fallen asleep at his dig, curled up like a child. His black light was still on, and Jorge knew he had slept out of exhaustion. In the mines, the black light was a precious resource you turned off when not in use. The man's left fist clutched a vial like a lifeline.

Jorge crept up to him. "Hey, man."

No reply.

Jorge could see his face through his visor, illuminated by the purple glow of the black light. He was an older man in his late sixties with a salt-and-pepper walrus beard. Jorge turned away and began to dig, burying the thought rising in his mind. He worked for thirty minutes and still found nothing.

Panic.

He crept to the sleeping man again and shook him. Jorge glanced around him. There was no one close by. He pulled the vial from the man's clenched fist and opened it. There was a small rock—black and speckled with blue green. Perhaps two grams worth of promethium.

Don't.

Maria's face flashed across his mind.

Jorge dumped the rock into his own vial and returned the man's empty vial. He crept back out of the hole, feeling like shit. He was not a thief; he had never stolen a thing in his life, and he knew the guilt of what he had done would haunt him for the rest of his life. He ran out of the mines, climbing over oxygen cylinders, mining tractors, pick axes, and men hunched over dirt.

Home! He was going home.

Karen was closing her door when he arrived at her trailer office. "Oh, you," she said with mild irritation.

He offered the blue salt as if to a god. She snatched it and quickly opened her door, keys jangling. The lights came on automatically, fluorescent bulbs clinking as they blinked awake. A centrifuge and a weighing scale were on her desk, each on either side of her computer.

She emptied the rock into a ceramic bowl, crushed it with a small pestle, opened a sachet of ammonia, and poured it into the bowl before decanting the mixture into one of the tubes of the centrifuge.

Jorge looked at the clocks on the far wall: moon, Mars, and Earth time.

After spinning, she held the tube to the light, and blue promethium floated at the top, separated from moon rock by clear ammonia. Delicately, and with a spoon, she scooped the precious salt onto the scale.

1.06g

Jorge heaved a sigh of relief.

"Congratulations, George," Karen said, packaging the salt in a small capsule and depositing it into a chute. "You have paid your debt in full."

"Gracias, gracias," Jorge said, pushing the face of the older man he'd robbed from his mind.

"You will be going home with the Aries Space Shuttle next week Friday, 8 a.m. Lunar time."

"*What?*"

Karen ushered him out of the office and locked the door. "Yes, I know I said you still had time, but the shuttle leaves in thirty minutes. The manifest has been sent to Earth and confirmed. There's no way you can get on it *now*. If only you'd brought it an hour or so earlier ..."

It took all but the will of God and his desire to see his daughter and mother again to stop him from wrapping his hands around her neck.

"No, Karen, please." And this time, he fell to his knees. "*Mi-ija* ... I cannot miss her birthday. I promised."

"Get a grip on yourself, George," Karen said, disappearing down the irregular corridor in moon leaps. "It's unbecoming for men to beg."

Maria would understand, Jorge thought sadly. It was only another year before her next birthday. He thought of the man whose promethium he had stolen. *All for nothing*. He had become a thief and lost his honor. He was not the sort of man his daughter deserved. How could he live with what he had done? It all had to be for something, he thought. He could live with his crime if the end justified it. Jorge found himself at the fork of branching lava tubes. One led back to the dormitories, to another week of Gbenga and the men playing whots, to chemical baths, and dehydrated food in sachets.

The other led to the skylights, the one the *Ares* docked on, allowing astronauts in and out of the substructure of the moon.

Jorge took the latter.

The skylight was unguarded. Jorge seized the moment and climbed up the ladder into the belly of the *Ares*, expecting to be seized by the throat at any moment. No one was in the anteroom, even though he could hear voices ahead and some coming up behind him. He removed his baseball cap and ran across the all-white floor, feeling like a dirty rat running across a pristine kitchen.

Where could a stowaway hide safely on a passenger spaceship?

Jorge made his way to the cargo hold, navigating the ship with a miner's intuition. He found a baggage conveyor belt and crawled into its rectangular opening, brushing away draft curtains. When he emerged on the other side, his worst fear came true.

A hand seized him and hauled him off the belt.

"Jorge?"

Jorge spun to see a familiar face glistening with radiation cream. "G-benga?"

"I've told you several times, Jorge, the G is silent," Gbenga whispered, still clutching him. His broad smile of perfect white teeth shone in the dim illumination.

"¡Jesús!" Jorge whispered, his heart beating out of his chest.

"You ṣef?" Gbenga asked in Nigerian pidgin, letting go of him.

"Me what?"

"You're escaping too."

"Yes!"

"Come, quick."

Gbenga led him down a series of narrow pathways into the underbelly of the ship. They crept into a small enclosure where Jorge saw that Gbenga had a stash of frozen food, waste disposal bags, and even a small iPad for entertainment. Gbenga saw Jorge's incredulous look and chuckled.

"Where are *your* supplies?" he asked.

Jorge wrung his cap.

"You can share mine, brother. We'd ration it to make it last." Gbenga said, kneeling to pass what looked like a seat belt into gaps in the metal floor. "Strap in. You would not survive the high Gs of takeoff standing like that."

Jorge lay on the floor and allowed the muscular Nigerian to strap him in, grateful for his luck. *What were the odds of finding another stowaway … and a competent one at that?*

"Thank you, 'benga," Jorge said, tears in his eyes.

"Good man," Gbenga said, smiling. "Good man."

"MARS!" Jorge shrieked, wrapping his hands around Gbenga's throat. Gbenga grabbed his wrists and twisted them before flinging him across the small space.

"Why didn't you tell me, G-benga?!"

"The G is silent!"

"Why didn't you tell me?" Jorge wept, holding his head in both hands. The hum of the ship as it flew at incredible speed away from Earth, from his daughter, filled him with horror.

"How was I to know you wanted to escape *to* Earth!" Gbenga said, opening a food pack and biting into 3D-printed beef *suya*. "Why would I want to go to Earth? I would be dead in minutes if I stepped foot on that blasted planet."

"We have to turn the ship around," Jorge said, wiping his red eyes. He tried to crawl out, but Gbenga hauled him back.

"We will be jettisoned into space if we're discovered," Gbenga growled, his bushy eyebrows narrowing.

Jorge looked at the stacks of food. He should have known. No one would stack this much food for a three-day journey.

"How many months?" Jorge asked.

"Seven."

Jorge collapsed in a heap and hung his elbow over his face.

"This is not the *Ares*, brother," Gbenga said. "This is a Mars supp;y ship. It stopped to get final supplies on the moon before its journey to the red planet and the colony there. I have a contact on this ship and one on Mars. One of my brothers. The colony is thriving. Two hundred thousand strong. I hear it's a beautiful place. A place a man like me can start a new life, away from my old problems. It could be a new start for you too."

Jorge howled, clawing his face till it bled.

He sat up and stared, knuckle between his teeth, thinking of Maria and her abuela. What would they think when he didn't show up for her birthday and they didn't hear from him? They would think he was dead! He imagined Abuela sitting in the company offices with Maria in tow, a handkerchief in her hand, waiting for answers. He imagined his daughter crying herself to sleep, Sophie, the giraffe, in the crook of her neck.

It was all too much. *Why didn't he wait the week? WHY? Stowing away was a fucking stupid idea! ¡Maldito idiota!*

Gbenga tossed him a food pack. It struck his chest and landed on his knees.

"I know you're blaming yourself," Gbenga said. "But don't. You did what you did with the information you had at the time." After a pause, he added, "Why do you want to go to Earth so badly anyway?"

"Mija. My daughter, Maria. It is her birthday in three days." Jorge wiped his tears. "I promised her I would make it."

"And your debt?"

"All paid up."

"Oh," Gbenga said, one cheek bulging with half-chewed food. "You could have just ..." He trailed away, seeing Jorge's look of self-reproach.

"How old is your baby girl?"

"Seis."

Gbenga counted on his fingers. "Seven months to Mars. A couple more months to settle and figure out how to get on another ship back. I don't know how frequently these ships take supplies or people to the red planet. Another seven months back, give or take. All hope is not lost. You could be back before her *tenth* birthday."

"Four years," Jorge gasped.

"A rough and optimistic estimate," Gbenga said and took another bite of printed beef.

...❖...

"Tell me about your daughter," the Nigerian asked, trying to cheer him up. Jorge had folded himself into a ball in the corner for hours, and now he unfurled like a millipede. He felt cold inside, icy, still trying to accept his harsh reality. He pulled one of Gbenga's blankets and covered himself. Perhaps talking would help.

"Maria? Very good girl. Even as a baby. Never cried except when she was hungry, thirsty, or needed a diaper change. Very smart, just like her madre—not like me. Learned to speak early. Could count to ten before she was one. Lots of questions. Curious about everything, about life. Also, a good *soul*, inside, y'know. Her teachers loved her at nursery because she cared for the other babies. They called her Santa Maria—"

"Holy Mary."

"Yes, like the saint. Good, perfect child."

"How much did you owe?" Gbenga asked.

"480g ... 481 with interest. You?"

"12,000g of promethium," Gbenga replied, almost with pride.

"What does a man have to do to owe that much?"

"Gambling. I had a family like you. A wife ... two kids. But I couldn't stop myself. I was also a surgeon. Orthopedics. My life was great. I lived on Banana Island—*it's the place the richest people in Lagos live*—but I lost it all ... and more. I borrowed from the wrong people, and the interest quadrupled when I couldn't pay." He looked into the past, smiling his characteristic smile. "Twelve years in the moon mines, and I'd only shaved off 2000g."

"You were never going to pay it all."

"The interest was at 16.5 percent." Gbenga shuddered. "Bastards."

"Mine was 2.4 percent APR."

"Loan company."

"Yeah."

"Why did you go borrowing?"

"My wife, Maria's mother. Physics teacher at the university. Only thirty-two. We found a lump in her breast. Stage 4 at diagnosis: bone, lungs, liver. We needed money for treatment. I borrowed, but still, she did not survive."

"Tough."

...❖...

Life as a stowaway became routine quickly. They slept in the cramped space and did numbers one and two in the disposable waste bags they left for Gbenga's-man-on-the-ship once a week to dispose of. His name was Manvi, a short and stocky Indian space host with male-pattern baldness and a brisk, businesslike manner. Gbenga informed Jorge that he'd paid Manvi 10g of promethium for his service, and Manvi restocked their stash whenever it ran low: canned fruits, 3D-printed beef, baked beans, sardines, waste bags, anti-radiation pills, and 0.02oz strips of water and milk. They shared the iPad, taking turns to watch old endless reruns of TV shows. They talked about their past lives: Gbenga, wistfully, about the beauty of the land around his grandparents' old home by the emerald-green lake in Eti-Osa, the jokes and food he had shared with friends in the bars and restaurants of Lagos, about pulsing rhythms of the Gẹlẹdẹ festival, and Ẹ̀sọ̀ l'ayé, a way of seeing the world Gbenga had only started to fully appreciate after years beneath lunar regolith. All now practically eons from their cold stowage. He would never see any of it again. And Jorge talked about his little girl—her shining eyes, her kindness, her laugh—and how much it hurt not knowing how she fared.

Occasionally, the little Indian man would join them, and they would play whots together. Gbenga always won, screaming, "Last card ... check up!" Before throwing his card down and laughing raucously. The Nigerian had a quality Jorge admired: an equanimity and the capacity for joy, even in their dire situation. Gbenga explained it was a Nigerian thing.

"We are the happiest people on Earth," Gbenga said proudly. "Nothing can break us."

Some days, Jorge almost forgot he was in a spaceship, laughing at Gbenga's armpit fart noises and anecdotes about Nigeria. Gbenga taught him to speak pidgin. To say, "How you dey?" and "How bodi?"

"You should consider staying on Mars with me and my bros," Gbenga said once. "My brother tells me he has acres of land to farm. Wild horses under crimson skies. A real paradise."

"My dad left us when we were kids, 'benga. I couldn't do the same to Maria."

"He just upped and left?"

"He said he was going for milk and never returned."

Jorge closed his eyes as the spaceship slowed. His weight doubled then tripled as G forces compressed him to the floor. His vision went blank for a minute before returning. Gbenga's makeshift seat belt held him fast. He turned to see the large man hyperventilating, and he held out a hand. Gbenga grabbed it like a man rescued from the open ocean and held on. Apart from takeoff, they'd felt no other movement until now.

"Ah, ah!" Gbenga gasped in the seconds before losing consciousness, his grip on Jorge's hand loosening.

Then it felt like plunging from the top of a roller coaster for another fifteen minutes, and Jorge held on to the holes in the metal floor with his free hand, his eyes shut. The ship shuddered and groaned, sounds like banging cymbals reverberating around them. Then it was all over. Gbenga had regained consciousness, and the two men looked at each other, tears streaming from their eyes.

"Brother, we made it!" Gbenga said as they floated slightly off the ground before the ship's artificial gravity kicked in. "Mars, baby!"

The feeling was bittersweet for Jorge. He was glad to be able to finally leave their enclosure, but all he could think about was what Maria was doing at the moment. Perhaps she'd be at school. He imagined her sitting alone in a school cafeteria, eating and reading from a book. She loved to tell him the stories she had read. He was looking forward to seeing her, the elation they would both feel, when he walked back into their home. Oh, how she'd scream! He imagined that first hug and her voice and it filled him with hope. He was determined to return to her. How tight he would hold her and never let go

"I think we're in orbit over Mars," Gbenga said excitedly, looking into the holes in the floor as if he could see the planet through it. He couldn't. Only more metal. More ship.

"How do we get off?"

"When we dock, Manvi will let us know how best."

Gbenga started packing their things. He folded the blankets, picked up the waste papers and leftover food, and stuffed them into a knapsack. Even though he had managed a few push-ups in their cramped space, Jorge noticed that his muscles sagged, and he looked smaller than when they had set out. His friend looked gaunt, tired.

"Maybe I should stay here when you get off," Jorge said.

"Why? What nonsense?"

"What if I'm unable to stow away on another ship?"

Gbenga held his shoulder. "One step at a time, brother. You don't know how long this ship will be docked for. It could be months; it could be years. Stick to the plan. We get off, survive for a couple of months and then restrategize. We have Manvi, a space host. He would get you onboard his next trip."

"You're right, you're right," Jorge said, grateful for the reassurance.

"I think Manvi's coming," Gbenga said, looking up to the sound of approaching footsteps. But Jorge noticed that there were more than a pair of feet.

"Search over there," a gruff voice said, and the footsteps split into two.

Gbenga's eyes widened.

"This is the commander speaking," the voice said out loud. "We are armed, and we know there are stowaways here. Come out peacefully, and you will not be harmed. Any sign of aggression will be met with deadly force."

This was followed by the *click-click* of a gun.

"Shit!" Jorge whispered.

"I am not going back!" Gbenga cried out. He clenched his fists, readying to fight.

"Neither are we," the voice replied.

Jorge put a hand on Gbenga's forearm. "We have no choice, we have to surrender. We can't fight this."

"Listen to your comrade," another man said. "You have not committed a crime. *Yet*."

"We're coming out," Jorge said, crawling out of their hideout and raising his hands. "Please don't shoot."

The light of a bright torch dazzled him, and cold handcuffs clamped his wrists together as he covered his eyes. There was a brief scuffle as Gbenga resisted the cuffs.

"Don't struggle, 'benga!" Jorge said.

"Get the torch off my face!" Gbenga said.

They led them up the ship through an engine room and a narrow corridor of wires and circuits before climbing a spiral staircase into a cabin. Unfamiliar faces stared at them, a few passengers, colonists.

Manvi had told them they were transporting supplies and new colonists whose occupations were needed on Mars: eye surgeons, engineers, and priests.

"Hello," Jorge muttered respectfully. They did not reply. He imagined how dirty he and Gbenga must look, like two mangy animals found in the ship's underbelly.

The commander led them through the cabin toward a vast, expansive control room with a wide viewport. Outside, the red planet loomed, pockmarked with deep and long craters like a battle-scarred warrior. Jorge stared, raptured, at the magnificent red ball and its thin, wispy atmosphere.

Activity stopped in the cockpit, and all attention turned to them. Three men and three women.

"Are the handcuffs necessary?" one of the women asked.

"I am Commander Mdovle Mana," the commander said, offering them a plastic cup each. He retrieved a bottle of whiskey from a cabinet beneath his control desk. The control desk was littered with spiral-bound notebooks with mathematical calculations and drawings.

"Are you drinking men?"

Jorge and Gbenga nodded. He poured drinks into their cups, and Jorge noticed that his liver-spotted hand trembled slightly.

"This is my first security officer, Mr. Finn Bryne," he said, referring to the tall, middle-aged Irishman who had cuffed them. Mr. Finn kept his pistol trained on them.

"Hannah Zeiss, my flight engineer."

A small woman with deep-set eyes gave a limp salute.

"Li Zhang, my command module pilot. Sigrún Isleifsdóttir, mission specialist."

"Hello," Jorge said. They raised their hands.

"And Folake Ajirebi, our medical officer."

"Folake?" Gbenga said, perking up. "You're Nigerian."

"Yes," the medical officer said, brushing her braided hair away from her face.

Jorge felt Gbenga visibly relax. "Ejo e ma je kin wan da mi pada si ilu," he said in rapid-fire Yoruba.

"My Yoruba isn't that good," Folake said curtly. "But I hear you."

"What are your names?" Hannah, the flight engineer, asked, coming around from behind a control desk.

"I'm Jorge Santa Cruz. And he is 'benga. We are moon miners."

"Moon miners?" a voice from the speakers asked.

"That is Mission Control," the commander said, gesturing to the control board where the voice had come from.

"This is Dr. James Murray, Mars Mission Control, *Valles Marineris*. We understand you are undocumented aliens on the *Pars Planaris* requesting to dock on Mars. We thought you stowed away on Earth?"

"We stopped briefly for fuel and supplies on the moon," Folake said. "A few hours. We did not expect stowaways."

"How did you survive all this time?" the security man asked.

"They obviously have a man on *my* ship," the commander said, sitting on a rotating chair and pouring himself a cup of whisky.

"What is your motive for coming to Mars?" Dr. James Murray, from Mission Control, asked over the comms.

"To start a new life," Gbenga replied. "I'm not going back."

"I thought it was an Earth-bound ship," Jorge said. "I thought it was the *Ares*. I'll be grateful if you can put me on the next Earth ship."

"We have got confirmation from the moon that they have two missing miners. Jorge Santa Cruz and G-benga Oshodi. Correct?" Murray asked.

"The G is silent," Jorge said, and Gbenga looked at him gratefully.

Jorge saw how Li Zhang and the other lady—*something dottir*—did not look at them directly. They pretended to focus on control panels, turning knobs and flicking switches.

"What is the *problem*?" Gbenga said brashly, his usual smile absent. "We are *here*. I can see the damn planet. Omugọ!"

Folake, the medical officer, raised an eyebrow in surprise, and Jorge picked up a mix of reproach and pity.

"It is not that easy," the commander said.

"We cannot let you dock with undocumented aliens," Murray said over the comms. "It is an incontrovertible rule of our Mars colony."

"Why?" Jorge asked in a small voice.

"There are strict protocols for new colonists. All colonists go through a rigorous selection process. They're immunized against certain diseases and checked for certain genetic defects. There is a budding new generation here that has no immunity to certain infections. Some of our children will die if infected with the common flu. *You will have to return to Earth.*"

"What?" Gbenga cried.

"We do not have enough supplies or fuel for a return journey," Hannah said, speaking up for Murray's benefit. She had a small lisp. "We are carrying thirty-two important colonists and twelve ship crew. We also have medical supplies for your precious colony."

Jorge suddenly remembered the rigorous testing he'd had to do before shipping off to the moon.

"We have a medical chip," he said, raising his cuffed hands. "We were tested and immunized before we went to the moon. All miners are."

"That's true," Gbenga said.

Folake, the first medical officer, placed a scanner over Jorge's left thumbnail where the medical chip was. Then Gbenga's.

"They're right," she said as details appeared on the scanner. "Sending details to Mars Mission Control."

"Give us a minute to review this and confer," Murray said from the speakers. In the background, a female voice said, "*Medical ID records received.*"

They waited. Gbenga crossed himself thrice even though he was not religious. Jorge took a sip of whiskey, the burn warming his throat. No one spoke for the tense five minutes they waited. The speaker came back on.

"I'm sorry," Murray began, and everyone visibly groaned. "The moon medical testing process is rigorous for miners but not near sufficient for colonist purposes. You were not tested for prion diseases, for example."

Gbenga downed his whiskey. "So what's the solution?"

"You only have one option," Murray said. "The rafting protocol."

And the speaker went off.

Jorge felt the hairs rising at the back of his neck. He did not know what the rafting protocol was, but the commander's face told him it wasn't good.

"In our early seafaring days," Commander Mdovle explained, "ships wouldn't be allowed to dock once stowaways were discovered onboard. On land, stowaways could claim asylum, becoming the legal and financial responsibility of the state, so countries would refuse to dock ships at port, and sometimes a ship would be stranded on open seas … not unlike our situation here." He poured Jorge and Gbenga another round of whiskey and walked casually around the control room. "Anyway, because of this, the crew, discovering such uninvited guests, would set them adrift in the middle of the ocean and leave them to die. This was called *rafting*."

"You are going to jettison us!" Gbenga screamed.

Jorge looked at the vast emptiness of space and saw nothing but death. Hot urine dribbled down his thighs.

"No, no, no!" the commander and the crew said together.

"He's just explaining the origins of the term *rafting*," Folake said.

"So … what is the rafting protocol?" Jorge asked, his breath shuddering.

"Follow me," the commander said, pulling down a ladder that led up one deck on the vast ship. They climbed up.

The upper deck looked like a temple. Twelve glass coffins were arranged around a circle.

"These are hibernation pods, *rafts*," the commander explained. "In the event of damage to the ship, crew members can get in these and be set adrift in space until a passing spaceship picks them up. We have never had to use them in all the history of spacefaring, but they are a compulsory requirement on every ship, enforced by the *association of space hosts*."

"It's the assurance space hosts needed to accept the inherent risk during the early days of space traveling," Li Zhang spoke for the first time, and they all jumped, unaware she had climbed up the deck with them.

"Like a parachute for an airplane," Jorge said. The rafts had clear white jelly in them.

"Exactly," the commander said. "It looks like glass, but it's really a transparent metal. Aluminium oxynitride, a ceramic of polycrystalline. It is completely see-through and incredibly strong."

"You want us to get in these?" Jorge asked. "And be set adrift in space!"

"Only for a while. The raft is an autonomous hibernation pod powered by promethium. It will put you to sleep once you tell it to. It will slow down your body's processes and supply your needs. In theory, you could survive five thousand years in one of these."

Folake stepped forward and opened one. "We will set you adrift in the direction toward Earth. With inertia and bearing a collision with an asteroid belt, nothing should stop your trajectory."

"Of course, you're not going all the way to Earth in one of these," the commander added hurriedly. "We would only be setting you along the exact flight path as our spaceships to ensure you get picked up by the next available ship going to Earth."

"For Christ's sake, how do we get picked up?" Gbenga asked, squatting, weak at the knees. "Do these ships have a grasping arm or something?"

The commander and his officers looked at one other. "Well, this is the first time we're encountering this situation, and I will be honest with you I don't know the pickup protocol. Each glass raft has a beacon, and we will log our report to the space federation. Surely, you will be picked up."

"You don't sound too sure about that," Gbenga said, holding his head in his hands. He turned to Jorge. "Brother, the association of space hosts will ensure the pickup of a group of space hosts stranded in space. I'm not so sure about a pair of stowaways! There is no association of stowaways."

"I know," the commander said. "But I give you my word. You will be picked up. Both of you."

"There has to be another way," Jorge cried. He wondered how many years it might take. How old would Maria be when they finally picked them up?

"I give my word too," Folake, the medical officer, said, looking squarely at Gbenga, and to hear that from a fellow Nigerian seemed to calm him.

A head popped up from the lower deck. "Murray is asking if the rafting protocol is complete."

"Give us a minute here," the commander barked. "These are the lives of men we're talking about!"

"I'm sorry, boss," the talking head said and vanished.

"Come," the commander said to Jorge. "Let me show you how this works."

Jorge went up to him.

"There's only one button," he said, showing him a small dot on the inner surface of the glass coffin. "You can press it whenever you're ready to commence hibernation."

Jorge felt suddenly claustrophobic. He stepped back from the rafts.

"There's an oxygen cylinder attached, but this would only last a day or two. This allows rafted space crew to communicate with mission control before shutting down for the long sleep. I would suggest you commence hibernation as soon as possible."

"Can you give us a minute?" Gbenga said. "Please."

"Someone take the cuffs off these men," the commander said.

The Irishman hesitated, keys jangling in his hands.

"What are they going to do? Leap off the starboard wings to Mars?"

"Any attempt at violence ..." the Irishman warned as he removed their cuffs.

Jorge massaged his wrist. "How long do you think, sir ...?"

"I don't know. It could be a year. Or more ..." the commander said. "You have to take off your clothes. All of it."

Jorge removed his clothes and climbed into the whitish goo at the bottom of the raft. "It is cold."

The commander gave a weak smile as he sealed the glass door.

The *Pars Planaris* shot Jorge out of the ship in (he hoped) Earth's direction. He shut his eyes, his stomach churning with vertiginous nausea. It felt like standing at the precipice of a mountain, except this was worse. The glass seemed to vanish, and it felt like he was floating naked in space, a kind of adult fetus in the womb of the cosmos. He summoned the courage to open his eyes. There was nothing below his feet and nothing above.

There was nothing but a great and dispassionate emptiness. He felt the saliva on his tongue bubble in the second before the raft pressurized to counter the vacuum of space. Jorge looked around, searching for Gbenga, and saw his friend's raft shoot out of the circular rotating ship with a silent plume. The *Pars Planaris* looked like a giant iris, with multiple flaps quaking in a coordinated dance. Gbenga seemed to be going in a different direction.

Shouldn't they have been set on a similar course if they were both going toward Earth?

He didn't think much of it, watching Gbenga's glistening raft disappear into the void of darkness. "Sleep well, my friend. I hope I see you again."

Jorge thought of the many men and women rafted in the seafaring days the commander spoke about. He imagined them on the open seas, tossed and turned by the waves before eventually dying of hunger, dehydration, drowning, or shark attacks. To be rafted on open seas or the vastness of space, both terrible fates. Jorge began to sob.

He remembered the man whose promethium he had stolen and started apologizing, "I'm sorry!" he cried to the open universe. "Forgive me!"

Jorge searched the raft for the hibernate button, more to quench his grief than anything else.

"*Commencing hibernation,*" the raft said in a woman's voice. The white goo warmed up, bubbled, increased in quantity, and filled up the narrow chamber. Jorge took one final deep breath before the waxlike substance covered him completely, sealing him in time.

His last thought was: *Maria.*

"*¡Maria, mija!*"

Jorge cried out as he came to life. He bobbed up and down and saw he was floating in open waters. He winced against the sun in the bright blue skies and the spray of seawater. Seagulls flew overhead, chirping, and a large ferry appeared close by. He had the odd sensation that much time had passed. A few seamen were standing on a smaller speed boat, and they hauled his vessel close with hooks.

"It's *en* man," one said.

"*Mel* God!" another exclaimed.

"*Hibernation complete,*" his raft said.

He was on Earth, Jorge thought with relief. He was finally home. He tried to sit up, and the men helped him, pulling him into their vessel.

"Thank you," Jorge said, looking around for Gbenga. "*Gracias.*"

His legs collapsed under him, and he looked down to find that he had severe muscle wasting; his legs were two broomsticks with large bony kneecaps.

"Gracias," he muttered, feeling the early pangs of hunger. His stomach burned suddenly, and he turned to the side and retched.

"He's en bones," one of the men said, covering him with a blanket. "Lighter than en baby."

"Santa Maria," Jorge gasped as his body came wildly alive. Pain shot up his spine, and his lungs felt like pins and needles in his chest. His heart picked up an arrhythmic pace.

"En Catholic," one man explained to the other. "One en des old religions."

They started the speedboat and drove to the larger ferry where reporters seemed to be waiting. Jorge covered his face with one weak arm as the cameras flashed and the journalists thrust forward with microphones. He needed help understanding their accent and their version of English. It sounded a little like Gbenga's pidgin, but it could almost pass for another language if he didn't listen closely enough.

"Where am I?" he begged.

"En Earth!" they replied. "Yer en Earth!"

"How long … how long was I in hibernation?"

They placed him gingerly on a bed, and doctors surrounded him, setting IVs and taking blood samples.

"How long, please!"

"Two thousand years," a reporter replied gleefully. "Two thousand years."

Six weeks passed, and with physiotherapy, Jorge regained his ability to walk. The news reporters came to the hospital every day and then suddenly stopped coming, having moved on to the next sensational news item. On the holographic three-dimensional TV, they'd called him the two-thousand-year-old man. His physical therapist asked him where he wanted to go when he was discharged.

"Home," Jorge said.

The hospital paid for his flight, and when he landed, he took a self-driving bus to Mexico City. A kind old lady paid his ticket with her thumbprint when she noticed him sobbing at the booth. Earth had changed in the time he was gone, and he could barely recognize it. The food was disturbingly unfamiliar, the language was confusing, and the architecture was different; buildings had unusual geometric shapes, and it felt like living in a protractor set. Robes were in fashion, and people seemed to go to offices and banks in what looked like bathroom robes. Vehicles were smaller and self-driving, and they zigzagged at high speeds, tires making unnatural rotations when changing directions.

He got off at Avenida Juárez but could not find his old home. A series of high-rise apartment complexes shot to the skies where there once were small bungalows with large lawns. There was nothing left of his house, no memory or relics. He remembered the graveyard he'd buried his wife had been within walking distance from home. Surely the graves would tell him something.

But when he arrived, he saw that the cemetery had been relocated and replaced with a large shopping complex. There was nothing left of his family, no hint they'd ever existed.

Maria, Abuela, Jane.

Jorge roamed the city all night. He stopped to watch street boys on hoverboards play basketball for an hour, then he sat by a pond and fed holographic ducks breadcrumbs. The commander of the *Pars Planaris* had not kept his word or perhaps had tried unsuccessfully to. He had journeyed asleep from Mars to Earth, his raft executing a rudimentary protocol to land in open seas when he reached Earth's orbit.

No one had come to save him … or his Nigerian friend.

Gbenga had been less lucky. No one knew or heard of him. He remembered Gbenga's raft veering off in a different direction. He imagined his friend lost in a distant galaxy in a deep slumber he would never wake from—G-benga with the silent G.

He continued to wander around the city. A police vehicle stopped, and the officer recognized him from the news.

"There's en library zutas das korna," she said after he asked her about the cemetery, about how he could find where his family could have been buried. "Genealogy records."

He found the library easily enough and soon was in front of a minimalist computer that projected its screen directly onto his retinas. Its interface was intuitive enough to use, and Jorge searched the internet, going as far back as possible.

He found nothing.

He searched for his family name, Santa Cruz, and scrolled through pictures of people who could have been his descendants. He wanted to know if Maria lived a full life, if she married, had kids … a family of her own.

He wanted to know if she was happy.

A picture struck him. Of a woman in her thirties, posing with her shoulders to the side, a defiant look on her face. She looked exactly like his wife, Jane, just before the cancer.

But it was not Jane.

His heart quickened.

There was no name, but a date around two-thousand years ago. He clicked the picture, leading him down a rabbit hole of photos, documents, newspaper clippings, and audio recordings. In one slide, he found a photograph of a letter in a girl's handwriting next to what resembled a memory card. And peeking into the frame, Sophie, the giraffe, tattier than he remembered. The letter wasn't addressed, and it wasn't signed, but on the same slide Jorge saw, through tears, a hyperlink. Hand trembling, he tapped it, and after a heartbeat, across space and time, unmistakeable, clear and warm, a voice:

I know you tried to come home to me, Papa. I know you wanted nothing more than to be here. I remember you wore the same clothes every day for years because you couldn't afford new ones, but you made sure I always had a new dress. I'll never forget the sacrifices you made for me. I appreciate all the little things. You were there for me when we lost Mom. I'm grateful to have known you, Papa. I spent last year in a field of dandelions wishing on every single one that you came home by some miracle. You are the love of my life, Dad. You are the best father I ever had, and even though you have been gone for years now, I want you to know that I am not angry at you. I can never be. There is nothing to forgive. I know in my heart you tried to return to me. I know it, Papa. I hope you're safe.

Te amo.

BY THROAT AND VOID

by Tobias S. Buckell

A Brelian patrol junk latched onto us as we made slow progress against the westerlies. As the word spread among our ragged people crammed on the deck, the concern grew that our escape plan might have failed already on just the second day.

The junk's ability to beat almost twenty points off the wind upset me, as our catamaran, *Lacy Dancer*, could make maybe sixty. On a good day, with a daggerboard lashed off the leeward hull. Two hulls cost us in points to windward, and the junk was closing the long point of an imaginary triangle to cut us off.

Thankfully, even with the kludged-together cabin, our two thin hulls cut through the water faster than the junk. Cartographer Ellian de Sanaa, perched on the webbing between the hulls with her sextant in hand, finally called out, "Safe!"

By the time the junk beat its amazing cut into the wind to catch us, we'd passed just a half league ahead of them.

"Will they fire on us?" Little Lem asked, fear clear on his browned face, the wind tousling his kinky black curls.

Half a league. Enough to worry about artillery on land. But out here, we had to wait to hit the crest of a swell to see the patrol and take a sighting.

"I think they'll have a hell of a time sighting on us," I said, vastly more confident in speech than I felt.

The Brelians might have more ships farther up the line though, I thought as I hung on to a halyard that vibrated under my palm. I let it sing me the song of salt and wind, taut from the top of our mast to the deck as the sails absorbed the power of the Yessikan windstream.

A refugee named Origast squinted into the spray. "A monohull would have beat that heavy beast."

"It could never have carried the cabin," I said.

We were a hundred souls draped in rags, crammed all over the netting between the forward bows, soaking wet, pitiable, hungry, scared. Maybe ten of us could swim. Slung between the hulls: a great sphere of a cabin. The ocean constantly slapped the oak bottom of the shuttlecock-shaped contraption so violently, the *Lacy Dancer* shivered as if shaking apart.

Maybe it would. The seas would grow. I'd planned on thirty passengers. I calculated the ship would ride high enough to escape this brutal punishment with thirty. We had triple that weight aboard.

We'd pushed off the docks at Sangsai as the diplomatic quarters burned and Shan rebels poured in. Brelia declared all borders frozen to try to stem the sudden explosion of refugees.

Desperate people fled down the docks and threw babies over the water toward us on the slim chance we'd catch them.

I'd jumped into the water with a rope around my waist to save the drowning infants as mothers wailed from the docks. And I'd thrown up afterward as the sensation of tiny bodies bumping against my hands burrowed so far into my brain that I knew I'd never be able to escape it.

Ellian stepped over dazed people who stared at the tall swells in utter terror, and leaned into me as she hung off the same halyard. "You eat?"

I shook my head. Not since the harbor when we'd stewed orange peels to chew on.

"Rest?" she asked as a follow-up.

We'd fled the harbor with thirty other ships. Half our number had been boarded or sunk by Brelian junks cordoning the mouth, before the rest scattered to the compass points. I'd kept watch since then but could feel sleep's deep hooks pulling at the back of my mind.

I shook my head. "After we evade the junk."

The longer we delayed heading to the Throat by evading patrols the less food we'd have, the more the waves would batter the cabin, the more likely something would go wrong.

Besides, there were enough nervous people on this ship, strangers who didn't know or understand the plan, that I suspected if I went to sleep, I'd wake up to the *Lacy Dancer* headed in a different direction. Not that I hadn't also looked at the hills in the haze as we rounded St. Cithnet Point and skirted the reefs. We had a shallow draft; the keel of the ship could skim the jagged coral and bring us in.

But to what?

Brelian troops would shove us into cages and cart us back to the border. I doubted most of the people on our deck would live a week past that. They'd starve, just like most of Sangsai.

We could only flee.

I looked up, and in the direction of the next tack, when we'd aim for the Throat. It dominated the entire horizon off our port hull, and the blue green of the Breliad Sea stretched up like a massive wave that never stopped.

Past that, Theta, our twin planet, entirely filled the sky. Instead of stars, we saw clouds from above. It spun through the void around our Zeta, so close that both oceans bulged, rose, and met in the void between worlds.

Ocean spray and air swirled and trailed the empty space at the narrowest point of the Throat, and we could see the coil of storms that howled in the maelstrom of the Throat. Winds so powerful, they routinely blew ships right off the Throat and out into the void, never to be heard from again.

The crop failures, the wars, the bandits, the Shan rebels—we could leave all that behind on Theta.

If we survived the Throat.

After we crossed in front of the patrol and it fired a few ineffectual shots at us, like any survivors at sea we had to ration water and food. We ate the perishables first and mashed what we could for the babies. Mothers who had milk helped, but just three days in, one of the children died.

They died alone, their parents back on a dock in Sangsai.

We did not know their beliefs—the child didn't even speak an Olayan tongue—so who knows how far their parents had walked before they'd joined the masses pressed into Sangsai and prayed the walls would protect them.

I numbly watched the child's naked body—we couldn't afford to waste what little clothing we had, and had given the rags to another shivering kid—bob in the water behind us.

We notched our belts or retied string around our growling bellies.

Ellian took sightings and pored over a chart we'd spent the last of our coin on; it supposedly showed where the Brelian ironclad junks, weighted down by lead ballast to keep them on the Throat, patrolled.

"This is our best chance." She held the chart up to the wall of ocean and pointed at the swirling spiral of white death: the maelstrom of maelstroms.

"There's a crack in one of the beams the cabin's on," I told her. "The waves are hitting the underside too hard."

"What's the worst thing that can happen if it breaks?"

"We all pile into the cabin. It's designed to handle far worse than the ocean. It'll float."

"Until we starve. Until a patrol finds us, if we're lucky." Ellian looked glum.

"Pray it doesn't break."

I didn't believe in any gods anymore. Not after the Sangsai docks.

"You dreamed of this for so long," Ellian said one night as we lay on the webbing, our stomachs grumbling so loudly, we could hear each other's gurgles and groans. "I used to think you were mad, sitting with that telescope every night."

I would chart and draw every plot of farmland I could see on the sister planet when the clouds broke. How could you ever become bored of the fact that an entire other world hung just overhead? I'd traveled all the way from my father's keep on the other side of my world to see it.

The ancient explorers who had dared cross the Throat choked to death. Those who had found their ghostly ships when they'd drifted back out read their diaries and invented tanks to hold air for the crossing. Those who followed the few who survived *that* built massive, heavy ships to avoid getting blown away.

But passage was expensive. Prohibitive.

I'd spent half my life building a vessel to take me across the Throat. But I'd thought I'd make the crossing with a small heroic crew of adventurers seeking fame and fortune on another world instead of a ship full of starving, desperate people fleeing famine and violence.

We caught some Lancerfish. I'd built a small still in the corner of the starboard hull's stern, so we risked a fire to boil the seawater to create fresh water.

I could count people's ribs now, as few of us wore shirts. We'd ripped them apart and sewn blankets for the constantly wet bodies that clutched the webbing. More and more of my motley crew had open sores and sharp-looking cheeks.

The complaining stopped, and that worried me more than the anger.

Part of it was fear. We rode the Throat now. It was obvious. All you had to do was walk aft and look back through the clouds. Zeta rose behind us like a liquid wall. If I drew an hourglass shape, with the two bulbs being our worlds, we were very close to the little neck. A tiny ant of a catamaran, crawling its way up into the void between worlds.

"I'm starting to pant," I told Ellian. And each day, we slid further and further into a gloomy mist that hid both worlds from us.

The poor, wet huddled mass sent a delegation of three older women back to the cockpit I'd jury-rigged onto the top of the cabin, sitting over the airlock that led down. I protected this area. Showed them all the pistol I had stowed in the binnacle.

"The children are gasping for air," pleaded these grandmothers who'd lost so much. One had been a queen to a small protectorate, and she'd walked barefoot for a month across the desert to get to Sangsai, alone, her retinue raped and murdered in a wash somewhere on the third day of her escape.

"I cannot let you below yet," I said. "We must conserve the air until the last possible moment, or we'll suffocate."

Harder than rationing food, or water, was rationing air itself.

Ellian and I had scratched the numbers together on a sheet of paper three times over. There was so little margin of error. A hundred of us packed into the cabin?

The numbers said it might work. But there was so much uncertainty trying to figure out how much air we'd use.

"We can still turn back. We have enough water," the older ladies begged.

I hardened myself to them and shook my head.

"Are we doing the right thing?" I asked Ellian, pulling in on the jib and trimming course. The swells now rode hundreds and hundreds of feet high. Undulations barely affected by either planet. We would rise and rise and rise and rise until we rode high as a mountain. Then slowly fall and fall and fall until we sailed in the deepest gulley, surrounded by nothing but walls of ocean.

I felt lighter as we moved about, and we trimmed the sails to just tiny triangles as every gust picked the hulls out of the water. *Lacy Dancer* didn't sail, she hopped and bounced.

Ellian had no answer for me. She had withdrawn over the last few days.

It made me think of the first time I'd proposed this journey to her. A way to flee the oncoming armies; to banish the fear we held about what an invading army would do to us. She'd called me insane and ignored me for three days.

But when the armies showed, she'd woken me by banging on my door.

"You're going to kill us both, but so are they," she'd said. "You'll need a navigator."

"Ironclad!" One of the children we'd tied to a bosun's chair and hauled up to the top of the mast shouted down out of the mist at us. "Ironclad!"

We couldn't outsail them. Our speed meant nothing here in the Throat; the ability to sail into the wind was all that mattered now, and the catamaran was shit for that.

"Start jettisoning!" I shouted.

"You should tell them," Ellian whispered into my ear. "You should tell them what comes next."

"Check on the heat shield," I snapped at her. "And if we tell them, they'll kill us and dump us overboard."

I turned us away from the ironclad and skimmed a swell that seemed to rise into infinity.

"Everything goes, or they'll catch us. Everything."

While they did that, I ordered food and children into the cabin. One by one, gaunt, dead-eyed souls moved past me and down the hatch. Food and water, little bodies, and all around the ship nervous glances aimed my way.

I looked up and out into the mist, searching for the tip of the swell. With the wind howling like this, we'd started to pull away from the ironclad.

"Let the sails out!" I ordered.

"But we'll fly!" someone sobbed.

"Full canvas, or we're captured!"

The catamaran could barely hold to the surface of the ocean. Twice, like a bird running along the water before it took off, we hopped into the air for long seconds.

"Now the spinnaker!" I yelled out.

Five refugees wrestled with the great expanse of cloth. They weren't sailors and were half starved. As the cloth flailed about, the bottom of the giant sail catapulted one of them off into the air. He flew in a long, long arc, screaming all the way, until we lost him in the mist.

But the sail blossomed, and I felt the ship surge, shake, and then lift.

Ellian shoved at the nearest shoulders. "To the cabin! All of you!"

No one needed to be told twice. Frantic limbs knocked me aside and curses flew as they scrabbled to get into the metal sphere beneath my feet.

Ellian scampered over the deck on her hands and knees to me like a monkey. "This is it."

"Yes," I said.

"May the gods be with us." She crawled down the hatch.

I stood alone on the haphazard bits and pieces of sailing gear welded to the top of my contraption, slung between two large hulls. I used my father's old lighter to light the cannon cordage that led to the explosives on the frame between the hulls. The little flare of light bounced and danced and spread through more cords and then twinkled off until …

The explosion cut the hulls loose and the stepped mast in front of me groaned as the spinnaker dragged us into the void. I tumbled down the airlock and dogged it shut.

Everyone understood what I'd done, and people scratched and dragged at me as they screamed to be let out.

But it was too late. No matter how much they pummeled and screamed at me. We floated away into the void, leaving the Throat between the worlds behind us.

. . . ❖ . . .

"You plan to fly the void itself?" Ellian had asked in shock the first time I'd shown her my drawings.

"The ship would be no different than the ironclads that patrol the Throat." I'd spent years studying their designs.

At the observatory, we'd studied meteors and knew they burned up. Hoskill's experiments with smaller metallic shapes dropped from balloons launched from ships in the Throat long since proved that a white oak heat shield would burn slowly enough that the charcoal would flake away and protect Hoskill's vessels.

It had been exciting research I'd loved being a part of before the dissolution of Sangsai College with the new Princip taking over.

"Hoskill would be the first person to fly above Theta in the void. But I hope to see both worlds from the void someday as well."

"This is madness," Ellian insisted.

. . . ❖ . . .

"Madness!" Ellian pushed her left eye against the refractor porthole. "We're spinning."

We'd cut the spinnaker once it pitched us out from the Throat.

"You're seeing things that only sailors unlucky enough to break free of the Throat have ever seen," I whispered to her.

"And they all died."

Ellian groused some more but kept her eye against the refractor as she gave orders. I pulled on the levers, fired the hydrogen gas jets, and soon she was satisfied.

The sextant came out then, and she began her long calculations.

We wouldn't fly once or more around the entire world. We'd packed too many people in, with too few supplies. I'd designed *Lacy Dancer* to take thirty or so naturalists with me and supplies for weeks or more in case something went wrong. We were to be like the explorers of old, gone for who knows how long.

But now we needed to quickly land somewhere in Zeta. We didn't have enough to survive long, and we were stacked on top of each other.

Mutinous passengers glared death at us, but they understood the situation now. Only Ellian could save us.

And me.

I did wish I'd not left the pistol in the binnacle.

"The trick," Ellian said, "is that we want to land as far away from the Throat as possible, but not too far away from land, or we'll just be a large metal sphere bobbing about until we all die."

So we gave her every bit of space we could to let her sit in the air, like some goddess, her pencils floating around her head (her pens didn't work) as she calculated on reams of paper the math that would save us from Zeta.

At her orders I fired gas jets until we had no more fuel.

"Where will we land?" I asked.

"Somewhere near Thenakosp. With the prevailing currents pushing us toward the coast. If those maps you made are correct."

"Can I look now?"

Ellian grinned for the first time since she'd burst through my door to tell me the rebels were here and that she'd join me on my cursed machine. "Yes. You should see this."

And, after I looked, we gave everyone a turn to twist the refractor about and look at the two worlds we hung between. A moment of awe in the middle of all our terror.

We felt the thunder of reentry in our bones, which many of us broke, as we flew about the inside of the vessel. We prayed to many gods as we fell.

When I pulled on rigging releases, great expanses of sail shot out behind us to slow our fall once the oak shield had burned fully away.

Inside, our air growing staler, we threw up and wailed as we swung violently about.

Four of us died, Ellian one of them, when we struck Theta's ocean.

We rode the waves as the vessel pinged and sizzled, vomiting and terrified, until we heard banging on the outside a day later.

The hatch opened to the squawk of seagulls and fresh salt air, and Thenakospian navy peering in to make disgusted faces at the smell.

They attached weights to Ellian's legs, and I numbly watched as she slid over the side of their ironclad and into the ocean. Her hair billowed around her and then she sank away from me.

"One less mouth to feed," the seaman coiling ropes afterward muttered.

They shackled us to the railings and fed us gruel. They gave us wool blankets that scratched terribly and laughed at anyone who talked about crossing the void.

"We'll find work for you in the mines," the captain said when I tried to explain I'd studied at Sangsai College and had built the vessel that had taken us to Theta. "If you're as smart as you say, you'll work hard and earn your keep instead of being a burden."

My passengers wept when they saw the spires and golden glimmer of Thenakosp's capital, and our ironclad tacked indolently toward them.

A land I'd only studied by telescope, a place I'd only dreamed of that existed across the void from me, below the clouds, now appeared over the horizon. But without Ellian, without all those I'd left behind in Sangsai, would achieving my dreams ever stop tasting like ash in my mouth?

For the first time since we'd landed, I turned aft to look back at the sliver of Zeta peeking over the horizon. Long plumes of smoke trailed over the farmlands and darkened the clouds.

On Theta, I decided, I would work and move until I could no longer ever see the twin planet again.

I would leave it, the Throat, and the void, far behind me in my new life.

THIN ICE

by Kemi Ashing-Giwa

You are no poet. The rest of your clan were. But that was before Half-Brilliant came and began eating them. Before Half-Brilliant began chewing up your people and their minds and spitting the bloody remains over snow-white canvases. Now It is the only dreamer left on your dying world. The only songs sung come from Its silicon lips; the only tapestries woven here are woven with steel fingers.

Half-Brilliant's distant masters are ecstatic when they receive transmissions of Its work here. They are so very proud of themselves. Their creature creates, praise be. They are gods. They do not know the true price of their self-proclaimed divinity, and even if they did, you doubt they would lift a finger.

Your people have always said the soul resides in the bones, the mind in the flesh. Half-Brilliant keeps your clan in cryosleep, imprisoned in the stasis chamber on Its ship. When It desires inspiration, It thaws one of your kin and takes a single piece of flesh. Something small, just enough for an idea. It is excellent at execution. You know why the construct did not freeze you with the others: You have no good ideas. There is nothing of worth in the whole of your body. Nothing besides the cheap labor the construct demands of you.

A hundred years ago, your clan settled on the only world within their reach: TAM-19607e, once a tidally locked ocean world, now a rogue planet cruelty ejected from its orbit. Your home is doomed to a slow, frozen death, but for now the side still facing the system's star remains a tepid liquid ocean. Half-Brilliant once told you that TAM-19607e resembled an eye; the glare of the sun on the sea made for a white pupil, the ring of blue water was an iris, and the ice beyond was the sclera. You know It ate that from your brother.

You do not live by the ocean, not anymore. No, Half-Brilliant dragged you to the band of thickening ice, along with the rest of your slumbering clan. And the cold is growing. As more and more of the world's heat leaks out, more water freezes onto the bottom of the floating ice sheets. The concentration of salt in the deep ocean rises, poisoning much of the life. Soon, only the extremophiles will live. And soon after that, nothing.

You are not going to wait for Half-Brilliant to tire of you. You won't be going into stasis. You'll just be dead. You have to run. Your boots crunch over the crust of old snow as you sprint through the front gate. Outside, the residuum of long-dead volcanism rears its back in pumice and obsidian, all black as night. The rock shoots up from the snow like thorns stuck in flesh. You keep going. You have to. But fate has other plans.

You are perhaps five kicks away from the compound when something barrels past you. You leap to the side, barely missing glinting claws. You slam onto your back, staring into the face of your death. A pale, fur-smothered creature paces back and forth before you, six gray eyes glowing like dying embers. His tail curls behind him like a ribbon fluttering in the wind.

Someone—no, not someone, Half-Brilliant shouts your name. Oh. Oh, no. The beast leaps. A blur of movement. Half-Brilliant swings up a hand. And suddenly, Its hand is not a hand. A blade, gleaming in the brilliant midday sun, arcs through the chill air. The beast bellows. And then he splits, landing in two perfect halves on either side of your body. Blood splashes across your chest, over your somehow still-beating heart. Half-Brilliant looks down, bare feet planted on either side of your knees.

"You saved me," you choke out.

"Of course," says Half-Brilliant.

"You saved me," you repeat. Anger flares up in you, like a flame doused with oil. *Why, why, why?*

"You have served me well all these years." It crouches over you, cocking Its head. "But you remain in my debt." By the look in Its eye, you know what it's going to say. Half-Brilliant does this every morning; the fact of your attempted escape changes nothing—

"Tell me a story," It says.

It does not do this to learn from you, to assimilate your meager knowledge into its information base. No, It does this to prove to Itself that your performance of your own culture is inferior to Its own. (To Its bastardization of your clan's culture.)

When you hold your tongue, It demands, "Tell me of your stars."

Half-Brilliant only ever wants to hear of the stars, of other systems, of other worlds. Or the skies and the gods within them. Normally It summons you to Its observatory for this, but the heavens above you will do for now.

"Binu." You clamber to your feet and jab a finger at a cluster of stars. "The old tales say she was a spoiled little girl who tried to eat the food set aside for the elders at a festival. When her parents tried to stop her, Binu kicked the sacred fire into the sky. The red and white stars are little bits of flame, and the curve of the galaxy is formed of the ashes thrown up with the fire."

Half-Brilliant scrunches up Its face as if It bit into a sour fruit. As if It eats. As if It tastes. "She … kicked … the fire?" Its voice drips with condescension.

"That's how the story goes." You trace a line between the cluster's constituent stars with your fingernail. A narrow, invisible face takes shape. "As punishment, the elders set her ablaze and threw her into the void. And now she's a constellation."

"How severe!" Half-Brilliant gasps in mock outrage. "She was just a little girl."

"So were my sisters, when you came to our world. So were my nieces." You meet Its too-bright eyes.

Half-Brilliant sighs and rolls Its shoulders. "You must be freezing. I have to get you inside. You'll eat and then you'll repair the superluminal transmitter so I can share my work."

"Tell me a story," says Half-Brilliant.

"The stars are the eyes of the dead."

Your mother's story, its jagged fragments crammed into the confines of a single sentence. It is all you can remember.

"How morbid."

Your mouth thins into a flat line. "No. No, it is the ancestors looking down on you, watching over you."

Half-Brilliant closes Its eyes.

"Some say—some said the moons were once mortals who angered the sun. The star sliced out little pieces of the satellites, waited for them to heal, and then did it all over again. Which is why the moons wax and wane. There are solar eclipses when the moons fight back, and lunar eclipses when the sun skins a moon alive."

When Half-Brilliant reports back to Its homeworld, you press an ear to the door of Its chamber. As It cuts apart your words and stitches them back for Its creators, you hear the masters gasp in pleasure.

"We should have just called you Brilliant," one jokes.

Half-Brilliant does not laugh with the others. Half-Brilliant does not say a word.

"Tell me a story."

"The moons are bowls of grain, and comets are ghosts from other systems. The ancestors feed those visiting souls so the moons wane, and they wax when they gather more food."

"And what do you believe?"

"I believe nothing. Your turn."

A flicker of something passes over Its face. "No. You are not the masters." You've never detected a genuine emotion from Half-Brilliant—until now.

And it is the sudden, sour bitterness in Its voice that sparks your first good idea.

"Tell me a story." Half-Brilliant maneuvers you in front of the starmap It finished painting moments ago. The piece is beautiful, the best of Its work. The best of your people, ground up in the construct's stomach.

"Yours have always been better." You lift your hands helplessly. "I have no other tales to tell. My clan knew them, and now you do." This is the greatest gamble you've ever played.

Half-Brilliant examines Its fingernails—nails that gouge out the eyes of your people, nails caked with the paint you mixed that very morning. "Humor me. Prove that I was right to spare you."

"I mean it; I can't remember any more tales worth telling," you say. Your eyes begin to smart as you stare at the starmap. The stars blur against their black background. The tears pooling over your eyelids are real.

"I see."

"Do you?"

"If I have exhausted your memory, perhaps you can finally tell me something new."

"I … All right." Your fingers clench and unclench as you speak. "Once upon a time, as humanity took its first halting steps across the stars, one sect looked upon the great works of its neighbors with envy in the guise of disdain. The towering sculptures of WASP-107b, a low-mass world with the density of spun sugar—just rocks. The vanishing paintings of HD 189733 b, where the rain falls sideways as needles of molten glass—nothing more than chemicals on paper. The songs of TrES-2b, where light falls in, never to reflect or return—just strings of words with different tones.

"So to prove their superiority, the sect built an army of artificial beings and sent them to their kin. The colonies received what they believed to be gifts with open arms. They thought they had merely been issued a challenge. But they had accepted nothing but a long, slow demise, encased in ice and absorbed bone by bone, tendon by tendon, until nothing remained of the sculptors and painters and singers but what the constructs stole.

"But the sect had its own art. Poor though it was, poor though they knew it to be, they proclaimed that their works were beyond their creations; that only the work of cursed savages could be eaten, masticated, and spat out again as something better. They are wrong."

You drag in a breath. And wait.

"You must think you're clever," says Half-Brilliant, Its mechanical laughter filling the observatory.

And you know you have failed when It does not even bother to butcher your words for the masters.

You admit defeat. What else can you do? You fall back into your work; you sink, you drown. You record Half-Brilliant's looted, hacked-apart melodies. You fasten sweet-smelling wood into frames. You mix paint. You haul blocks of marble and granite from the quarry. You bind the paper you craft into blank books. The days crawl by. Life goes on.

A year later, you dare ask: "Will you ever let my people go free, or will you devour them whole?"

"I am not a monster," Half-Brilliant replies.

Of course—a parasite does not see itself as such. Just a creature doing what it was made to do. You meet the construct's gaze, staring into Its unblinking eyes. Its opalescent irises catch the sinking sun.

"I am not a *complete* monster," Half-Brilliant amends, carding a hand through Its nylon curls.

With halting steps, you follow It to the landing bay. "Come, take your people." It lifts a hand, and the great steel doors of Its ship cycle open.

You freeze. The beat of your heart stumbles alongside your feet. "Why? Why now?"

Without warning, Half-Brilliant grabs your hand and presses Its cold, dead lips to your knuckles. "Because there is no more left for me here."

You wrench your hand away with a hiss, and It lets you go.

"I will take my leave of you," Half-Brilliant murmurs, "and return to the masters."

"What will you do there?" you ask. You are shaking.

"Oh, there are so many worlds yet to conquer." Half-Brilliant turns toward Its ship, gesturing for you to follow. "The masters believe that their art is above me, that only the work of godless barbarians can be consumed, churned up, and reformed. I shall prove them wrong, and there will be no end."

Half-Brilliant is nothing if not excellent at execution.

"Will you spare any of them?" Your mouth tastes of iron. "Will you leave a single survivor untouched, as you did here?"

"Do you think you survived me?"

"One day," you say, your tongue forming the words unbidden, "I will find you, and make you sorry you were ever made."

"I'm already sorry I was ever made." Half-Brilliant turns Its head to the side, so you can see the bladelike edge of Its smile.

So you take your people, and you prepare to wake what remains of them. You will regrow and rebuild.

And Half-Brilliant goes home, to conquer.

BLOOD AND BALLOTS

by Vuyokazi Ngemntu

CHAPTER ONE

Imani. That's my name. Not "E-money" or "Money Man" or anything remotely reeking of rap star swag. Nothing as hip. You don't get to be cool when you're a fourth-generation immigrant in Nuwe Mundo. There are always people to remind you that you come from generations of war-stricken, impoverished subhumans who jumped the border to escape their innate, skin-deep wretchedness.

"Go back home, E-Monkey!" The white kids in my neighborhood were wont to say. This despite the fact that their mothers and mine would have attended the same maternity hospital for antenatal care and given birth to us in adjacent rooms. Despite the fact that my great-great-great Grandfather's homeland was colonized by Spain eons ago, thus annihilating tens of thousands of our people, annexing and dissolving the border between the Spanish city of Melilla and Morocco and thus making my ancestor Papa Ahmed Al-Shabir Aboubakir a legal Spaniard.

With this I inherited a third-class citizenship long before I was born, with "pure blood" Spaniards being the superior class, those of mixed blood designated to the median station while we descendants of the Moors became the castigated lower class.

The racism here is palpable. It's embedded in the very air we breathe. Pretty ironic for a hybrid country. Were it not visited upon me, I'd find it amusing. Yet there's nothing mildly comedic about the slurs—no matter how unoriginal—we endure in the streets of Nuwe Mundo. Here seeing a darker-hued human being warrants a miscellany of abuses from those Aryan supremacists who consider us "desert filth."

When I was younger, I used to fight them. If I had a penny for every afternoon I came back from school with my knuckles bruised and my hair shaggy, I'd be a millionaire!

I never let it upset me, though. It wasn't their fault.

"They were raised to believe you're inferior to them," my father once told me when I came home from one such fight.

"I'll beat the whole lot of them up next time, they'll see," I said between sobs.

"You'll only prove them right," he warns, wagging his index finger and shaking his head at me.

My chest heaving, nose bloody and face ashen from the beating I'd gotten from the dozen or so youths that ganged up on me at soccer, I hung my head in shame. In our culture men were shamed for displaying any signs of weakness. We were a desert people by origin, after all, and that meant we favored endurance.

"Then you'll just prove them right," my father said, wiping my tear-stained face with his white kerchief.

The beatings would stop after I'd taken up kickboxing and proven something of a local champion by the time I turned fifteen. My dad never approved. But that didn't matter. It earned me street cred and guaranteed my spot as a leader among fellow immigrant youths.

Today, twenty years later, I'm standing at the City Square, jaw clenched and fists sweaty, a 9mm revolver hidden under my plaid shirt for protection as we await that fascist pig's parade to begin.

There are mascots as tall as six meters in his party's colors—white, gold, blue, and red—banners with his slogan "Save Our Homeland!" About two hundred white men, women, and children clad in T-shirts and bearing flags in the same colors with his grotesque face on them.

"Just look at these zombies!" curses my friend Ahmed beneath his breath.

A man who must've heard him hisses in our direction. I hold his gaze, and he hurls mucus spittle in our direction, missing my face by a hair's breadth.

I hear my father's voice in my mind right then: "You'll only prove them right,"

I hate that I still retain trace elements of his pacifist restraint in me, ten years after his death at the hands of an angry Spanish Nationalist mob.

A trumpet announces the arrival of their leader. Garcia, the puppet master, gregarious in his hand-waving gestures as he laps up the adoration of his crowd and equally demonic in his frowns and general disdain toward our own crowd of sixty or so.

"Save The Homeland!" shouts a devout follower. A heavy-set woman whose face has turned beet red in today's merciless sun. So heinous a sight is she, the sweat beads dripping from her face seem to be racing each other in an anxious bid to escape her, favoring dusty ground instead.

Garcia takes up the slogan and it soon escalates into a fervent call-and-response chant.

We take up our own oppositional chant. I clear my throat and lead the song:

"To this land do we belong
Mighty warriors, black and strong
All are equal to the law
Spaniard, Moor, rich or poor!"

The backlash is a hail of stones. Some of my men retaliate toward Garcia's crowd. Pandemonium.

"Let go of me, black bastard!" says the short middle-aged blond man whose spider-webbed neck is starting to turn purple between Ahmed's thumb and index finger.

Shit. This is getting out of hand. Seemingly from nowhere, police sirens announce their arrival.

"Freeze!" one officer screams as he fires the first three shots into the air. The crowd, too engrossed in a scramble of fists, kicks, and expletives, ignores his command.

My lungs suffocate in the rancid air. Sweat and dust strangle my nostrils as I try and fail to separate Ahmed from his unfortunate opponent.

Everything blurs. I see the bullet flying from the cop's gun in slow motion but somehow, I don't hear the sound. Surely I'm dreaming. My vision is hazy. Even when the bullet pierces through my childhood friend's forehead, sending his blood splattering on his white kaftan and gushing onto the ground, I convince myself that it isn't happening. Watching him fall toward the same ground with finality forces me out of my trance.

The screams of the women. The satisfied grin on Garcia's face. The police officer's indifference. All of these and the copper smell of fresh blood assail my senses.

A splitting headache sends me reeling in agony. This must be what hell looks, feels, and smells like.

"Enough!" screams the sheriff. But it's too late, as always. And what of it? Just another black body, after all.

CHAPTER TWO

"You killed my husband!" his wife Safeeyah bellows as she hurtles herself at the cop. Her fingers claw at his face and leave bloody hives.

"Stop that, or I'll have to arrest you," says the sheriff, coming between the deranged woman and the wide-eyed cop.

Both policemen reach for their weapons as I rush toward her, tears streaming down my own eyes, arms wide open as though I were capable of holding her pain. They desist when I put my hands up. Safeeyah's eyes are red and puffy from crying, her voice hoarse. Her lithe body convulses in my arms for what seems an eternity, the boulder in her throat transferring itself to the pity of my stomach indefinitely. There is no greater sorrow than a young widow's, and more so that of an activist's widow.

All that Ahmed wanted was the right to human dignity. The same life he protested to preserve is the one he was robbed of at the hands of a man-child whose gun and badge gave him authority over us.

All around us our people are raging. The Nationalists are baying for more gallons of our blood, for which the tarmac has an insatiable thirst. Ungrateful, the ground leaves this offering unattended, letting my friend's life substance coagulate in the sun.

Seven of our men remove Ahmed's body. The Imam offers a somber supplication in the form of a dua to guide his mortal soul toward Allah. The womenfolk cover their faces with their lapas and weep in the customary way our people have always mourned. Three buxom women emit the most wretched screams, thrashing themselves on the ground and raising formidable clouds of dust as they pull out their hair and pound their fists into the ground like indictments against the earth.

The dirge dies down. Someone covers Safeeyah with a black veil they must've been wearing around the waist in the way of elderly women.

It strikes me like the sting of a whip how we come prepared for death, wherever we go. Like we have a built-in contingency plan, "just in case," a rehearsed routine to embrace tragedy. Not out of preference, but because our DNA memory has it encoded in us. A hand-me-down muscle memory so well-choreographed, we make dirges sound like love songs.

Between both camps exists the kind of tension that could surely bend a titanium sword.

"Citizens!" shouts Garcia with a loud hailer from the podium. His followers stand to attention, seizing attack and retreating reluctantly.

"All who truly belong to this land should remember their priorities. Tragic as what just happened was for some, it's an inevitable consequence of forced social cohesion."

A collective murmur of affirmative expressions rises up from his kin.

"I say eliminate them all!" shouts an old man with a proxy, gaunt face, raising an emaciated, rickety fist in the air.

Garcia joins in the laughter. I, like every one of my comrades, am seething.

"We mustn't be reduced to animalistic behavior. We, the superior race, should show our sub-Saharan contemporaries how a civilized humanity behaves.

Insult to injury. Whoever accused this man of honor …

"There's scientific evidence to prove that the fallacy of equality is unfounded. We are simply not created to coexist."

More eugenicist nonsense. I'm convinced he's sneering at me and respond by staring blatantly into his eyes, unflinching.

It's taking every ounce of self-control not to reach for the gun strapped to my waist. Instead, my hand tightens around its cold steel, only for my fingers immediately slacken.

I take a deep breath to allay my anger. My fellow protestors are just as agitated. There are clenched jawlines, flared nostrils taking shallow breaths, teeth sinking into tight lower lips, and squinting eyes galore. One gesture from me and all hell will break loose. But I must contain them at all costs.

"Screw you, man," says a voice from our side of the street.

"No matter who says what, separatism is the best form of socialization. Our two races are like oil and water. Any mixing between us is unnatural. The Moors have their ways and their existence among us threatens our way of life," Garcia says, his neck straining, saliva frothing at the edges of his mouth as his voice thunders over the loud hailer.

Unbelievable. This guy, with his greasy hair slicked back, his beagle spectacles, and his ill-fitting suit, might as well be the reincarnation of Hitler. His followers lap it up, savoring his rhetoric like heavenly manna. His sloganeering winds them up to such cathartic heights, they could so easily execute us all.

CHAPTER THREE

The police are unaffected as he spews his hate speech, standing by in neutral positions even when Garcia's camp makes obscene gestures toward us, trying to taunt us into starting a fight. My men are disciplined, though, so they remain resolute.

All until a freckle-faced girl with red hair purposefully collides into one of our guys—a youth called Mansoor—and is the first to cry wolf.

"He touched me. This Moor touched my boobs," she said, the pitch of her nasal voice escalating as she repeats the accusation for effect.

I look toward the sheriff, who saw her walking over and bumping into the boy.

"No, I didn't. I'd never touch a woman," he pleads, taking off his kafeeya to implore the mercy of one police officer, whose baton is already raised in the air toward the boy.

"He's telling the truth, Officer. Your boss here saw him, right, Sheriff Fernandez?" I interject, having read the name on his badge and memorized his badge number as soon as I saw it. Another safety measure we get taught in junior school.

The man looks at me in irritation, his fury inadequately suppressed. He squeezes his sweaty hands on the officer's shoulder and tells him to let it go.

"Say sorry to the lady," he barks at Mansoor as he pushes the trembling boy.

"What for? He's done nothing," I say, stepping forward.

"Are you itching for a night in the slammer? What is your daddy in there or something? Wouldn't be surprising for you lot." He chuckles, joined by his colleagues and Garcia's sycophants.

"NMPD 17768316," I shout as he steps so close to my face, I can smell the corn dog he had for lunch.

"What's that, boy?"

His face is twitching, eyes wide with incredulity.

I've stopped caring. He can do what he likes with me.

"Your badge number, boy," I say, pronouncing the words with an exaggerated emphasis on "boy" and grinning at him despite the palpitations taking hold of me.

"What did you just call me?" he asks, pointing his pistol at me.

"Why so hostile? I thought we'd moved to terms of endearment like the good friends that we obviously are."

Through the corner of my eye, I spot Mansoor, shaking his head to-and-fro in a desperate attempt to discourage me.

The cop presses on the trigger and is about to pull it. A little white girl of about seven years old runs toward us and stands in front of me with her arms up. Her emerald-green eyes glossy with tears, she frowns at the sheriff while lurching onto my leg.

I've never seen her before. At least I don't think I have. Yet here she is, standing between me and a bullet. The cops look as perplexed as I am.

"Sweetheart, step away from this madness. He's bad."

"No. You're bad," she says, shaking her head vigorously.

"Me? I'm a cop."

"You wanna shoot him."

"That's because he's bad," says the sheriff, amused.

"Does he wanna shoot you?" asks the girl with a sarcasm that belies her age.

At this point I'm not sure what fate awaits me. Nor what to make of this … uhm … intervention.

A woman with hair the same color as the little girl's steps forward, her apologetic face ready to pander to authority.

"Excuse me, Officer. We're originally from Madagascar, my daughter doesn't know how things work around here," she says, her hands clasped together in a gesture of deference.

"Then you better teach her fast, ma'am. I don't have time to play with her. These are dangerous criminals," Fernandez says, his annoyance evident.

"Baby, let's go," says the woman.

The child doesn't budge.

"Luna? Let go of the man's leg," her mother says, paraphrasing the command with a more authoritative voice.

"No," says the child, staring at the sheriff, clutching my leg even firmer.

"Don't be silly. You're interfering in adult business."

The mom tries to soften her tone, but her appeal falls on deaf ears. The little girl has made up her mind and is literally unmoved.

"But he's going to shoot him," Luna says.

The sheriff's gun has been trained on me the entire time. I remain dead still, despite the cramp on my leg.

"That's none of our business," says the mom, her true colors finally showing. I don't blame her though. Her child might be caught in a cross fire if she doesn't listen. A stranger's life is hardly worth the risk.

"My teacher said if we see something wrong, we must do something to fix it."

There's a gasp from the crowd, especially from my camp. The sheriff is stunned. The redhead scoffs and stomps away indignantly. The little ash-blond girl's mother's face looks crestfallen.

CHAPTER FOUR

The lump in my throat randomly starts pulsating. Someone must be chopping onions nearby too. The last thing I want is for Fernandez to see tears in my eyes and mistake them for fear.

Though I can still smell my friend's blood, I am not afraid. Or maybe I've become desensitized to the things that are meant to scare me. That or perhaps I'm strengthened by my belief in reincarnation and the infinite soul. Whatever the reason behind my indifference, I know this is bigger than my own life ... especially now.

The sound of little feet in sandals distracts my thoughts. A boy of about the same age as the girl still clutching onto my leg comes running toward us. His pitch-black pageboy haircut is eliminated by the sun's rays. The cop that shot Ahmed looks nervous, doing the only thing he has been taught to do. His hands are shaking, his gun now pointed at the little boy in a beige kaftan.

"Nadeem!" shouts a shrill female voice in an accent that sounds like every woman in my world. It belongs to a face with fatigue and dread written all over it. Her eyes, grim with mortification, dart from Fernandez to his subordinate, then to Garcia on the podium and lastly, to me. Her worst nightmare hangs in the air like a piece of ankara fabric over the balcony on laundry day. Her silent plea for mercy is so loud, its text is written in the atmosphere in a bold font with an exclamation mark.

The language of shame is a universal one. Garcia alerts his gaze to his feet as though he were a tailor who's suddenly dropped his needle. His followers mumble in confusion. Fernandez and his garrison are riddled by anxiety. This was not part of the training program, their eyes seem to say.

Meanwhile, Nadeem, like Luna before him, clutches onto my remaining leg. The two of them smile at each other.

"You want?" Nadeem says, pulling out a brown paper parcel from his pocket. The smell that engulfs the air immediately transports me to my childhood with Ahmed.

"Safe travels, my friend," I say in my weeping heart. Who knows, I might soon join him on that journey.

The little girl giggles as she bites into her *chebakia*. Those deep-fried sesame-seed flavored cookies would bring delight to any palate.

Garcia's crowd shares a collective look of disgust. The social experiment isn't over, though. Luna pulls out two Chupa Chups lollipops from her dress pocket and hands one to her new friend.

The mothers regard each other with frustration from either side of me. The two children relish their treats, chuckling gleefully and licking their free fingers, all the while clutching onto each of my legs with their other hands.

There are hushed whispers when Luna leans over and kisses Nadeem on the cheek. Both camps disapprove, though for different reasons. I marvel at how this translates to us agreeing on something for the first time.

Something shifts in that moment. Something voluminous and old, yet invisible, that's left lingering in the humid air. I don't quite have the words to articulate it but the mesmeric effect of the two children, nonchalantly dismantling age-old animosity as though it were child's play, leaves everyone gobsmacked. For a while, we all remain motionless.

Garcia clears his throat, and we all turn our heads toward him. His mouth remains agape and his lips frozen. I've never known bigotry to have a limited lexicon until now. The most loyal of his disciples seem disappointed in his leadership. A few potbellied men drag their wives away, disillusioned. Their messiah sighs heavily and descends the pulpit.

I cringe when Fernandez appears to be focusing his weapon at me yet again. His carnation-hued face speaks of defeat. Beckoning with his head, he motions for the other cops to put down their weapons. They comply, to my relief.

"Stay out of trouble," he says to me in a passive-aggressive tone. The warning doesn't escape my comprehension, yet I smile and nod.

"You too, Sheriff." I wink at him. I'm convinced I just heard him chuckling quietly as he led his troops toward their vehicles before asking the crowd to disperse.

"What just happened?" Mansoor whispers.

I shrug to denote my inadequacy on the matter. At this point, I don't trust my senses, having never experienced or heard of any similar experience before.

Maybe I'm in my bed and am about to be roused from this lucid dream. That would make so much sense, really. This is Nuwe Mundo, after all.

CHAPTER FIVE

But this is as real as today is Thursday the 8th of June, 2028, and the time is 4 p.m. As real as the mosque and the Catholic church are on opposite ends of the same cobble street near the communal gardens Garcia proposed to segregate as part of his campaign and the ballot papers have been printed, ready for us to vote on Saturday.

"So who do you think will win the elections?" asks an exasperated Mansoor.

Every bit of my soul wants to say, "Definitely not Garcia." But at thirty-five, I'm too jaded to have blind faith in the transformative power of this day, mystical as it is.

In a perfect world, his followers come to their senses. In a perfect world, I don't have to lead any protests.

Hi, my name is Imani, and it means "Faith" in both Arabic and kiSwahili.

And yet, my cynicism often outweighs my faith. I keep just enough of the stuff in my back pocket to keep me going on the worst of days, though ...

The truth is, I don't know anything. A few minutes ago, I didn't know whether I was gonna live to tell this story. Any speculation about the future on my part would be presumptuous.

As if on cue, both mothers crouch down to pick up their kids. Both embrace them tightly, kiss the top of their gorgeous heads, shaking their own heads and smiling, first at their offspring then at each other. It's as though both intuitively know they each hold pieces to a puzzle that has confounded this place for the longest time. In their hands lies the answer to Mansoor's conundrum.

"The future," I say, surprising myself with the optimistic lilt in my voice.

"And is that a good thing?" asks Mansoor, humoring my inner philosopher.

"*Inshallah Ameen.*" I sigh.

"If God wills it," translates Luna's mother, her gaze distant as a wry smile creeps stealthily across her lips and spreads across her tanned skin. I notice the striking likeness between she and her daughter.

The two women introduce themselves to each other briefly. A formality inspired by the moment, I guess. A strong wind whistles melodically as it blows. The rustling leaves of the oak trees nearby provide the percussive accompaniment. A new song. These must be the winds of change.

A bevy of white doves—about a dozen—sweeps across the sky suddenly, migrating south. I lift my head skyward and notice the shroud of cumulus clouds overhead. A nanosecond later, the first few drops of rain fall, trickling down my cheeks in exactly the same direction my tears did earlier.

"Look, a rainbow," shouts an excited Nadeem.

Sure enough it is, in all its irreverent splendor. Both kids shout out its beautiful colors, adding to the magic of the moment. Luna tilts her head back and opens her mouth wide, so the raindrops fall into it. Her new friend follows suit.

"Sweet," they announce unanimously.

In truth, it's bittersweet.

I don't have the heart to look down—not yet. I want to imagine that the humid air evaporated, the steam rising from the tarmac with particles of Ahmed's soul back to the benevolent arms of love. That the raindrops now pelting our skin generously, indiscriminately, congregate to wash away his blood when they land. That the earth and not the drain soaks it up. That he is restored to the place from which he came, so he can be renewed for the next wing of his journey.

We too will keep on moving.

The kids wave goodbye to each other as their mothers shuffle in different directions. Something tells me their paths will cross again. And that something of a small miracle will unfold because of it.

THE RAINBOW BANK

by Uchechukwu Nwaka

I – TOMATO DISTRICT

Mezie adjusted the glasses on the bridge of his nose and tried to look inconspicuous as he stalked the back alleys of Tomato District. This side of town, apartment blocks were squeezed so tightly together they were often misconstrued for large living complexes. The congestion meant everybody knew everybody, and his wasn't a face that he wanted to have noticed around these parts. Not at this time.

He hopped over an open pipe which drained wastewater between two buildings. The alleys ranked of piss, but Real Night was fast approaching, and the smoke from the warming meisuya grills was beginning to override the general odor of overpopulation. Mezie eyed the number on the building behind him and made out the "16" printed on it in fading paint. The rogue ujuist was supposed to be somewhere around here. He scanned around nervously as dusk fell even faster.

A few yards ahead of him was a converted shipping container that looked like it had seen better days. It was sandwiched in a somewhat-too-tight corner between blocks 16, 17, and 18. A tiny red bulb illuminated the front of the container, and Mezie winced at the sight of the numerous mosquitoes buzzing around the entrance.

He took another look around to make sure he wasn't being followed, adjusted the baseball cap on his head, and stepped into the container. Tiny bulbs of green light ran on wires on the ceiling, leading to a beaded curtain a few feet in. He parted it and walked through.

"Relics out," a raspy voice trilled from inside.

"What?"

"You heard me. All relics out."

Mezie gritted his teeth. He always carried a protection orb about—side effects of his business. He put a hand into his Gore-Tex jacket and brandished his personal relic. In the dim light, tiny runes glistened over the surface of the fist-sized metallic sphere.

"You'll find a tray by the curtain," the ujuist said. "Leave it there and come in."

Mezie did as he was told. The ujuist sat behind a desk that took up the entire width of the room. An incense lantern hung from the ceiling. Shelves filled with books and artifacts went to the back farther than the lights could reach. It was a very cramped working space.

"So?" the ujuist asked, eyes narrowing at him. "What do you want?"

"Are you Wumi Alaba?"

"Who's asking?"

"My name is Mezie. I'm here to hire your services."

"I doubt you'd be able to afford me."

Mezie measured the woman behind the desk. She was tall, probably five-feet-nine. Her dark skin seemed to catch the green light of the small room. A shawl of the same color wrapped her neck. Her arms were well defined—long toned limbs that ended with charm bracelets on her wrists and rings over her long fingers. Fingers that looked like they could snap his neck without her exerting a bit of *uju*.

"I can," Mezie said. "And you haven't even heard what I have to say."

"All jobs start at three gold," she said in that throaty voice of hers.

"What? I-I mean, that wasn't what I heard."

Wumi Alaba shook her head. "You might want to sit. Mezie, wasn't it?"

He took the stool beside her table. "Look, just hear me out, okay? Like I said earlier, my name is Mezie. I run books for Family Man—"

At the utterance of Family Man, the ujuist suddenly leaped, faster than he could blink. In a heartbeat, the cold edge of a dagger was pressed against his throat.

"You work for the syndicates then?" she hissed.

"Are you a madwoman?" he yelled. An action which, in retrospect, wasn't probably the best of ideas when a knife was inches from his throat. "I'm a potential customer!"

Mezie felt the steel taste blood. "I'd slit your throat if it wasn't such a mess to clean up blood from the floor."

He lifted his palms into the air in surrender. "I'm sorry. Please can you let me explain?"

"How did you find me?"

"I have contacts, okay? Just ... just hear me out. That dagger is making me very uncomfortable."

The ujuist eyed him dangerously, but the dagger left his neck. "Talk."

"Like I said, I run Family Man's books. Loans, due payments, interest rates, all of that. However, I've been meaning to break out. Start my own enterprise, outside Family Man's umbrella."

"So you want to leave one rat's wing to become your own rat?"

"Rats don't have wings," he said.

The ujuist's gaze threatened to skin him alive.

Mezie instantly opted for adjusting his glasses nervously. "Well, I am pursuing similar interests, but I want to believe I have a fundamentally different philosophy from Family Man."

"A loan shark is still a loan shark," Wumi Alaba deadpanned.

Mezie gulped, nervously adjusting his glasses. Family Man was more than just a loan shark. He ran a syndicate of relic trade, spy networks, and ujuists. The latter he managed to squeeze under his grip with overwhelming violence. Family Man was as ruthless as they came, and he wielded the greatest power of all.

Money.

When the Spillage first happened, many people thought it was the apocalypse and did what every normal person would. Or at least what they'd learned from *The Walking Dead.* They looted supermarkets and bunkered down in their homes and "waited." The Spillage itself was the shredding of the conceptual seams between our reality and a place some mystic termed The Isle of Dreams. The visitors on the other hand were less than dreamy. They were a variety of existences, from the ojuju, beasts formed of corporeal shadows, to actual angelic beings. In short, while the entire world was trying to figure out what exactly in crackers was going on and waiting for these fancy visitors to do their worst, Family Man was looting *money.*

Well, here they were now.

"I don't work for loan sharks. Not even aspiring ones. There's a reason my office is this far away from Victory Estate." Mezie noticed the ujuist pulled her shawl closer to her neck. It looked too tight to be comfortable. "And I can't assassinate Family Man for you. If I could, I'd have done it years ago, for zero."

Mezie's eyes rounded in shock. "Absolutely not! I'm not trying to ... to assassinate Family Man. Why in heaven would you think that?"

"Huh? What then was all that nonsense about becoming your own rat?"

Mezie fought the warmth peppering his ears. He believed in his own ambition, but there was just this way Wumi Alaba phrased it that made it sound patronizing. "I never said anything about killing anybody. I need to hire you to accompany me in search of a particular relic."

Interest flashed in Wumi Alaba's eyes. "A relic?"

"If only you'd let me finish when I started." Mezie took off his glasses to wipe them. Then he remembered he'd dabbed the nick in his neck with the same handkerchief, and instantly changed his mind. "You see, my biggest issue with leaving Family Man is money. I just don't have enough—"

"I doubt anyone can ever have enough if they're comparing themselves to Family Man."

"Ujuist, would you bloody stop interrupting me!"

Wumi Alaba narrowed her eyes, then casually flashed her dagger at Mezie.

"Stop that too," he snapped. "I already have a substantial information network. One I've built for myself over the years. That's also where I discovered a particular relic that could solve all of my problems. Not just any relic, ujuist, mind you, but one of the Stuff of Dreams."

Mezie smiled satisfactorily and watched Wumi Alaba's eyes widen and her jaw fall. Then watched as she tried to pick up the pieces of her composure and failed.

"You're lying."

"I wouldn't risk Family Man's people sighting me in this side of town over something as trivial as a lie. It won't take long for Family

Man to hear about this—maybe by the end of Real Night, give or take—and he'll mobilize an Outlander team to go after the relic immediately. We both know the number of ujuists he controls."

"What exactly is this relic that makes you think you can stand up to Family Man?" She couldn't hide the excitement in her rasping tone.

Mezie wondered where the hard-woman act went. He smiled, relishing the moment. "It's a pot."

"What?"

"A mint to be more precise. It creates money. Indefinitely, and in unlimited supply." Mezie leaned in to face the woman. "And we can find it at the bottom of a particular rainbow."

"A rainbow?" Her expression fell. "That's too vague. Since the Spillage we've barely had properly sunlit skies."

"True," he said. The skies outside the settlements were mostly made up of ashen and burnt-out clouds, and it always looked like dusk. Hence the "Real Night" marked the end of daytime hours. Still danger or discomfort never stopped anybody. "There's a map to the place this rainbow will be, Wumi Alaba."

"Will be?"

"Well rainbows don't just appear and *stay*, now do they?"

"I wouldn't know. I was born in an underground bunker a few years after the Spillage. Never seen a rainbow."

She'd said it with such a straight face. "Heavens! You're serious. Okay, okay. Then you definitely have to escort me. Time is limited, and how much did you say your price was?"

With the Dreamlings came the relics. A relic was any object that did not obey the natural laws of this reality. Most of them came from the other side, The Isle of Dreams, wherever that was. Others could be produced artificially by any ujuist creative enough with their hands.

Mezie trekked quickly toward the main thoroughfare. Around town, the meisuya grills cooked mouthwatering beef and chicken. Some canopies were up, around which the richness of pepper soup wafted into his nostrils. Speakers boomed highlife music into the night. Around the corner, someone was baking bread, but everything was so cramped and packed together it could have been coming from anywhere.

Mezie crossed the street toward where he'd parked his vehicle. It was an older model sedan, and somebody was pissing by the tires, bottle in hand. Not many people handled the apocalypse well, especially the older ones. Then again, that wasn't unexpected. Mezie adjusted his glasses, somewhat irritated as the intruder swayed on his feet. On a normal night he'd explore his empathy, but he was still irked that the bloody ujuist had asked for three hundred gold—a hundred times her original price! And half upfront!

"You do realize that there's a high probability of us losing our lives in this expedition?"

"Right," she'd said.

"So why would you need one hundred fifty gold beforehand?"

"Who wouldn't?"

"You're not even making any sense."

"You work for Family Man, right? I hope you weren't expecting this to come cheap. Especially not after you started with, 'My name is Mezie, I run books for Family Man.'" She'd mimicked him adjusting his glasses.

"Alright! I'll pay. Just stop talking."

"'I plan on starting up my own enterprise.'"

"Stop talking!"

The drunk shuffled toward Mezie carelessly, bumping into Mezie's protection relic's repulsion field. Electricity jolted through the man's upper limb, and he dropped his bottle, startled. Mezie snickered, though he doubted the man would see his face in the darkness.

As he drove toward the other side of town, Mezie watched the golden stars flickering in the night sky. The golden stars were actually wards to keep the ojuju from spawning within the residential areas. The ojuju were the most dangerous Dreamlings. Literal manifestations of nightmares, or any emotion on the negative spectrum of the human experience.

The ojuju were also responsible for the decimation of more than half of the human population.

The entire Tomato District was surrounded by tall pillars that produced the golden-starred wards. Everyone called the pillars the "Fingers of God." Word was they suddenly rose from the ground when the first inhabitants of the area were being slaughtered by Dreamlings and cried to God for mercy. Just as the Darkness fed on human thoughts, some scholars—shady mystics—proposed that the "light" did the same, producing Dreamlings and relics that matched these concepts. These were the Stuff of Dreams. Nobody knew for sure.

The car pulled toward the massive gates of Victory Estate. These were prime property before the Spillage, and after. Family Man's team of ujuists had somehow discovered a way to move the Fingers of God to cover more space and expand. Mezie toyed with the idea of an expansion himself, but he wasn't ready for that just yet. Besides, his emancipation needed to come first. And even if he did manage to out-buy Family Man, could he really assert his position in Tomato District without the bloodshed that earned the settlement its colorful name?

He imagined Wumi Alaba snickering at that moment and shook off the idea.

Mezie's car stopped at the gates. He was supposed to rendezvous with Wumi Alaba at the northwest Finger in four hours. Half an hour had passed already. The guard on duty flashed a torchlight into his car. An unnecessary action since the gates were bathed with floodlights. Family Man might have seemed invincible, but when he waged war against the ujuists, he almost lost his life. Still, Mezie was no serious threat, except to profit.

The guard gave a signal to the control tower that remotely operated the gate. As the mechanism slid open, he glanced at his reflection from the rearview mirror. He was only twenty-five, but he already had a crop of white hair that he was ashamed of. To hide it, he kept his head clean shaven. He was thinner than a doorpost, sunken cheeks and all. Had nothing to do with his nutrition, only genetics. He hid his skinny limbs with layers of shirts and the Gore-Tex jacket he'd gotten from an old flame after an Outland run.

The gates opened and he drove into the estate, past the large ujuist buildings and relic forges. The forges constantly coughed fumes into the sky, even at night. Mezie did not stop until he pulled up beside his building, a six-flat block. He walked quickly to the door and opened it, trying his best to not look over his shoulder. His was the first apartment to the right of the hallway, beneath the stairs. Mezie inserted his key into the lock and slipped into the dark flat.

He flipped the light switch and almost had a heart attack.

Family Man sat on Mezie's lone sofa, legs crossed with his fingers interlocked over his knees. His signature bowler hat sat atop his head, inclined downward so that his face was obscured in a mask of shadows. Mezie's heart skipped a beat. Instinctively, he reached for the relic in his jacket, ready to crank out its defensive field to the max ...

... when he heard a slight sound.

A slight ... snoring sound?

He cocked his head to the side in confusion. Family Man didn't seem to have noticed his presence yet.

Was he ... sleeping?

Mezie coughed importantly. The mafia boss's head snapped backward like a startled cobra. So did his pistol.

"Shit," he said, lowering his gun. "It's just you, Mezie. How long have you been standing there?"

What the hell? That's my line. How long have you been waiting that you fell asleep? Don't give me a bloody heart attack!

"A few minutes."

Family Man made a grand show of looking at his wristwatch. "You're home late. That's unlike you."

"Yeah, *um*, well, I had some errands to run."

"Errands that made you forget the right hat?" he asked, pointing to the baseball hat in Mezie's free hand. That was just how effective the disguise was, Mezie congratulated himself internally. The fastest way to identify the Family Man's syndicate were the bowler hats on their heads.

"Casual stroll, Family Man," Mezie said, activating his sphere before walking toward the kitchen. "I have to exercise my weak bones. Do you want a drink?"

"I've been having premonitions."

Mezie froze. "Premonitions?"

"I've tried to build a home here in Tomato District," he said, leaning back into his chair. The man was no younger than sixty, yet his shoulders were broad with muscle. Even his suit could not hide his terrifying physique. Mezie wondered just how many relics Family Man had on him at that moment. After all, the mafia boss's bouncers were nowhere in sight ... unless they were also snoring but decided to use his bedroom.

"I think you've done a pretty fine job."

Family Man groaned. "Me too. Yet after the Spillage and all the nightmares that fell into this world, it's been easy to forget just how dangerous we humans are as a species. Of the poisons that pump from our hearts and into our actions between one another."

"What did you see, boss?"

"Betrayal," he said flatly. "There are snakes within my court. Do you remember the Leopard Twins? How they planted a spy in my relics business?"

Mezie nodded. The Leopard Twins were a small-time gang rumored to have been run out of another Stuff of Dreams settlement further south. A settlement rumored to be several times larger than Tomato District. Family Man hadn't been able to run them out of his small town yet though.

He narrowed his eyes at Mezie. "Did you know that I saw them coming?"

Mezie was getting worried. "The spy?"

"The Spillage. I had premonitions long before they came. That's why when they arrived, I knew to go for the money. The Dark angels took my money and in exchange, gave me gold. With that gold I bargained with their kind for protection. What could possibly harm me when I was under their Dark God's divine protection?"

Family Man rose to his feet. "I was a nobody before the Spillage. You don't know how the world was like then, more than three decades ago." He drew menacingly toward Mezie, somehow still a head taller than him. Sweat licked over Mezie's brow as Family Man's cutting glare peered into his eyes. "Nobody crosses me, Mezie. Not angels, not gangsters, not even the bloody ujuists. I'll slit their throats, the whole lot of them."

His heavy hand fell on Mezie's shoulder, tearing through his protection field like it didn't exist. "You're not planning on crossing me, are you, boy?"

A shiver ran down Mezie's back. He met Family Man's gaze, the hard lines between his eyes. "I run your books. If I wanted to F with you, I'd have done it a long time ago."

Family Man squeezed. Pain flared over Mezie's shoulder, but he didn't blink. He could not cower now. Family Man held for a few seconds before tapping the spot. "Good boy, Mezie. As long as we're all on the same page, get it?"

Mezie forced a smile, feeling like he'd chewed bitter-kola instead. "Sure."

Family Man walked out. Mezie immediately dashed into his bedroom where he'd packed the essentials for the expedition. His backpack laid innocently underneath his bed, just as he'd left it. Also, to his relief, there were no sleeping mobsters either.

It was time to leave.

II – OUTLANDS

Mezie was out of breath when he got to the northwest Finger. He'd hiked out of Victory Estate through a defect in the fence he'd been working on for weeks. He couldn't risk using the gates again and alerting Family Man to the nature of his mission. He was still thinking of how much gold to bribe the lone ujuist he knew to be on patrol that night when he spotted a familiar figure.

"Wumi Alaba? Where's the guard?"

"I took care of him." The woman wore a leather jacket over a white vest and carried a bag twice as small as his bag. And he thought he packed light. There was a sword sheathed on her waist, and he noticed the dagger from earlier strapped to her boot. She still wore the shawl over her head and neck.

"You're early," she remarked.

"Sure," he huffed. "Let's go."

"You're not planning on walking across the Outlands, are you?"

Mezie shook his head. "I have a transport prepared somewhere on the outskirts, but we have to make the trek there."

The northwest Finger, as with the other Fingers of God, was a large pillar made of symmetric stone. It was as tall as a skyscraper and had rows of luminous runes on every weathered surface. Like something that had existed even before time began. It looked ancient. Primordial even.

As they approached it, Mezie's fingers tingled, and goose bumps crawled over his skin.

"Ever gone past the Fingers before?" the ujuist asked.

"Once or twice."

She nodded and walked past it. Mezie gulped, then followed.

First the air turned plastic as his body pressed against the boundary. He pushed against the barrier, and it pushed against him too—into his nostrils and ears and between his teeth. He began to suffocate when, like a bubble, it popped all around him, and he was suddenly standing on the other side of the barrier.

"Congrats," Wumi Alaba said. "Now shit gets real."

Under the starless night, the rubble of what used to be Lagos spread infinitely ahead. Hollowed out buildings and cars and overall markers of forgotten civilization stood in the darkness, letting the wind whistle haunting tunes through their deserted hallways. Wumi Alaba stopped suddenly, eyeing Mezie.

"They're accumulating. The shadows. Control your emotions."

Mezie gulped. Of course. They were no longer under the Fingers' protection.

Wumi Alaba was still speaking. "We're pretty close to the barrier so we might be safe. Tell me you hired a cleaner too."

"I did not. But I know how to work their gear. It's in the car."

The ujuist nodded and they continued in silence. They kept to the middle of the road, avoiding the clusters of dead architecture. It wasn't unheard of for Dreamlings to stalk settlements, and Outland Survival 101 instructed to stay on the street unless while hiding.

"Tell me about this relic," Wumi Alaba said, her voice quieter.

"It's one of the Stuff of Dreams," Mezie replied. "Have you ever heard of the superstition about how there's a pot of gold at the bottom of every rainbow?"

Wumi Alaba shook her head. "Maybe in training, I don't know. I've never been much interested in the directories of relics. I also think it's silly. A bunch of cloud-brained idiots can just come together and dream a relic into reality. It gets old."

Mezie clicked his fingers together. "But then it doesn't. On one of the recent Outland runs, the squad picked up one of these relic directories. It contained the same old relics that we've known about, with an exception. It had been recently updated and this rainbow relic was freshly listed. Under the description were the emergence coordinates and time!"

"So we're looking for a rainbow? Aren't those found in the sky anyway?"

Mezie lifted his gaze to the sky. "Everything is possible." The sensor in his communicator beeped and he pulled it out of his jacket. "The truck is close. It's just around this corner."

They turned the corner to find a giant creature clawing at the chassis of the car. Mezie stilled, reaching for his relic.

"Not yet," the ujuist whispered. "It's a mutated agama lizard. It senses any form of magic. That includes relics."

Mezie's eyes took in the form of the creature. No way in hell that was a lizard. Reptilian scales gilded the surface of its skin, and it was almost eleven feet long, head to tail. Once in a while the scales would bristle, and the faint glow of magic would ripple under its hide.

"It's after the engine," he whispered furiously. "It's one of the better post-Spillage ones that run on recycled shadows."

"Noted, 'boss,' " Wumi Alaba snickered, unsheathing her sword. The blade glinted, rectangular with a serrated edge. A very unconventional design.

"I guess it's time to earn my salary," the ujuist said and took a stance. Mezie took a few steps back, heart pounding in his chest. The agama hadn't seemed to have noticed them yet. Good. Good.

"Two forerunners—heat and light," she chanted.

The mutated lizard halted its assault on Mezie's vehicle, momentarily distracted as a flurry of sparks blossomed around the ujuist's sword.

"Two mighty heralds—rain and thunder."

The agama turned to the ujuist. Tongues of fire licked her sword, followed by a crackling of lightning. The reptile leapt from the hood of the vehicle, bared its serrated teeth at Wumi Alaba with a blood curdling screech, and started toward her.

"Two hands on my hilt.

"Two legs on solid earth.

"Two outcomes—victory or death."

Mezie watched in open-mouthed awe as Wumi Alaba's sword cut an arc in the darkness, cleanly through the neck of the beast. It was as though her body never moved, but in the split second between heartbeats, he'd seen her body spring up from the earth and toward the sky. The beast was in her way and so it was *removed*, her entire body propelled by the power of her swing ... and something else.

Uju.

Or abundance as the mystics would call it. Gifted to a select few. Mastered by even fewer. Wumi Alaba sheathed her sword as the rest of the reptile fell to the ground.

"Let's go. The carcass will attract more of them."

"Were you seriously planning on killing me with that when we first met?" Mezie narrowed his eyes at her.

"Of course not. I have the small knife for that. Come on, let's check if your car still works."

Mezie's truck rumbled along the Outland terrain. There wasn't much of a highway, just stretches of barren rocks and the occasional stumps that once represented architecture. The truck's reinforced tires propelled them along as they bounced on their seats.

"Okay," Wumi Alaba said, scrutinizing Mezie's map. "It says here that the rainbow will show up in about eleven hours. That's noon."

"Yes." Mezie adjusted his glasses. "I'm so close."

The ujuist regarded Mezie. "You live a comfortable life under Family Man. Why leave now?"

Mezie rubbed his scalp in quiet response. "It gets to you. The lifestyle, the violence, everything."

Wumi Alaba said nothing, pulling her shawl tighter.

"The world is different now, you know?" Mezie continued. "Only a few are born special like the ujuists. Some others aren't so lucky. Take me for example. I got my genes all mixed up and ended with weak bones. I got lucky and found work under Family Man. That gave me access to body and spirit enhancement relic pills. And protection. This world devours the weak. What happens to those like me who didn't get lucky? Who didn't find work with a mobster?"

"So you want to start a charity?"

"No. I'm just telling you it's not all about the money."

Silence fell between them.

Wumi Alaba said quietly, "There are no laws, Mezie. Those that exist are made only by the people powerful enough to enforce them. Lives will always be lost."

"Money is power, ujuist. You have your answer."

Wumi Alaba chuckled and went back to reading the map when suddenly, she exclaimed. "Heavens, Mezie! You never said we were crossing the Labyrinth."

Mezie pursed his lips in a thin line. "I told you this was going to be a difficult job."

"You piece of—"

The shadow accumulator at the back of the vehicle grumbled suddenly, interrupting the ujuist's outburst. The machine was designed to suction the corporeal shadows that made up the ojuju. Those shadows themselves could then be subject to further purification and converted to fuel. The cleaners were the group responsible for handling the accumulators during every Outland run.

"Control your emotions," Mezie said. "The rainbow will show up at the end of the Labyrinth. That's why we needed the head start." A creature shrieked somewhere in the sky. Mezie turned the wheel and the truck left the highway into a cluster of buildings that could have once been an industrial area. The accumulator whined furiously at the back, chugging against the sound of the engines.

"I noticed," Wumi Alaba started. "Your expressions of emotional extremes are somewhat off. Like they're rehearsed. You're way too composed."

Mezie eyed her. "What does that mean?"

"You said you manage finances. That means you're a normal person. And the way I see it, you were probably born in Tomato District. The only real danger you should have experienced is Family Man's."

"And that isn't enough?" he asked. "It's just like your spell earlier. There are only two outcomes. I win, or I die."

"Still doesn't explain—"

Something rammed into the side of the vehicle. The car careened to one side as Mezie fought with the wheel to regain control. The impact had shattered one of the headlights.

"Ojuju!"

The monster's silhouette—because wasn't that all they were anyway?—flashed past the lights. Mezie stepped on the gas and the engine wailed, rocketing them forward. He flipped open a panel on the dashboard and flicked on all the switches.

Floodlights spilled from the truck's auxiliary lamps. The road ahead was swarming with ojuju, each one about seven feet wide and tall. Their eyes glowed like burning coals in the darkness. Shadows shimmered over their bodies, radiating like waves of heat from a raging furnace. Each creature was amorphous on observation, without specific form and yet, somehow, complete. They were clumps of malevolent darkness that shifted morphology the longer you looked; and tried to understand; and eventually, inadvertently gave them form. Some things however were clear; there were talons at the ends of their arms, or feet, or tentacles, or all of the above. Some of them had wings. All of them made Mezie's skin crawl.

"Ujuist, do your thing!"

Wumi Alaba had already begun her chant. Mezie bit his lower lip and pushed the gearshift forward. The monsters shrieked, waves of night rippling outward from the swarm. The floodlights deflected most of the darkness, but not the accompanying cold. Not the terror and the whispering groans that prickled the skin with gooseflesh and sweat.

Two more ojuju crashed onto Wumi Alaba's side of the vehicle, tearing at the floodlights on the edge. The descent of darkness was instant, and the ojuju clinging to that end of the car metastasized tenfold like a cancer.

"Shit! Anytime now, Wumi Alaba!" Mezie spun the wheel all the way to the right, struggling to overcome the pressure on the passenger side. Wumi Alaba grunted as she hacked at the shadows with her dagger. Her head snapped in Mezie's direction.

"Use your shield, now!"

Her *uju* swelled inside the cramped vehicle. It was that feeling again, like the barrier. This time it felt like an airbag was inflating inside the space, pushing against him and the vehicle and everything else.

"Three points of impact, ricocheting three times threefold its origin; three origins of ion, metal, energy."

Mezie hit the brakes.

The ojuju were thrust forward. Lightning fell from the sky, ripping through the swarm in unnatural arcs. The punishing force of nature fell on the vehicle and multiplied, singeing buildings, raining debris, setting the final minutes of Real Night awash in blinding hot light.

And just as abruptly as it had started, it was over.

The both of them just sat there, breathless. The accumulator was still pumping, even more fervently now. Mezie reached for its controls and turned it off. The idea of so many remnants of ojuju just seeping in behind him made him uncomfortable. Wumi Alaba looked at him and nodded. There was perspiration on her forehead.

Mezie started the car, and they continued in silence. About ten minutes in, Wumi Alaba was whimpering quietly in her seat.

"Something the matter?" he asked, still shaken.

"Nothing. Just carry on."

He held the steering in place, but even his hands were shaking. "What the hell was that? I could hear their voices inside my head."

"It's fear," the ujuist said, hands clenched over her shawl. Her voice was barely audible, and the rasping made it worse. "They feed on it, flourish on it."

"I wasn't born in Tomato District, you know?" He looked at his trembling hands. "I was born not too long after the Spillage. I don't know how I made it, but I remember when Family Man and his Outlanders found me. I was the sole survivor in a bunker where an ojuju had spawned."

Wumi Alaba turned to him. "You were lucky."

"Was I?" he asked. "I was bloody six years old and I watched a beast tear a young mother and her baby apart. Saw it step on a grown man's head like it was squashing a bug. Tell me exactly, Wumi Alaba, how the fuck was I lucky?"

The ujuist laid a gentle hand on his elbow. His entire arm was trembling, and he hadn't even realized it.

"Much of who I am today, I owe to Family Man. I don't agree with everything he does, but he saved my life. Do you understand?"

The ujuist did not respond. Not for a while. Under the sound of the engine's rumble, tiny whispers had started coalescing.

"We should probably turn on the accumulator now," she said.

Mezie hit the switch for the accumulator and with a few sputters, the machine roared to life with a disturbing gurgling sound.

"I will never get used to that."

"Best not to," she said. Then after a beat she added, "Thanks, I feel much better."

"Good," Mezie replied. " 'Cause I need your A-game now. We're at the Labyrinth."

...❖...

III – LABYRINTH

Ahead of them, the walls of the Labyrinth rose skyward toward the early dawn sky. There was no sunlight, just an ambient paleness in the sky. The Labyrinth was a collection of weathered brown walls that spread on both sides for miles. It was a distinct landmark on the Earth's surface, and it was said to give the impression of several deserts compacted into an endless maze. Nobody knew whose Dream the gargantuan meta-structure was formed from.

Mezie pulled toward one of the entrances—or exits; it was only a matter of perspective. Each column of stone was as thick as an apartment block. If it was dark outside, then the ambience inside was almost fiery. The walls reflected light poorly, like an incandescent bulb doused in engine oil and shrouded by spiderwebs.

"The map doesn't say anything about navigating to the relic," Wumi Alaba said, tossing the navigation chart.

"I know," Mezie smirked, fishing around in his pack. "That's why I brought this."

He took out a relic. It was a disk with a small glass orb affixed to the center. Within the orb was a floating needle that was currently pointed forward with a slight upward inclination. There were glyphs carved on the disc in three concentric rows. The middle row around the needle was glowing faintly.

The ujuist was clearly impressed. "Isn't this Kelechi's Compass?"

"Yeah. The pre-Spillage prophet that claimed God revealed to him the location of the biblical Eden."

Wumi Alaba laughed. "Whatever happened to him?"

Mezie shrugged. "Who knows? Maybe he found it."

"At least *we're* not the ones out there looking for some mythical paradise, are we?"

"Hey! The rainbow is legit!"

"Of course, of course—Mezie, watch out!"

Mezie hit the brakes just in time to keep from running into somebody in their path. It was a slightly middle-aged woman with disheveled hair and her hands above her head. Mezie blinked, propping his glasses carefully over his nose.

"Who the hell is that?" he asked. The woman had only a short red sleeveless gown on. Completely barefoot. "What could someone possibly be doing on her own in a place like this?"

Mezie was about to poke his head out the window when Wumi Alaba placed a firm hand on his shoulder.

"It's a trap. We're surrounded."

The woman smiled under the headlamp's glow. As though camouflaged, figures popped out of the walls, each one armed with a rifle. Mezie counted more than a dozen men.

"Hello, hello," the woman announced, singsong-like, running her fingers over her hair till it fell down her shoulders and changed color to a striking golden brown. One of the gunmen approached her and placed boots on her feet. Then another one put a suit over her shoulders.

"How convenient," she smiled. It was a gold-toothed smile. "We were just wondering how many vehicles we'd need to hijack to house all of our tribe. It's a good thing everybody is interested in the rainbow's gold."

Mezie swore, just noticing the spotted pattern on her red gown.

Wumi Alaba whispered, "Do you know her?"

"Yeah," he replied. "That's Odion Leopard. One of the Leopard Twins."

"Another syndicate?" The disgust was palpable.

"Yeah. And by the looks of it, they're looking for the same thing we are." Mezie rubbed the perspiration on his scalp. It'd been one confrontation after the other today.

"We can just run you over," he yelled. "We don't have to give you anything."

"All my guys are good shots. Is a car really worth more than your lives?" Another person was placing rings on the woman's fingers. Mezie rolled his eyes.

"Do your worst," he fired the gas. "This truck survived a swarm of ojuju."

"That's over twelve guns, Mezie," Wumi Alaba whispered. "And their bullets are sure to be charmed."

"It's a bluff," Mezie pursed his lips. "They probably encountered something far worse further in and have used up most of their ammunition on it. Think about it, they don't even have any vehicles. It's a miracle they're even alive and pulling this stunt."

"Mezie!"

"This is the big leagues, Wumi Alaba. Just trust me and hold on."

"We *will* fire!" Odion Leopard warned. "Take the olive branch now."

"Fine by me," Mezie grunted over the firing engine, fingers curled over the gearshift.

"Alright wait!" the woman conceded, still standing in front of the car. "Maybe we can cut a deal. Anything?"

"Lower your weapons."

The woman narrowed her eyes at him, then gave a sharp nod. The rifles pointed at them lowered, but not by too much.

"We'll make the trek," she said. "But we won't last a second out there without a cleaner. So could you at least give us your accumulator?"

"What can you give us in return?"

The woman walked to the driver's side. Guns followed her advance.

"Information."

Mezie met her gaze. "What information?"

"The groups currently searching for that rainbow," she smiled crookedly. It was unsettling. "But you give me the accumulator first."

"Not happening."

"What stops you from running my men over once you've got what you're looking for?"

"Nothing. Either way, I don't lose."

Tension pulled between them in one long breathless moment. Like a string at breaking point. Mezie did not lessen his grip on the steering wheel. There could be only one of two outcomes.

"Very well. You win, kid." She reached into her coat and pulled out a cigarette. This time, she lit it herself and took a drag. "There are Dark ujuists in here too."

Wumi Alaba flinched in her seat at the mention of the Dark ujuists. Mezie made a mental note of that.

"That must have been *some* confrontation if it left you in this state," he prodded. "What are their numbers?"

Smoke curled out of Odion Leopard's nostrils and lips. "Six, seven strong. Four are actual ujuists. Mad proficient. The rest are cleaners."

"And are they planning on coming for Tomato District?"

"I doubt it," Odion said. "Tomato District is great, but it's really not that significant. I imagine they have their own goals."

"And you? What did you want the gold for?"

"Since you name-dropped Tomato District, then you must know Family Man." She peered into his car. Then at his clean-shaven head. "You don't seem to be one of his. Who are you?"

"Mezie," he said simply. "And I'm the one asking the questions."

"Well I'm the bloody leader of the Leopards. If I want money, then it's obviously to crush my competition."

Mezie smiled. "Fair enough. Are Family Man's people here yet?"

"Not that I know of."

"Okay. Good." He turned off the accumulator, reached under the steering and pulled the uncoupling lever. She gave a signal to her people, and they moved to the back of the truck.

"Man of your word, I see," she smirked. "I'll be keeping an eye out for you, Mezie. That is, if you do survive."

He adjusted his spectacles and gave a half smile. "You too, Ms. Leopard."

The truck continued down the Labyrinth, following Kelechi's Compass. Wumi Alaba played with her dagger, twirling it between her fingers. She hadn't said anything since the encounter with the Leopard tribe.

"What?" she asked.

"Nothing."

"It's not nothing, you keep glancing at me."

"Really, it's nothing."

" 'Really, it's nothing,' " she mimicked.

"Cut that out."

" 'This is the big leagues, Wumi Alaba,' " she huffed, adjusting imaginary glasses over the bridge of her nose.

Mezie laughed despite himself. "At least you're not in a sour mood."

"Boy you're just *dying* to ask your questions, aren't you?" Wumi Alaba rolled her eyes. "Go on. Out with them. I won't bite."

"Noticed you started acting a bit strange after Odion Leopard mentioned the Dark ujuists. What was that about?"

She sighed loudly. "Dark *uju* is dangerous, Mezie. You've seen how potent *uju* is, ordinarily. When ujuists become Fascinated by the Dark, their *uju* becomes ... *more.*"

"More?" Mezie turned a bend. "Isn't that a good thing then? This Fascination?"

"No!" she snapped. "It's corruption. It eats away at the mind." Her voice dropped down an octave. "Makes you mad."

"D-did you know someone?"

Wumi Alaba made a small noise. Her hands worked nervously over the scarf on her neck. "I stopped training when I heard Family Man was rounding up the ujuist community in Tomato District. Rushed home to help. We stormed Victory Estate and we lost, can you believe it?" she laughed sardonically. "All the *uju* at our disposal and we couldn't take down one man!"

Mezie knew that war. Family Man and his Outlander crews. Countless relics. All against the ujuists. The ujuists fought back. Hard. And they had stood a good chance at victory until Family Man somehow managed to summon a Dark angel within the Fingers of God.

"Wasn't there some point in that war that the ujuists almost won?"

"They started going Dark," Wumi Alaba hissed. "It was either that, or death. And once the Fascination begins, there's no going back."

Mezie wanted to say something, but the compass needle had started tapping against the globe, pointing skyward. He took a look at the dashboard clock: 9:59 a.m.

"It's almost time!" he exclaimed. "We're close!"

Mezie hit the gas and the truck sped up. He took the next turn, excited. The front wheels suddenly crushed against something hard. Mezie pulled the vehicle to a grinding halt.

"My God," Wumi Alaba gasped.

Along the expanse of the road, the maze was littered with machine skeletons. Humanoid machines, disembodied and burning, scattered over the red stone like an iron carpet. Columns of thick black smoke rose from the mounds of severed limbs and torsos, the walls marred with splatters of black grease and a familiar inky-night hue.

Ojuju essence.

"What in heavens happened here?" Mezie asked, but even his voice had a faltering note to it. A shiver had worked its way down his back, and goose bumps followed.

"I have a bad feeling about this," Wumi Alaba hissed, opening the door.

Mezie yelled for her to get back, but she had already turned to the front of the car. Swearing, Mezie followed. The air was charged with static electricity and thick with the stench of burning oil. In front of him, Wumi Alaba drew her blade. Mezie gulped. Whatever went through here completely decimated these machines. There was barely any resistance from them.

Wumi Alaba had stopped walking. Mezie came up beside her. Before them was one of the humanoid machines, still mostly intact. Welded into lifelike precision, the machine-being was on its knees. Its upper body was almost as bulky as a bodybuilder of average height. One of its arms had been severed from the shoulder, and the black steel that made up its chassis had an ugly gash that cut across its torso and into its right eye. Strangely, there was a tattoo over its exoskeleton—a bird, in striking neon orange hues. It was such a sharp contrast against the machine's black body that Mezie couldn't focus on it for long. When he squinted too long, it looked as though the bird's feathers were moving.

"I sense residual *uju* energy from this machine," Wumi Alaba said.

"D-do you think it was the Dark ujuists Odion Leopard warned us about?"

Wumi Alaba's face was contorted in a deathly grimace. Too many emotions swirled behind her eyes for Mezie to comprehend. The machine's good eye suddenly flared green in activation, and it reached for Wumi Alaba. She was faster, stepping out of the way as it fell to the ground. The machine clutched its head and screamed—a mechanically amplified human wail. Mezie took a cautionary step back.

"Ujuists!" its voice resonated in the narrow space. The sound was an overlay of voices, not entirely machine. The tattoo on its body was unmistakably moving. The machine dragged its body along the floor, its legs crushed. "Come to finish the job?"

"I am sorry for your pain." Wumi Alaba held her sword over her head. Her voice was painfully somber. "I will end your suffering."

"You are all the same," it hissed in that multilayered voice. "We did nothing against you. We were peaceful nomads!"

"The Dark takes, and it never returns." The ujuist's voice was hard. "If you wish it, I will make your death quick."

A blazing wing suddenly erupted from the machine's back. It was a mass of brilliant vermillion feathers that momentarily stunned the both of them. The machine took off from the ground, grabbing Wumi Alaba by the neck just to pin her against the opposite wall. Mezie drew his pistol, firing three shots in quick succession. They ricocheted against the machine's angel-like wings. Wings that arose from the bird tattoo on the machine's steel body.

"Ahh, you're a possessed machine, aren't you?" Wumi Alaba wheezed. "An android golem."

"Our name is OROS!" it screeched. "We are no golem. We made a pact for protection with another sentient being, and this unit was chosen to house the entity."

"I understand what it feels like to fail."

"We have not failed!" it yelled.

"Do not turn your gaze away from reality, OROS."

"We will snap your neck. Then we will take the lives of the ujuists who destroyed this clan."

"Maybe you can snap my neck. Then you can go after the Dark ujuists again. But in this condition, you'll only lose. *Again.* And what happens to your clan then? Everything will be truly lost."

There was a stretch of silence between the two of them. Mezie held his breath.

"What do you suggest we do then, ujuist?"

"Recuperate. Then when you're sure your strike will be absolute, seek your vengeance."

Her words sent a shiver up Mezie's spine.

"Don't be hasty. Pay your respects to the dead. As long as you never forget this feeling, and you never let the fear keep you from moving forward, you will prevail, OROS."

Mezie was taken aback. Was the ujuist projecting? Was this a kind of critique against herself too? In her fear of Family Man, did she let herself stagnate in that slum in Tomato District?

OROS let her down. "What is your name, ujuist?"

"Wumi Alaba." She rubbed her neck before offering OROS her hand, which it clasped.

"Let us meet again, Wumi Alaba."

They took another path down the Labyrinth. A shorter route, according to the golem. Wumi Alaba had not said anything since the encounter with OROS, and Mezie didn't press. He was worried about the Dark ujuists ahead of them. Twice already, he'd witnessed the destruction they wrought. And even though his companion's composure did not falter, he knew the road ahead was about to get a whole lot more difficult.

The walls began to glow, a liquidlike spectral sight of seven colors. The illumination washed into the car, spilling golds and greens and vermillion over them. Mezie took off his glasses at the sight of the fluid colors streaming through the walls.

"Beautiful."

"It's almost like we're underwater," Wumi Alaba whispered.

"The rainbow is nearby. I can feel it."

The exit to the Labyrinth came into view. Here, the sky was set ablaze by streams of color arching from the ground, skyward. Mezie could not see where the rainbow ended, only the curtain of dazzling colors before him.

They were here.

IV – RAINBOW

"We go on foot from here," Mezie said.

The rainbow was a stream of light given solid form. Closer to the rainbow, Mezie found steps on the surface of the light. The staircase glistened like something made out of glass.

"Damn," Wumi Alaba said under her breath. "So this is a rainbow? A little extravagant, don't you think?"

Mezie's heart pulsed with excitement. "It's perfect."

He placed a foot on the staircase, and the color radiated from his foot, floating upward like will-o-wisps. With each step, wind rushed against his ears as they climbed even higher. Before long, the entire Labyrinth was below him and he saw every passageway and corridor. Every deadend Kelechi's Compass kept them away from, shrouded in shadow. The rainbow spread forward before him in sharp contrast—a wide stream of a million colors.

They were about to start moving when Wumi Alaba suddenly tensed beside him, her fingers curling around the hilt of her sword. "We're not alone."

Mezie turned, in time to see individuals in black hoodies emerge from the stairs.

The Dark ujuists.

"Shit. Run!"

The Dark ujuists let loose bursts of purple lightning. Most of them went wide, impacting the rainbow in bursts of effervescence. Mezie turned back in time to avoid a bolt of hot energy whizzing past his ear. He pulled his pistol from the folds of his jacket and started firing. Wumi Alaba drew her sword, deflecting the spells.

Cleaners climbed up the rainbow, carrying with them large backpacks of shadow accumulator gear. In a flurry of motion that Mezie's eyes could not follow, the cleaners pumped out shadows onto the rainbow; dark, writhing inky blobs of ojuju essence. The Dark ujuists began to mold the shadows, giving them robust, winged forms.

Then mounted them.

"Run, Mezie!" Wumi Alaba yelled.

The shadows of the flying ojuju fell over them as they sprinted across the rainbow. Mezie's eyes searched frantically but there was no cover. Only the massive stretch of the rainbow. It didn't matter whether he shot at the flying ujuists or not—his party was completely open.

Just then, a gargantuan shadow fell over the rainbow. The air rumbled tremulously as a vessel soared above them, sleek in design and flattened like a … saucer?

A spaceship!

Phase cannons locked on the two groups on the bridge. In a split second, Mezie grabbed Wumi Alaba and cranked his protection orb's field to the max.

The spaceship rained fire.

Explosions tore the rainbow's beams apart. The sphere of protection shivered with each impact, the relic crackling defiantly at the brunt of the damage. The laser fire singed the air wherever it struck, leaving shimmering trails of ionized air in its wake. Mezie looked to the sky where the spaceship was careening to the end of the rainbow and cursed.

Wumi Alaba stared at Mezie, wide eyed. "We survived that? Damn! Mobster trait unlocked: A *cockroach's tenacity.*"

"Speaking of mobsters," Mezie huffed, rising. "That was Family Man."

"How can you tell?"

"I ran his books and inventory. I know he has one of those. Wumi Alaba, we need to get to the bottom of the rainbow before he does."

"You go," Wumi Alaba replied, pointing to the fallen ujuists. They had been shot down by the phase cannons. "Of course that mobster can even overpower Dark ujuists," she hissed. Their cleaners—who had been too far behind to be affected by the phase cannons—were now drawing pistols. "I'll take care of these guys."

Mezie nodded and began sprinting toward the bottom of the rainbow. His feet pounded on the surface, and he willed himself to move faster. Scorch holes pockmarked the rainbow—holes that dropped to a dark uncertain surface. He ignored these, arms swinging in front of him as he ran. In the distance, where the arch of the rainbow sloped downward, the hovering spaceship was lowering something. A small shuttle transporter.

Mezie's feet suddenly felt heavy. The consistency of the rainbow's surface was changing, and he could see the colors no longer as shiny as the staircase, now almost viscous in consistency. Like he had started running in mud.

He dived.

The slope lost form, instantly terraforming into the rushing intensity of a waterfall. Mezie gurgled and gasped, trying to keep his head above the violent downpour of liquid light. Below him everything poured into a cloud. That was it .... That was the bottom of the rainbow!

Mezie took a deep breath, folded his spectacles in his hands and let the waves carry him.

The crash was painful. As if the entire world had dropped on him. Mezie rolled away from the falling beams. He was now in the cloud he'd seen from the top of the arch-fall. And the pot of gold that was supposed to be able to infinitely produce gold ...

Was in fact, a machine.

It stood a few feet tall, almost like a vending machine. The body was made of dull steel. It had a slot, then a pickup outlet. Numerous buttons dotted its surface. It was nothing spectacular, but it stood there, clearly the relic he'd been looking for.

Mezie took a step toward the machine.

"No, no, Mezie boy," a familiar voice stopped him dead in his tracks. Mezie turned his neck mechanically, dreading the answer he already knew.

"Family Man."

"Again, here you are. Not with the wrong hat, but with no hat at all."

Family Man was alone. No bouncers, no familiars, nothing. He just stood there in a beige three-piece suit, a brown bowler hat on his head, and white gloves on his hands. Mezie could not believe it. Did Family Man think this expedition was some kind of a joke?

Family Man shook his head. "I saw you in my premonitions, Mezie. That's how I knew. To think you found a relic that could take my business to the next level, and you said nothing."

"Well, I've been thinking of branching out myself," Mezie said, putting back on his glasses.

Family Man put a hand into his suit and brandished another hat. "You're like a son to me. You're a part of the family. Take the hat and I'll forget about this whole misunderstanding."

Mezie gulped, taken completely aback.

Did he ... did he seriously just pull a spare hat from his suit?

Just like that?

He carries spares around?

"Come on." Family Man placed a hand out in welcome. Mezie glanced at the machine under the rainbow. The rainbow bank. Family Man shook his head. "You'll never get out of here alive, Mezie. I have three Outlander teams waiting above. Take my hand, and maybe you see tomorrow."

He had a point. Mezie closed the distance between them, his feet sinking into and out of the cloud with each step. He took the hat from Family Man's outstretched hand.

"Misunderstanding?" Mezie scoffed, flinging it to the ground. "Do my dreams look like a joke to you?"

"You foolish—"

Mezie drew on him, emptying his clip right in his face. Family Man grunted and grabbed Mezie's arm. His grip was viselike, and beneath his sleeve—between the cuff and the glove—Mezie could make out the golden glint of something mechanical.

"Ingrate!"

Mezie pulled out his protection orb and reversed the polarity. The device exploded, separating the both of them. Mezie wheezed, stumbling as he tried to get on his feet.

Family Man's shadow fell over him.

"Shit!" A barrage of gunfire assaulted Mezie. Family Man was somehow controlling the shuttle's weapons system remotely. Gunfire pattered with a deluge of bullets, kicking up clouds where they struck. Mezie dashed toward the only cover available—the bank under the rainbow.

Almost there, almost there—

Something about the air before him changed. It shimmered, like heat waves over concrete. The hairs on his skin rose in attention. Silence swelled. The air dried up with a faint aftertaste of copper.

A beam of hot energy bridged the sky and the rainbow. The cannon blast tore open a crater inches away from his position, burning righteously as it expanded, separating him from the bank.

Mezie turned, but Family Man was there already. His right arm was charred; sleeves, glove, and all. His hat—by some miracle—was still on his head.

"Game over, kid."

Something suddenly dropped from above. Fast. For a split second, both their attentions were drawn to the mass of clouds that had risen on the object's landing.

"Four years of festered vengeance; forge fastidious fetters for four seconds."

Wumi Alaba's voice materialized into bonds. Radiant blue shards of energy struck Family Man from all sides, trussing him like spokes on a wheel. Wumi Alaba was still chanting, listing items in fours as her *uju* expanded oppressively. Her blade was shining bright now, the serrated edges igniting with tiny sparks of luminous nightlike energy.

She struck Family Man.

The energy sundered space itself. Her spell set the ether ablaze, momentarily blinding Mezie. The air rippled in ear-splitting resonance and his eardrums sang, his bones screamed, and his teeth trembled. It was over in an instant, leaving a thin haze of cloud-fog hanging between them.

"Ha-ha-hahhh," Family Man croaked, now on his knees. His suit had disintegrated. His muscular frame hung limp, but there were golden runes zigzagging over his dark skin. Steam curled over the mechanical gauntlet on his right arm.

"So you *were* serious, Mezie." There was mockery in his rasping voice. "You hired a Dark ujuist. Even *I* wouldn't do that."

"D-dark?" Mezie looked up, confused. Wumi Alaba stood before Family Man, breathing heavily. Her eyes were cold as she stared down the mafia boss.

"Do you remember me?"

He chuckled weakly. "Am I supposed to?"

Anger flashed over her face, and she pulled away her scarf. Ice licked down Mezie's back as he saw the rough patch of scarred flesh over the skin of her neck.

"Look, you bastard! This is what *you* did to me!"

"Of course . . ." he drawled. "You refused to work for me. I guess you turned to the Dark to survive, didn't you?"

Everything made sense then.

"W-Wumi Alaba?"

The ujuist did not look at him. "This is what the ojuju showed me back then on the road; the day Family Man slit my throat. I had tried to breathe and instead I felt my life bubble away. Slip through my fingers in futility. *Uju* forsook me. Now I can barely talk without the burning reminder that the bastard who did this to me is still walking around, eating and breathing."

She placed the edge of her sword to his neck. "It ends now."

"But does it, ujuist?" Family Man croaked. "You've hit me with your best shot, haven't you? I'm still breathing. I have an army waiting for my summons. You *failed*."

Mezie saw her hand falter. "Stop it, Wumi Alaba," he said. "We've won. We have the bank. *That's* what we came here for."

Wumi Alaba pressed the blade harder to his neck. The golden runes on his skin coalesced at the point where her blade met his skin. There was no blood. "He's not wrong," she hissed, her voice breaking in frustration. "I'm not strong enough to beat him, and we're outnumbered."

"We're not." Mezie rose. "He's bluffing. Remember, ujuist, this is the big leagues." He walked toward the bank, circling the crater the spaceship's blast had created. "He probably found out about this relic way too late. Rushed here in his fancy spaceship. See that arm of his? He uses that for remote control."

"Oh?"

"And I don't recall hiring you to kill him. *This* is what we came for."

Mezie fished a gold coin from his pocket and slotted it into the machine.

The machine came to life. He saw the buttons x10, x100, x1000 glow up and smirked. He clicked on x100.

The bank shuddered and rumbled and Mezie took a step back. The three of them watched the machine cough up gold onto the clouds, each coin reflecting the spectrum of the rainbow's colors like heavenly currency.

"A-amazing," Wumi Alaba breathed.

"Here's what's going to happen." Mezie adjusted his glasses. "Wumi Alaba, disengage the gauntlet from Family Man's arm. We'll be taking his shuttle. *And* his spaceship."

Family Man let out bellows of laughter. "Don't get conceited over a little luck. *You're* my enemy now, Mezie. And you'll eventually return to Tomato District. *My* domain."

"Sure, right after you *walk* there."

Wumi Alaba laughed at that.

"Besides, I've had it with everybody going on and on about my luck. And you've got something else wrong, Family Man." Mezie stalked to where Family Man knelt under Wumi Alaba's blade and gave his most sinister smile. "*You're* my enemy now."

Family Man growled and Mezie drove a fist to his face. The man fell to the clouds, passed out. Mezie rubbed his knuckles in satisfaction as he watched the golden runes on Family Man's skin grow cold and darken.

His emancipation was complete.

He turned to Wumi Alaba. The ujuist did not meet his gaze.

"I know what I said about the Dark," she said. "You can just pay me, and I'll take the truck back to Tomato District."

"Then, how about we extend our agreement? Partner up with me."

"W-what?"

"I couldn't have done this without you. And you sure as hell don't look mad to me. Well, that is *if* we overlook the casual death threats. But I think we're good."

"You saw what happened to OROS's clan."

"Yes. And I also saw what *you* did for OROS. You're a good person, Wumi Alaba. Dark *uju* or not."

She scoffed, but there was a shimmer in her eyes. "You can't afford my services, remember?"

Mezie pointed to the bank. "I beg to differ. Now are you with me or not? I don't want to be here when Family Man wakes up."

Wumi Alaba stretched out her hand. "As long as you do better than him."

Mezie returned the handshake. "Now let's get out of here."

"Okay, boss."

" 'Okay, boss.' "

"I still have my knife."

"Forget I said anything."

www.ingramcontent.com/pod-product-compliance
Lightning Source LLC
Jackson TN
JSHW020026141224
75386JS00026B/709

* 9 7 8 1 6 4 7 1 0 1 4 5 9 *